DISCARD

# THE SCENT OF
# LEMON LEAVES

D1320229

# THE SCENT OF LEMON LEAVES

## CLARA SÁNCHEZ

TRANSLATED BY

JULIE WARK

ALMA BOOKS

ALMA BOOKS LTD
London House
243–253 Lower Mortlake Road
Richmond
Surrey TW9 2LL
United Kingdom
www.almabooks.com

Originally published in Spanish as *Lo que esconde tu nombre* by Ediciones Destino, S.A., in 2010
First published in English by Alma Books Limited in 2012
© Clara Sánchez, 2010
© Ediciones Destino, S.A., 2010
Translation © Julie Wark, 2012

Clara Sánchez and Julie Wark assert their moral right to be identified as the author and translator respectively of this work in accordance with the Copyright, Designs and Patents Act 1988

Cover image: Trevillion Images

Printed and bound by CPI Group (UK) Ltd, Croydon, CR0 4YY

ISBN: 978-1-84688-185-5
eBook ISBN : 978-1-84688-198-5

All rights reserved. No part of this publication may be reproduced, stored in or introduced into a retrieval system, or transmitted, in any form or by any means (electronic, mechanical, photocopying, recording or otherwise), without the prior written permission of the publisher.

This book is sold subject to the condition that it shall not be resold, lent, hired out or otherwise circulated without the express prior consent of the publisher.

# THE SCENT OF
# LEMON LEAVES

# 1

## In the Hands of the Wind

### Julián

I knew what my daughter was thinking as she watched me pack my bag with a trace of fear in her piercing black eyes. They were like her mother's, and her thin lips were like mine but, as she grew older and her body filled out, she looked more and more like her mother. If I compared her with photos of Raquel from when she was fifty, they were two peas in a pod. My daughter was thinking I was an incorrigibly crazy old man, obsessed by that past that no one cared about any more, unable to forget a single day of it, a single detail, or face or name – even a long, difficult German name, although it was often a great effort for me to remember the title of some film.

However hard I tried to look cheerful, there was no way I was going to stop her feeling sad because, apart from being old and crazy, I had a blocked artery and, although the cardiologist had tried to reassure me by saying that the blood would seek an alternative route bypassing that artery, this gave me no illusions about my chances of coming back alive. So I kissed my daughter with what, for me, was the last kiss – doing my best, of course, to make sure she didn't realize. There had to be a last time she'd see me, and I preferred it to be when I was alive and packing my bag.

The truth of the matter is that, given my state, such a mad idea would never have entered my head if I hadn't received a letter from my friend Salvador Castro – Salva – whom I had not seen since the people at the Centre put us out to grass. The Centre, which had been established with the aim of hunting down Nazi officers scattered all over the world, was going into retirement itself as its targets were reaching the limits of old age and dying. Those moribund monsters were escaping from us again. In most cases, it was fear that had kept them alert and helped them to get away. They'd only had to learn how to sniff out our hate and they were off like a shot.

When I picked up the envelope in my house in Buenos Aires and saw who the sender was, it was such a shock that I nearly died on the spot. Then I was flooded with immense emotion. Salvador was a kindred spirit, the only person left on earth who knew who I really was, where I came from and what I'd be capable of doing to stay alive. Or to die. We met when we were very young, in that narrow corridor between life and death that believers call hell and that non-believers like myself also call hell. It had a name, Mauthausen, and it never occurred to me that hell could be any different or any worse than this. And while my head was struggling once more to get out of this hell, we were cruising through the sky among white clouds and the hostesses left behind a pleasant fragrance of perfume as they walked past me, comfortably stretched out in my seat, more than twenty thousand feet high and in the hands of the wind.

Salva told me that he'd spent several years in retirement in Alicante, in an old people's home. It was a very good home, a sunny place, set among orange trees, just a few kilometres from the sea. At first, he came and went as he pleased, since the home was like a hotel, with a room and bathroom just for him and an *à la carte* menu. Then he began to have health problems (he didn't specify what kind) and now had to rely on other people to take him to and from the town. Whatever ailed him, he hadn't stopped working in his own way and without anybody's help. "There are some things you can't just leave as they are – right, Juliánín? It's the only thing I can do if I don't want to start thinking about what lies ahead of me. Remember? When I went in *there*, I was just a kid like many others."

We had a deep mutual understanding, and I didn't want to lose him, just like you don't want to lose an arm or a leg. We both knew what "there" meant – the concentration camp where we'd met working in the quarry. Salva knew what I'd seen and suffered and I knew what he'd seen. We felt we were damned. Only six months after we were liberated, looking ghastly and trying to cover it up with a suit and hat, Salva had already found out that a number of organizations had been set up with the aim of locating and capturing Nazis. That was what we were going to do. Now freed, we signed up at the Memory and Action Centre. Salva and I were only two among the thousands of

Spanish republicans who'd been sent off to the camps, and we didn't want people to feel sorry for us. We didn't feel like heroes. Plague-ridden, more like it. We were victims – and nobody wants victims or losers. Others had no alternative but to keep quiet and suffer the fear, shame and guilt of survivors, but we became hunters, Salva more so than me. Basically, I was swept along by his rage and spirit of revenge.

It was his idea. When we left there, I just wanted to be normal, to join up with normal humanity. But he said that this was impossible, that I'd have to keep on surviving. And he was right. I've never again been able to shower with the door closed, and I can't stand the smell of urine, not even my own. In the camp, Salva was twenty-three and I was eighteen, but I was physically stronger than him. When we were liberated, Salva weighed thirty-eight kilos. He was scrawny, pale, melancholic and very intelligent. Sometimes I had to give him a scrap of what went by the name of food there – boiled potato peelings or a morsel of mouldy bread – not out of compassion, but because I needed him in order to keep going myself. I remember the day I told Salva I didn't understand why we were struggling to stay alive when we knew we were going to die anyway, and he retorted that we were all going to die, including all the people in their houses sitting in an armchair with a drink and a cigar. For Salva, the drink and the cigar represented the good life that every human being should aspire to. And happiness consisted in finding the girl who'd make him feel like he could walk on air. He also believed that every human being had the right to walk on air at some point in his life.

In order to overcome his terror, instead of closing his eyes and trying not to see or know, Salva preferred to keep them wide open and gather as much information as possible: names, faces of guards, rank, visits from other officers to the camp, as well as the general organization. He told me to remember as much as I could, because one day we were going to need it. And it was true that while we were trying to remember everything, we forgot a bit about fear. I knew straight away that Salvador was convinced he wasn't going to end up in that quarry – and I wasn't either if I stuck with him.

When the gates were opened, I ran, stunned and crying, while Salvador came out with a mission, although he could barely stand up. He managed to locate and bring ninety-two high-ranking Nazi officers before the courts. With others, we had no option but to kidnap them, try them and execute them. I wasn't as proficient as Salva. Quite the contrary. I was never able to close a file successfully. In the end, it was either others who nabbed them or they escaped. It was as if destiny was making fun of me. I located them, hunted them down, cornered them and, as soon as I got close, they slipped away, vanished. They had a sort of sixth sense for saving themselves.

In his letter Salva sent me a clipping from a newspaper published by the Norwegian community on the Costa Blanca with a front-page photo of a couple called Christensen. Fredrik was eighty-five and Karin a bit younger. It was easy to recognize them, because they hadn't thought it necessary to change their names. The article did not reveal who they were, but was merely about the birthday party this respectable-looking old man had held in his home, attended by a large number of his compatriots. I recognized those eyes – eyes of an eagle hovering over its prey, eyes that are bound to stay engraved in your memory for as long as you live. The photo wasn't very good. It had been taken at the party, and they'd published it as a birthday present. And, incredible as it may seem, Salva had managed to see it. Fredrik had been merciless, up to his neck in blood. Perhaps, being a non-German Aryan, he had to prove his trustworthiness, earn the respect of his superiors. He had served in several Waffen-SS units, overseeing the extermination of hundreds of Norwegian Jews. I had an inkling of how cruel he had to be in order to become the only foreigner who was awarded a Gold Cross.

The photo showed them sitting side by side on the sofa. His large bony hands lay flopped on his knees. Even seated he looked enormous. It was very difficult for him to go unnoticed. She, in contrast, was more difficult to recognize. Age had disfigured her more. I didn't need to rummage around for her in my memory. She'd been one of those young, round-faced, ingenuous-looking blondes with arms raised in a Nazi salute who filled my files.

"I can't see very well, my hands are shaky and you'd be a great help to me, so if you've got nothing better to do, I'll be waiting for you. Who knows, you might even find eternal youth," Salva wrote in his letter. He must have been referring to the sun, the drink and the cigar. And I wasn't going to let him down. After all, I'd been lucky enough to marry Raquel and have a family, while he'd given himself body and soul to his cause. Raquel had the gift of turning bad into good, and I took it as yet another punishment that she'd died before me, leaving the world bereft of her good thoughts while mine remained. But after a while I realized that Raquel hadn't totally abandoned me, and that thinking of her gave me peace and filled my head with small rays of sunshine.

My daughter wanted to come with me, as she was frightened my heart would fail. The poor girl thought that at my age everything's harder – and it's true. Yet it was also true that I preferred to die doing this rather than torment myself about whether my blood-sugar levels were rising. Then again, things might be different for once, and Fredrik Christensen's heart could fail before mine. Even though he is very old, he must think he can live a little longer, and would be very upset if we cropped up in his life and put the fear of God into him right at the end, after he's managed to elude us for so long.

It was great to think that Salva and I could get to that sofa and that Fredrik would be shitting his pants as soon as he saw us.

## Sandra

My sister let me have her beach house so I could think calmly about what would be best for me – whether to marry the father of my baby or not. I was five months pregnant now, and less and less sure that I wanted to have a family of my own, although I'd foolishly left my job – just at a time when it was so difficult to find a job and so hard for me to raise the baby alone. For the time being, I was getting around with the baby in my belly, but then… Jesus! End up in a marriage of convenience? I loved Santi, but not as much as I knew I could love. Santi was a hand's breadth – just a hand's breadth away from being the great love. Though it might be that the great love only existed in my mind, that it was a figment of the imagination, like heaven, hell, paradise, the Promised Land, Atlantis and all the other things we can't see and, as we already know, we'll never see.

I didn't want to make any final decision. As long as there was food in the fridge and the baby hadn't come out and wasn't asking me for anything, I was happy just to let my thoughts float around without getting weighed down by the various possibilities that were as intangible at the moment as the clouds. It was a comfortable enough situation, but one which unfortunately wasn't going to last long, as my sister had found a tenant for the month of November.

It was now the end of September, and we could still swim and bask in the sun. The neighbouring houses had already been shut down, to be reopened the following summer or to be used for some weekends or for longer breaks. Only a handful, like ours, would be occupied throughout the year, and there were so few of them scattered around that when their lights were on they looked incredibly lonely. I liked this feeling, until I began to miss having someone to talk to, or someone who'd just be there making a noise, and then I'd start thinking about Santi. These were moments of weakness, moments that conspire to keep couples together for a long time – like my parents, for example. I only had to think about them to pluck up enough courage to overcome my loneliness. I knew that if I didn't deal with this now, I'd never again be able to deal with it for the rest of my life.

To get to the sandy beach I only had to get on my little motorbike, a Vespino. My sister, brother-in-law and nephews had told me over and over again not even to think about parking it without chaining it. As soon as I had breakfast and had watered the plants (one of the duties imposed by my sister), I'd take some old magazine from a wicker basket and put it in a Calvin Klein plastic bag, grab a bottle of water, a peaked cap and a towel, then head off to lie on the sand. Out in the sun there were no problems. The tourists had practically disappeared. Most of the time I met the same people along the route: a lady with two little dogs, a few fishermen sitting next to their taut rods, a black man in a jellaba who seemed to have no better place to go, people running along the beach and, under a beach umbrella splashed with large flowers, a retired foreign couple with whom I exchanged greeting glances.

And thanks to them that morning I didn't pass out and fall flat on my face in the sand, but only sank to my knees and vomited. It was too hot, one of those days when the thermometer shoots up as if broken. The peaked cap gave very little shade, and I'd forgotten my bottle of water. Sometimes people were right when they said I was a disaster. Everyone who was close to me said the same thing. If they didn't say it sooner they said it later – you're a disaster – and, when everyone tells you that all your life, there has to be some truth in it. When I sat up on my towel I felt sick, and everything started to spin, but even so I managed to stagger to the water's edge to cool off – and it was then that I could resist no more and threw up. I'd had too much for breakfast. Since I got pregnant, the fear of losing strength made me eat too much. The foreign couple came running over as fast as old people can run on burning hot sand. They took for ever to get to me and I was sinking my hands in the wet sand trying to get a grip on it but it kept melting away, again and again.

*My God, don't let me die*, I was thinking when some large bony hands took hold of me. Then I felt the coolness of water in my mouth. A hand wet my forehead and ran water through my hair. I could hear their words, strange and far away, and didn't understand a thing. They sat me on the sand, and I saw that it was them. The man brought over his umbrella to shelter me from the sun.

His first words in Spanish were, "Are you all right?"

I nodded.

"We can take you to the hospital."

"No, thank you. I must have had too much for breakfast."

The woman rested her small blue eyes on my belly sticking out over the bikini in a slightly rounded bump. I didn't give her time to ask.

"I'm pregnant. Sometimes my stomach plays up."

"Just rest now," she said, cooling me down with a fan on which I saw, double, the words advertising the Nordic Club. "Do you want some more water?"

I drank a little as they stared at me without blinking, as if trying to sustain me with their gaze.

After a while, by which time they must have been dizzier than me, they accompanied me to the motorbike and then followed me in their car in case I felt sick again on the way. We were moving so slowly that all the drivers were tooting at us and, when I turned into the track to my sister's house – which looks as if it has been eased in with a shoe-horn on the left-hand side – I beeped my horn and waved goodbye.

Perhaps I should have asked them in and offered them something to eat or drink, or to sit for a while on the porch, which always had a very nice breeze wafting through. I hated myself for not being friendlier, since I'd ruined their morning on the beach, though it was also true that interrupting the monotony of these old couples who spend all day brooding over the past wouldn't do them any harm either. I showered under the hose and lay in a hammock in the shade.

I didn't want to think about the dizzy spell on the beach, because I didn't want to feel weak. From now on I'd be more careful: the fact was that my body wasn't the same any more, and it was constantly taking me by surprise.

## Julián

It bothered me that I had to spend some of my savings on a business-class seat, but I did so to set my daughter's mind at rest, and also because I wanted to reach my destination in the best possible shape, so the journey wouldn't be in vain. And because of that, I drank only alcohol-free beer with my meal and, after shaking off my demons as best I could, slept the sleep of the just while my fellow passengers downed one whisky on the rocks after another.

I wasn't counting on Salva's coming to meet me at the Alicante airport. He hadn't even answered my letter telling him the date of my arrival. What would he be like now? Maybe I wouldn't recognize him. Or he me, of course. In any case, I looked at the signs people were holding up behind the security barrier and made myself as visible as I could, in the hope that Salva would suddenly come over and hug me. After around fifteen minutes, I decided to go to the bus station and take a coach that would get me a hundred kilometres away to Dianium, the town where I'd booked my hotel. The Christensens were living in the surrounding area and only a little farther away was Salva in the old people's home.

When I got out of the bus, rather than go directly to the hotel, I got in a taxi and asked the driver to take me to Tres Olivos, the old people's home, and later drive me back to the centre of town.

I put my bag in the boot and we headed off inland, swathed in the fragrance of sun-warmed pines. After a while, the driver asked me, somewhat surprised, whether I was going to be staying in the home. I didn't take the trouble to answer, but pretended to be absorbed in the landscape – which in fact I was. Dusk wasn't far off, and it all looked wonderful to me: the red soil, the small woods, the vineyards, the orchards, the birds coming down to peck about on the ground... it reminded me of when I was a kid, before anything was important, and my parents took us on holidays to the beach. I patted my jacket pockets to make sure I'd left nothing on the plane or the bus. I worried that tiredness might be making me lose reflexes without my even noticing.

The home had a smaller garden than Salva had led me to believe, but it was in the middle of the countryside and this seemed to be a good thing, although we elderly folk usually prefer to see people than trees. There was no need to ring the doorbell: the door was open, and I entered a room where they were starting to lay the tables for dinner. I asked the waitress if I could see Salva, saying I'd come a long way to visit him. She looked at me in surprise and led me to a small office where a solidly built woman told me that my friend had died. When I showed her his letter, she told me that he'd asked them to post it immediately after his decease. Decease. What a word to use. They'd had him cremated and sent his clothes to a local church in case some poor person might want them. He'd died of multiple organ failure. His body had packed it in. She told me, without my having to ask, that he had not suffered.

I went out for a little walk around the garden and imagined Salva there, weak, shrunken, still holding out, sometimes looking at the sky as he reflected on what he had on his plate, without ever losing sight of his objectives. We'd had no contact for many years, ever since the people at the Centre had stopped thinking we were useful and I'd preferred to spend my time with my family and make the odd enquiry by myself without ever achieving anything. I tried to tie up the loose ends of the cases of Aribert Heim, the world's most wanted Nazi criminal, and of Adolf Eichmann, but never had any luck. It was difficult to believe that Salva would have stopped working during all these years. He would certainly have kept gathering material and passing it over to others on a plate, so they'd get all the glory. Now it was my turn. He'd left me his last discovery, and it would only be significant if I was able to make it known to others. When he realized he was about to die, he thought of me, remembered this friend, and the legacy he left me was a poisoned chalice, as was anything else coming from our tormented souls. I would have loved to talk with him, to see him one last time. Now there was nobody who knew everything about me, nobody who knew what my hell was really like. A dull, pearly light was bringing the afternoon to a close.

I got back into the taxi and, after asking the driver to go to the Costa Azul hotel, I took the handkerchief out of my pocket and blew my nose. The sight of Tres Olivos disappearing in the distance filled my eyes with tears – feeble tears that only wet the rims of my eyes, but that meant I was alive. I'd outlived Salva without wanting to, just as I'd outlived Raquel against my own will.

The taxi driver glanced at me in the rear-view mirror. There was such a gulf between his youth and my old age. There was no point in saying anything, trying to explain anything, telling him that my friend had died, because he'd think it's natural to die at our age. But it wasn't natural, because otherwise we wouldn't find it so strange and incomprehensible. Was I still worthy of seeing these beautiful silvery fields? Raquel had told me off for having such thoughts, had called me a masochist, a misfit. After all, Salva and I hadn't seen each other for ages, since I went to live in Buenos Aires with Raquel, while he continued with his itinerant life. I would never have imagined him secluded in an old people's home. And, as he himself used to say, we're not the only ones who die. Everyone, the whole of humanity dies, and we have no option but to resign ourselves to that.

After arriving at the hotel, I unpacked my bag, put my clothes in the wardrobe and then studied the map of the region, trying to locate the house of Fredrik and Karin Christensen in a wooded area called El Tosalet. Since I didn't want to go to bed too early and was trying to fight the jet lag, I went down to the bar to take my evening dose of pills with a glass of hot milk. A girl in a red waistcoat, busy doing a juggling act with glasses and ice blocks, asked me if I wanted a dash of cognac in my milk. I said why not, and entertained myself by watching her as she served me. She gave me a radiant smile. She must have had a grandfather who needed cheering up from time to time. When I was starting to feel woozy in my tiredness, I asked reception if they could answer a couple of queries I had about the map and booked a car for the following day. I wasn't surprised when they asked me if my driving licence was up to date, since this had been happening to me quite a lot recently. If I'd had time, I would have felt offended, but I had other matters in my head that were more pressing than being old and being treated as such. I had to fulfil Salva's mission.

The room was nothing special. It looked onto a street, and you could see the lights of a few bars through the lace curtains. I stretched out on the bed, feeling more relaxed than I had in a long time. I'd gone back to the old habit of being alone in hotels and not telling anyone about what I was really up to, with the difference that I expected nothing now, because after this there was nothing more to be expected.

It didn't matter that the whole world was stronger and younger than I was. I had the enormous advantage of not expecting anything... feeling – how can I put it? – resigned. When I realized I was nodding off, I undressed, slipped into my pyjamas, turned off the air conditioning and took out my contact lenses and put on the thick-lensed glasses I used for reading in bed. At least my teeth stayed put. Oh for the times when I needed only myself, without all the paraphernalia, when I was moving about. I closed my eyes and delivered myself to Raquel and Salva.

The rays of sunlight coming through the net curtains woke me up. I showered and shaved with the electric shaver that my daughter had put into my bag, very unwillingly as she said that it was silly not to use the shaving kit supplied by the hotel. I shaved my face smooth. Not even when I was ill in hospital, not even in the most difficult moments of my life had I stopped shaving. My wife used to say that my meticulous way of shaving was my personal trademark. Maybe she was right. I had more than usual for breakfast, because the buffet was included in the price of the room, and so I'd only need a snack at lunchtime. I was planning on having an early dinner.

The rented car was only being delivered at twelve, so I strolled down to the port and, for twenty euros, bought a panama hat at a stall on the Paseo Marítimo. That provided more shade than the peaked cap I was wearing. My daughter had insisted that I shouldn't pack so many things I could easily pick up here, but I thought it was a waste to leave them behind when they weren't going to know what to do with them later. Although it was quite hot, I had no choice but to wear a jacket – fortunately a light one – because I needed pockets to hold my glasses in case I lost one of my contact lenses (I'd taken my sunglasses out of their case and put them in my shirt pocket), and take my wallet with money and credit cards, a notebook and my little box of pills. When I was young I also carried my packet of Marlboros and a lighter. Luckily I could leave my mobile phone at the hotel because it had stopped working as soon as I had crossed the Atlantic. I liked carrying everything distributed evenly among my pockets as this balanced out the weight. My daughter once bought me a backpack but I'd left it behind, as it didn't feel like something that belonged to me. Whenever possible I've worn a suit or, at least, trousers and a jacket and, in winter, a mid-calf-length beige wool overcoat. To tell the truth, I wouldn't know how to survive without my little quirks.

I sat down at a terrace bar to have a coffee and kill time studying the map again. Coffee was the only health-damaging habit I hadn't given up and wasn't planning to give up either. I refused to move on to green tea, like the few friends I had left. The worst thing about being old is that you're left more and more alone, turning into a stranger on a planet where everybody's young. But I still had my wife somewhere deep inside me, and my daughter had to get on with her own life without taking on the burden of mine and all the bad things that had happened in it. On my scales, hatred weighed heavy but, thank God, love also weighed in. Yet I must say, and regret to say it, hatred had encroached too far into the territory of love.

I thought, as I was sipping my coffee on this terrace – quite a good espresso, by the way – that when you've known evil, goodness is never enough. Evil is a drug, evil is pleasurable and that's why those butchers kept on with their exterminating and were more and more sadistic. They could never get enough of it. I took the label off my hat, put it on and tucked the peaked cap into my pocket. If Raquel was alive, I'd buy another hat for her. She looked good in any hat. Then women stopped wearing them and thus lost some of their elegance. Not long ago, a doctor told me that, at my age, memory is crystallized memory, meaning that you recall long-ago events better than recent ones. It was true and now I set about remembering, in minute detail, the hat Raquel wore the day we got married, back in 1950, one bright spring morning.

## Sandra

The next morning I didn't risk going to the beach. I didn't feel like using the motorbike, so I just walked to the little supermarket some five hundred metres away to buy some juice. I had all day long to make myself healthy meals, read and take it easy. The lemon tree and the orange tree gave the small garden an air of paradise, and I was Eve. Paradise and me. My sister had left me piles of dirty clothes to wash. I had to water the garden morning and afternoon, put the washing into the machine, hang it out, bring it in, fold it up and, if I was in the mood, iron it. If I took her seriously I could spend the whole time working. Where did she get all those dirty clothes from? I think she let me move into her house to oblige me to do something and, as she saw it, I'd end up being useful, if only for this. Maybe she'd even spent a few days getting the clothes dirty. She liked being bossy, but in such a way that she didn't seem to be giving orders. Even I had taken years to wake up to the fact that she was bossing me around and, without my realizing it, making me do things I didn't want to do.

It was precisely when I was doing my afternoon watering chore, after my siesta, that I saw a car pull up next to the ironwork gate at the entrance. I heard car doors closing and the sound of slow footsteps advancing. It was the old couple who'd helped me on the beach. They seemed happy to see me, and I was happy too. I'd been spending too much time mulling things over all by myself. I turned off the hose and went over to greet them.

"What a surprise!"

"We're happy to see you've recovered," he said.

They spoke very good Spanish, although with an accent. It wasn't English or French. Or German either.

"Yes, I've been resting. I've hardly been out."

I invited them to come and sit on the porch.

"We don't want to bother you."

I served them tea, in a beautiful teapot that my sister kept in an imitation antique cupboard. I didn't mention coffee because I hadn't found a coffee pot yet. They drank it in small sips as I told them about the father of my child – that I wasn't sure whether I was in love with him and that I didn't want to make a mistake at this stage in my life. They seemed to understand as they listened in silence, and I didn't care if they knew all these things about me – or at least what was bugging me more than anything else right now – and it didn't bother me that they were strangers. It was like telling the air.

"The uncertainties of youth," the man commented, taking his wife's hand. You could see he'd been really in love with her and now he couldn't manage without her. She was something of an enigma.

He wasn't a man who smiled, but he was so well-mannered he seemed to be smiling. His enormous height made the wicker chair look like something out of a doll's house. He was very thin, and his cheekbones were prominent. He looked elegant in his grey summer trousers and a white shirt with mid-length sleeves.

"If you like, we could come and get you tomorrow, take you to the beach with us and then bring you home again," he offered.

"It would be a change for us," she said. Now she really was smiling with her little blue eyes, which might have been pretty once, but were ugly now.

Instead of answering I poured them more tea. I was weighing up the situation. It had never entered into my plans to make friends with a couple of old people. In my normal life, the only old people I had anything to do with were members of the family, never friends.

They glanced at each other, communicating with their eyes, and let go of each other's hand so they could pick up their cups.

"We'll come at nine, not too early and not too late," he said, and they stood up.

She seemed very happy: her eyes had become lively. She certainly seemed to be the one in charge. She was the one who decided what to do and the one who had her little whims. I might have been one of this lady's whims but, in principle, that was neither good nor bad. She clutched my arm, as if trying to stop me from escaping.

"You don't need to bring anything. I'll see to it all. We've got a portable fridge."

"Fredrik and Karin," the man said, holding out his hand.

I held out my hand too and gave Karin a kiss on her cheek. I hadn't known their names before now and hadn't even realized I didn't know them, perhaps because they hadn't mattered until now. The totally detached from me, just people going by in the street

"Sandra," I said.

I'd never known my grandparents, who'd died when I was a little girl, and now life was compensating me with these two old people, and I didn't mind being their favourite granddaughter or, better still, their only granddaughter, the depositary of all their love and... all their worldly goods, these fabulous goods for which you shouldn't have to struggle or even want because you deserve them from the moment you're born. Maybe what I hadn't been given by blood ties was being handed to me by destiny.

## Julián

The following day, what with one thing and another, I didn't manage to set off in the car until one o'clock. I opened the window because I preferred the air outside to the air conditioning. I had to stop at a petrol station and then a newsstand to ask where El Tosalet was. I ended up on a long winding road, so it was impossible for me to ask anybody and, after that, I went into a wooded area in which the houses were submerged among fifteen-metre-high trees and where the only thing you could hear was a dog barking. It took me quite a while to find the street where Fredrik and Karin Christensen lived, maybe because my reflexes had deteriorated with age, but in the end I got in front of their house, Villa Sol. Nothing remarkable about that name round here.

The house was built like a fortress. It was practically impossible to see anything inside, and I didn't want anyone to catch me nosing around because, even if I couldn't see them, it didn't mean they couldn't see me. Silence reigned, and the scent of flowers lay heavy everywhere. What could this have to do with suffering, humiliation, wretchedness and boundless cruelty? Like the newspaper article, the letterbox did nothing to disguise their names. It said: "Fredrik and Karin Christensen".

The iron gates were painted dark green – both the sliding gate for the cars and the smaller one for people – and the ivy growing around threatened to cover them. I pretended I was admiring the climbing plants, hoping to hear some sound or notice some movement inside, then I went back to the car, which I'd left parked in a more open area two or three streets higher up. I now realized that this could be a good vantage point, given that their street was a cul-de-sac and that they could only leave through there.

But that could happen any time, and I couldn't hang around all day. It was already three thirty – time for me to have a bite to eat, take my pills and lie down for a while. I didn't want to squander the little energy I had on the very first day.

I struggled to find a parking place close to the hotel and, when I finally managed to, it was around quarter-past four. I went into a bar and asked them to make me a French omelette and an orange juice, which I rounded off with a coffee with a dash of milk. The coffee was as good as it had been in the morning. I was feeling slightly euphoric, pleased with how things were going, and called my daughter. I tried to calm her fears, saying I was feeling better than ever, that the change of air was doing me good, expanding my lungs. I didn't tell her that my friend Salva had died.

I told her that we'd already located the Christensens' house and that we'd soon be starting our surveillance. My daughter wasn't at all happy to hear this. Anything that sounded like obsession to her had her saying "Enough of that!" – so I changed the subject and told her it was a perfect place for a holiday, with a large community of old foreigners. Then I added something I knew she'd like: that I'd use this trip to go looking at houses for rent or for sale with a porch and a little garden, where I could retire and where she could come and spend all the time she wanted.

"With what money?" she asked, because that was what she always said when she started to like an idea.

I'd probably been too self-centred with Raquel and, sad to say, was continuing to be so with our daughter. I didn't give her breathing space. I never let her forget about evil. I constantly reminded her of it as I pursued my demons. She always told me she didn't have time to put the world to rights. She just wanted to be a normal person, despite all the things her family had gone through. At least she had a right to that. Didn't she?

And I was asking myself whether it was right that Karin and Fredrik should be living surrounded by flowers and innocence.

\* \* \*

16

When I got to my hotel room, I lay on the bed still dressed, half-covering myself with the bedspread, and turned on the television. I didn't want to go to sleep, but dozed off anyway and, when I opened my eyes, it was getting dark and I could feel the remote control tingling in my hand. I was rested, but also feeling groggy, and went staggering off to the bathroom as if drunk. I hadn't taken out my contact lenses, and my eyes were stinging. I decided to go out for a stroll, down to the port, to breathe in some fresh air from the sea.

The road to El Tosalet was full of curves, so I didn't fancy going out in the car at night. I'd wait till the next day, although with a great sense of having wasted time. I wasn't here on holidays. I didn't have time for holidays. Holidays were for the young, for people with a whole life ahead of them, while for me the long slumber was waiting just round the corner.

The beautiful lights of the port were nothing to me in comparison with the lights that might be coming on now in the Christensens' garden. Those lights made sense. They were signs that fitted into my world, guiding me to a lost inferno.

I walked up and down the Paseo Marítimo, noting that the stall where I'd bought my hat was still open and working out a plan of action. I'd have an early breakfast in the morning and then go up to El Tosalet. I'd wait for Fredrik to come out and then tail him. I'd take note of what he was doing. In two or three days I'd have an idea of his routines. He might have been a highly decorated Nazi officer, an escape artist moving from country to country, changing houses and cities, but he wasn't going to escape the clutches of old age. And old age is built on routine – that's what keeps it going.

I still wasn't sure how I was going to use the information I would gather, but I knew I'd end up using it somehow. Knowing someone's habits and the people around them is like knowing the doors and windows of a house. You finally see a way in.

So let's see: what was I going to do once I verified Fredrik's identity? Capture him and bring him before a court, accusing him of crimes so monstrous as to be unthinkable in a human being? That time was past. Old Nazis weren't being brought to trial any more. At most, it was hoped they'd die off and with them would die the problem of having to extradite them, try them, imprison them and stir up all that murky, stinking shit once again. And I thought, as I contemplated the stars, that, though old and on our last legs, Fredrik and I were still here, and we could still raise our eyes to admire their beautiful light. And I thought I could still manage to make that swine tremble, that I could die with the clear conscience of having done my duty. I know Raquel would ask me who I thought I was fooling, would say I was doing it purely for my own satisfaction and pleasure – and she might be right – but, whatever name you might care to give to what I was feeling, that was not what really mattered.

# 2
# The Red-Haired Girl

## Sandra

The beach was very comfortable like this. Fredrik sometimes brought us an ice cream or cool drink, the shadow of his wide bony shoulders falling across us. Karin liked waffling on about Norway and about their beautiful home, an old farmhouse by a fjord. They'd stopped going there because of the climate, the damp that got into their bones. But she missed the snow, the pure air of the bluish snow. Karin wasn't all skin and bone like her husband. She must have been slim in her youth, fat in her mature years and now she was a combination of both, a deformed mixture. She looked at you with this difficult expression, somewhere between friendly and suspicious, and you never knew what she was really thinking. Better put, what she actually said must have been a thousandth part of what was on her mind, like all old people who've lived a lot only to end up enjoying small things. It wasn't unusual for Karin to bring along, in her straw basket, one of those novels with a man and woman kissing on the cover. She loved romantic stories and sometimes regaled me with some tale of what was going on between the boss and the secretary, or between the teacher and the student, or between the doctor and the nurse, or between two people who'd met in a bar. None of them was anything like my story with Santi.

It was very pleasant letting myself go with the flow. I walked along the water's edge, from the Norwegians' beach umbrella to the rocky promontory, and from the rocky promontory back to the umbrella. I didn't throw up again and we had all the cold water we wanted in the portable fridge, which was a very good one, of a kind that didn't exist on the Spanish market. Hardly any of the things they used were from here, except for her sarongs, which she bought at the beachside stalls.

Above all, they were placid. They moved slowly, didn't speak loudly, rarely argued and, at most, they'd change their mind about something. They were completely different from my parents, who always made a mountain out of a molehill, however slight the setback. I hadn't even told my parents I was pregnant, because I didn't feel up to dealing with one of their dramas. They made the most of any opportunity to throw a wobbly, to go berserk. Maybe that's why I got involved with Santi, simply because he has a good character and is patient and well balanced. Yet, as you see, it didn't work. After half an hour in Santi's company I'd be swamped by an intolerable sense of wasting my time, and this was the main reason why I couldn't imagine myself with him after one or two years.

The Norwegians and I went to the beach only a few times, so I wasn't getting too fed up with them. When they dropped me off, they sometimes didn't even get out of the car. They said goodbye through the car windows and left me to it.

## Julián

I wanted a bite to eat before going back to the hotel, as I've always believed that eating in hotels is more expensive than outside. I steered away from restaurants because I didn't care to spend two hours over a dinner I didn't really want, so I went into a bar and asked for a serving of Russian salad and a yogurt, plus a large bottle of water to take back to the hotel. My daughter had made such a fuss telling me I mustn't drink tap water that drinking bottled water was something like an act of loyalty to her.

The hotel receptionist was the same one I'd seen when I arrived. He had a large freckle on the right cheek, which gave him quite a raffish look and ensured I wouldn't forget him. I'd immediately registered it in my mind, which is what I used to do when I was young, when I automatically filed away faces without any chance of confusion among them. As he handed me the key to my room I asked him if his shift hadn't finished yet. He seemed surprised that I should be concerned about him.

"Within the hour," he said.

He must've been about thirty-five. He glanced at the bottle.

"If you need anything, the cafeteria's open till twelve, and sometimes even later."

I turned, looking around for it.

"There, at the end," he said.

It would be the place where I'd had the glass of milk. I don't know what could have prompted me to tell him not to succumb to any temptation of getting the freckle removed, because this mark could help him to be a cut above the rest. This got me thinking about the V-shaped scar at the right-hand corner of Aribert Heim's mouth, which, with age, must have been camouflaged by wrinkles. For years I'd been so obsessed by it that every time I saw an old man of eighty or ninety with something near the mouth that looked like a scar I was hot on his heels. Even with his eye-catching stature and this mark he'd managed to slip out of sight, over and over and over again. He'd blended in with the other members of his species and sometimes he'd been confused with other Nazis as giant-sized and long-lived as Fredrik Christensen, who looked very much like him. During the five weeks I was in Mauthausen between October and November 1941, Heim had been busy performing needless amputations without anaesthesia, just to see how much pain a human being could endure. His experiments also included injecting poison into the heart and observing the results, which he meticulously wrote down in black-covered notebooks. He did all this without ever dispensing with politeness or his smile. Fortunately, neither Salva nor I coincided with him in the camp. Others of our countrymen couldn't say the same. Without any exaggeration, they called him the Butcher and, in all likelihood, the Butcher was sunbathing and swimming in some place like this. He and the others would be enjoying things that didn't remotely resemble them, things that weren't made in their own image. Salva had had the courage of not wanting to forget anything.

"What a day! I'm quite tired," I said, taking my hat off and casting off, too, the image of two Jews sewn together back to back, howling with pain and begging to be finished off for once and for all. Who could have done such a thing? Someone who was affected by those cries of pain in the way the rest of us might be affected by the squealing of a pig being slaughtered or of a rat caught in a trap. It was impossible to go back to the point when you'd never seen such a thing. You could pretend to be like other people, but what you've seen remains with you. This old spectre in my head must have suddenly aged me because the receptionist said, looking quite serious, "As I say, if you need anything, don't hesitate to call me."

I waved my thanks with the somewhat crumpled hat in my hand.

Truth to say, I wasn't tired but I was so used to being tired and to saying I was tired that I said it. Being tired fitted so much better with my profile than not being tired.

After the customary ritual that took me three quarters of an hour, I got into bed. I watched television for a while, then turned off the light and started mentally visualizing Fredrik's house and street, the newspaper photo and what I knew about him. The photos of him as a young man, of which I only had two in my office files and a few more in my mental archive, were a sufficient reminder of what he was really like, a monster who, like Aribert Heim, believed he had power over life and death. Also like Heim, he was one metre ninety, with an angular face and pale eyes. Arrogance is more visible in a young man. It's in the body, in the way of walking, in the longer neck and the consequently higher head, and the firmer gaze. In old age, decrepit bodies disguise evil as goodness, and people tend to see the elderly as harmless, but I was old too and the old man Fredrik Christensen couldn't pull any wool over my eyes. I'd reserve what strength that remained to me for the aged Fredrik, and the rest of the world would have to manage without me, I told myself, wondering what Raquel would have thought of all this, although I imagined she'd tell me I was about to throw away the little bit of life that remained to me.

I woke up at six the next morning. I didn't feel bad, as I'd slept through the night. I had a shower, took my time getting dressed, listening to the news on the radio alarm with its big red numbers next to the telephone. This got me up to date with local politics and the efforts of local ecologists to stop further construction along the seafront.

I was one of the first into the dining room and had a good breakfast, a lot of fruit especially, practically as much as I'd need to get me through the day, and I also took away an apple in my jacket pocket. I went out and walked to the car, noting the fresh morning air, which was quite cool at this late stage of September.

I went up to El Tosalet, crossing with cars going faster than me, probably on their way to work. In some sense I was going to work too, although I wasn't getting paid for it. Anything that entails an obligation imposed by oneself or by others could be called work, and my work was waiting for me in a small square with several streets running off it, one of which was Fredrik's. I took up my position in such a way that, from a distance, I could keep an eye on the thick ivy of the house, which almost covered over its name, Villa Sol. Since Christensen had never seen me in his life, I didn't have to conceal myself too much. I only had to act naturally if our paths crossed.

And our paths were going to cross, because I hadn't been waiting an hour when an olive-green four-by-four nosed its way out of the Villa Sol fortress. My heart missed a beat, that missed beat my daughter feared so much, and I barely had time to get into the position to follow it. I was just finishing the manoeuvre when the tank-like vehicle driven by Fredrik Christensen cruised slowly by like a vision. Sitting next to him was a woman who had to be Karin. I moved onto the main road behind them. After about five kilometres we turned right. I didn't have to worry about them seeing me. For them I was just a neighbour taking the same route and this gave me a certain degree of freedom because I wasn't at risk of losing them.

Some kilometres farther on, a young woman came out of a small holiday house and got into the car with them. They continued on their way to the beach with me behind them. Sometimes I let another car come in between us so they wouldn't notice me, but I didn't want to take any chance on losing them either, or to have to resort to any kind of urgent or strange manoeuvre. Not that he'd be up to too many flourishes either.

We drove along parallel to the beach for about ten kilometres until he turned right and parked in a street at the end of which you could see a snippet of sea, a dazzling blue slice. How could hell and paradise be so close? The waves, if you paid proper attention to them, were the work of a prodigious imagination.

They got out of the car and, fearing I was getting too worked up, I breathed in so deeply that I started coughing. It was him, still very tall with long arms and legs, broad-shouldered but skinny. He opened the boot and took out a beach umbrella, a portable fridge and two deckchairs. I wouldn't have recognized his wife, however. She was walking unsteadily and her body seemed quite out of kilter. She'd put on weight and looked deformed. A plastic bag hung from her shoulder.

She was wearing a shapeless pink beach shift with slits up the sides, while he was in shorts, a loose-fitting shirt and sandals. The girl was wearing a T-shirt over her swimsuit and a peaked cap. A towel was slung over her shoulder and hanging from her hand was an attractive plastic bag, not the supermarket type. Once they'd put up the beach umbrella, they were all mine to monitor, so to speak, so I occupied myself looking around for somewhere to relieve my bladder and have a coffee. It wasn't easy but, in the end, I even obtained two bottles of water, which I left in the car. My daughter would never forgive me if I died of dehydration.

I took off my shoes and socks so I could walk on the sand, which was very agreeable. As soon as I found time I'd have a swim. The Mediterranean conjured up images of youth, love, beautiful women and carefree times. I spotted Fredrik and Karin under the beach umbrella. He was looking at the sea, she was reading and they occasionally exchanged the odd remark. Their heads were in the shade and bodies out in the sun. There weren't many people in the water, typical holiday stragglers and foreigners without a care in the world, like these two. The girl had gone down to the water's edge. I was concentrating so hard on the two Norwegians that I didn't realize that something had happened until Fredrik went over to her. It seemed that a wave had carried away the magazine she was reading and he'd jumped up to grab it. I took off my sunglasses to see better but the light struck my eyes so intensely that I had to close them. When I opened them again, Fredrik was striding back with the magazine in his hand. He very carefully opened it and spread it out in the sun on top of the umbrella, after which he got an ice cream out of the icebox and took it over to the girl. Full of curiosity and somewhat drowsy, I sat down by the wall separating the sand from the thistles, rushes and bushes that spread out behind me.

They seemed to be very considerate and kind with this girl who wasn't of their Aryan race. It was terrifying to see them being nice. They were acting as if they'd never come to be truly aware of the evil they'd done. Generally, in normal life, good and evil are quite mixed up together, but, in Mauthausen, evil was evil. Never in all my life have I come across pure goodness, but I've certainly been in the midst of Evil with a capital E, caught up in its devastating power, and there's nothing good at all there. Seeing Fredrik right now, you'd imagine that this man was once young, had struggled through life, worked and then retired to take things easy. And there was no way you'd discover you were wrong and that you'd go on being wrong every time your path crossed with that of a heartless man.

We were there for a couple of hours. When I saw that they were starting to put down the umbrella and the girl was shaking out her towel, I went to the car and waited. The three of them soon appeared. They got into the four-by-four. The two Norwegians sat in front and the girl in the back seat. They headed off inland where the houses had a more rural, more authentic look about them, and there were vegetable gardens and a lot of orange groves. Then they turned off onto the narrow track where they'd picked up the girl earlier in the morning, but it seemed too risky to follow them, so I went on ahead and waited on a patch of ground by the roadside until the large square snout of Fredrik's car made its appearance and I saw it driving off. They'd certainly be going back to El Tosalet, where I could head later. Now I'd have a closer look at the girl on the beach because I wanted to know what it was about her that interested the happy couple. Hence I parked the car slightly more conveniently and got out.

I was looking right and left along the track amid barking dogs that furiously hurled themselves against the fences, apparently trying to kill themselves. Then I spotted her, next to a bougainvillea, lying in a hammock. She was young, about thirty years old, neither fair nor dark but with brown hair, some of it dyed deep red. She had a black-and-red tattoo that looked like a butterfly on her ankle, another on her back, plus some black Chinese or Japanese lettering. She was lying half on her side, so she might have had more tattoos on the other side. The garden was small, with an orange tree and a lemon tree besides the bougainvillea, although it might have been bigger at the back of the house. There was a clothesline with a bikini, underwear and a towel hanging from it. She was alone. A perfect victim for the Christensens. They might have met her on the beach and singled her out to suck her young blood, absorb her energy and defile her freshness. At bottom, people don't change much and, as far as Fredrik was concerned, a fellow human was someone to be taken advantage of, someone to steal something from. He wouldn't be changing in two days or in forty years, and neither had I changed in any essential way.

What could this girl know about all this? How could she discover evil in those two old people who were concerned about her? I didn't want to frighten her and I didn't want anyone to think I was a dirty old man, entertaining himself with the vision of a slumbering, defenceless girl. I still had some sense of modesty, in spite of everything, although I didn't care what people thought of me. I left off my scrutiny and kept walking down towards some end to this track, searching for "For Sale" or "To Let" signs, so as not to be completely disloyal to my daughter. Lying to her over such a small thing, deceiving her by saying I was looking for a house I wasn't looking for, seemed to me more miserable than doing something on a bigger scale, something dangerous, something that really warranted hiding. Hence, in order to stick to what I'd promised her, I'd have to spend my free time looking for a nice house for us, and I'd even have to consider the possibility of coming to live here. I didn't want to end up being, along with everything else, a bigmouth that held out false hopes to the people he loved. Not that.

At the end of this winding, shady track where the red-headed girl lived, there were more and more tracks bordered by houses, next to which the girl's cottage was dwarfed, almost a little storybook house. Since I didn't find any sign and couldn't see a clear exit to anywhere, I decided to return to the car and, walking past the cottage again, I glanced at the bougainvillea. The girl was gone. Someone, and it must have been her, had opened a window. I kept walking. It was time for me to take my pills and lie down for a while.

I went back to the same bar as the previous day, but I was still very full from breakfast and only asked for some juice and a coffee so I could take my pills. Then I went up to my room to rest. It smelt fresh, of detergent, with the bed perfectly made and the doors to the small balcony over the street left ajar. Nonetheless, I couldn't get my mind off things, relax and go to sleep like a normal pensioner making the most of what remained of his strength, like my friend Leónidas who got up early and went to bed late so he could live more, but then spent the whole day nodding off. The time would come, and it wasn't far away, when I wouldn't be able to drive or catch a plane by myself, and the time would come when there wouldn't even be a Fredrik Christensen. Life placed me in a world I didn't want, an inhuman world without dreams, and now the finale of this world was approaching, like a film coming to an end.

# Sandra

As time went by there were fewer neighbours – none, to tell the truth – the days got shorter and the silence grew. Sometimes the silence was so tremendous that any small movement of leaves sounded like a tempest, and when a car came down the track it felt like it was going to come through the wall and crash into the bed. Thank goodness it didn't take long before I stopped being deceived by distances and, if I heard a drop of water plopping on the floor in the passageway, I knew that it was actually falling on the porch. It was on one of these afternoons that I felt the baby's first kick and, if I'd known where Fred and Karin lived, I'd have hotfooted it over there to tell them about it. I was sure it wouldn't have bothered them if I'd suddenly turned up on their doorstep. Of course I resisted the temptation to call Santi, who'd desperately seize on our baby's first kick as an excuse to come and see me, and I didn't want to phone my parents either, because they'd be giving me a sermon about my being alone.

I seemed to remember that the Norwegians had mentioned something about El Tosalet, but the villas in El Tosalet were widely scattered over a very extensive zone of pine woods and palm trees, so it would be like looking for a needle in a haystack. So I kept lounging there with my hands joined at the nape of my neck, waiting for the next kick. Until I couldn't stand it any longer, until I felt I just had to share this moment with somebody, until it clouded over and threatened to rain, and I had the whole afternoon ahead of me, and couldn't resist the impulse to act. I had nothing better to do than to go looking for the Norwegians' house. I don't know why, but as I was getting on the motorbike that grey afternoon it occurred to me that the Norwegians had never invited me to their house. They'd never given me their address or telephone number. They'd be very surprised to see me turning up there if I did manage to track them down, and then I'd feel uncomfortable, as if I'd crossed some invisible line drawn by them and them alone.

In any case, I didn't mind going on a nice tour through the peaceful streets of El Tosalet. Even before they'd got wet, the smell of damp earth and flowers mingled with the moist air from the sea. It was opening up my lungs, I was breathing better than I'd ever breathed and it would be very good for the baby. After all, I was his or her door and window onto the world and not much would filter through. Oxygen, music sometimes, my heartbeats and possibly my moments of sadness and happiness. This would be getting through, but the baby would never know that it was, and that it would be his or her baggage for a whole lifetime. That's why, even from kindergarten, people have a very marked character, so I was wondering how I'd be marking the character of my baby right now.

I went as slowly as I could, staring at the houses that would seem to fit with my new friends and checking names on letterboxes. The latter course was more reliable because, what was I expecting to find, a Norwegian farmhouse? When it comes to houses, people are quite surprising. There are some people who get around looking very stylish and yet live in a pigsty, and vice versa. My parents, for example, had a disastrous, intense, crazy way of being in the world but they were incredibly orderly with their papers and bills, and the house was very tidy too, with everything in its proper place, so whenever a light bulb blew it would be replaced immediately. That's why I wasn't sure whether the dwelling would be a true reflection of the dwellers.

I went deeper inside the housing estate and parked in a small square, chained up the motorbike, and when I looked up I saw a restaurant on the other side. It was closed, which was a shame, because they might have given me directions. A few heavy drops of rain had begun spattering here and there but I kept walking. This was a perfect moment, as long as I stopped thinking. Almost all the villas were closed down, well and truly under lock and key, with stone walls and metal gates everywhere, as if they didn't want to see or be seen, as if they had everything a human being could possibly need inside. It was raining, then it was pouring, and, before long, it was wildly pelting down. I was soaked through and didn't know where to go, as there was no jutting roof or overhang under which I could shelter.

Finally a woman in a car, opening her garage door with a remote control, asked me if I wanted to come in until it eased off. She didn't have to ask twice. I went into the garage, walking past the car in my sopping-wet sandals, and, from there, into the garden. There was a pergola in the garden and I told this lady, a foreigner like Karin, that I'd sit there in the pergola for a while.

Before I could tell her myself, she'd guessed that I'd got lost. I told her I was looking for the house of a Norwegian couple called Fredrik and Karin. I assumed that didn't ring a bell with her, because she marched off to her front door without another word. She went in between the Doric columns on either side, as I wrung out the water as best I could, wondering how much time I'd have to spend on the alien planet of that woman – who didn't have very good taste by the way, although she evidently had plenty of money. In this case, dwelling and dweller seemed to match up. After ten minutes of daydreaming about what I'd do with that block of land and how I'd try to salvage the façade of the house, the lady came back, holding up an umbrella and trailed by the racket of several small dogs. Now she was smiling as she came over with a towel in her hand. She held it out to me so I could dry myself, but I didn't dry myself, because it was a beach towel with signs that it had been used by several people, so I just stood there holding it in my hand as she told me that she'd phoned Fredrik and Karin and that Fredrik was on his way to get me.

"Poor Karin," she said. "Her arthritis is really playing up today. Any change of weather is the death of her."

The little dogs were now yapping at my ankles and jumping up around me. In the middle of all the hullabaloo I said it had been a real stroke of luck that she knew my friends.

"Around here we know everyone," she remarked. "They live three hundred metres away."

She looked down at my belly, letting her gaze linger there for a moment, but didn't make any comment so as not to put her foot in it in case it was a false impression. At that point I was still wearing very summery clothes with a waist-length T-shirt and low-cut trousers with my belly button in the air. I could feel my feet squishing in my platform-soled sandals.

"Don't go catching a cold now. That's not a good idea. You'd better dry yourself."

The little dogs shook out their well-groomed pelts.

"Don't worry," I said, handing her the towel.

"Have you known the Christensens long?"

"We met on the beach a few days ago and we like spending time together."

The lady stuck the closed umbrella between the slats of a wooden bench inside the pergola. She was wearing a white ankle-length dress that was transparent enough to show her knickers. Although she was more or less Karin's age, she looked agile and not much aware of her years. She smiled at me pensively.

When we heard Fred's horn, we all went over to the gate, the youthful old lady, the little dogs and me. As I'd imagined, Fred looked at me with some surprise. He asked me about the motorbike and if I'd come alone, and I told him what you say in such cases, that I was passing through here, that I remembered having heard them say they lived in El Tosalet and that… When I got tired of explaining myself, I stopped talking. It wasn't such a big deal. Next to the entrance there was a very beautiful bit of mosaic work showing the number 50. The elderly young lady pulled out a small packet from one of the pockets of her dress and handed it to Fred.

"Thank you, Alice," Fred said. "Thank you very much."

I got into the car feeling a bit awkward and worried that I might wet the upholstery.

"Karin's making tea. We'll be there right away," he said, with a cheerfulness that wouldn't have been just because of me, as we wound through streets and more streets in which it was a miracle that the four-by-four could fit and emerge without a scratch.

It said "Villa Sol" at the entrance to the house. We then descended into its depths and rose again by way of some stairs into a vestibule.

Karin was in the kitchen, a kitchen of thirty square metres with well-used authentic antique furniture, not imitation antique like my sister's. She didn't ask any questions and was happy to see me. She was walking with more difficulty than on other days and a few more lines of suffering were etched into her face.

"My whole body's hurting today," she said.

"Yes, that lady told me about your arthritis."

"Ah, Alice! Alice is very lucky. She's got incredible genes. Impossible as it may seem, she's a year older than me."

Then Fred put the little package in Karin's hand and her eyes lit up.

"I'll be back in a moment," she said.

She soon reappeared with a pink silk dressing gown in her hand and she made me go into a small bathroom next to the stairs to take off my wet clothes and put it on. She ordered Fred to go to the garage to get me some plastic sandals. Villa Sol looked nicer to me than Alice's villa. It was less pretentious and more personal. There were more flowers and the architecture was the traditional style of the zone, with an ochre façade, tiled roof, Mallorcan-style shutters and dark-green parquetry. We adjourned to a small sitting room where they must have spent a lot of time because it smelt like Karin's perfume. It had a fireplace and looked out onto the garden. In one corner there was an armchair that I liked from the moment I set eyes on it, so I went to sit there. Fred brought me a little footrest. The cups were decorated with gold, as were the plates and teapot.

"In two weeks we'll be starting to light the fire at night. This zone is very damp."

"I'm sorry to have turned up unannounced."

"Don't worry, dear," Karin said. "I want to show you something. Look, I'm making a pullover for your baby."

Fred picked up a newspaper and I drew closer to Karin. I couldn't believe they'd been thinking of me to such an extent.

"Today I felt a kick, two kicks actually."

Karin smiled at me through her difficult wrinkles, which gave her smile a slightly diabolical effect, as if she was saying how lonely you must be when you have to tell a perfect stranger something so intimate and important. But, since she didn't actually pronounce the words, I couldn't reply that the reason I was telling a stranger about it was that I wanted to tell a stranger, and that maybe I wanted to tell it but not share it.

She set aside her knitting needles and the ball of wool because, with her arthritis, she couldn't do anything just then. She let her hands drop to her lap and clasped them.

"I hate the winter," she said. "I used to like it when we were young, with the sparkling snow, the icy cold on your face. The winter never bothered me then. I could cope with everything, but now I need the sun and its warmth. Days like today make me feel sad and I start thinking. And do you know what the worst part is? Thinking. If you think about the good things you miss them, and if you think about the bad things you feel bitter. When it's very hot and I'm on the beach I don't think about anything at all."

It was more or less the same thing with me. On the beach, with the sun sizzling my brains, I was in seventh heaven.

"Don't you worry about anything, dear. You'll have plenty of time for forgetting. You're so young…"

The two of us sat there looking out at the garden, without speaking, thinking, watching the drops falling from the roof and the trees. I closed my eyes and dozed off, not because I was sleepy but because it was very agreeable. Forget what? Santi? That wasn't such a drama either. Even if I didn't want to get married or share my child with him (I wasn't crazy about the idea of going to the park with him and the kid), I was fond of him. When I opened my eyes and sat up in the armchair I started being nagged by the guilt of feeling much better with Karin than I'd ever felt with my mother, of preferring to be under the same roof as Fred leafing through the newspaper than with my father. They soothed me. I drank what was left in my cup, now cold. Karin said that, if I wanted, she could show me how to make some baby clothes.

I liked the idea of learning to do something useful, using my hands, and I thought it would also be quite nice working with clay in the middle of all this peace, on days when nothing at all happens. I didn't need to be asked twice when Fred announced at eight o'clock that it was dinner time and they hoped I'd stay and eat with them. I set the table while Fred made a salad that was a bit on the light side. He had a beer and Karin and I drank water. After clearing away the serviettes, which had probably been embroidered by Karin, and the plates decorated with shields, Fred got out a pack of cards so we could play poker precisely when I could have seized the chance to take my leave. But I settled for moving a little farther away from my world and fully immersing myself in Fred's and Karin's dimension. Then again, it was better to keep trying to find out about what lay in store for me, when I wasn't going to be able to enjoy the luxury of getting bored.

Karin held the cards in her tortured fingers and kept casting vivacious glances at her husband. According to her, Fred had won several poker championships. He was very good, the best, but the trophies were in their farmhouse in Norway, along with those he'd won at target-shooting. Fred was trying not to change his expression despite all the flattery. He didn't raise his eyes from the cards and let himself be praised. When he finally looked at us, his eyes were shining like a child's.

We only interrupted the game when someone rang at the door.

It was two guys. One of them was not tall, not short, broad-shoul-dered, with close-cropped hair and very fine sideburns outlining his jaw. A black singlet hugged his large chest. They called him Martín. Martín looked at me intrigued and Fred took him by the arm and led him into a small den just off the living room. The other one stayed by the door. He was verging on skinny and you could almost say that his light-brown hair, by comparison with Martín's, was long.

"Are you a friend of Fred's and Karin's?" he murmured, holding out his hand. "I'm Alberto."

I gave him my hand and the contact was too intense. His hand was very hot. Or was it mine? I pulled it away as if it was burning and scurried into the kitchen. I didn't want to be looked at any more by those slippery eyes, which seemed to be moving behind a layer of oil. It was impossible to know what he was thinking while, with the other one, it was easy to see that he was surprised to see me there. This one didn't show anything. He was like an eel.

When I came out of the kitchen he wasn't there any more. He'd left with Martín.

They wouldn't let me go back home. Someone was waiting for me maybe? We played cards till late and it didn't stop raining, so Fred would have to take me to the motorbike in the car and then I'd have to go down through all those horrible curves in the middle of the downpour. Well, what for? To sleep in my own bed?

"We've got spare rooms," Karin said.

Fred said nothing, which made me hesitate, until Karin nudged him.

"Say something," she urged. "Stop acting like a nincompoop."

"If you spend the night here, we can go to the beach together tomor-row, or maybe you'd rather swim in the pool," he added.

I let myself be persuaded for a few minutes and I stayed. We spun out the evening a little longer until they led me to a very nice room, with blue-flowered wallpaper and a set of white shelves.

"Fred made them." Karin pointed at the shelves.

I thought that my parents might be happier if my mother admired my father like Karin admired her husband. But it must be something genetic, because I hadn't managed to admire Santi like this either. Karin lent me an off-white satin nightdress with a fabulous cut. It must have been from the days when she would have been tall and slim and they made fabrics to last your whole lifetime. It looked great on me and I felt bad about wearing it in bed and getting it crumpled. I normally slept in a comfortable old T-shirt and knickers. I didn't need anything more. It didn't make sense to get between the sheets as if I was at a high-class party... well, until now, when the silk or satin was swirling round my thighs and clinging to my princess-like breasts. It could even be that if my baby was going to be born with good self-esteem and able to move confidently through a future life, he or she would need a mother who slept in vampire nightdresses.

Although I was missing some of my sister's back-dated magazines and wanting to know what had become of Princess Ira von Fürstenberg, I started nodding off at once because it was impossible to resist that bed, although I did take the time to ask myself what I was doing in this room, in this bed, among these little blue flowers and wearing this nightdress.

Like every other night for the past couple of months, I had to get up to pee at least once or twice. I woke up slightly disoriented, vaguely remembering that there was a bathroom in the passage. As I was looking for it, I kept hearing that noise that beds make when... together with the odd moan. Would these two old people be... Could they really be making love? I had no idea of the time and when I got back into bed I could still hear a distant murmuring, words here and there as if they were discussing how it had gone, so I covered my head with the pillow, almost embarrassed about having listened to them without wanting to. Hence, I wasn't surprised to find it was striking ten when I awoke next morning. When I first got up, I thought I was the lazy one because I couldn't hear a thing, but when I saw that the front door was bolted I deduced that they must be still sleeping. I drew back the curtains in the living room and opened the doors. It was a marvellous day. The sun was making the wet leaves shine and the birds were singing their lungs out. I made myself a milk coffee, which I was drinking on the porch when they appeared, yawning, Karin in her nightdress and Fred in shorts with an enormous polo shirt with elbow-length sleeves. They were happy. They asked if I'd slept well and Karin seemed more agile than she'd been the previous day.

"I'm going to get breakfast," Fred said.

He didn't give me time to announce that it was quite late and I was leaving. Karin was one jump ahead of me, setting out the dainty embroidered serviettes on the porch table. While she was getting dressed, Fred made orange juice and the customary tea. OK, I said to myself, as soon as we finish I'll be off so I can keep reading the life of Ira in instalments. It's not that I had great things to do, but here I had the impression of neglecting them, the impression that everything I wasn't doing was very important.

Fred and Karin were very vivacious, chatting about the television series they watched, recounting whole episodes for me. I joined in with anything that came into my head but, all of a sudden, as I was talking, I caught them looking at me, terribly serious, as if they were going to leap on me and devour me. Was it because of something stupid I'd said without realizing? It lasted half a second. Then they looked at one another in the way they usually did and, a second later, everything was back to normal. Their faces changed back to being very agreeable. It had been one of those mirages you hardly notice. When we left the table, Karin suggested that we could lie in the hammocks in the sun. I thought, oh well, in for a penny, in for a pound and, after all, it didn't really matter if I stayed a while longer and if I had another rest before getting on the motorbike.

Karin and I lay there, our faces turned towards the sun, eyes closed. I had no intention of going back to sleep but was simply thinking how comfortable the hammocks were and that my sister would do well to buy some like this and throw away the ones she had. Half an hour in them was about as much as you could stand.

For such an old man, Fred didn't get tired. He cleared the table, washed the dishes and then locked himself away somewhere to work and, at about four, after serving us tea and biscuits, which only I ate, set off to the shopping centre since it seemed that we'd eaten up everything they had in the fridge. I thought I could get a lift back to the motorbike, but by the time I managed to react he was already out of the garage. We went back to the hammocks. Karin's arthritis was better now. Even her fingers were straighter and she was quite sprightly getting out of the hammock, as I could see just then. She came back with the skein of wool, her knitting needles plus another skein and needles for me.

"You can have a swim if you like," she offered, "and it doesn't matter if you haven't got your bikini. No one's going to see you here."

The water was cold. However sunny it was, it wasn't swimming-pool weather, but it felt good. It cleared my head and I could sunbathe practically naked, making the most of Fred's not being around, because I wanted to respect his age and customs, although after what I'd heard in the night I felt kind of embarrassed to think about his customs. When I calculated that he might be about to arrive, I got dressed and picked up the knitting needles. Karin showed me how to cast on. It was pleasing to keep advancing, making the band grow on what was going to be a little lemon pullover, even if my stitches weren't all that regular. I thought I could keep rotating magazine, pullover, strolls, meals, and my life would be full.


## Julián

I was trailing Fredrik for several days and keeping watch on his house. Almost every morning he and Karin went to the beach or to buy things at the zone's biggest shopping centre. I think she was doing some kind of rehabilitation therapy, because some afternoons they went to a gymnasium where she spent an hour before coming out, during which time he went off to fill up the car and get it washed, or headed for the Nordic Club. You might say they led a normal, discreet existence.

He'd got into the habit (with so many years ahead of him) of pushing the shopping trolley and reading the labels of products, no doubt making sure they didn't contain sugar or fats. He was polite to people and seemed unperturbed by the hotchpotch of races swarming around him, the inferior beings that were going to survive him and take over the planet. How they must have turned his stomach! This was an aversion that he bore deep inside. His success in life was inseparable from the fact that he was revolted by part of humanity and, besides Karin, he must have needed other beings of his kind with whom to share his sentiments. Were there others of their ilk here, or were they alone?

It was as if I had eyes that were different from those of other people, because, where they only saw an old couple, I saw the young Nurse Karin.

She was four years younger than Fredrik and had suited him beautifully, though now they were on the scrap heap. With her pretty face, pretty body, wavy blonde hair and her being sufficiently tall so as not to look like a dwarf at his side, she was the typical Nordic woman, although not a stunning beauty. They met as students and it seems she was the one that pushed him to join the Nazi party and to prosper in it. The information I had at my disposal suggested that Karin was the brains of the two, the one who did the manipulating, the one who'd made the most of her husband's limited, rigid ideas to get him – and, by the by, herself – to the top. A mediocre tale, except for the massacred lives it entailed. Fredrik had been a good sportsman. He'd played ice hockey, like his friend Aribert Heim. In addition, he was a horseman, skier, mountaineer, a fit man. In any case, they weren't people to whom I would have devoted a lot of time, but just enough to know who they were, probably because I'd spent the best years of my life running around after the Butcher of Mauthausen, after Martin Bormann, after Léon Degrelle, after Adolf Eichmann and others of that breed. Sometimes, as they say, you can't see the wood for the trees, and I hadn't given Fredrik the attention he warranted, had considered him a second-ranking Nazi until now, when I'd gone back to extract from my files information as old, dry and wrinkly as he was, and as I was too. Then I realized that everything I'd been doing up to that point had led me to this place and to him.

I couldn't keep still that afternoon. Sometimes we old people get very fidgety. It's as if fatigue affects our bodies but not our brains. My brain had a lot of work to do and these flaccid, debilitated muscles of mine were in revolt and, lying there, I tried to sink into the bed as much as I could, so that the mattress would do its restorative work. Thus with an hour's rest, during which I'd drowsed off for fifteen minutes, I was in good enough shape to go up to the little square in El Tosalet and keep watch on Villa Sol. Sooner or later they'd be having visitors and, with a bit of luck, they'd be visitors like themselves, their comrades from hell who'd been drawn together in the mutual attraction of wanting to feel more secure. I was dying to find out more.

I took the binoculars I'd brought with me from Buenos Aires which, according to my daughter, were going to add considerably to the weight of my bag, but they were old-style Canon binoculars of a kind they don't make any more. I'd been using them for so long that they adjusted to my eyes almost by themselves and there was no way I was going to fork out money unnecessarily to buy new ones here. They were a pro's binoculars, made for observing important life-and-death matters. I'd never use them to sneak into other people's lives, to see something it was no business of mine to be looking at. I'd already had too much intimacy in the camp. In our hut we slept piled up in three-tier bunks and I had to squeeze my eyes shut in order not to see what was not for me to see. Ever since then, I've never been able to witness intimate scenes, not even in a film. This was different. My binoculars were strictly focused on the enemy. My binoculars had always been at war. I also had a tiny camera that made no noise, a gift from my daughter who, even while she was trying to make me forget, also understood that there were some things that had come to be part of me. Otherwise, my way of working was very homespun. I had neither time nor inclination to get up to date.

In the car I also had several bottles of water, of a litre and a half each, two notebooks, a couple of biros and the apples I kept taking from the hotel buffet in case I got bored and started feeling hungry. I put the mini-camera in my pocket. All my jackets ended up out of shape, almost invariably with a rip in the lining of the right-hand pocket and the two front corners pulled out of alignment. Thus equipped, I went to take up my position in the small square in El Tosalet from where I planned to monitor Villa Sol. However, it wasn't necessary for me to go all the way since, before starting the upward climb through the bends, I crossed with Fredrik's olive-green four-by-four. He was coming down slowly, hogging the whole road. These people were also voracious in monopolizing centimetres.

This sudden change of circumstances made my heart rate shoot up. I urgently needed to do a U-turn and follow Fredrik. Damn road. I had to risk my life as soon as I saw the chance and the space to bring off the abrupt U-turn. From the great beyond Raquel told me I was crazy, that I was also endangering the life of another person who might have crashed into me. Raquel said that nobody should keep paying because of Christensen or anybody else. On this point, Raquel and I had never agreed. She told me to stop worrying about it, not to waste any more time because these bastards would end up dying like everyone else and there was no way they were going to escape from that. They'd end up as skeletons or ashes, would die, would expire, would disappear. When I used to tell her that I wanted them to suffer in this life, that what I didn't want was precisely that they should go off to the next world having escaped from me and my hatred when I couldn't escape from them, from them who'd had no reason to hate me, then Raquel would say that I was giving too much of myself, that it was as if I'd never really succeeded in getting out of the camp, and that they were even sucking up my hatred. I missed Raquel so much.

I drove recklessly so as not to lose him and, in effect, when I reached the bottom and got onto the straight part of the road I could make him out in the distance. I overtook as much as I could until I was a couple of cars behind him. The good thing about the four-by-four was that it was very easy to spot. When I realized he was heading for the shopping centre, I relaxed. My heart rate suddenly slowed down so fast that I almost got dizzy.

In the shopping centre I had him by the balls because, while it covered a very large area and had many sections, Fredrik's head would always be sticking up somewhere. Yet, at first glance, the four-by-four wasn't visible in the car park. It didn't matter as I only had to think about what I'd have to buy for myself to know what he and Karin would be needing. Bottled water, calcium-enriched yogurt, fruit and fish. Anything else was bad for them. I might also find him at the shelves with herbal teas, or in the bathroom section buying shower gel, disposable razors and toilet paper. I covered the route at a good pace until I spotted him in the central zone chatting with another man of similar age who was wearing a fisherman's cap.

They were both wearing shorts, Fredrik showing long skinny legs ending in a bulky pair of Nikes, and the other man shorter, stronger legs, or legs that must have been strong in other times but that were fat now. Fredrik was so neat and tidy that the other man looked coarse and sloppy beside him. Both of them were leaning on the handlebars of their shopping carts. The solid fellow, whose face I couldn't make out very well because of the cap he was wearing and my contact lenses, which played up in enclosed spaces, was pointing somewhere off to the right and they set off in that direction. I could have taken a photo of them with my mini-camera but, though it appeared that nobody was paying any attention to me, it wasn't a good idea to do it in an enclosed precinct like this where security cameras would necessarily be installed, so I pushed my cart in that direction. Unlike these individuals, I didn't have to buy anything as I was living in a hotel, because I was alone, and because I had more important matters to deal with: them. From the time I retired to the present, alone and in Raquel's company, I'd frequented places like this, where once again I had the feeling of not being like other people, although pretending to be like other people was very agreeable, and such moments had perhaps been the only happy ones of my life. There are people who've suffered much more than us, Raquel used to say, and everyone suffers in his or her way. At bottom, it made me feel bad that Raquel should have made such an effort to turn me into somebody it was impossible for me to be. She did it out of love and that's the only reason why I tried hard to pretend that I'd forgotten.

Fredrik and the other man were looking at some shirts on special offer. Three denim shirts for the price of two. It turned my stomach to think they should be there chatting about shirts, that they should be there checking the sizes, and I was indignant that they should be happier than me, and that Fredrik, after everything he had done, should still have Karin. They were at large among their victims, crossing paths with people they would have been only too happy to gas.

Fredrik remarked in German that he wanted to buy a sea bass because they had a dinner guest, so they said their goodbyes. It's curious that I used to eat much more before going into the camp than I did after I came out. I never went back to eating a lot. It was as if my respect for a simple bit of meat and a few carrots was enough to satisfy me. People will do anything for food: steal, whore or kill. Raquel was only just spared from being sent into the camp brothel along with the Polish women, although a lot of officers and Kapos preferred boys, especially Russian boys. What would have become of those children? There was one Kapo in the camp who sometimes went into the hut with ten at a time and nobody could do anything to stop him.

Fredrik went to the fish stall, but there were a lot of people milling around there, so he took a number. I calculated he wouldn't be served for at least half an hour. He must have had the same thought, because he got a bit of paper out of his pocket, a shopping list no doubt, read it and went off to the cooking-oil section, where he took two bottles, after which he took the shirts out, stood there staring at them as if he wanted to hypnotize them and then resolutely turned his trolley around to retrace his steps. I could have sworn that he was going to change them or dump them, because suddenly he didn't want to be wearing the same shirts as the other fellow. He must have been too carried away by a sense of brotherliness, or he'd picked them up to get rid of his pal as soon as he could.

I got there before he did and positioned myself behind some beach towels hung out full length so people could see their designs. The shirts were the pièce de résistance of the offers and they were jumbled up together on the display table. Fredrik took those he had in his cart, put them back where he'd found them and stood there gazing at the ones he'd passed over the first time. Then I had the urge to say from behind the towels, "I know who you are. You're Fredrik Christensen and I'm going to get you, but first I'm going to get Nurse Karin."

Having said that, I still wanted to say more, to get rid of some of the venom that had rushed to my throat, but it was better to keep cool, be succinct and let his mind get to work.

Exactly the same as what would have happened to me, he stood there paralysed for a few seconds, not reacting, not knowing where to look, although the voice had come from behind him. He must have been getting by for too long without any frights and he'd let down his guard. The problem was that it was difficult for me to turn my cart around because of this propensity of supermarket carts to go sideways. Maybe I should have just left it there but I was slow off the mark and, when I realized what was happening, he was a few metres away. He was coming up behind me. I didn't want to turn round and let him see my face, but I could feel it was him, knew for sure it was him, because when I started walking faster so did he, and his cart sounded like a train rattling off the rails. So did mine. I was going as fast as I could to escape his enormous strides and had the advantage that my head didn't stand out, which meant I could disappear amongst the drums of washing soap. I abandoned my cart in the first place I could and then hid behind a mountain of books. I heard the clattering of his cart moving away and slipped out, heading for the exit. I got into the car and waited, mopping up my sweat and calming down. It wasn't time yet to take the nitroglycerine tablet I always carried in my shirt pocket.

It was almost another half-hour before he came out. He stowed his purchases in the boot (it seemed that not even an incident of this calibre was going to make him adapt his programme), his face contorted and with a ruthless look about him. I felt more in command of myself than ever. I was going to do things my way. I'd let myself be guided by intuition and experience. I'd reached the end of the world and, when the end of the world comes, nothing has the same value as before. The step I'd just taken certainly wasn't prudent but, on the other hand, I wanted to rattle him, wanted him to make some move and, in any case, what was done was done.

Now I had to be cautious and follow him at a greater distance, because, even if he didn't know me, he'd be able to detect me as an unwanted presence.

We went up to El Tosalet, not to Villa Sol but to another villa some three hundred metres away which showed no name, only the number 50. I parked some distance below and when, having waited an hour, I saw that he wasn't coming out, I left. I now had the place in my sights and it wouldn't take me long to discover who lived there. I was absolutely certain it was one of them.

## Sandra

At six Fred hadn't returned from the shopping centre and Karin started getting anxious. There was no way of contacting him. They didn't have mobile phones. None of us was very interested in telephones. In my case, when the card ran out, centuries could go by before I got another one. It seemed an absurd way of throwing away money I didn't have. And they hadn't got used to the new technologies. They didn't use a computer either. So I thought it wouldn't be very nice to leave Karin in this situation of uncertainty and I kept working on the pullover. It was looking better and better, and all the stitches were more even now. In spite of Karin's worries about Fred, she'd occasionally lean over to see how I was doing.

At about half-past six we went back inside. A little later I opened the door to the thickset guy from the other night, the one called Martín, who was wearing the same black singlet, jeans and worn trainers, and the skinny one, the Eel, who was much less concerned about clothes and his image than Martín was. The Eel asked if Fred was home. He looked as if he couldn't imagine what I was doing in that house. He came over and whispered in my ear in a way I found intimidating, "So you've moved in here?"

Thank goodness Karin came at once. She zipped out from the living room to the front door with amazing speed.

"I'll see to this," she said.

And she ushered them into the office-cum-den on the ground floor where, on walking past, I'd seen a table with papers, an old-fashioned typewriter and a few books. I could hear her telling them that Fred was unexpectedly late and she was worried.

"They help Fred with the accounts and running messages," she offered, referring to their visit when she returned to the kitchen where I was hanging around not knowing what to do because I'd suddenly found myself caught up with lives that meant nothing to me. "They say they'll wait for a while before going out to look for him. Sometimes Fred runs into somebody, gets chatting and time flies by without him noticing."

Then she held her head in her hands, not indulging in dramatics but in order to think better. A few anaemic curls, a memento of the days when they must have been beautiful gold ringlets, covered her fingers.

"If anything happened to Fred, it would be the end, do you understand?"

Yes, I did have an idea, but on such occasions it's better not to dig too deep so I said nothing. As for me, I'd hang around a little longer because if I left now I wouldn't sleep with an easy conscience. It wasn't so easy to move in and out of situations as if nothing's happening. From outside everything looked different, just as my baby inside me would be seeing it all in a completely fantastic way.

When Fred finally opened the door with his key and came in with his bags of shopping, I felt a huge sense of relief, as if he was very important to me when, in reality, he was of almost zero importance. Karin set her knitting aside, got up and literally ran over to Fred. I carried the shopping into the kitchen while they were talking in their own language. Since I couldn't make out a single word, I concentrated on the intonation. First of all, Karin expressed natural relief mixed with happiness. In his neutral, deep, verging-on-monotonous voice Fred was telling her something important, not something trivial like getting a flat tyre. Karin listened in complete silence, after which she responded with surprise and also alarm. Her voice had got its strength back. Clearly they had a problem.

* * *

It had gone nine when I convinced Karin that I needed to stretch my legs and that I was going to stroll back to the motorbike that I'd left in the little square a thousand years before. Fred was still with his helpers or whatever the visitors in his office were and whatever that room might be.

I went through the curves, back down to sea level, as slowly as I could. I'd never forgive myself if I crashed. I don't know why I'd left the Christensens' house more afraid than I was when I entered it, with a fear that was vague and indefinable, a fear of everything. What would Karin do if she were left alone and had an attack of arthritis? I still had the luxury of fending for myself, of being autonomous. When the baby came, we'd see. I think that Fate, or God, or whatever, put Karin in my path so I'd wake up to the pitfalls lying ahead, so I'd be able to appreciate what I had: youth, good health and a baby on the way.

I didn't see them again for several days.

## Julián

Once they entered Villa Sol and closed the metal gate, you couldn't hear anything from outside so I headed back to the hotel. I had dinner nearby, breathed in the fresh air of the night and even sat down for a while in a terrace bar to have a decaffeinated coffee and contemplate people's semi-naked bodies, navels, backs, legs, which I enjoyed because they weren't totally naked. I went back to my room without a very clear idea of how to get out of this impasse, how to provoke them and make them reveal who they really were. I couldn't go to the police and just assert without further ado that a dangerous war criminal lived here. Dangerous? But nobody who's got one foot in the grave is dangerous, they'd say. Would they have enough life left in them to be brought to trial? But what could be done, with the necessary proofs, would be to publish their crimes in the newspapers, so they'd have to deal with the revulsion of their neighbours, so they'd no longer be able to stroll around the supermarket, the hospital and the beach like any other person. It would make their lives a misery. It would oblige them to flee, to sell the house, pack their bags and start all over again, which, at their age, would be true martyrdom. They were certainly dreaming of spending their last days here. But it would be me who'd be spending my last days here, not them. They had no right to die in peace. What would Salva have wanted to do with them? He'd left me a legacy of the object but not the objective. In the last years of her life Raquel used to tell me, whenever I was tempted to do what I was doing now, that I was behind the times, that things worked differently now, that there were other means of investigation and that I should stay home. Well, whatever the case, I was aware that nobody was counting on me, that nobody remembered me or my services, that my old comrades were like me or even worse, that the newcomers thought I'd died, that the world was in other hands and that I'd have to go about things my own way.

On returning to the hotel at night, I was intercepted by the concierge with the big freckle on his cheek. He looked at me in alarm and asked me to sit down in one of the armchairs in the lobby. Something bad had happened.

"Is it my daughter? Has something happened to her?"

He waved his hands saying no, it wasn't that, and I calmed down. If my daughter was all right, it couldn't be all that serious.

"Something distressing has happened in your room… It's been ransacked."

I listened to him wide-eyed. "My room?"

"Yes, your room. Somebody got in and turned everything upside down. They also slit open the mattress and the upholstery on the armchair. We have safes here. If you've brought anything of value with you, it would have been better if you'd hired one."

I'm certain that the composure with which I received the news made him shift from discomfort to giving me a ticking-off.

"The hotel can't be responsible for this kind of oversight."

"I don't have anything of value, if what you mean is money, jewels or something like that."

He'd stopped seeing me as a helpless old man and was trying to look beyond the wrinkles and the decrepitude.

"Yes, but well… what about drugs?"

I didn't laugh at his question because I'd just understood that Fredrik had found me out and given orders for me to be given a good fright. I didn't know how, but after the supermarket episode he'd managed to locate me. More alarming still was that Fredrik wasn't alone, or at least not surrounded only by geriatrics, because he couldn't have done it by himself. Something like this required strength and speed.

45

"I think that whoever did this got the wrong room. I can't think of any other explanation," I said.

The concierge apologized and suggested that they should change my room. I could have a drink in the bar while they took my things to another floor. I accepted, thinking that what I ought to do was to go to another hotel, but on second thoughts I realized they'd find me again. They would most probably have found the file I'd taken out of my personal records. Fortunately, I'd stowed the newspaper cutting in my jacket pocket along with the only two photos from their youth that I possessed. She was dressed as a nurse and he was in a T-shirt doing gymnastics.

I sat at the bar in the cafeteria and asked for a decaf, thinking that, now I'd been found out by Fredrik, the whole situation had changed and, what was more frightening, Fredrik was more alert than I'd imagined. Furthermore, he had people working for him and I was alone. Would they be capable of killing me?

After an hour, Freckle-face came back to inform me that they'd moved my luggage but I could go back to my old room to check that they hadn't overlooked anything.

"It's the first time that something like this has happened in the hotel. Please forgive the inconvenience. We are very, very sorry about this."

I gestured with my hand as if to say he could stop apologizing. It made me feel uncomfortable and also guilty.

"Don't worry, we old people are an easy target," I remarked, getting my wallet out of my pocket, in vain as it turned out since he wouldn't let me pay.

All that was left in my room was my lens case and one of the two notebooks I'd been jotting things in. The other one was in the car. It wasn't surprising that they'd missed it, what with all the things strewn around on the floor: the pillow, the pillow case, stuffing from the slashed cushions and mattress, the blankets out of the cupboard, the little bottles of shower gel and shampoo from the bathroom, the drawers of the writing desk, a few cheap pictures, and bottles and bags of nuts from the minibar. The radio alarm too. They wanted me to get the message that they were after me.

"Good Heavens!" I exclaimed. "They got it wrong, no question about it."

"In any case, check that there's nothing missing. The hotel detective will have to speak with you tomorrow. I hope you don't mind."

In compensation for the fright they'd moved me to a suite on the top floor. It was a pity my poor Raquel couldn't have been here to enjoy it. There was a living room with armchairs and sofas and, embellished with huge-leafed tropical plants, there was a large terrace from which you could get a glimpse of the port. Raquel would also have loved the hydro-massage bath, the flowers, the basket of fruit and the bottle of champagne. Nonetheless, I was happy that my daughter hadn't come with me, because, this way, I only had myself to worry about. I breathed more easily when I noticed the file mixed up with my shirts and trousers. Fredrik's thugs hadn't unearthed it.

"Enjoy your stay here. Let me know if you need anything else. My name is Roberto."

I told Roberto to take the champagne, to enjoy it with his wife, because I wasn't supposed to drink alcohol. Roberto smiled and said he'd send a chambermaid to take it away.

I checked the locks on the hallway door and the terrace door to see how I could reinforce security. When I was in there it would be very difficult for them to set upon me by surprise. The problem would arise when I went out again.

Fredrik would imagine that after the incident at the hotel I'd go running back home again. The message was clear. They could slit me open like the mattress and cushions. They could trample on me as they'd done with the pictures. It's not that the possibility didn't scare me, but I had nothing to lose, and retreating at this point would cause me great mental fatigue. The idea that they might kill me made me feel really bad about my daughter. I didn't want to make her suffer, but it was also true that the writing was on the wall and I'd be dying well before her, so she'd have to bear my loss one of these days. I therefore decided to sleep like a log and almost managed it. I was awakened by some tepid rays of light crossing the suite.

Whatever the case, I was in no mind to do anything crazy. Given the circumstances, I'd give the Christensens a breather, at least for today. With the new day, a better plan had occurred to me: I'd go over to the house of the girl with the red streak in her hair.

It was Saturday, around eleven. The sun was shining but not scorching hot. Summer was on the way out. Before leaving my room, I decided not to let myself be stymied by whatever amount of technology the enemy might be wielding, and to resort to the old tricks I'd always used. As I went out, I hung the "Please Do Not Disturb" sign on the door handle so the chambermaid wouldn't come in, then took some tiny bits of transparent paper cut from the cellophane that had been used for wrapping the bottle and lodged them between the door and the frame, and between the bottom of the door and the floor. They'd necessarily move or fall when the door was opened. I didn't have time to get up to date with things or to try anything more sophisticated. I had to be myself, an old fogey who couldn't even count on his own people.

## Sandra

When somebody was going along the track, when the postman came or workers from the gas or electricity company, or when some motorbike went by, crushing pebbles and flattening the ground, the ghostly life of the neighbourhood was revolutionized. The man in the Panama hat who stopped at my house and rang the doorbell didn't imagine he wasn't interrupting any kind of activity. It was rather pure and simple inactivity that was sending me off to sleep. He interrupted such thoughts as I-should-be-sewing-something-for-the-baby-to-wear. He interrupted my simultaneously not wanting to be with anyone and wanting to be with someone. He also interrupted thoughts of who-would-have-said-some-time-ago-that-I'd-be-hanging-around-with-these-two-old-foreigners? Of course I was thinking about Fred and Karin, who'd given no signs of life since I'd left Villa Sol some days before. One of them must have fallen ill, or they'd gone off on a trip, or some relatives had come to see them and their daily routine had changed. All kinds of things were running through my head. I had to admit I was missing them. This was idiotic, because they meant nothing to me, but even so, I'd stop watering if I heard a car on the gravel at the entrance. Their faces were engraved in my mind, maybe because they had something slightly out of the ordinary about them. All faces end up having something special sooner or later but these had had it straight away, almost at first sight.

The man at the wrought-iron gate would have been about eighty, or more perhaps, and he looked as if he needed to rest, so I invited him up to the porch. He said he liked my little house. He said "little house" as if I were a gnome or a princess. He can't have taken a good look at me. He spoke with an Argentine accent that refined his already very good manners even more. I took advantage of his interest in renting the house to show him round and to spend a bit of time chatting with someone. He conveyed this sense of neatness that thin old people tend to have. He had light-coloured eyes, or they'd turned light over the years, and it was probably also the case that the years had made him shorter, so now he was about the same height as me, a couple of centimetres short of one metre seventy. As I was showing him round the little house I had a great sense of anxiety that I was wasting my time, precious time in which others were finishing university degrees, getting work experience, becoming bosses, writing books or appearing on TV. I don't know, I really don't know how I could have got to this point without having done anything useful except for this little baby I was carrying inside me, and not even this was my own work. I was the bearer, the person responsible for bringing the child into the world, and at least I wanted to be in good shape to do this, so I stopped smoking and drinking as soon as I knew I was pregnant and, though I've been tempted many times to smoke a cig out in the moonlight in this place at the arse end of the world, responsibility won the day.

I told him that I'd check with my sister about the possibilities of her renting out the house. But I didn't feel like calling my sister, didn't want to talk to her, didn't want her to start giving me a sermon, or to remind me that I can't keep living in this pro-tem way for ever. I didn't want her to ask me if I was watering the plants, or doing the washing, or looking after the house.

About to leave and fanning himself with the hat, he told me his name was Julián. And I'm Sandra, I said. Sandra, he repeated. And he went on to say that I'd been very kind to him, that I should take care because the world was full of dangers that don't show their face until they're on top of you and, come what may, I should always put my physical well-being first. Then he apologized for being such an alarmist, saying that I reminded him of his daughter when she was my age. I felt a bit strange because he was speaking to me as if he knew me, as if he knew something about me that not even I knew, but the strange feeling passed when I started thinking about how old he was, that he belonged to a time when women were less independent, and that I should try to see what he was saying from the standpoint of his experience.

As soon as my visitor left, I got out the Calvin Klein plastic bag in which the magazine with the story of Ira's life travelled to the beach. Fortunately, it had dried without the ink blurring.


## Julián

I parked the car in the same place as before, on the patch of ground by the roadside, and then walked along the picturesque narrow street where my demons were now calling. The sun shone directly down on the girl's little house, making it look bright and happy, and there were white clothes hung out on the clothesline. I could hear music, which meant she was inside. I rang the bell next to the metal gate and waited. Two minutes later I rang again. Finally she came out into the small garden. She was wearing a bikini, which gave a better view of her tattoos, but I averted my gaze from her body. I didn't want her thinking I was a dirty old man because, moreover, that would have been a completely false impression. I've never been tempted by women younger than myself, just as I've never been tempted by Ferraris and mansions. My world has its limits and I like it having limits. I sensed that she was disappointed to see it was me. She might have been expecting somebody, Fredrik perhaps? I didn't believe it, didn't believe that she could be disappointed about not seeing someone of my age group.

"I'm sorry if I'm bothering you. I was told that this house is for rent."

"Well, you've been misinformed. It's not for sale or rent."

Her hair was several colours, ranging from red to black, longer in some parts than in others. She also sported a small stud in her nose. She had greenish-brown eyes and an aquiline nose. The sun, striking her forehead, gave her a slightly ironic expression. If I was her age I would have fallen in love with her right then and there. She reminded me of Raquel as a young woman, her simple, direct way of seeing life and people.

"That's a pity, because it's such a lovely house. It's the one I like most in the whole street. My wife insisted I should come and have a look."

She looked around me as if searching for an invisible woman.

"She stayed in the hotel as she's not feeling well. You wouldn't know of any house similar to this that might be for rent?"

I took off my Panama hat and starting fanning myself, although I wasn't actually hot. I did it to prolong the moment and to avoid having to go leaving it at that. The ploy worked because she opened the gate.

"Come in and sit down. I'll bring you a glass of water. It's still hot."

"Just out of curiosity, how many bedrooms does it have?"

"Three," she answered from inside. Then I heard water running and some other sounds.

"It's really nice here," she said, handing me the glass. "All day long you're coming in contact with nature. You can see for yourself, the trees, the flowers, the air, the sun. It's the best thing for me right now."

It was clear she had the problems typical of her age, not knowing what to do with her life, fear of solitude, and energy.

"Thank you for letting me sit for a while. I'm taking heart medication and it brings down my blood pressure a lot."

She told me she understood all too well, because just after arriving here she'd had a dizzy attack on the beach and it had been awful. She took a T-shirt off the clothesline and put it on.

"I'm five months pregnant."

Five months, I thought to myself. This complicated everything. How was I going to get a pregnant woman involved in this mess? I stood up, ready to leave, as if I'd rested enough.

"Where are you going?" she asked cheerfully. "If you like the house, I'll show it to you."

I followed her inside, to the upper floor. Yes, she did have a bulging, rounded belly. Raquel's now long-ago pregnancy somehow connected me with this girl. I knew something about these things. It wasn't Greek to me. She wasn't worried about letting me look into her room with its rumpled bed. She seemed to find it all normal, natural. She was chatting, saying that in this house she felt as if she was in a monastery, that she'd come here to cut herself off from people and reflect about her life. I didn't ask any questions. It was better for her to tell me what she felt like telling me.

"I didn't tell you the truth before. This house belongs to my sister and she rents it on a seasonal basis. It might be free next summer. If you want, I could speak to her."

51

I said that would be fine and I'd tell my wife.

"My name is Julián," I told her, holding out my hand. "If you don't mind, I'll drop by again some other day."

"Sandra," she replied, not smiling but not serious either. In any case, she didn't have to smile to be agreeable. "Drop in when you want." Then she added with some concern, "I had some friends and we went to the beach a few times but now they've disappeared. They've stopped coming to see me without any explanation."

She must have been referring to Fredrik and Karin, which, combined with the episode at the hotel, meant that my presence had made them very jumpy.

"Don't worry, they'll be back."

"Well, they're old and maybe one of them is ill."

"That's also possible," I said, as much for her sake as for mine.

As soon as I arrived at the hotel, I decided to phone my daughter to tell her that I'd finally found a little house that was ideal for the two of us, but it wasn't free at the moment, although in all likelihood it would be next summer. I'd also tell her that my stay here would be longer than originally planned. She'd insist on coming here to make sure I wasn't going to do anything crazy, but I'd tell her it'd be better to save the money and put it towards renting the future house. Naturally, I'd keep mum about the suite, not because I wanted to have it all to myself, but because, in these circumstances, occupying a suite doesn't entail any pleasure.

But things rarely turn out the way you plan them. No sooner had I set foot in the lobby than Roberto came over to tell me that, at about eleven, some individual had asked whether I'd left the hotel. Luckily it was Roberto's shift.

"I told him that this information was confidential," Roberto stated, "but when he insisted and said he wanted to talk to the manager, I thought it best to tell him that you'd left the hotel. I don't know whether I put my foot in it. He must've been about thirty, olive-skinned, quite beefy and shorter than me."

"Thank you," I replied. "I don't know anyone who looks like that. As I said, I think they've got me mixed up with someone else."

Roberto looked at me, somewhat defensive. He no longer believed everything I was telling him.

"Then I'll give the order to my colleagues that they're not to answer any questions about you."

I smiled and threw out my arms in a gesture of impotence and to signal that I wasn't hiding anything, that I was the object of some absurd mix-up.

The door to my room was just as I'd left it. When I opened it, the transparent scraps of paper fell to the floor and I picked them up. It wasn't good news that Fredrik had followers (like the one that had been asking about me, like the ones that had destroyed my room), young neo-Nazis maybe. It would be better if they were hired louts because they'd be less fanatical. I went back to feeling like a David against a Goliath, a feeble David. Then again, what would Roberto be thinking about me?


# Sandra

I missed working on the pullover I'd started knitting and missed these adoptive grandparents who'd entered and exited from my life, as if my life was the metro or a bus, but, most of all, something didn't seem right. It was beyond all logic that they could be more scatterbrained than me. I've always regarded myself as the queen of all-over-the-place and foggy ideas. I thought that, when you got to their age, doubts would be history, because the path had already been walked and there was no need to beat your brains out over what you were going to be doing in ten minutes. It could be that I'd unwittingly said or done something to upset them. After all, we were from different cultures and different generations so it wouldn't be surprising if misunderstandings arose. I still remembered that look they gave each other when I was talking, which I found totally incomprehensible. Or, more simply, Karin had had a relapse of her arthritis. And was it all that important to me if Karin was consumed by pain? Partly it was and, then again, I'd watered the plants, hung out, taken in and folded more clothes, and I knew almost all there was to know about Ira. I needed to go back and see people who were familiar to me, who'd welcome me, give me human warmth, and I didn't have to go looking for them because they were there within my reach. I only had to get on the Vespino and start it up.

Hence at dusk, before starting the ride up to El Tosalet, I put a change of clothes in a backpack in case I stayed the night. Basically, I was trying my luck going up there at that hour, as my secret intention was not to have to come down again at night. Although it would be beautiful to ride among stars, trees and mountains in the moonlight, it also accentuated the feeling of risk, danger and helplessness. Fear of everything and nothing had got into my body, had taken over me, a senseless cowardice. Or it might have been caution. The cars sticking to my back were getting desperate because it wasn't easy to overtake with all the curves, but the sheer drop I had on my right impressed me more than it did them. Fuck you, fuck you, I growled at the cars. To top it all, halfway there it started to drizzle with drops that were getting bigger and bigger. It was nerve-racking because I couldn't stop and couldn't see well. So I breathed easier when I got to the residential zone of the Norwegians.

I rode through the streets until I got to Villa Sol. The drops had now turned into silver needles that seemed to have their own light brightening the darkness. Night had been closing in. What was I doing here? Neither my parents nor Santi could possibly imagine that, right now, I'd be looking for the house of some foreign pensioners in strange surroundings, in the middle of a downpour. I don't know why I was doing this. I was doing things that didn't make sense, because now I didn't have a job and I didn't have any discipline. But having a job meant giving a superficial meaning to life, false security. I wasn't convinced, either, that life's panacea was having a fixed timetable and being tied to a salary. And what if Fate had put me in Fred's and Karin's way so I could be liberated from such a mediocre existence? Villa Sol, the farmhouse at the fjord, the olive-green four-by-four and the black Mercedes had to go to someone when they died. And they could die any moment now. I wasn't guided by self-interest. I'd risked my life coming up here, because, in my present circumstances, I felt better with them than without them, but this didn't prevent me from weighing up the chances of their being a good influence on my future. I could already see myself raising my child in this house and driving him or her to school in the four-by-four. I'd sell the Mercedes and rent out the top floor so I could live comfortably. I'd put a small ceramics workshop in the greenhouse and devote myself to craftwork.

I might be able to sell some pieces in the Thursday street market. All this would be for me because Fred and Karin loved me like a real granddaughter, or more than a granddaughter, because our relationship was spontaneous, chosen by us and not because of blood ties.

I parked in the deserted street and rang the bell. No one opened and I felt a bit deflated. I rang again and... nothing. What a let-down! I hadn't thought about this possibility and didn't dare to go back home in the rain. This was no time to be reckless and yet I was soaked through, except for my head which was covered by the helmet. It was then that it occurred to me to go to Alice's house, where I sheltered from the rain the first time I came up to El Tosalet. Maybe they'd gone to visit her. It wasn't likely that they would have ventured farther in this weather. I was right. I saw the Mercedes parked there, not the four-by-four but the black Mercedes, a few metres from Alice's house. Fred must have thought that this was a chance to get it out. There were more luxury cars bordering the kerb, so Alice must have been throwing a party. Music was coming out of the house, distant music that the rain was bringing and taking away in gusts. I leant the motorbike against the wall and climbed up to stand on the seat. Through the windows overlooking the garden I could see people dancing and thought I could make out Karin walking around in a white evening dress. Maybe she'd been infected with Alice's eternal youth. I didn't have time to see any more because I felt a presence at my back.

"If you fall you're going to hurt yourself."

It was the Eel, Alberto I think his name was, whom I'd already seen in Karin's house. He had an umbrella and looked very pissed off. I felt embarrassed. I'd been caught out snooping and the Christensens would find out about it. Alice would find out about it. My inheritance was evaporating before my eyes.

I held out my hand so he'd help me to get down.

"I wanted to know if Fred and Karin were inside. I've been by their house... I'm soaking wet... I don't want to take the motorbike back down in this rain."

Once on firm ground again, I got under the umbrella and took off my helmet.

"I know you," he said.

"I know you too," I replied, as if we were speaking in code.

"Why didn't you ring at the gate?"

55

"I did ring," I lied, "but they can't have heard me."

"Where's the bell, on the right or on the left?"

"I don't remember."

"Liar."

The umbrella was forcing us to be too close, with the mist of our breath in each other's faces, and he didn't like me. It was strange because, even though I was up to my eyeballs with this vague fear of everything and nothing, this jerk had something about him that didn't make me afraid. He wasn't like the nothingness filled with stars. He wasn't like the road in the middle of the night. He was none of that. He was as mortal as I was, and he didn't make me feel afraid of everything.

"If you can, tell them I came to see them. I'm off now," I said, putting my helmet on again.

"Not so fast," he said.

"Not so fast? So, are you a cop or something? Don't fuck with me."

"Don't even think about moving," he ordered, getting out his mobile and leaving me outside the umbrella.

He moved away a little to talk, without taking his eyes off me. He had to wait for an answer, which annoyed him. I imagined Fred and Karin, giddy with the dancing, having to take in the news that I was spying on them over the wall. I was also waiting, arms crossed, helmet in my hand. He was behaving like a nightclub bouncer, like a minder, like a security guard. Today he was wearing a suit and tie with his hair combed back behind his ears. Finally he closed his mobile.

"I'm taking you to Villa Sol and we'll wait there for them to come."

The guy called Martín came out from inside the house and gave him some keys. I didn't have it in me to get into an argument. I just wanted to get dry, watch a bit of telly and get into bed.

Him taking me was a manner of speaking. I was the one who drove the motorbike with him sitting behind, holding up the open umbrella. When we got there, he took some keys out of his pocket and opened up the gate and the front door. I shrugged my backpack off, letting it slide down to the floor.

"Don't get any ideas about sitting on the sofa while you're wet," he warned, guessing my intentions.

I still didn't feel like talking. I picked up the backpack and went up to what I considered to be my bedroom, the one with the little blue flowers. The satin nightie was still under the pillow, just as I'd left it. The clothes in the backpack were damp, except for a T-shirt, so I put the nightie on. I knew what it might look like but didn't care. Didn't give a damn. Might as well be hung for a sheep as a lamb.

"I don't know what your game is. You don't fool me. And they'll end up seeing you for what you are. They're not stupid, you know."

This was his response to the spectacle I offered as I came downstairs. He watched me, leaning against the wall with his feet crossed. With the black suit and wet hair combed back, I had to admit he wasn't bad-looking. And suddenly this impression rattled me. The nightdress looked too good on me, even clinging to my belly. It slithered over my breasts and the straps slipped off my shoulders, the kind of item worn by women who aren't into beating around the bush.

I replied by twirling around making the skirt ripple.

"Think whatever you like. But if you think I fancy you, you're dead wrong, loser."

He looked at me with infinite contempt, but I knew, my instinct was telling me, that he liked me more than he wanted to. He couldn't keep his eyes off my tattoos. He was your typical fetishist. He was one of those guys in whom you start discovering things, more and more things until you can't hold back any more. I decided not to let him get to me and went into the kitchen. His steps, the footsteps of new shoes, followed me. I opened the fridge, poured myself a glass of milk, heated it in the microwave, and started drinking it slowly, sitting on the sofa and watching television. Now I could feel him behind me. His clothes smelt wet.

"Who gave you permission to put that on?"

"I don't need any. It's mine."

"Yeah sure, you carry these things around in your backpack."

I felt a bit cold, but put up with it until he went into the office-cum-den, which he also opened with a key, and then I picked up a shawl of Karin's and wrapped it around me. It smelt of her, of her perfume, which gave me a slightly disagreeable sensation, because it wasn't the same as putting on one of my mum's pullovers. I didn't get on with my mum, but her smell was as familiar to me as Christmas dinner. Karin's smell on my body gave me the creeps.

When I was sleepy enough I took it off and, without a word, went up to the bedroom and got into bed. At first I was alert, because there was no bolt on the door, but then I relaxed. Alberto might be an eel but that's about all he was.

I dropped into a sound sleep, thinking that Alberto probably wanted to be the Norwegians' favourite grandchild too, and then the sound of the front door opening and closing woke me up. There was an exchange of muted words and yawns. I wondered whether I should come out or if that would make it worse for everyone, because then we'd have to talk about what had happened and that would keep us awake. To tell the truth, I didn't know what to do. I went barefoot to the stairwell and saw that dickhead Alberto leaving. And I saw Karin in her gorgeous white dress with soft feathers at the neckline, which looked like a disguise on her. I was really surprised to see Fred wearing a uniform that I'd seen a thousand times in Nazi films, cap and all, which made him seem even taller, highlighting his already stern features. It suited him better than her dress suited her. It was just like Alice to be giving fancy-dress parties for her friends, in the style of the old days when the world was elegant and the women wore evening dress every night.

I got back into bed, turned the light off and tried to go back to sleep. After a while I heard them wearily climbing the stairs. There'll come a time, I thought, when they won't be able to get up the stairs any more and they'll have to fit out the library-den as a bedroom and live downstairs. It'd be a lot more practical, I thought, closing my eyes. But just before I completely slipped away from this world, I heard my bedroom door opening and bare feet padding over to the bed, felt eyes looking at me for a while, after which they moved off and the door closed. Or was I already dreaming?

In the morning they were waiting for me in the kitchen, Karin still in her nightdress and Fred all spruced up to go out to some appointment, with pale-grey trousers, blue jacket, shiny shoes and cheekbones and eyes gleaming more than ever. He was standing there having his last sip of tea.

"We thought you didn't like this house or us after the way you left the other day. Taking French leave, I believe you call it," Karin said, smiling at me in a way that made me feel embarrassed.

But her husband cut her off and I didn't have time to offer any kind of explanation.

"I'm glad you're here, because you can keep Karin company."

My look of bewilderment flustered him too, and we stood there staring at one another. My questions were: company? How long?

"I have to go away on a trip and I don't want to leave her alone. I'll only be away for a day or two," he said, then stood there thinking. "Of course we'll make sure you're properly recompensed. It'll be good for you to have something put aside for the arrival of the baby."

"More than anything else," Karin intervened, "you'd be doing me a great favour. You'll be fine here and won't lack for anything."

Making some money for a change seemed like a good idea. It was better than daydreaming about some improbable inheritance.

"We employ a woman to come and do the housework every day. You'd only be expected to do some shopping and keep me company. Can you drive the four-by-four?"

"No problem."

Fred's presence didn't bother me. He was silent and friendly, but even so I had the feeling that the house would lighten up without him. On the other hand, I wasn't mad on the idea of being fully responsible for Karin. What if she fell ill? This might have been the ideal time to ask them why they'd given no signs of life all these days, but I thought I already knew, that they wanted me to be the one who came to them, because otherwise it would mean I wasn't sufficiently interested in them. They'd be wondering about the extent to which I'd want to be hanging around with a couple who were in their eighties.

After she gave me the wool and needles, and while I was trying to reach Karin's level of perfection, she brought some paper and envelopes from the library-den and started to write some notes. Her birthday was coming up and she wanted to celebrate it. Under her reading glasses, the letters unfolded slowly in very beautiful handwriting that looked like German, but, to tell the truth, I had no idea of what Norwegian would look like.

"Do you know German?" I asked as I was counting the stitches.

Karin took off her glasses to get a better look at me.

"A little. A bit of German, a bit of French and a bit of English. I'm very old and I know a few things."

"Yesterday you looked lovely in that white dress I saw you wearing at Alice's party," I remarked so that my espionage would cease to be a taboo subject.

"Yes, I know you were looking. I would have been looking too if I could have climbed up on a motorbike," she said laughing.

I limited myself to a smile, because that totally innocent action seemed to have been given undue importance, and still more so now with some distance and in the light of day.

"What I don't understand is why you didn't ring the bell. You know Alice."

"I don't understand it either. It was a stupid thing. I think I didn't want to be an intruder, to gatecrash, to get into a party I wasn't invited to."

From Karin's expression I could see that my explanation had left her totally satisfied. It left me satisfied too.

I made the most of the moment to tell her I'd left my nausea pills down there (we'd started to refer to my sister's house as "down there") and I was worried about having a dizzy spell. Deep down, I was desperate to be alone for a while. I just wanted to listen to my own thoughts or none at all. It did my head in being so contradictory, first wanting to be with them and then wanting to be without them. Since it was getting dark, she told me to take the four-by-four. She probably thought that the motorbike was too flimsy and she wanted to be sure I'd be back, which I understood. It's very easy to be brave when there's nothing to stop you.

The four-by-four was so big that I parked it on a patch of ground by the roadside just before my street. As I closed the door I had the most idiotic sense of freedom, because nobody was retaining me and nobody was obliging me to do anything. Even so, I took in a deep breath, to get the smell of my street. The dim street lights revealed a man standing by my gate. An old man. I looked more closely. I knew him. It was Julián, the one I'd shown round the house. He didn't hear me approaching, and when I spoke to him from behind and touched his arm I feared he'd be startled. It was like thrusting my hand into the same bubble of fragility in which Fred and Karin were also trapped. But, no, he turned around, looking calm and with a smile on his face.

"I'm happy to see that you're well," he said as I let him in.

He'd come about the matter of renting the house. He said he'd missed me once, that this was the second time he'd tried to see me and he apologized for the lateness of the hour. I told him it was pure miracle that he'd caught me. We chatted for quite a while or, rather, only he was talking, mentioning his wife whenever he got a chance and showing interest in my Norwegian friends, maybe because he was intrigued by the fact of my having friends of his age. And he listened with great attention to whatever I told him. I'd always heard people saying that old people love talking about all their little battles, but this wasn't the case with the ones I was coming across, because it appeared that neither the Norwegian couple nor this one had any little battles to go on about.

When he left I busied myself watering the plants and bringing the towels in from the clothesline. I folded them slowly and left them on the table. I got my pills, picked up the keys and turned the light out. I had a growing feeling of being closer to Villa Sol than to this house.


## Julián

I had to go to the hospital, to the Emergency Department. I knew the symptoms of feeling faint with cold sweats. I didn't want to cause any more problems in the hotel, didn't want them to be thinking I was the worst client they'd ever had. I liked it there, they knew me and Roberto had decided to be a sort of accomplice in an affair about which he had not the faintest idea. Basically, I knew the terrain and could defend myself better there than I could if I moved to another hotel. This thought got me planning to check out the installations, stairways, meeting rooms and lounges, toilets for public use and kitchens as soon as I felt better. The good thing about being alone is that you don't worry anybody. You don't have to go through the double anguish of feeling ill and seeing someone else suffering because you're ill. It was marvellous having Raquel by my side all those years, managing to make each day fuller with life, but there were times, some bad moments when I would have preferred to be alone and not to have to pretend that I was fine so she wouldn't suffer. Sometimes one wants to experience what's happening exactly as it is, in all its dimensions, but not to the point of hurting the person at one's side, so I had a certain sense of freedom as I headed for the hospital alone in the taxi when I noted something wasn't quite right. I've never been able to stand people who throw their solitude in the face of others, or the ones who experience it as an affront. Solitude is freedom too.

Just as I'd imagined, they asked me at the hospital if I had anyone with me. I said no. I was having a few days' holiday alone. The doctor shook her head pensively as she contemplated my solitude. She said that, in these circumstances, I'd have to spend the night in hospital, under observation. It was nothing serious, a rise in blood sugar and metabolic decompensation. I said that would be fine. What difference did it make to me whether I slept in the hotel or in hospital?

What bothered me most was that they took their time about giving me the all-clear and letting me go in the morning. At midday I told them I couldn't wait any longer and that I was leaving. I looked like an old grouch, some old crank, but I had a lot to do and I was perfectly able to see that my system was stabilized again. They made me sign a document taking responsibility for my decision, so that if I died it would be the result of my own negligence. That seemed only fair. A simple signature was enough to reassure everybody.

I hadn't slept well because of the inordinate snoring of my roommate and because the nurses kept coming in every few minutes and making a racket, but I felt fine, in good shape, and I could even go and have a little dip in the sea when I'd seen to the main task. And the main task consisted in going to Villa Sol, but this was too dangerous right now, at least until I managed to change my car. Hence it would be better to go to Sandra's house to see if the Christensens had turned up there again.

My clothes had a hospital smell about them. I felt in my pockets to make sure I had everything with me. It was an extraordinarily beautiful day. I parked the car in a different spot for caution's sake, although I didn't think there was any way they could possibly link me up with Sandra, and walked down through the streets to the little house.

Nobody came out when I rang the bell. The shutters were ajar, there were towels hung out on the clothesline and the hose snaked over the flagstones. I couldn't see the motorbike in the garden or hear any music. I therefore went back to the car and drank a little water from one of the bottles I managed to have always within reach, thinking that the most likely explanation was that this was the time that Sandra would be on the beach, and probably with the Norwegians. I headed off in that direction.

\* \* \*

62

They weren't there, at least not in the place they tended to go to. There were only a few children running around and a couple kissing. I walked almost a kilometre along the top in the hope of spotting them somewhere until I decided to abandon the project and go back to the car. I felt a lot sprightlier than I had before going to the hospital. Even though it wasn't overly hot, the water was so blue and the foam so white, and since Fredrik's thugs or a heart attack might put an end to my life at any time, I decide to strip down to my underpants – which, fortunately, were boxers going halfway down the thigh so they almost looked like bathing trunks – and have a dip. I was committing what Raquel called an act of madness, because what for a young person was healthy activity could mean pneumonia for me, but by the time I decided to take that into account I was already in among the waves, with a continuing feeling of great wellbeing in the cold. Why not enjoy paradise when it's within an arm's reach? Raquel always used to say that people like us who'd suffered a lot were afraid to enjoy things, were afraid to be happy, and she also said that there were many kinds of suffering in the world and nobody was totally free from suffering, so we shouldn't feel special about it either. To tell the truth, I really admired frivolous people with a great capacity for enjoying their lives and for having fun with everything. Going shopping, playing a game of cards, having dinner with friends, with no more than that to think about. For me, their way of life was desirable and unattainable. Innocence was a miracle more fragile than snow. It was easier for happy people to join my fold than for me to join theirs. Deep down, I wanted the frivolous, corrupt and perverse Fredrik and Karin to join my fold, wanted them to suffer, to discover what pain is. I could see it clearly now: justice would never be done in the way I wanted it to be. If Fredrik had his thugs, I had my hatred.

I dried myself by raising my arms and doing a few little jumps on the sand, then sat down to receive as much vitamin D as possible from the sun. I felt better than ever and closed my eyes. Right then, I was less afraid than I should have been.

In the interests of precaution I changed bars at lunchtime and asked for the set menu. I still felt the salt on my skin and also noted that my hair, the little I had left, was scruffy and all over the place. One

63

of these days I'd have to get it cut. The swim had made me hungry, along with the fact that I'd hardly touched the hospital breakfast, which bore no resemblance whatsoever to the buffet they offered at the hotel. Though I still had enough energy to keep going and head off for Christensen territory, I realized that I didn't have my pills with me, so I went back to the hotel.

At the reception desk Roberto stopped me in my tracks with a concerned expression on his face. He spoke very quietly so as not to be heard by the other concierge or by the other hotel guests leaning on the counter.

"I was worried. The chambermaid told me you didn't sleep in your room."

It was obvious that, with somebody like me, one could only surmise that if you haven't slept in your bed it's because you've died in some other place.

"No, it's nothing to worry about. I went off on an excursion and it got so late that I spent the night in another hotel. Thank you for your concern."

And then I added in a confidential tone, "Anything new?"

"Not that I know of. Ah yes... the detective wants to see you."

Without consulting me, Roberto picked up the phone, informed someone that I was in the hotel now and hung up.

"The detective's called Tony and he's waiting for you in the bar. Have you had lunch yet?"

I said I had, wondering whether I should or shouldn't go up to the room to get my pills.

"Then you can make the most of the occasion to have a coffee."

I beat my hat against my leg, letting fly a bit of sand. Then I went off to the bar.

Roberto must have provided a good description of my appearance, because no sooner had I entered than a solidly built young man, who was going to be fat in a couple of years, came over to me, holding out his hand. He led me to a small table, a pedestal table, Raquel would say, on which a little lamp was lit even in daytime, but this didn't make the bar any less shadowy than it always was, because the idea was to create an atmosphere of intimacy.

"We very much regret the incident in your room the other day."

"Well, these things happen."

Tony had a bottle of beer clenched in his beefy hand. I asked for a coffee – which was very good, by the way – and as I savoured it, Tony apologized again. He was wearing a jacket that looked as if it was going to split down the back when he leant forward over the small pedestal table.

"I've been in this job for a long time," Tony said, staring at me with his slightly protuberant eyes, "and everything always, and I mean always, has an explanation."

I mulled over his words for a while, holding the cup against my lips.

"Then, son, you'll be able to tell me what happened."

I don't think he liked me calling him "son", and I wouldn't have liked it either, but I did it on purpose to test how sure he was of himself. Not very.

"I can't yet, but I will," he ventured with a more serious expression. "Are you planning on staying with us for a while?"

"I hope so, as long as the weather's good."

"I'm told you believe you've been mistaken for somebody else."

"Wouldn't that be the most reasonable explanation?"

"Maybe," he said, taking a long final swig.

I also drained my cup. We stood up.

"I hope there'll be no repetition of this," he said.

His words seemed to be deliberately aimed at me. I got his drift. He tried to rearrange his jacket, wriggling inside his second skin. I was dredging up my past, trying to find someone like Tony. I found a few. They weren't exactly Nobel Prize winners, yet they managed to make the world conform to their own vision of it.

I was almost certain that Tony had wrecked my room at the orders of Fredrik Christensen, or that he'd let others do it. There was something in the movement of his eyes that betrayed him. On the way to the lift, I told Roberto that I needed to get another car, since the one I had was giving me some problems. Roberto assented with a gesture of already having entertained this possibility. He no longer looked me in the way he'd done on the first day, but with more respect and interest now.

I had to use the bottle of water from the minibar to take my pills, which vexed me, because everything in the minibar was several euros more expensive. And every extra euro I spent was filching from my daughter's inheritance. Nobody was going to compensate either her or me for this service I was doing. Nobody cared. There were other things to think about, other enemies. I'd been left behind, in my world, and that's where the objects of my hatred, my friends and my enemies were. I had neither energy nor mental powers for any more than that. And, if I'm to be sincere, this was the first time I didn't expect remuneration or recognition, the first time that no one would know whether I'd succeeded or failed, the first time I didn't give a shit about other people's opinions, and I felt free.

I had a sleep and it was dusk when I woke up. Now the sun was setting a minute earlier every day, pretty much like what was happening in my life. A minute was a long time. I didn't regret having slept too long, as I needed to rest. Good God, it was ages since I'd felt so well! If it weren't for the expense of the call, I would have phoned my daughter to tell her, but one call leads to another, and if I missed phoning her one day she'd get worried, so I preferred to tell her in my thoughts. My wife had certainly got to the point of reading my mind. I'd had confirmation of this on numerous occasions and she used to say jokingly that if I was going to cheat on her I'd better be careful, even if it was only a thought, because she'd be able to read it, and I blindly believed her. I was certain that those black eyes of hers were capable of penetrating the bottommost depths of my mind.

I spent half an hour on my reconnaissance of the hotel, the general stairway, fire escape, roof terrace, lifts, service entrances, kitchens, restaurant, all the nooks and crannies, and the basement. I still had to check the laundry, the toilets for public use, and explore the passageways, one by one, as well as the pantry. If the guests had any idea of how deficient the security system was they'd be running away instead of leaving their savings here, but such is life. Some knew and some didn't. I'd make the most detailed plan I could and design an escape route in keeping with my limitations. I wasn't tired and felt so full of energy that I went out for a while. It was getting cool and my jacket didn't bother me in the least. I wanted to forget for a moment that I was an ailing old man. The air was laden with the fragrance of flowers. This could be the perfect time to go over to Sandra's house and see if she'd come back.

I drove slowly, savouring the moment of going into the narrow street and approaching the little house, but also fearing that I might not find

Sandra there, fearing that I wouldn't be able to exchange a few words with this girl who could be my granddaughter, a granddaughter sent so I could give her only the good things that life had given me. Of all the people I'd met after arriving here, she was the only one who made me feel that I had a bit of life ahead of me, that there would be a life after Fredrik and Karin. The track was almost dark and not even the little house had its porch light on. A girl in her state… I only hoped nothing had happened to her. From our earlier conversation I'd deduced that she didn't have friends around here, and yet everyone knows that young people, being as they are, make friends quickly. While I was ruminating on such matters, standing there motionless next to the metal gate somewhat bemused, hoping that maybe the lights would suddenly go on, I heard someone behind me and also felt a hand on my arm, which startled me, although I made an effort not to show it.

"Ah, it's you?" Sandra said.

Sandra, Sandra. She'd arrived. She was here.

"I'm very glad to see you," I said, trying to disguise my happiness.

More than Sandra, I saw shadows of Sandra. The hair, the arms, shadows of edges of things falling on the shadow of her trousers.

"Forgive me for turning up at this hour, but I've only just been able to talk things over with my wife. I hope I haven't startled you."

Sandra laughed. "I'm not easily frightened. I've been in tighter spots than this."

She laughed again, although she didn't seem to be the sort of girl who expressed happiness by laughing. I think she did it for me, to make me feel comfortable.

"Come in. Don't just stand here," she said as she opened the gate.

Then she opened the door of the house. I waited, walking around the garden, breathing in its fragrance, then all at once the porch light came on and the plants were visible. Sandra came out and settled in a hammock.

"I was going to offer you a beer but I don't have any. I haven't had time to go to the supermarket."

"Don't worry. I prefer not to drink alcohol."

"Me neither. Now I'm pregnant I don't drink or smoke, and I'm not handling it at all well. Right now I'd love to have a cig."

She was a trusting girl who believed in her right to be in the world without anything bad happening to her, without anybody attacking her or harming her. I was certain that it had never as much as occurred to her that things could be otherwise. I sat down on one edge of the other hammock, without reclining.

"Well… I've come about this question of renting the house. We can wait till next summer if that suits your sister."

"I'll speak with her about it but not right now. Right now I don't want any hassle. I couldn't stand it if she started asking me if I've thought about what I'm going to do with my life."

"Take your time. There's no hurry. By the way, did your friends turn up, those elderly foreigners?"

Sandra sat up. "Yes, they did, and I've just come from their house. Fred's just gone off on a trip and she needs somebody to help her and I've got nothing to do. You'd certainly like that house. What a garden! Swimming pool, barbecue, summerhouse, fruit trees. Three storeys, counting a sort of loft, and a greenhouse."

"That's too big for us. The maintenance costs are too high. They must have a lot of employees."

"Don't you believe it. A gardener and a helper they pay by the hour."

"And do they have friends? These rich retired folk only get around with people like themselves."

"Yes, I think that's true. But there are some young guys who go there. At least two Spaniards who turn up from time to time and speak with Fred. Karin's teaching me how to knit. She's very nice, very understanding, and she cares about me."

"It's curious how two such different people can get on," I remarked.

"I don't see why. All of us are pretty much the same."

What would Sandra be like now if she'd been one of Fredrik's and Karin's victims? I was really glad that her soul hadn't been in contact with anything like that, glad that she was generous, that she opened up the door of her house to a stranger like me, and I was glad that evil hadn't caught up with her.

"I have to go to the supermarket tomorrow. Do you want me to pick up anything for you and bring it here? In your state you shouldn't be carrying bags or any weight."

"Don't worry. I'll be going back to Villa Sol in a while and tomorrow I'll most probably be spending the day in and out of the swimming pool. If you give me a telephone number I'll call you after I speak with my sister."

I gave her the phone number of the hotel and the number of the suite. I was running the risk that she'd talk about me with the Christensens, but then again our meetings had too little relevance to be talked about.

"Sometimes people aren't what they appear to be," I said in a desperate attempt to get her to read my mind as Raquel used to do.

"Now you're going to tell me you're a satyr or something like that." I half-smiled.

"Maybe," I said. "One never knows where the danger is until one discovers it."

Sandra waved goodbye to me and went inside the house yawning. She was wearing wide-legged Indian silk pants and strappy sandals. Sandra didn't know what she was getting into and neither did I, which bothered me. I hadn't counted on this, on running into somebody who was going to need protection.

Raquel would have got angry. No, she would have been incensed. She would have told me that what I was being unscrupulous, that I should leave this girl alone, that I shouldn't drag her into this and that there was no reason why she should be yet another victim. But things aren't so easy, Raquel. They are the ones that have taken her into their terrain. It wasn't me who put her there. It was them, and she's let herself be led like a lamb. Yet it was true that, if she didn't have a clue, if she was totally ignorant of the kind of people she was dealing with, the danger would be minimal. As long as Sandra saw Fredrik and Karin outside of hell, she'd see them as angels and not devils. Maybe angels didn't exist and absolute good didn't exist, but I could vouch for the fact that absolute evil certainly existed.

# 3

# The Venom of Doubt

## Sandra

I had to take Karin to the gym in the four-by-four. We said "gym" so as not to call it rehab. The gym was in the centre of town, in the main street where it was impossible to park, so I went to look for a spot thinking I'd go for a walk. I'd return after an hour to collect her, wondering how much they'd be paying me for doing this and also thinking that Fred would be feeling some relief at being liberated from these obligations. Apart from the gym, there were the medical check-ups and going to the shopping centre. She also liked the street markets, hunting for old bits of junk, going to the hairdresser, having a stroll along the seafront if she wasn't up to walking on the beach. She loved raving on about her childhood in the Norwegian farmhouse, about the incomparable beauty of her mother, about the manly beauty of her father, and about the beauty of her brothers and sisters, not to mention her own. About the beauty of the salmon they tended to have for dinner and the beauty of the lights in the middle of the night. When she got tired of this, she asked me about my life, because she couldn't stand silence. I fell into her claws too. Over the time I'd been living in her house I'd been getting used to her, and Karin didn't need to go out of her way to ensure that my priority was to keep her happy.

I wondered what was going to take her fancy today. I left her at the door of the gym, drove off. When I got to the corner, a man waved at me, taking his hat off as he did. I recognized Julián, the one who wanted to rent my sister's house. I waved back, but he came over to the car.

"Can I get in?" he asked, opening the door.

He asked me if I'd like to go and have a cool drink. He'd discovered a place at the lighthouse where they made fresh fruit smoothies. What about it? Would I risk going up there with him? I told him I had to be on my way back within the hour and, as soon as I got the words out, what I said sounded strange, as if it wasn't me, who always arrived late everywhere. That was when I realized that I wouldn't be able to stand Karin's look reproaching me for making her wait.

We set off, without my suspecting that from then on Villa Sol would never be the same again, as if the curtains in a theatre had opened up and at last there was a story. I didn't get it straight away. At first I didn't want to get it. It scared me. Julián was serious. He was frowning and there was a sad expression on his face. He pulled a press cutting out of his pocket, an ad about some house for sale maybe.

"And your wife? I never see her," I asked with a sense of something tense or disagreeable in the atmosphere.

"My wife died. She's never been here."

I immediately thought that when we got out of the car I'd get rid of him with one good kick in the balls. I thought I could push him over with one hefty shove and he'd take so long to get up again I could put kilometres between us in the meantime.

"I'm sorry I lied," he said, "but it's better like that."

"I don't understand you," I replied, feeling him looking at me. I didn't take my eyes off the road.

"I would never have got you involved in this, I swear it, but the fact is that when I met you you were already involved."

Involved? What could I be involved in when I was spending my life with the plants in the garden and hanging around with old people?

"I think it's my duty to tell you what your real situation is."

I didn't like it in the least that someone should be trying to manipulate me or play games with me, so I raised my voice louder than I should have.

"I already know what my situation is!"

"No, you don't know," he said as I parked the car.

With the page of the newspaper in his hand, he led me to a stone bench looking out over the sea.

"How do Fredrik and Karin treat you?"

"Fred and Karin?"

"The old Norwegian couple."

I had no idea where all this was leading when I said fine, they were affectionate, they knew how to respect my space and I knew how to respect theirs. When I talked about space, he smiled vaguely. I didn't like him finding something funny in what I'd said. It put me in a bad mood.

"I didn't want to have to show you this," he said, holding out the page from the newspaper.

On the page there was a photo, the photo of a couple. Right then, that's all I saw because he'd put me off with that ironic smile and I didn't care about anything else.

"Look carefully, please. Don't you recognize them?"

"I don't know what's so funny about saying they respect my space."

"Because it's a cliché. It doesn't suit you."

I took the page and looked hard at the photo. They were… they were Fred and Karin. I concentrated so as to study it better.

"Yes, it's them," Julián said. "Nazis, criminals and dangerous. Fredrik Christensen murdered hundreds of Jews. Do you understand what I'm telling you?"

I was perplexed. I didn't know what to think.

"Are you sure?"

"I've come here after him. I don't want him to go off to the next world without having to recognize his guilt, without paying in some way for what he did. He might be the only one of them left alive at this stage."

"Why are you telling me this? Why don't you tell the police?"

"When I arrived here, that's exactly what I thought I'd do, make it public, make their life a misery, but that would be a poor revenge, and now I think that they could lead me to others. You're going to and from their house and they don't suspect you. If you weren't pregnant, if I didn't keep thinking you could be my granddaughter and if I didn't feel such a toad asking you, I'd ask you to tell me what you see there."

"I haven't seen anything special and, anyway… they're my friends."

"Your friends? I told you I don't want you to be in any danger, but get that idea out of your head. These people are nobody's friends. They're vampires feeding on the blood of others and they love your blood. It gives them life. Be very careful."

We didn't have the smoothie. Julián knew very well where he could speak with me without anybody seeing us. We looked like the typical couple of an old man and young woman, half hidden by the trees. I already had the telephone number of the Hotel Costa Azul where he was staying in case I wanted to contact him, but under no circumstances could I go there in person because he was being watched and it was dangerous. The most sensible thing to do would be to disappear from the lives of the Christensens, from Julián's life and to go back to my own normal existence. He begged me to resist the temptation of saying anything to my Nazi friends, to contain any desire I might have to tell them about this because I'd be glad about that later.

"You take it," he told me, holding out the newspaper page. "Keep a close eye on them."

I folded it and put it in my pocket.

What did I know about Julián? I knew nothing at all about him. He'd turned up one day at my house and now he was saying these strange things. I could believe him because I knew that the Nazis had existed. Everyone knew that the Nazis had existed, that they got turned on by the swastika and all that. But Fred and Karin? I knew them. Karin put a cushion at my back to ease my kidneys when I was sitting in my favourite chair. It was winged, high-backed, and had a footrest. Fred didn't talk much. When he was around, he limited himself to going out and buying cakes and serving us tea. It was Karin who wore the pants in our group. Karin was teaching me how to knit, and Fred sometimes had visitors and spent time talking with them. But what was so special about that?

Julián had inoculated me with the venom of doubt. He'd just told me terrible things about my friends. He'd informed me that Nurse Karin was a depraved criminal and that she'd helped to kill hundreds of people to advance the career of her husband, who'd been decorated by none other than the Führer. "Do you know how many people you have to kill to be deemed worthy of getting the Gold Cross?" He'd forced me to have doubts about Fred and Karin, and about him too. He was no longer the kindly old man in the white hat who was always going on about his wife. Now I didn't know who he was. Maybe this wife of his had existed and maybe she hadn't. Perhaps he wasn't even interested in renting the house. I didn't like the idea that he'd been making a fool of me. At least the Norwegians hadn't lied to me, though it was true they hadn't told me about their lives either, which was unusual for people in their eighties, but for the moment the information I had about them was what I'd seen and heard for myself, and my own conclusions.

I decided not to argue with him. The most sensible thing would be to ask no questions and not to want to know anything more. The best thing would be not to dump this weird man here but to take him back to town and, once there, go back to being with Karin.

And what if it was true? Even if I eventually decided to leave them, I still had to go back once more. It would seem very strange if I didn't and left there the few clothes I'd taken with me, along with calcium tablets, stretch-mark creams and all the rest. They'd be worried and would come down to look for me, would ask a lot of questions and the whole thing would go from bad to worse. I wouldn't be too happy about it either, and wouldn't even sleep well that night. Then again, to be sincere, I had to confess that my curiosity had been aroused. And if I got out of this situation now, as Julián suggested, if I didn't go back up to Villa Sol and disappeared, I'd regret it because I'd be left without knowing anything. Life, or destiny, had brought me to this winding road, and it was less complicated to keep going than to turn around and go back.

Just as I feared, when I got to the gym Karin was waiting for me and very testy too.

I apologized, explaining that I'd run out of petrol and, when we got back to Villa Sol, I went to my room and put the newspaper item in the bottom of the bag in which I'd brought my clothes.


## Julián

I was very clumsy with Sandra; I scared her, but I had to open her eyes at some point. I'd been going up and down to Villa Sol too often and couldn't keep waiting till one of Fredrik's young brutes beat me up on some corner, in which case she'd never know whose hands she'd fallen into. There was no time to waste. On the one hand, Sandra would have been in less danger not knowing, but on the other, she wouldn't have known what she had to defend herself against. She was still in time to make her escape, to leave the whole thing behind her, to remember it as one of the strangest things that had ever happened in her life. Maybe it would help her to do justice to what she'd left behind her when she came here.

My choice, in contrast, was made. I'd keep going to the end, probably my end, but they weren't going to get rid of me in any amicable way. Well, yes, I was very worried about the amount of money I was spending and what I had put away, not so much for me to get by in my old age as for my daughter in her old age. My wife wouldn't approve either. We'd only had one daughter, and Raquel used to say that we couldn't spare her the upsets and wrongs of life, but at least she shouldn't have many problems with money. And I was spending it on something necessary or on a caprice, depending on how you looked at it.

Even for changing my rented car I had to fork out more. As soon as they gave me the new one, I embarked on a new round of following Fredrik, now with a certain degree of peace of mind, at least until they discovered me once again.

I tailed him comfortably to the car park of the Nordic Club, which was full of very classy gleaming cars. It was the second time I'd been there. I left my car in a discreet place and, as soon as I saw that Fredrik had gone inside, I went in after him. I'd taken my jacket off and wrapped up the binoculars in it, but had left my hat on, which gave me the appropriate air of a foreigner. I was counting on the doorman letting me in and, almost before he could open his mouth, I announced I'd come with Fredrik.

"I was parking the car," I offered by way of explanation.

Whether he took me for a chauffeur or a friend, the fact is he let me in as if it were the most natural thing in the world. Fredrik's head would be sticking up somewhere and I went looking for him, but his long legs that propelled him along as though the soles of his feet were burning, raising his shoulders with every step, had borne him out of my range of vision. I looked into a series of lounges and found him in one of them talking to an individual who would have been very strong once but now was fat. He had light eyes, a sizeable set of jowls and you could still see a sabre scar on his face. He could very well have been Otto Wagner, founder of the ODESSA Organization, engineer, writer and various other things, a restless bastard and apparently in good health, who certainly wouldn't be content with just playing golf. I leant against the wall trying to calm down. I was churned up and sad, although in my state being churned up was less recommendable than being sad. After about five minutes, and having taken in a few deep breaths, I managed to end up with only the sadness. It distressed me that these monsters were enjoying life in a way that Salva never managed to do, or me, or Raquel, however hard she tried, or even my daughter. I was distressed by their robust health and their zest for life and enjoying themselves.

I watched them getting into a buggy and moving away over the grass. The Nordic Club was incredible: porches with beautiful cool wicker chairs, tennis courts, paddle tennis, indoor and outdoor swimming pools, restaurant, pub-style lounge, billiards room, library, plus all the things I couldn't see and, in the background, the green undulations of the golf course. I wondered how much water was needed to maintain it. But what did that matter? The important thing was that Fredrik the giant and his buddies could get a bit of exercise.

What hole would they be at? I saw this sport as something that was light years from me. I leant against a tree, as far as possible out of the field of vision from the terraces of the club, and hung my binoculars round my neck. I did a sweep through the middle distance and found a group of octogenarians, Fredrik and Otto among them, who were leaning on their golf clubs and having a chat. There were a couple of young men too. The old ones were carrying on like men of seventy. It was incredible. Perhaps feeling superior to everybody else gave them all that energy. I lowered the binoculars, pondering this, when I spotted some sort of commotion. I raised the binoculars to my eyes again and saw one of them, but not Fredrik or Otto, lying on the grass. One of the young men was talking on his mobile and, a few minutes later, a man with a doctor's bag appeared in a buggy with others running after him. I wrapped the binoculars in my jacket, despite the fact that no one was paying any attention to me. At the end of the day, you're as old as your years, I thought. I could hear the ambulance. That one's had a heart attack, I thought.

The lounges of the Nordic Club were abuzz with the news. At last, something new to jazz up the everyday golf routine. The news ran like wildfire and I watched from the car how they put whoever it was in the ambulance, a corpse, but not totally covered up and with an oxygen mask so as not to alarm the members of the club, although, at bottom, it would have been disappointing for the members of the club if it had all turned out to be a false alarm. The way things were, they'd have something to keep them talking for days. The ruse didn't fool me. When you've seen so many dead people you can recognize a dead man at a glance.

They all left as fast as they could. The soles of Fredrik's feet seemed to be sizzling more than ever. He was bounding rather than running to his Mercedes, the kind you see in those catalogues that come with your newspaper.

I followed the man I thought was Otto through all the damned curves leading up to El Tosalet. He took the same route as his friend Fredrik but didn't stop at Villa Sol. He went three hundred metres farther to a mansion that displayed the number 50. Fredrik had led me to Otto and he'd lead me to more of them. The whole bunch of them were bound by a blood pact.

## Sandra

Fred paid me more than I expected for keeping Karin company, taking her to the gym and doing a hundred thousand errands for her. Maybe Fred realized that I was feeling too tied down because Karin loved getting out of the house and coming with me under any pretext, and her slowness getting in and out of the car ended up getting on my nerves. But it never pushed me to the limit because Karin was tremendously observant and immediately aware if I was getting impatient. Then she'd ease up, leave me to my own devices and, at the weekend, I could go back to my house down below and breathe. It wasn't bad being able to save almost everything I was being paid. I was buying my future freedom.

From what Fred had given me I put a bit aside to buy some pearl-cotton skeins and some new needles to start a second pullover. I'd keep the first one as a memento because it had served its purpose in trial and error, but the one my baby was going to wear would be this other one, into which I was going to put all the tender loving care in the world. When I got to the armhole I'd definitely have to ask Karin for help. The rest I'd manage by myself.

Hence, after lunch, as Fred and Karin were getting dressed to go to the funeral of one of their friends, at the hour when, on other days, Karin got under a blanket and had her siesta on the sofa with the television on, I got out the skein of cotton and knitting needles from the purple velvet bag that Karin had given me to keep them in and set about clacking away with the needles – well, OK, slowly – until, after about a quarter of an hour, thoughts started buzzing like a hornets' nest in my head. They were zooming by, one after another, appearing and disappearing, but the matter of the uniform and the press cutting Julián had given me was a constant. According to Julián, they were Nazis, which tied in with the SS officer's uniform I'd seen Fred wearing the night he came back from the party at Otto's and Alice's house. The uniform, a uniform gigantic enough to fit Fred, would that have been hired or did it belong to him? If Julián was right, he'd be keeping it somewhere. Although, leaving aside his suspicions, I could also assume that people have the weirdest fantasies and, in this case, they might have nothing to do with what the uniform meant. Compared with people who get off sexually by dressing up as comic-strip characters, Fred's thing could be permissible. It might be his way of getting it up with Karin. But why should I want to deceive myself? Fred was the perfect Nazi in that uniform. The thing is that, out of uniform, in normal clothes, I didn't know what a Nazi looked like. How would I spot it? They wouldn't let anyone spot it.

And what about me, what did I care? Yes, yes, I did care, or maybe I was curious. I don't know. Anyway, I put the knitting back in the velvet bag and went off to explore the house. Until that point, I'd never had the temptation to snoop. In some ways I was going back to childhood, when it used to be such fun opening up drawers and poking about to see what was inside without anybody knowing that I was looking. But now pleasure was mixed with caution.

The house consisted of two storeys with a basement, a greenhouse, a junk room, a garage and, right at the top, a loft with no stairs leading to it or any other kind of access. That was understandable as there was already too much house for the two of them. Scattered round the bedrooms were some very beautiful old trunks and large chests in which they kept the bulky eiderdowns and rugs in the summer, and then there were cupboards. When I was old and couldn't be getting out all day I'd also like to have a very big house like this one, so I could go from one room to another without getting bored. It took Karin a lot of effort to get to the top floor, dragging herself up as she clung to the artistically carved mahogany banister. When they came to live here she certainly wouldn't have had any idea that she'd end up like this. And maybe the worst was yet to come. She therefore tried to stay on the ground floor until bedtime and more and more of her knick-knacks were ending up downstairs when they should have been upstairs. She was leaving them here, so she wouldn't have to go and get them herself or send me to fetch them. I suggested that to avoid having so much stuff lying around – shoes, dresses, the odd pullover, a jacket – I could stash it all away in a trunk in the library-den, but she told me to get that idea out of my head, because only Fred was allowed to go into that room, and he was very particular about the way his books and papers were ordered. He went mad if anyone touched his things. This is why the door was always locked, so nobody could go in there by accident and problems would therefore be avoided. Yet when his acquaintances like Martín, the Eel or Otto had to wait for him, they were allowed to be in there alone, which, on reflection, was no concern of mine, so I held my tongue. It was evident that the door was closed to me and me alone.

I went upstairs to the bedrooms making the minimum amount of noise possible, even though nobody else was there. You could only hear the tick-tock of an old porcelain clock, which must have been very valuable. Normally, you'd be hearing Karin's snores too. She tended to sleep for three quarters of an hour, snoring her head off. The doors hadn't been greased for a thousand years and all of them creaked. According to Karin, they functioned as alarms that would warn of the presence of any intruder. The wardrobe doors squeaked too. I opened them and was awed by Karin's beautiful evening dresses. Not just the white one she'd worn to Otto's and Alice's party. There must have been at least a hundred of them, all tucked away inside cloth covers. Each one must have cost a fortune. I could only see a few by lifting up the covers, but not the whole dress. Embedded in the wardrobe wall was a safe where they certainly must have kept her jewels, because with dresses like these she'd have to wear equally valuable jewels. Then I opened up Fred's part of the wardrobe. It was even tidier than Karin's. The covers here were transparent and there was no uniform in any of them. I stood there for a moment, fascinated by the perfect arrangement of ties, handkerchiefs and socks. I closed the door and peeked in the trunk at the foot of the bed and, as I imagined, it contained an eiderdown. I went out and closed the door with the sensation that my fingerprints would be all over the place, an absurd notion arising from groundless fear.

I also went into the guest room and checked out the chest of drawers and the wardrobe in there. I looked into the three remaining bedrooms. At the end of the passageway there was a door that was also locked. There were lots of places where the Nazi uniform could be kept, but it could also have been hired and returned. I wasn't keeping track of the time it was taking me to go from one room to another, opening and closing wardrobes. Then I heard the front door opening and Fred's long strides coming up the stairs.

I asked him about the funeral and he asked me if anything had happened in the house in their absence. I said no but could see that he still wanted to know what I was doing upstairs, so I told him I'd gone to lie down on my bed and now I felt dopey so I was going out for a ride on the motorbike to clear my head.

I went down to the town and headed for Julián's hotel. I recalled that he'd said something about never going there, but I don't take these things too seriously and thought it slightly excessive, so I parked for a moment, wrote a note telling him that I'd be waiting for him at the lighthouse the next day at four, walked into the lobby, pretended to be looking at a newspaper, slipped over to the lifts, got to his room and slid the note under the door. I slipped out as I'd come in, trying to make sure nobody noticed me, but I didn't know whether I'd managed that.

## Julián

The day after the ruckus at the Nordic Club we had a funeral. It was none other than Anton Wolf, commander of a Waffen-SS battalion notorious for its part in the massacre of four hundred civilians in an Italian village, most of them women and children. Salva would certainly have located him, but I hadn't been capable of spotting him and, once again, one of them had escaped right under my nose, even if it was to the next world. I'd had him there in my binoculars and hadn't recognized him. It seemed that I was forgetting more than I thought. I'd been so caught up with what Fredrik and Otto were up to that I hadn't noticed Anton Wolf. Now he'd got out of my clutches. He was buried in a grave overlooking the sea.

Despite the horror he created in his life, his burial was surrounded by beauty, but at least he wasn't there to enjoy it. His wife, Elfe, was there crying quietly and restrainedly, standing between Karin and Alice, both of whom looked as if they wanted to get the whole thing over and done with. Now why should Elfe be crying, I wonder. Yes, Elfe, you people die too, and all that cruelty has been in vain. You did all that and your life has still slipped by like a sigh. You don't even remember very well the atrocities you lot committed. Do you remember how we had to dig our own graves? You didn't know anything? Yes, you knew, and you aren't sorry because you believed you had the right to do what you did. You're going to die too, Elfe, and nothing and nobody will be able to prevent it.

I put all I had into these thoughts so they'd be transmitted through however many neurons it took for her to get the message. Drawn by my power, she looked over to where I was but couldn't see me, because I was hiding behind the tomb of an eight-year-old boy, which was finished with an impressive carved marble angel. Then she started to weep louder and louder, which was frowned upon by her Aryan brothers and sisters, especially when a very tall old man joined the group, a man bearing a close resemblance to Fredrik, although fleshier, walking slightly stooped forward as if the engine of his body was in his head. I could have sworn it was Aribert Heim, the *Butcher of Mauthausen*, the very same man who'd been with Fredrik that day in the supermarket when I gave him a fright, but it didn't occur to me then to imagine that this coarse, fat, unkempt, verging on dirty man could possibly be the lean, dandyish Heim of the old days. The famous V-shaped scar seemed to be there next to his mouth. What a shame, Salva, that you can't share this moment with me, and that we're not able to plot together what we should do with them. They all greeted Doctor Death with respect, the kind of respect that also covers up a certain degree of revulsion. They got Elfe out of there between two of them and the rest went back to the gleaming cars they used for funerals.

There was nothing more for me to do there, so I chose the best bunch of flowers from Wolf's grave and put it on the tomb of the little eight-year-old boy and left. Remaining behind me was the angel with its big wings and ahead of me was a grey sea that had adopted the form of the arch of the cemetery. Further down the road, Heim was lumbering towards the town. I certainly didn't expect this. I dug my nails into my hand to stop my heart from pounding excessively. I was following a probable Heim. And why not? What did anyone know of his whereabouts? No one was sure whether he was dead or alive. People speculated that he was living in Chile protected by Waltraut, the daughter he'd had with an Austrian lover, or by her daughter, his granddaughter Natasha Diharce, in Viña del Mar. However, neither this daughter nor the two other offspring who lived in Germany had claimed the life-insurance policy worth a million dollars and deposited in a German bank, which was the best proof that he was alive and laughing at all of us. It was also said that he could have died in Cairo and, then again, that there were signs that he was hiding in some residential estate in Alicante.

It was likely that, right now, there before me, in jeans, a cagoule and a battered sailor's cap, doggedly walking as if trying to anchor himself to life as much as he could, was the Butcher of Mauthausen. In that place that stank of burning flesh and where beings like Heim were the lords of life and death, I'd stopped believing in God, or had stopped liking God. If the God of green fields, of rivers like the Danube, of stars and of people who fill you with happiness was also the God of Heim, of gas chambers, of those who got pleasure out of making others suffer, this God didn't interest me, whatever name he was given in the thousands of religions of the world. I couldn't trust in a God from whose energy good and evil came out at the same time, and had therefore begun to do without him in living out the life I hadn't even asked for.

He was walking so fast it looked as if he was going to fall flat on his face. He was heading for the port, but I needed to have that face just a few centimetres away from my own, to see him front on and to be able to examine him for a few moments without drawing attention to myself and without raising his suspicions. I couldn't let him get away without confirming that it was him. So, with some difficulty, I sat down on the ground and shouted.

"Please, can you help me?"

Heim turned around, hesitated for a moment and finally came and held out his hand. That this torturer and killer should be holding out his hand to help me stand up was incredible. He didn't do it because he wanted to, but because it was what was expected of him in the milieu in which he now lived, just as in that other milieu he was amputating the prisoners' arms and legs without any need, without anaesthesia, and carrying out all kinds of macabre experiments. He was helping me to stand up, me a resident of that lovely holiday home called Mauthausen. It was difficult for me to get on my feet and I wasn't pretending, so he had to lean over a little more, and I saw it. I saw it clearly, the scar at the corner of his mouth, the light eyes and the inward-looking gaze, directed at a world made in his image and likeness.

I thanked him and he didn't reply but went on his way. A wind was getting up. The sea started to roar. He clamped his cap to his head with one hand, and then put up the hood of his cagoule. I could follow him without a care in the world because, unless he turned round completely, he wouldn't be able to see me. He went on board a very beautiful wooden boat with the name *Estrella* painted in large green letters. It must have been the name it had when he bought it and he hadn't scrapped it in order to give it a new name. New lives, new names, new habits, but the same soul. Heim, you'll never change, I told him in my head.

What a discovery. I thought I should perhaps phone one of our old friends from Memory and Action and tell them the whole story, but I feared that by the time they reacted it would be too late and, more than anything else, they'd bungle it for the simple reason that you can't brief somebody in a moment, relaying the endless string of small details that had to be borne in mind if one is to be on the same wavelength as this group. Because this was an organized group.

Neither did I know whether I should mention this to Sandra. Sooner or later, she'd end up seeing this inoffensive old man at some or other of the group's gatherings and it wouldn't be in her best interests if he could read in her eyes that she'd recognized him. For her own safety, it would be better to keep her in the dark.


## Sandra

Fred and Karin took it for granted that any native was born knowing how to make paella. I had to beg them not to oblige me to cook, because I didn't have a clue, had to tell them that I preferred Norwegian cooking to Spanish, and that I'd eat anything they cooked, so that, without actually intending to do so, I liberated myself from this task and the most I did was stack the plates in the dishwasher while Karin stretched out on the sofa to watch some soap or other on TV until she dropped off to sleep and Fred shut himself away in the library-den. I took advantage of this time for my meetings with Julián.

I got to the lighthouse at five to four, and went to the place we'd decided would be our meeting spot. We would sit on the same bench, surrounded by rocks, stones and the wild pygmy date palms that grew all over the place. Pulling them up was prohibited. The sea in front of us allowed us to sit there in silence.

Julián was already there. He always wore the same light-blue jacket, no doubt because when he decided to come here he didn't imagine he'd be staying so long. He'd added a cravat to the outfit, which, along with the Panama hat, gave him the dapper air of someone out of an Italian film, but it wouldn't be long before he'd have to buy himself something warmer. He asked me how I was. Then I couldn't hold it back any more. I told him about the night I'd seen Fred dressed in a Nazi uniform and that I'd been looking for it in the wardrobes at the house but hadn't found it, so was wondering if it might have been fancy dress.

"I can assure you it wasn't. If they could, they'd wear it all the time. And, if they could, they'd fence off a bit of land, the stoniest, driest land they could find, stick us all in there and kill us to use our bones, teeth, skins and hair, and to force themselves on us as superior beings."

And who was Julián? Would that be his real name? Why should I trust him more than Karin and Fred? What if he was a bit mad? Yet it was also true that I hadn't mentioned anything about the Nazi uniform to either of those two. I didn't have any proof that it was the real thing and, even so, I'd avoided mentioning it. Instinct had told me that I mustn't make them feel uncomfortable or oblige them to give me any explanation.

"They don't feel guilty," Julián went on. "I've never known a single one of them that's shown the slightest sign of remorse. They think they're victims of a world that's changed and that doesn't understand them. In some way," he added dejectedly, "this absence of any feeling of guilt has saved a lot of them, including Fredrik and Karin. They've escaped and have managed to survive very well. You can be sure that in their intimate life they keep nourishing their fantasies of superiority."

He gazed at me, testing my reaction, but I didn't have any, because I hadn't seen any real sign in them that they saw themselves as Nazis. I just had suspicions.

"And if you're right, what am I supposed to do? I've already told you the little I know."

"Nothing, I don't want you to do anything. I want to warn you so you can get away in time. If you get any more involved with them you won't come out of it well. They always win... until now. I'm going to have no compassion."

He wasn't going to have any compassion? But what did he think he was doing, this scrawny old guy dressed up as an Italian? What was I doing listening to him? How can you find out if somebody's got senile dementia?

"And if I got it into my head to do something, what would I have to do?"

He sat there staring at the sea down below us, pressing dark blue against the horizon.

"The Gold Cross. If you find the Gold Cross, it will clear up any doubts we might have. Or rather doubts you might have, because when I came here I already knew who he was."

"I need to think about it," I said.

I didn't want to believe that Fred and Karin were Nazis. Nazis were incomprehensible beings. The last thing that would have crossed my mind in this life was that I'd ever meet one. I'd seen them in films and documentaries and they'd always seemed unreal. The uniforms, the boots, the banners, crowds of people with their arms raised, the Aryan race, the swastika, and so much and such twisted evilness. It was amazing that people, I mean people with a brain, should have taken them seriously and should have let them do all the things they did.

"I'm repeating it once more. You mustn't do it. You mustn't let yourself be intimidated by them and you mustn't let yourself be exploited by me. You shouldn't be in this story. You should be with a boy who loves you, with someone who makes you happy. Don't fritter your life away."

"I don't know how not to fritter life away."

"Being happy, being content, enjoying life. Fall in love."

"I'd really like to, but it's not that easy."

"What about the father of your baby?"

"Santi? Sometimes I miss him, but not like I'd miss him if I was in love."

"Do you know what? Falling in love happens."

The rest of the time we were talking about my feelings. You could see he'd loved his Raquel very much, so she must have really existed. Then I asked him how he knew he loved her, what he'd felt to know it. The question took him by surprise and he was lost in thought for a moment.

"Because sometimes she made me walk on air," he answered.

He told me that he'd come to this same place at four in the afternoon in two days' time in case I needed to talk with him.


## Julián

So Otto lived at number 50 with a woman called Alice who was the very image, from head to foot, of a camp guard. I knew that icy look, so like that of Ilse Koch, who was notorious among all of us because of her collections of tattooed human skin. Alice revolted me almost more than Otto, but no more than Fredrik and Karin. The one who got the repugnance prize was Heim, the man with the most putrid brain ever to have walked this earth, the man who was now taking up fifty per cent of my attention. I filled the two notebooks I'd brought from Buenos Aires with my jottings and had to go to a stationery shop to buy another two. If anything happened to me, or if I wasn't able to nab them one way or another, I wanted to leave a record of these days, of poor Salva's sleepless nights, of my own, and Sandra's as well. Sandra deserved to have somebody who could tell her child what kind of mother he or she had. When I mentioned Sandra, I wrote "she" in case my notebooks fell into other hands, and I had to think hard about who they should be sent to if things went wrong, because I didn't want this whole investigation to vanish into thin air as Salva's had. The problem of being old is that nobody takes you seriously. People think we're anchored in the past, unable to understand the present, and that's certainly why they would have thrown out Salva's papers. I was also making a note of what I was spending. I wanted my daughter to understand that I hadn't spent the money on mere whims but on petrol, car hire, paying for a suite at the price of a modest room, warm clothes, notebooks, contact-lens solution, the lunchtime set menu at the bar and a few coins for the launderette so I wouldn't have to pay the hotel washing and ironing rates. I'd brought enough supplies of my medication with me, but if I ran out I'd have to go to the hospital and explain my situation, because the pills were too expensive.

The launderette was two streets from the hotel and I used the time waiting there to write my reports. I went when I didn't have a single pair of socks or underpants left. I sometimes washed the shirts myself, using the little bottles of gel in the bathroom and hanging them from the bathroom rail nicely pulled straight on a coat hanger so they wouldn't need ironing. I sometimes sat on the terrace for a while to write, wrapping myself in a blanket, so that I could breathe fresh air and not feel cold. I'd got so used to this room, this terrace, getting into the car to go and watch decrepit Nazis, that it didn't occur to me that I could be doing anything different. It felt as if the whole thing had been planned down to the last millimetre by Salva and Raquel from some out-of-the-way corner of my mind so I'd be able to find some sense in what life was left to me.

Now I'd added to my previous itinerary the house of the deceased Anton Wolf. It was tucked away off the road leading inland, where small farms with market gardens had been renovated and modernized while still conserving a rustic air. I only had to go to the land registry to find out the address. The place was in Elfe's name.

It wasn't easy to get there. You had to go down a dirt track, which I did perfectly brazenly as if I'd got lost. Before I entered the property a dog was already barking. At the front door of the house, which was surrounded by a garden so wild that it looked more like the country-side, I started turning around to leave with the front of the car pointing at the way out. I did this slowly, giving Elfe time to appear. There were two cars under a carport, one brand new and the other old.

The woman was on her last legs. Her eyes had got smaller from crying and her hair was dirty and unkempt. At another point in the history of humanity I would have felt sorry for her. Her grief aroused my curiosity, but it might have been the pain of a woman who'd once had everything and now she didn't. She took some water to the dog and then came over to me.

"I'm sorry," I said. "I think I've made a mistake. I'm looking for…"

"Frida's house is a little farther on, the third bend to the right, with a black letterbox on the track."

It was evident that whoever came to this lonesome place was looking for Frida, never for Elfe, and Elfe was resigned to it. I thanked her, convinced that Elfe wasn't going to last long. She'd lowered her guard, talked too much. They couldn't take the risk of her blabbing what she knew. And, lo and behold, without even trying, I'd located the house of this Frida. One more to keep tabs on.

From the track you could see several cars but not much of the house. It was quite isolated and, from my vantage point, I was exposed and risked being seen, so I didn't dare to get out my binoculars and follow this one up. I'd instead go and check out Heim and take a photo of his boat with my mini-camera.


# Sandra

I never paid attention to what Frida, the helper they called their maid, was doing. She came in three hours a day and, while she was sorting out the house, we used the time for errands or to spend some time in the garden, especially when she was cleaning on the lower floor. However, if we did stay inside she was as silent as a ghost and all you could hear were the sounds made by a few pieces of furniture that seemed to be moving under their own steam or by windows that opened all by themselves, and it also seemed that the floor was in charge of shining itself. On one of the days when Karin was in such good form that she decided to go and play golf with Fred and Otto, I saw the helper opening up the library-den to clean it, no doubt thinking about the party Karin was planning to throw, then closing it again when she was inside, which surprised me because Karin had told me that nobody went in there.

As cheeky as you like, I opened the door and went in. She was standing on the library stepladder dusting some books that didn't look at all like Karin's love stories. The atmosphere was cosy. There were leather armchairs in which the visitors must have comfortably lolled as they waited. The helper turned round and asked me in a German accent if I was looking for something, and it was then that I understood that, if Julián's suspicions were well-founded, she had to be one of them, so

I didn't take any chances. I said that I was thinking about going out shortly and asked her to leave the house properly locked.

I didn't go out. I made a noise with the motorbike and stayed. I watched from the garden how she was shaking out things from the window of the library-den and how she hung a large Persian rug that she'd just vacuumed over the window sill. I could easily see how she opened up a very beautiful cupboard, in apple green with an antique finish, which contrasted with the seriousness of the bookshelves, and which my sister would have loved. I nearly let out a scream when she took out the Nazi uniform and methodically brushed it down, after which she got a cloth and polished some black boots almost as tall as I am. I'd just discovered something important, another sign to support Julián's theories, and nobody in this house must realize what I'd found out, so I went into the garage and took the seat off my motorbike ready to pretend that I was fixing some problem in case Frida stuck her nose in there, which fortunately didn't happen. She didn't even come into the garage. When her time was up, she locked the house, got on her bicycle and rode off without a second glance.

The Christensens hadn't come back and this was an ideal chance to go poking about in the basement and the bedrooms once more. I put the motorbike seat back in place, got my keyring out of my trouser pocket and opened the front door. There was a very pleasant smell, as if Frida had been scattering lavender all over the place. What was this lavender? I don't know, but Frida had a very healthy-looking face, gave the impression that she carried lavender around in her pockets, and she had extremely chunky calf muscles after all the pedalling she did on her bike.

I'd never thought about Frida. I'd seen her arriving and sometimes leaving, but nothing in between, and yet she'd registered in my mind. She was blonde, about forty years old, though her rosy cheeks were like a fifteen-year-old's. As she zipped around so fast on her bicycle, the fresh air stuck to her skin and clothes and had turned into her personal smell.

There wasn't much in the basement, or I wasn't able to see it. After the uniform, I guessed there had to be more bits and pieces stowed away here and there. The only thing that caught my attention was a sun with its rays etched into the floor and painted black.

# Julián

I couldn't find a safe enough place in my room to hide the note-books. I didn't trust Tony, the hotel detective, and had the impression that he was watching me. I was also increasingly wary of Roberto, the receptionist. At first I carried my notebooks around in my jacket pockets but I was getting to have too many, so I only took the one I was currently using to take notes and left the others in the car under the floor mats, which wasn't a very good idea, as anyone who got it into his head to inspect the car would find them for sure and, if not, they'd end up in some scrapyard lying among the wreckage of bodywork. It also appalled me to think that they could connect me with Sandra, thus putting her in danger.

The last thing I'd jotted down was that I'd have to go back to Elfe's. Elfe herself didn't interest me much. What I did care about was what she might let out, what I could worm out of her now she was so disoriented and in such bad shape. At the cemetery, she didn't give the impression of being on very good terms with Karin and Alice. They were standing next to her but they didn't touch her or console her and barely even spoke to her. Maybe they were old enemies or simply hadn't managed to hit it off. It could be that Elfe wasn't in the same league of evil as Karin and Alice. Or maybe she'd outshone them. I knew nothing about her. She'd escaped my attention. I'd have to ask for information at the Centre and I didn't have either the time or the inclination to do that.

I cautiously approached the pretty house of the widow Elfe. In the carport, a solid construction in wood, were the two cars I'd noticed the previous time. One would be for everyday use and the other for going to play golf or to the houses of the other officers, that is, if they were ever invited. The dog threw itself at the car window, barking. I waited for a while to see whether Elfe was going to come out and then tooted the horn. Nothing. Yet the cars were there. The dog went to the door, barked and then ran back. It seemed to be trying to tell me something. OK, I said, I'm getting out now. I got out of the car and the dog barked, but without showing its teeth, making a great fuss jumping all around me. It was quite large but it wasn't about to set upon me.

I went to the door and rang the bell. I looked in through the kitchen window. There was nobody in sight. The dog wanted me to do more. It was agitated, but I didn't know what else to do. I couldn't force the door, and what if she wasn't inside? Then the dog went round to one side of the house and looked at me as if to say, come here. It pointed with its muzzle to the ground, to a large copper flowerpot. Making a huge effort, I moved it, cursing both the dog and Elfe. There was a trapdoor leading down to the cellar. I opened it up and the dog went in like a shot, almost knocking me over. We went down into the cellar and came up again into the vestibule of the house, alongside the stairs. The dog ran upstairs and barked at me from the top, but after all the effort I'd made with the flowerpot I had to take it easy and went up slowly. I always carried a nitroglycerine tablet in my shirt pocket just in case and in the hope I wouldn't have to use it. I don't know how, but I knew my time hadn't come yet.

I rested a little more and looked in where the dog was indicating. You could be making action films, I told it. After Sandra, it was the most admirable creature I'd met in recent times.

The bedroom stank of alcohol and vomit. Elfe was lying on the bed, in all likelihood unconscious. Whatever the case, I decided not to call an ambulance. I sent the dog out so it would stop licking up all the muck, and closed the door. I looked to see whether there was an en-suite bathroom, wet a towel, wrapped her head in it and stuck my fingers down her throat. I didn't know whether she'd taken pills along with the alcohol. When she finished throwing up everything she had in her, I made her stand up and, with further exertion that was undeserved by Elfe, I got her into the bathroom and turned the shower on. She screeched and I ordered her to shut up. The water fell on her reeking skirt and blouse. Then I wrapped her up in a dressing gown and put her in another bedroom, which was clean. I folded back the bedclothes and told her to get into bed. She mumbled something in German, which sounded like a protest, like repentance, like I-can't-take-any-more. The dog came in and stayed by her side, wagging its tail. I was certain that if this animal had had hands like mine it would have done everything I had done, or better still. I went down into the kitchen to make some coffee.

Jars and tin containers were tidily set out. The crystal of the wineglasses was tinged slightly purple after so much use. I took a cup and fortunately the coffee jar still had enough in it for the coffee pot. I made coffee. The kitchen emanated sadness, woeful loneliness, drama.

I took a tray up to her room. I didn't have a coffee, didn't want it to keep me awake and, most of all, didn't want to drink Elfe's coffee or set my lips anywhere they'd set theirs. The dog rubbed its head against my leg and I stroked it.

"What's the dog's name?" I asked Elfe.

"Thor, like the god."

"Quite right too," I said, sitting on the edge of the bed. "If it hadn't been for him I wouldn't have been able to get in."

I put a cup in her hands and poured her some coffee.

"Sorry, I didn't bring any sugar up."

"It doesn't matter, thank you. I never thought anyone would come to save me, least of all a stranger."

I didn't ask her if she'd tried to kill herself. I didn't care. It might have been a combination of alcoholism and suicide.

"I came to express my condolences. I knew Anton from the golfing group. Thor wouldn't let me leave. He showed me where the cellar trapdoor is, which is how I got up here to you."

She put her hands up to her hair, pushing it back behind her ears. At some time in her life she must have been pretty, but now she was a spine-chilling sight.

"I got into bed soaking wet and now the bed's wet too," she said mournfully, apparently not remembering the state in which she'd left the other bed.

"Don't worry. I'll sort it out when you feel better. Rest now. I'm leaving you the coffee pot. Thor will look after you."

"No, please don't go. They don't want me. They think I'm weak. I'm sure they'll never come to see me and they'll leave me completely alone."

"Do you mean the friends that played golf with Anton?"

"Yes," she said, sinking her head into the pillow. "Them and their stupid wives. They've always left me out of things."

"You must have been much prettier than they were when you were all young."

She raised her body, supporting herself on her elbows.

"What did you say your name was?"

"Julián."

"Well, Julián, what you're looking at now isn't me and, if you don't believe me, ask Anton."

I didn't remind her that Anton had died. Hence, in her world right now, Anton could be out playing golf, I could be a friend of hers, and the dog a god.

She got up with the dressing gown over her wet skirt and blouse and, barefoot and clinging to the banister, she went downstairs and into the living room with me following behind and Thor getting there before us. She opened up a box, took out a photo album and there I saw her as a young woman in 1940s clothes, hair blowing in the wind and a gaze in which you could somehow detect that she would one day end up like this. Arms held up. Swastikas, Anton Wolf as an officer. Karin as a nurse in another photo. I asked about her.

"I didn't know Karin in those days but when we met later she gave me the photo and then we parted ways."

All of them, now middle-aged, in swimming costumes on a beach. Alice alone in a swimming costume. Them and others in uniform. The album was a real treasure and I wanted it.

"Just out of curiosity, how long have you been living here, Elfe?"

"Since 1963. In 1970 we had to leave for three years but then we returned. The house was still as we'd left it. Nobody had touched anything."

"And Karin? And Otto and Alice?"

She ignored my question. She wanted to tell me about every one of her photos but I told her, as I stowed the album in its drawer again, that I'd come back and see her again very soon and then we could have a better look at them.

"Right now you've got to get well again. You need to rest and, if you like, as soon as we have a sunny day I'll take you to the beach. The sun cures all ills."

Down below, I watched as she wearily climbed the stairs, and when she was out of sight I opened the front door but, before leaving, went back into the living room and took the photo album out of the drawer. I closed the door quietly but didn't shut the trapdoor to the cellar. The dog could do that.

Although she'd stained my jacket I was happy when I left. I'd clean it up myself or even spend a bit extra and send it to the dry-cleaner's.

Now I'd have to find a safe place for the photo album.

# 4
# Open Sesame

## Sandra

The Gold Cross looked like the proof I needed to confirm that Julián's suspicions weren't mere fantasies and that I wasn't going crazy. I had the idea that there were two places where he might be keeping it: in some box under lock and key in the library-den or in the safe together with Karin's jewels, in which case it would be impossible for me to get to it. I'd have to work out the combination in order to open it, and that was impossible right now. Yet it was easy, just a matter of saying "Open Sesame!"

That afternoon, the "Open Sesame!" afternoon, we'd been to buy a dress and some shoes for Karin's birthday party. We'd spent several days preparing for this, working non-stop. All the small frictions or, better said, misgivings and doubts seemed to fade away with the preparations that were keeping us in the four-by-four all day long, running here and there to get a thousand things. The wine from a village in the interior, the salt fish from another, cakes and tarts from a special bakery. The fish and shellfish we ordered at the fish market, and so on and so forth. The most boring thing was having to find a new dress (a rag in comparison with the ones she had in the wardrobe) and some shoes.

The dress was red chiffon. It gave off metallic glints and, when she put it on, Karin looked like a gift, a gift of which the most beautiful thing is the wrapping paper. I convinced her that the shoes shouldn't be red as well, because then she'd look as if she were going to a wedding, but rather a neutral tone of beige and, then again, she couldn't wear shoes with much of a heel, as her toes were deformed by the arthritis. Karin listened to me, trying to make sure I'd enjoy being involved in all her stuff. She loved talking about it till she was talked out, even though it was her feet that were half twisted, and it was no hassle for me.

"Some large diamond earrings or a necklace would go well with this dress," I said distractedly without giving much thought to what I was saying.

"I think I've still got some diamonds. If I remember rightly, I've still got a diamond necklace."

I was vaguely shocked by the remark, but not as much as I should have been, because my attention, which Karin was sucking out of me, was fast fading. Fluttering about in the depths of my mind was the comment of somebody who refers to her diamonds as if she's saying she doesn't know whether she's still got a few grapes left in the fridge, somebody who hasn't had to buy them, or pay for them, or even choose them. Nobody talks like that about her own jewels, even if she's got money to burn, which wasn't actually the case with Fred and Karin. They hadn't got to the point of owning a private aeroplane or a yacht or mansions scattered round the planet, which seem to be the possessions that would go best with so many diamonds.

We finished shopping close to dinner time. When we got to the house we said hello to Fred, who was happy because his wife was so hugely entertained and because he was watching a football match. As the world was gradually rolling over into darkness, Karin made me go upstairs with her to the bedroom. Even though I'd seen it before, I'd never felt enough at ease to take in many details. It was very big and rather childish, with a lot of cushions and what looked like a collection of antique dolls, which Frida would have to clean with enormous care. The cupboards, the chest of drawers, the bedside tables and the writing desk were full of curves, as were their drawers, legs and mirrors. The little lamps on the bedside tables had pink pleated satin shades with bobbles. The bedspread, the curtains and the other lampshades were also in pink satin, while the finishing touches on the furniture were done in gilt. You didn't have to understand much about rugs to know that these were real Persian rugs. It was all very, very expensive. And this pink bed would be where they made love on those dreadful nights when I'd thought they were dying or something like that.

Karin took what we'd bought out of the bags and laid it all out on the bedspread. She arranged the dress and shoes on top of it as if she was a pink rose inside them. It's gorgeous, I told her. I sat down on a corner of the bed because I had no desire to intuit what these two had been up to there.

"I think we got it right," I said.

And then she did something as simple as opening the wardrobe, leaning over the safe and opening it. When she took out a box from inside it, a wooden box, I was looking away so she could see I wasn't interested in how she opened it. She placed the box on the bed next to the dress. She put her hand inside and took out a diamond necklace from the bottom. There was another necklace with several strands of pearls and a matching bracelet, earrings, the odd tiara and several rings. If I hadn't known that this was the real thing, I would have taken it for costume jewellery, the stuff they sell for a euro a piece, and her hand was rummaging around in it as if it were junk.

"Once, when I put my arm in the box, the jewels came up to my elbow," she said.

She placed the necklace on the rosy neck of the satin body offered up by the bedspread. It went marvellously with the red of the dress.

"Can I?" I asked, moving my hand towards the little flashes escaping from the box.

"Go ahead, dear," she said in that slightly old-fogyish way of hers. "You can try on anything you like. All of it is real."

I picked up some ruby earrings and dangled them from my fingers in front of my ears, but without going so far as putting them on, because I didn't want to put on any earrings that had probably been snatched from somebody, maybe even along with her life. I looked at myself in the gilt-framed mirror and saw that she was observing me.

"You're still not of an age to be wearing these things," she said, trying to discourage me from taking a fancy to them.

I put them back in the box and kept taking out pieces and holding them up to the light, keeping my eye on a little box right at the bottom.

"Why don't you try on the necklace with the dress?" I suggested. "I'd love to see the whole outfit."

While she was getting undressed, I pretended to be distracted by looking at the jewels, and when she'd got everything on and was engaged in ecstatic contemplation of herself in the mirror, ogling the legendary Nurse Karin getting ready for yet another party, I opened up the little velvet box and, inside, saw a cross, the cross I'd seen in films, pinned to the Nazi uniforms. My heart missed a beat, my hands began to sweat and shake, and I put them inside the box to close the little case properly and, when Karin turned around, I took out the pearl necklace and made it click through my fingers. I grabbed at the pearls to calm myself down.

"Beautiful, Karin, really beautiful. Do you want Fred to see you?"

"No!" she said, acting as little-girlish as she could. "Let it be a surprise."

I covered up the little case as best I could with the jewels and, when Karin had changed and was about to return them to the safe, I told her she should have a good look to make sure we hadn't dropped anything. I said it because I needed her to trust me. She actually heeded me and ran her hand through the jewels several times, as if she knew what was there by touch alone. Everything was there, so I left her to close the safe.

Before meeting Karin, it wouldn't have occurred to me to think that evil is always pretending to be doing good. Karin was always pretending to be doing good and was most likely putting on her act as she was killing, or helping to kill, innocent people.

## Julián

At four o'clock, as agreed, I was at the lighthouse. I didn't go directly to sit on the bench but wandered nervously among the palms with a thousand things on my mind.

Anton Wolf had been living here since 1963. There was no doubt that the members of this community had been coming and going right under the noses of everyone, as if they were invisible. They'd gone from being youngish senior citizens to being very, very old senior citizens. This was total infamy.

Sandra was late, which made me even more apprehensive.

What would I do without Sandra? I had to recognize that nothing would have been the same without her. Sandra was my witness. What I was doing was not going unnoticed, was not wholly useless, because Sandra was watching, even if I hadn't told her everything. Sandra was the answer that Salva had left behind him. And if Sandra took seriously the idea of leaving, a big part of the edifice we were constructing would come tumbling down. What we'd now accumulated was so much, the burden of what I knew was so great, that I needed more than two hands to sustain it. Thank goodness I heard the sound of the motorbike, the marvellous sound rolling over the pebbles and then stopping. I didn't want to go to meet her, so sat down as if I'd been there the whole time, feeling her approach me behind my back. Sandra had the long flexible stride of the sportswoman. When she was already standing next to me I turned and then I saw her face of stupefaction. That was the word, out of all the words I knew, that best fitted the face I saw.

"I can't believe what's happening," she said. "It feels like I'm in the middle of a dream, or a nightmare more like it."

I didn't want to interrupt her thoughts, so I concentrated on tying my cravat more neatly. It was evident that she had some sort of news, because she was staring very hard at me. Since I'd met her, such a short time ago, her gaze had changed to become more mature, the look of someone more in command of herself, less prone to meandering around her surroundings, and more discerning.

"I saw the Gold Cross."

"Are you sure?"

She nodded.

"Until now I've doubted everything. If you go looking, you can find things that fit with what you're looking for and yet they give a false impression. But seeing the Gold Cross has been decisive. You told me yourself. The Gold Cross is real. Why would they have something like that if it wasn't theirs?"

I nodded in agreement.

"I already knew," I said, "but you needed proof."

"And what are we going to do now?"

"Leave that to the professionals. You go. You've done enough. I'm serious about this. Later might be too late."

"Not yet. They don't know that I know, and nothing's changed except that I'm not that airhead they found on the beach any more. Why would they want me?"

"It could be for nothing in particular. They want you because of what you're doing, bringing a bit of joy into their life, bringing more life, your life, into theirs. You're doing them a favour."

"I'll convince myself that I don't know anything, that I haven't seen the Gold Cross, and I'll keep going as I have been up to now. Tomorrow we're celebrating Karin's birthday and I don't know what to give her. I want it to be something she likes, something that would help me gain favour with her so I can get a better idea about her life."

"But, Sandra, we already know who they are and, from now on, you'll be finding more and more skeletons in their closets and in their heads. Now that you know the basics, you'll become aware of many more things, and we can't go on like that indefinitely. We need to give a twist to the situation, get them jumpy, force them to betray themselves, making sure they never know where the shots are coming from."

"How do you do that?"

"It comes out. You only have to exert a bit of pressure. Come on, let's go and buy your gift. We'll put it on my account."

Sandra protested, but it was the least I could do at this point when I was getting carried away by a bad but necessary idea. I took her to a pet shop that sold dogs and cats. I'd seen it in the shopping centre and Sandra thought that it was a great idea.

## Sandra

Karin, on the last day, the day of her party, wanted me to do her make-up. It looked like she was going to celebrate this birthday as if it was the last one of her life, and she was probably right about that. All her friends were coming and she was very excited and hardly noted her arthritis. She'd feel it when it was all over and she relaxed, and then I'd better make my getaway. What for her was great fun was a pain in the neck for me. In the end, I was totally fed up, and the worst of it was that, with only one day to go, I still hadn't got her a present. It was Julián who suggested that I should get her a puppy. He was certain that the real Karin would love dogs and especially one particular breed. And he kindly paid for it. It was a black-and-brown Rottweiler pup, a cute, soft little ball. I'd planned to present it to her in a wicker basket with a flowery lining and a great big red raffia bow on one side.

I dressed up fairly formally to fit in with the rest of them. I was wearing a strappy dress with a shawl over it and, in my hair, a flower I'd picked in the garden, bigger than a rose, but I wouldn't know what it's called. In fact, everything looked lovely and Fred set about lighting candles all over the place. As soon as the first guests started arriving, champagne corks began to pop and a waiter hired for the occasion passed around trays of canapés made by the best restaurant in the area. Karin introduced me to everyone as if I were family, with the exception of Alice and Otto, who knew all too well who I was, and who limited themselves to greeting me coldly, and Martín and Alberto. They came to the party with a few more like them and these guys asked me if I was in the Brotherhood until Martín muttered something to them, after which they moved away. Frida was there too. She'd baked the fish and had made some colourful salads with lettuce, beetroot, pickled peppers and salted fish. And she'd pushed several tables together to make one long one in the greenhouse, which, with all the plants and the candlelight, couldn't have looked nicer. I don't know why but, sitting there amongst all those people who were asking who I was and who were talking to me out of strict courtesy and a very big dose of curiosity, I had a certain sense of guilt, because I'd never taken so many pains to organize a birthday party for my mother. It had never occurred to me to spend several days preparing a party for her. And now I was here, amid these strangers, celebrating a birthday that meant nothing to me. What was I doing with my life? I was drifting, like when I rode the motorbike down to the town at night with only stars and an abyss before me.

You don't know what kind of mother you're going to have, I telepathically addressed the baby. I'm not ready to be a daughter or a mother. I'm lazy, erratic, I'm nobody and I'm going to have a baby that will depend on me. I don't even know what I'm going to call you and now you're here, in this greenhouse in the middle of a set-up that's not your thing, and it's not mine either. As I was feeling more and more out of place, the faces around me were getting redder and the voices more and more excited. Food and drink never fail when it comes to making a tribe happy. I began to have clear images of the men dressed up in SS uniforms and the women in dresses like the ones Karin kept in her wardrobe. If they had been young, the dinner might have been followed by an orgy, but now they couldn't even get down on all fours. And there among them, paying tribute to them, venerating them, were Martín and his cronies. They'd got dressed up in suits and ties but they looked like thuggish nightclub bouncers, except for the Eel, who was watching it all out of the corner of his eye and keeping his head down. He was the one who spent the most time talking with Alice and Otto, and the one I most often caught stealing sideways glances at me.

I still felt like crying when the cake with its ten symbolic candles appeared. You can't stick eighty-two candles into a cake, so I'd suggested using two wax numbers, but Karin didn't like numbers. Then I suggested one candle, but she thought one candle seemed ridiculous, so in the end we opted for ten, which filled it up nicely.

She blew them out and, after the singing and the champagne toasts to her, Karin opened several gifts, saying it was the happiest day of her life, that she never thought that she'd reach this age surrounded by friends, after which she said a few words in German. I slipped off to the garage. That afternoon I had left the puppy in the four-by-four, so if he whimpered it wouldn't be noticed. I let him suck my finger so he wouldn't make any noise until I entered the greenhouse and presented him to Karin.

I'm not much given to smiling, but I managed a half-smile as I handed her the basket. Karin looked at me with that deep wrinkle etched between her eyebrows and then peered inside the basket. The puppy wriggled and whined. She took it out with her right hand, on which she was wearing a ring that matched her diamond bracelet.

"What is this?" she said, taken aback and staring at the pup.

"Have I got it right? Do you like him?" I asked.

Karin didn't thank me, didn't answer me, didn't look at me. She put the pup back in the basket and put it down with the other gifts. There was no comment. The silence was only broken by Bolita, as I called the puppy, and the sound of leaves when somebody brushed past the plants. Then Fred said that we'd go and have drinks in the house, and everyone wandered off. I stayed behind in the greenhouse. I couldn't drink alcohol – I wanted to do at least that properly and not pass on to my baby anything bad that could be avoided – so I got in amongst the plants not knowing what to think.

Not only was she not pleased with the puppy, but her reaction had been strange, which meant she wouldn't be keeping it. Now, this really was a problem. What was I going to do with a puppy? I wanted to cry but held back.

Behind the greenhouse glass, the moon trembled slightly. It was enormously big and shiny. I'd heard people saying that we're nothing so many times, but now the words came back to me. I'd taken shelter between two large tropical-looking plants and had the stupid sensation that any moment now their giant leaves were going to wrap themselves around my body so they could devour me. There was something human about them. I heard what sounded like breathing, and it wasn't fantasy, because when the sound accelerated I turned round and the Eel was standing there staring at me. The moonlight shone on two terribly brilliant eyes. I shuddered and moved towards the table where the presents were, to put some distance between us, but the opposite happened. I had to brush my whole body against his in order to avoid a cactus. It was a matter of choosing which type of thorns I preferred to hurt me. He didn't move, but just watched what I was doing, which made me even more nervous. If only I could have turned invisible, disappeared, but no, I couldn't. I had to stay cool whatever happened.

"Why are you still here? Aren't you coming in to have a drink?"

The puppy whimpered loudly. Soon it would be barking its lungs out.

"I can't drink alcohol."

No sooner were the words out of my mouth than I regretted them. I'd just made myself too vulnerable. I didn't like the way his slithery eyes went down to my belly. I clamped my lips together with the intention of not opening them again. Whether I stayed or didn't stay in the greenhouse, it was no concern of his. I picked up Bolita and held him next to my face. He licked me. It was time for his bottle. I'd counted on Karin seeing to his needs, thought that the pup would amuse her, and now look what I'd gone and brought upon myself, all off my own bat.

"Do you like dogs?" I asked him.

"You really put your foot in it," he answered. "And I think you don't even know you have. Who suggested that you should give this dog to Karin?"

I'd already talked too much. There was no way I was going to blab Julián's name.

"It was by chance. This was the one I liked the most. Now it turns out that Karin doesn't like animals, so that's that. So now what are we going to do with him?"

He was looking at me trying to understand. Understand what? I pulled out the flower I'd put in my hair. I was sick of it and threw it in a pot.

"I'll do you a favour. I'll take the dog, I'll look after it and, in return, you'll come out with me one of these days, okay?"

What was worse, taking charge of the pup or having to stand those eyes of his opposite me throughout a whole dinner?

105

I handed him the pup in the basket.

"Wait here a moment," he said, marching off quickly.

I barely had time to reflect upon the situation because he was back in no time with some milk in a bowl. Bolita lapped it up and I almost felt sorry to be giving him up. I thought that in all probability I wouldn't be in this house tomorrow.

"Don't hurt him," I said.

"What do you take me for?" He looked at his watch. "I'm running late."

He walked away to the gate with the basket hanging from his hand and soon I heard a car engine.

I could get out the motorbike and escape from here, go to my sister's house, to the "little house", but the tenant, a secondary-school teacher, had turned up earlier than planned and was about to move in. I could also go to a hotel. I had money, though this money wouldn't last long and a hotel room would guzzle it all up, and, most important, it was cowardice go stampeding off like that because I felt hurt by Karin's reaction. A mother, a future mother, should know what to do in any situation. I wasn't a little girl any more and couldn't throw in the towel just because of some setback. Tomorrow I'd probably see everything in a different light. Then again, I had an appointment for an ultrasound test. I'd thought that Karin could come with me, that I could share with her the moment of discovering the sex of my baby. But I'd just had a change of heart. I'd go alone and maybe call my mother from the clinic, because Karin wasn't my mother and my baby couldn't mean anything to her. Life constantly throws up completely artificial situations. And my relationship with Karin was artificial, because it hadn't existed a couple of months earlier and it wouldn't exist later. It was like an inflatable mattress floating in the middle of the sea.

The best thing would be to go to bed and try to sleep.

I timidly entered the living room. Some women were dancing and others were seated. The door to the library-den was half open, so you could see, without really seeing, what was going on inside, sufficiently to know that the young men were in there with Fred, Otto and the rest of them. The smell of tobacco and dope wafted out. They were laughing. A hand closed the door. Outside there was only one German, a short, dark-eyed fellow who looked Spanish.

He was yawning as he sprawled in an armchair. He didn't seem to be interested in anything. When he saw me he smiled slightly, not at me but to himself.

"Having fun?" he asked.

I was about to say yes, but I said no.

"No, I'm tired."

"Would you like to have a walk in the garden?"

"I was on my way to bed."

He'd already stood up and gave a slight bow with his head by way of farewell, something that nobody had ever done for me in my whole life. So I wrapped myself up in my shawl again and went to have a walk with him.

"Don't those piercings hurt?" he asked, looking at my ears and nose, although I doubted he could see them in the tenuous light of the garden, so he must have spotted them earlier.

"No, once the hole is made, they don't hurt, although I'd never have one in my tongue."

"How awful!" he exclaimed, admiring the moon. "You young people are crazy – young people are always crazy. We also did terrible things."

"What terrible things did you do?"

"They did not seem terrible to us in those days. We did these things because we could and they seemed normal. Like putting a ring in your nose."

The conversation was starting to make me jumpy. I didn't know whether we were talking in code.

"I can do a lot of things that I don't do. I could kill somebody and I don't do it," I said.

"Because you would not find it easy and you would be traumatized. Whether they found you out or not, you would have become an outlaw, and you would feel you had sinned or were simply a criminal. But imagine if there existed a system in which it was legal and patriotic to kill a certain kind of person and nobody would be pointing the finger at you afterwards or wanting explanations."

He took out a cigarette from a silver case that made a pleasant clicking sound when he closed it, and lit up. He didn't offer me one, so I guessed he knew I wasn't smoking. When he was young he must have been very dashing, and it didn't look as if his friends were making him crazy with joy.

"In the end, what is done is done and there is no turning back. Moreover, life is short and, when you reach the end, it seems as if you have just woken up from a five-minute sleep and in your dreams you have done things that do not make sense."

"Like sticking a steel ball in your tongue," I suggested.

"For example."

"As long as you only do damage to yourself..." I added.

"You are right. In the end the damage to yourself is the only thing that can ease your conscience."

He was leaning against a tree. I moved away from him and put an end to the conversation. I didn't want him to say anything more to me. He might have been drinking and the next day he'd regret what he'd said to me, and I had no wish to be hurt by those people. I left him finishing off his cigarette, engrossed in his past with the moon casting all its pallor over him. He didn't turn towards me and looked like an unbearably melancholic statue. And I wanted daybreak to arrive and the sun to come out, so its rays could drill into my head.

He must have been an elegant man once. Now he was wearing a dark-grey suit with cuffed trousers and a black polo-neck sweater underneath. He was the image of a black angel, though I didn't know what that might have meant for other people. But that was the first thing that came into my head, a black angel. He could have been the most intelligent of the whole bunch. He didn't seem to be dominated by the atmosphere in which he lived and yet he couldn't move out of it, so he must still have been afraid of solitude. None of the women there was with him. Perhaps he was a widower. It must have been very exasperating having only the past left to you and not being able to share that with anyone, which was why he'd spent a minute sharing it with me. The problem was that this occurred to me later. Luckily for him, he could still share it with these monsters even though he couldn't stand them sometimes.

So many things in a few hours. Fuck Karin's reaction to the dog, fuck her not looking at me, fuck the black angel and fuck everything. I'd go upstairs to my room as fast as I could. As if it was so easy to go up to your room! I had one foot on the first step when a hand firmly gripped my arm.

It was Alice.

You couldn't consider her old; she didn't look old, her skin wasn't loose and nothing sagged as you'd expect at her age. She looked about sixty, but in reality she must have been over eighty. And it couldn't have only been due to sport, sun and drinking natural juices. She gave the impression of having submitted herself to some experiment. You could even see the biceps in her arms.

"Do you want to dance with me?"

I was stunned by her proposal. I couldn't refuse her, couldn't be rude the way things were, and I needed to observe Alice for my own ends.

They were playing a slow song that I'll never forget as long as I live, 'Only You'. I stepped off the stair I had mounted and took her by the waist. She was wearing a very elegant dress of dark-green velvet, sleeveless with a V-neck front and back. It was slithery velvet that hung fantastically. It was full length. Close up, she had the typical freckled skin that's been in the sun. I stroked my hand over the velvet, not for pleasure of course, but out of curiosity. I was curious to know what Alice's waist was like, if she had any small roll of fat or just hard bones. And, surprise surprise, it was quite a normal body, or better than normal, perfect. I think Alice interpreted my exploration as something more, and she drew closer in a way that made me uncomfortable, although I was only uncomfortable for a second. What the hell! Alice, though suspiciously young, was a woman, and I preferred a woman to take liberties with me than Martín, or his friend the Eel, or the Black Angel, or Otto or any other one of that lot. A bit of human warmth wouldn't hurt me. I needed to be hugged and kissed. And that's what Alice did. She embraced me and rested her lips on my hair until the song ended, at which point I removed myself from her arms and, with a slightly droopy face, informed her that I was tired. She said something in German and I looked at her. It was a difficult language to interpret and you couldn't know whether what she said was good or bad.

"How young you are!" she went on, taking my hand in a way that frightened me. If she could have, she would have ripped my youth right off me.

Her eyes, normally inexpressive, gave me a hard look. She knew what I had, something difficult to steal. I escaped as best I could from the contact of her hand on mine and hurried upstairs so nobody else would detain me.

I really wanted to bolt the door, but there was no bolt. Suddenly I realized that all the rooms had bolts except this one. I had a shower to banish Alice's lips from my hair, then pulled out the nightdress from under the pillow and, as usual, threw it over the armchair. I put on my sleeping T-shirt, turned on the little lamp and, from the small bookcase, took out one of Karin's romantic novels, in Norwegian, with well-worn covers. I could hear the racket downstairs, the music, the voices, the front door opening and closing when somebody left, the cars starting up. The indecipherable pages of the novel were sending me off to sleep. My vision was moving over a story that was happening right before my eyes without my understanding it. I turned off the light, covered myself up to my neck and the noises didn't bother me. They were happening in another world, a distant world full of strange people.

I didn't wake up till the light came in through the window, filtering through the curtains since there were no blinds anywhere in the house. It was a pensive awakening. I'd had strange, heavy dreams, had felt the faces of Fred and Karin observing me, and Alice's too. And Alice's was the one that had made me most jittery. This uneasiness was with me all day long.

I went downstairs at nine when they were still asleep. Frida was already there tidying up things after the party with her usual stealth. In fact, I didn't see her but intuited her presence in the good smell and the shine that had started to appear on the furniture and floor. I was getting my breakfast when her voice made me jump.

"I won't be able to clean your room today. I've got a lot of work down here."

"It doesn't matter," I replied. "I'll make the bed later."

Frida was taking more and more wineglasses out of the dishwasher and, set out all together on the kitchen bench, they created an intensely luminous effect that almost hypnotized me.

I was cold. It had cooled down a lot and the sun wasn't warm enough any more; I'd have to buy myself some winter boots, socks and an anorak too. In the hall, by the front door, there was a built-in wardrobe with raincoats hanging inside, along with umbrellas, jackets and everyday shoes for going out into the garden or walking along the beach. I put on some well-worn sneakers of

Karin's. They were a size too big but I didn't care. I didn't want to catch a cold in my state. I also took a woollen jacket with pockets that drooped from all the times that Karin had stuck her hands in them. I buttoned it up well and started the motorbike. The four-by-four was too unwieldy to park and, besides, I didn't dare to take it without Karin's permission, as I had the impression that something had changed overnight and that we weren't on the same wavelength any more.

The wind sneaked up under the edges of the woollen jacket and chilled my bones. I thought the bloody winding road was never going to end. I parked near Julián's hotel because I wanted to tell him about the dog and, more than anything else, I wanted to talk with somebody who wasn't from the Brotherhood. Brotherhood: someone had pronounced this word and it was the most fitting one for this tribe into which I'd fallen without meaning to.

The receptionist, a man with quite a large freckle on his right cheek, told me that Julián had gone out for a walk. I thought about where I'd like to go for a walk at such an hour and headed for the port. As I walked, the jacket started to annoy me, so I took it off and slung it across my shoulders and then I began to shiver. I walked around the port seeking Julián with my gaze, until I spotted a white hat among the catamarans and sailing boats.

"Hello," I said.

Julián wasn't surprised to see me.

"I'm taking in some vitamin D. Do you want some?" he said, making space for me on the stone bench he was sitting on.

I sneezed and put the jacket on again.


## Julián

I hadn't slept well, despite the sedative I'd taken. I took it because I had a bad conscience and knew that, at some point in the night, either in dreams or in my waking thoughts, Raquel was going to appear with her reproaches. My wife wouldn't have consented to my involving this girl, without her consent, in such a twisted affair. She would have forbidden me from using her. She would have told me that I'd become like them, that I'd been contaminated by their evil.

111

Fortunately, Sandra was here, sitting next to me, but my remorse prevented me from looking into her eyes. I asked her how she was, watching the slight rocking of the *Estrella*, Heim's boat, in the distance.

"Fine," she said, and then went on to tell me more or less what I'd imagined was going to happen with the damn dog.

"I don't get it," she said. "They've got so much garden and the house is so big that a dog couldn't bother them. It would keep them company and protect them. Then there's Frida, who could feed it. I was destroyed by Karin's reaction."

"I'm sorry," I said, feeling truly sorry, sincerely repenting but without confessing to her that dogs of this breed were what Fredrik and Karin used in the concentration camp to terrorize the prisoners (and this was one of their best-known and most clearly identifying features, so her reaction confirmed who they were beyond all doubt). They were animals that the two of them killed when the Allies came in and they had to flee. Six pedigreed dogs, as strong and murderous as their owners, were left lying on the ground each with a shot in its head, as if they were the shades of Fredrik and Karin. I didn't tell Sandra because I needed a little more of her innocence.

I felt much more of a swine and really wretched when she told me she was nervous because they were going to do an ultrasound test to determine the sex of her baby. Her fingers were interlaced and she was wearing large rings on both middle fingers. The sun fell on her red streaks that were now longer than they'd been when I first met her at the little house, but cut in layers as was the fashion among young people. The small nose ring was shining. She was so beautiful and natural, despite what she wore and did to herself, that I thought I didn't deserve to be sitting beside her, didn't deserve to speak to her or to look into her greenish eyes. I didn't deserve her smiling at me or considering me a fellow creature. Although we were here together, I belonged to another planet, had belonged by force of circumstances to an unpardonable past. I could also be sitting beside a rose of velvety red petals or next to a rock or under a radiant star, but that wouldn't make us the same. She told me that, deep down inside, she had the feeling that she'd be betraying her mother if she let Karin share this moment with her. Sandra had moral dilemmas that were so beautifully ingenuous that she made you want to hug her and protect her in a glass bubble.

112

"I could come with you, if you like. I'm not a woman, and you won't be betraying your mother. I know about these things. I have a daughter and you could be my granddaughter."

I shouldn't have said that. Would I have treated my own granddaughter as I'd treated her? Would I have exposed her like this?

"Yes, I think you're the person I want to come with me," she said.

Before her appointment we went to the street where all the shops were, because she wanted to buy some winter boots. She got some black rubber-soled ankle boots, six pairs of special-offer socks and a capacious waterproof anorak. She put on a pair of the socks, the boots and the anorak, and bundled the trainers and woollen jacket she'd been wearing into a bag. I bought myself a three-quarter-length coat, which Sandra liked.

"Now we can go and do the ultrasound," she said.

In her boots, she was as tall as me. She walked through the streets like a queen and I liked being at her side. Sometimes she sneezed as if she'd caught a cold. The wind was coming in from the sea, bearing some chilly drops with it.

When we got to the clinic, we sat down in the waiting room until they called her. I didn't get up at first, but told her I'd wait for her there. She asked me to go in with her. It's not so much that I was feeling uncomfortable but I was aware that I was in a situation that wasn't mine to be in, and I didn't think I was capable of giving her the support she needed.

We went into a very small room into which we only just fitted, Sandra lying on the examination table, the woman doctor sitting on a revolving chair next to her, and me in a corner holding the bag with the trainers and woollen jacket, Sandra's backpack and, on top of all that, my hat.

"It's a little boy," the doctor said.

After a silence Sandra asked, "A boy? Are you sure?"

"I'm sure. Look, that's the heart."

I poked my head forward to look at the screen, but it was all very hazy. It could have been a baby boy or anything else. I must recognize that, for the moment, I forgot about everything, even who I was and what I was doing in that place.

"Is he okay?" Sandra asked.

"Perfectly fine," the doctor answered, rubbing some absorbent paper over Sandra's belly and whipping off her gloves.

"Congratulations," I said.

"Are you her grandfather?" the doctor asked mechanically.

We didn't answer as we both thought it unnecessary to lie to somebody who wasn't remotely interested in us. I held out the anorak to Sandra together with the backpack and carried her other bag myself.

"A little boy," Sandra murmured.

I thought the best thing was to smile.

"I don't even know what name to give him. I can't stand people who seem to have a baby just to give it the name they've wanted to use for a thousand years."

"Something will occur to you. You've got time. How about celebrating this? Let me invite you to lunch. We'll go and find a nice restaurant."

I was being foolish. There was no way I should have let myself be seen with Sandra in town. I relaxed and decided to trust in luck, in the chance that nobody who recognized me would see us together. Poor girl, she'd gone from the viper's nest to the poisonous snake.

I asked her where she'd parked the motorbike and suggested going in my car to some inland restaurant, somewhere less touristy, where they served local food and, along the way, we could have a look at any interesting place that captured our attention. I asked her to wait for me in a terrace bar while I went back to the hotel to get my pills.

Roberto waylaid me on my way in to tell me that a girl had been looking for me, a girl somewhere between redhead and brunette, almost a punk.

"She's not a punk," I protested. "Punks wear chains, leather, crests. Anyway, there are hardly any punks around these days."

Judging from the expression on his face, I deduced he found my remark amusing. I'd noted an increasing respect from him as if, beneath the wrinkles, in the bag of bones, he was discovering a life.

"That's fine then. It looks as if you know who I'm referring to."

I waved goodbye to him on my way to the lifts and again on my way out with the pills in my shirt pocket.

\* \* \*

114

When I got back to the terrace where I'd left Sandra, I found her with her face propped in one hand and immersed in the deepest reverie. Anyone might have thought that this girl was bored, that nothing in her surroundings interested her, but I knew that the exact opposite was the case, that Sandra had a lot to think about. Right now, life was totally hers and, if she'd wanted to, she would have left the rest of us with nothing. She needed to concentrate on this power, so I sat there for a few minutes without speaking.

I asked her to drive. She got into the car humming.

"When we get back, I'll phone my parents from some bar. I can't keep this to myself. It's impossible."

"My mobile doesn't work here, so I never take it out of the hotel."

"It doesn't matter. It's not urgent."

"You shouldn't have gone to the hotel. It's not safe," I told her.

Sandra shrugged.

We had a good time. We went to see a few small villages and, next to a narrow road, we found a restaurant where they served oven-toasted bread sprinkled with olive oil on which we could spread delicious home-made aïoli. We got stuck into the cured sausages and salted fish while Sandra told me that she'd never been much good at studying or holding down a job, that both things bored her hugely. With great difficulty she'd completed a vocational training course in Administration and her father had managed to get her into the offices of a construction company. Before a week had gone by she was filled with great sadness, by six months she'd lost six kilos and, after a year, she couldn't even understand television newscasts properly. Santi helped her a lot. He was a mid-level manager and one day he asked her to go and see the company doctor, who gave her sick leave for depression. Santi was very good to her, was loving and always unflagging in finding qualities in Sandra that she didn't know she had. He advised her to make the most of her time off with the depression and then, at the end of her sick leave, to get out of there because it wasn't her thing. She had a more artistic spirit. Not everyone in the world was apt for being closed up in four walls for eight hours at a time. In a nutshell, she wasn't suited for anything.

"When I found out I was pregnant, I thought about aborting. I don't know if I'm doing the right thing having this baby. I don't know if

I'll know how to raise him. If I can give him everything he needs. I don't know if…"

"Don't worry, children raise themselves and are capable of living in conditions you couldn't begin to imagine. All you have to do is love them and feed them. I don't think your family's going to let you both die of hunger."

Sandra was about to start crying and this alarmed me. She shook her head, challenging my words.

"This baby deserves to have an intelligent mother, a mother who's got some qualifications and who's capable of making beautiful pullovers."

"This baby deserves to have a mother who doesn't think such things about herself. You're very brave, braver than you believe and, when some years have gone by, you'll understand this. You'll look back and see that you were splendid and that, with what you had, you did all you could and in the most honourable way possible."

She looked at me with tear-filled eyes. She was bearing an emotional burden that was greater than I'd believed. I knew that better than she did. She couldn't see, from the outside, the labyrinth she'd entered. This is why, when you get to my age, when we can see it from above, we want to go back and retrace our steps without stress or anguish.

I passed her my paper napkin so she could blow her nose.

"And now you're going to have a slice of chocolate cake with cream, while I have a coffee with a bit of milk. And, as for tomorrow, God will tell us."

All of a sudden, as if answering a question I'd unconsciously put to her, she told me that one of Fredrik's and Karin's friends was going to take the puppy. His name was Alberto, but she called him the Eel because of the slippery expression on his face. It was likely that her head too was exploding with information that she wasn't a hundred per cent aware of. Having to process data and details she didn't know how to fit together was probably making her anxious. We believe that we're only harmed by things we know are harming us, but there's a host of memories and images that cause great distress because we can't make any sense of them.

"He says I have to go out with him some day."

I was left staring at Sandra, trying to work out what the fellow wanted from her. From the way she'd described him, he didn't seem to be the typical mindless fanatic. This one had the reek of a psychopath.

"You mustn't trust him. Try to do what he expects you to do. What we don't know is what he wants of you."

"I'm going to tell him I can't. I don't want to talk with him. I'd rather go out with the Black Angel. I trust him more."

The Black Angel? Black Angel? German, olive-skinned, my height, elegant, affable, apparently level-headed, intelligent, the brain of any organization. From what Sandra told me, he might have been Sebastian Bernhardt. No, that was impossible, as the official story had it that he'd died peacefully in Munich in 1980. Nevertheless, it might also have transpired that he'd been yearning for his marvellous Spanish refuge. These rats went in one hole and came out of another, and were well accustomed to dying and being resuscitated. It was a relief to know they weren't eternal, though they'd tried to be, though they'd desperately been trying to get their hands on the elixir of eternal youth. And at what a price. Ask the prisoners, the victims of maniacs like Heim.

"Wait a moment. I'm going to fetch something from the car."

Sandra didn't answer. She was pensively nibbling her cake, little bits of cake, off the end of her spoon.

When I came back with Elfe's photo album, she was still in the same position, thinking about her son, or the Black Angel, or the Eel, or maybe Karin or her mother, who wouldn't have the slightest idea of the situation her daughter had got into.

"Look," I said, opening up the album. "Look at this man."

It was Sebastian. He was wearing a suit, which made the identification easier. A dark suit, receding hairline, eyes also dark.

She looked at him as she emerged from her private ruminations.

"Could he be the Black Angel?" I asked.

"Could be. He smokes in the same way."

I hesitated over revealing to Sandra who the Black Angel was, because the more she knew the worse it would be for her. She'd look at him differently, or might let his real name escape her lips, and she wouldn't talk about him with the healthy ring of ignorance. Sandra was a candid, sincere girl with nothing to hide, and they'd immediately read what she knew in her eyes. Then again, I didn't feel capable of manipulating her to such an extreme. She had the right to know about the vipers' nest she'd fallen into. She'd let me participate in a beautiful event of her life and I mustn't fall so low as to betray her, to stand by and watch her plummeting down without having warned her that the abyss was waiting for her only ten metres away.

"You have to decide," I told her. "You have to tell me if you want me to tell you who this individual is. Bear in mind that every piece of information you acquire will take you one step closer to hell."

# 5
## Monsters Also Fall in Love

### Sandra

It was hard to recognize them from the photos Julián showed me. Physically speaking, they were other people now. Some still had features they couldn't hide, like the exceptional height of Fred and Aribert Heim, the *Butcher of Mauthausen*, who now had only a couple of white hairs left on his head. He walked bent over as if he couldn't hold up his enormous skeleton. I recalled having seen him only once at the Norwegians' house, at Karin's birthday party, and he seemed to be a friendly man. He held out his hand and flashed me a smile. The scars crossing Otto Wagner's face and his blue eyes had become less noticeable, were fading away. And the Black Angel, who was apparently called Sebastian Bernhardt, had no outstanding features, was quite ordinary-looking though he did dye the little bit of hair he had left on both sides of his head.

Julián assumed that the man I'd previously thought of as the Black Angel had died in Germany, when in fact he'd returned to this village, where he'd previously been living from 1940 until some time in the Fifties. He and his family possessed a villa presented to him by Franco in recognition of his services, which had been nothing more nor less than convincing Hitler to give his support to Franco. I swore to myself that when I got back to my normal life I'd read more about these things. How could someone that old still keep going? His wife, Helen by name, had probably died and his children would have retired by now. Sebastian had always enjoyed the reputation of being unpretentious and agreeable and he continued to be so. I can vouch for that. Julián immediately suspected that this mansion of Sebastian's was what was now known as Villa Sol. He'd probably sold it to the Norwegians and retired to a more comfortable apartment. There was a sort of background feeling of comfort at Villa Sol, most likely left by Helen and her children. I didn't understand how somebody who looked as reasonable as Sebastian did, someone so understanding, could be one of them, or how he wasn't revolted by the things they'd done. I wondered what could have gone on in the mind of somebody in order for that person never ever to feel remorse about anything. Basically, he was the only one of the whole tribe who had a human gaze. The rest of them were fakers. Had any of them killed again after the War, or had they had their fill for ever? Would any one of them be capable of killing on his or her own account, or did they need to be part of an organization?

I didn't know any of these things before and would never have known them if it hadn't occurred to me to come and spend a few days by the sea. Mauthausen. Auschwitz. How many times had I heard these names? But then they were light years away and belonged in the realms of Orion at the very least, in a past that wasn't mine. Now I had them a metre in front of my face, and sometimes just a few centimetres away.

Aribert Heim had held out his hand to me and, when I discovered what those hands had done, I felt marked and that there was no way I could walk out now, although there was always the possibility that this was merely a case of mistaken identity, because all old people look alike. If only it wasn't true that I'd shaken hands with the Butcher. Just thinking about it made me feel sick. For the moment, there was nothing but the Gold Cross that could confirm Fred's identity. All the rest was conjecture.

Could I put on an act, Julián had asked me. Could you dissemble to the point that it would never enter their heads that you might be interested in that old story of Nazis and the Holocaust? Actually, they never talked about politics in front of me. Nothing that could sound important was ever mentioned, although sometimes they let slip a few words in German, which you didn't have to know in order to twig that they were a departure from the general tone. I was sure that such precautions were not because of me, but because they were used to taking them, which is why they'd slipped through Julián's hands over and over again. If I hadn't known they were Nazis, they would have continued to be normal people for me. But now, everything, whatever it was, had a meaning. Those marked features of Fred's were Aryan features, and Alice's strange youthfulness came from God knows where. Maybe it was simply that she trusted in her genetic superiority. We decided that we'd never mention their real names as a precaution against their slipping out when I was talking with them.

## Julián

As before, Sandra arrived at the lighthouse on her motorbike, parked it, and came into the ice-cream parlour. I saw her through the window. We always sat at a table from which you could see the cars coming and people entering and leaving the place. It was one way of avoiding unpleasant surprises. When she sat down at the table, she sighed and put her helmet down beside her. I thought she didn't look well and was possibly too thin for a pregnant woman, but it was just a passing impression and not a conscious assessment. More than an idea it was an image. The present was escaping from me too fast, without giving me time to savour it. Birds flew very fast, air was lost before it was felt, faces changed instantly, smells disappeared, and it scarcely mattered. My whole life was in the past. I had the sense that I'd been left in this world after Raquel died to atone for some wrongdoing, to suffer a little more, and that my having survived her made no sense. Sandra functioned in the dimension of the present and I in the past, even though we could see each other and talk.

When I confessed to Sandra that I'd bought the dog deliberately and for morbid reasons, without calculating the risks, when I confessed that I'd used her to make the Norwegians uneasy, she would never look me in the face again and would very rightly consider that I was as wretched as they were. But I had to say it. I couldn't die with this on my conscience.

I thought about writing her a letter and giving it to her when we said goodbye at the lighthouse, but I immediately thought it would be an act of cowardice not to say it to her face, so I looked her in the eye.

"I've got to tell you something. I'm not asking for forgiveness, I don't want anything. That's life, one despicable thing after another. You shouldn't have anything to do with somebody like me."

Sandra didn't blink. Sometimes her gaze was so fixed it was uncomfortable. It was as if she'd forgotten to change its direction.

"It's about the dog, the puppy you gave to Karin."

"Poor Bolita," she said. "I've been thinking about him too. I shouldn't have given him to the Eel. I shouldn't have washed my hands of him. I feel really bad about it. I wonder what they've done with him."

"Remember how surprised you were by Karin's reaction? Such a beautiful dog, such a big house. It's impossible to understand how she could reject it, isn't it?"

"I felt really bad about it, as you know. It was a tremendous slap in the face. Karin's never mentioned it again or said sorry or offered any explanation. I feel like I've done something terrible without knowing what, but now the only thing I'm sorry about is what would have happened to the dog."

In a few seconds, I was going to rip from Sandra a little bit of her good heart. From now on she'd be minus another scrap of her good heart. And the fewer the good hearts abroad in the world the worse it would be for everybody.

"It was my fault. Totally and absolutely my fault," I said, almost closing my eyes so I didn't have to see her. "Karin hates this breed of dog, because they used them to terrorize the prisoners in the concentration camps where they'd been sent. I'm not going to tell you any more. They trained them for that and their presence reminds her of who she was and who she continues to be. Basically, people don't change, don't improve. They only get old. Sad to say, it's as easy to get worse as it is to get better. And I've just realized that I, too, am worse than I believed."

Sandra was disconcerted. She'd probably never imagined I'd be capable of such a dirty trick, of putting her in danger or at least in a difficult situation. Her expression had changed, had turned a little sad, as if she was very tired.

"If I respect you, appreciate you and think you're marvellous, and yet am capable of doing such a thing, imagine how far they might go."

I couldn't bear Sandra's not saying anything. When Raquel got really angry with me, she didn't speak. Rage sewed her lips together. At first I used to get desperate, trying to bring her back to me, to make her look at me, to accept me again, which only made things worse, until I understood that it was better to wait and not force matters. I used to go into another room, or to have a walk, taking a distance, trusting that Nature would do her work. And now I was thinking of doing the same, although Sandra wasn't Raquel and neither had I ever done such a rotten thing to Raquel as I'd done to Sandra.

I called the waitress over, paid and stood up. Sandra remained there looking dejected. I left a two-euro tip on the saucer and the waitress looked at me with infinite contempt. Something must have happened to her at Sandra's age with someone of my age, something worse than what I'd done to Sandra.

## Sandra

I'd almost succeeded in forgetting about Karin's party when Julián made his confession about the dog. I felt so let down and betrayed that I acted like an idiot. At the time, I didn't see that if he'd warned me about what he was thinking of doing, I would have given myself away in front of everyone when Karin rejected Bolita. Of course I wouldn't have reacted so naturally. Julián had got carried away by his zeal in wanting them to feel that their cover had been blown and that they couldn't keep on living like that without a care in the world. He could have chosen not to be sincere with me, and then I would never have had a clue. If it was only because of his having exposed himself to the shame of confessing, I wanted to give Julián my vote of confidence. It also occurred to me that Julián had offered me this explanation about the dog so I'd pull out of this situation for once and for all. I didn't believe he was faking when he was fretting about my safety, and when he kept insisting I should leave. Maybe he'd had the idea about the dog in order to force my retreat, which wasn't part of my plans any more. I wanted to do something important.

Since I didn't know to make a good job of the small things in life, I'd have to do something outstanding so I wouldn't go on feeling I was such a complete good-for-nothing. I'd never believed this stuff about opportunities that life places in your way because I'd never played this opportunities game, and because, in order to find them, first you have to go looking for them, and what opportunities would be suitable for me? I never knew until I landed in the Norwegians' house, until I met Julián and began to enter into this terrifying story that everyone's heard of, and yet there were very few people left who'd actually lived through it. I felt caught between victims and executioners, between the Devil and the deep blue sea. Then, lo and behold, life ends up thrusting an opportunity right in front of my nose, the chance to help Julián unmask this scum. Any woman can be a mother, but I didn't want my son to have any old mother. I wasn't a little girl any more, I'd never go back to being that, and life was giving me an opportunity. This was no time to be running away.

I'd also forgotten about the Eel and my promise to go out with him. It was something I'd put out of my mind as best I could by thinking about what name to give my son now I knew the baby was a boy. I wasn't sure whether I should call him after someone in the family, or after Santi, his father, or whether to give him a completely new name not associated with anyone. I was also thinking about how to decorate his room, without knowing which house the room would be in. I'd stick a starry sky on the ceiling, which would shine when the light was turned off so he could see it when he opened his eyes. If only you could do everything just by thinking about it. By thinking, then, I'd have enough money to set up a shop selling clothes or costume jewellery and I'd contract an assistant so I wouldn't feel tied down. By thinking, I'd fall in love to the point of swooning, like in Karin's novels and, by thinking, Fred and Karin would be two normal old people of the kind I wouldn't have to suspect or fear in the least. But what you think is going to happen rarely does happen.

On Monday, when we got back to Villa Sol from Karin's gym, we found Martín there chatting with Fred and, from the expression on his face when he saw me, it looked as if he was waiting for me. On the kitchen bench there was a small packet, which he must have brought. Karin picked it up at once while Martín handed me a piece of paper with a malicious air about him.

Handwriting with rounded, absolutely feminine letters informed me that he'd be coming to pick me up at seven. It was signed "Alberto". It was the Eel.

"Have you read the note?" I asked Martín. His head was even more close-shaven now and on his cranium he was sporting a tattoo of a sphere.

"I wrote it myself," he replied, enjoying the fact that he'd thrown me off balance.

"And why?"

"Alberto asked me to do it. He had a little matter to deal with and didn't have time."

"Well, you've got very pretty handwriting."

"Really?" he said, rubbing his hand over the tattoo.

I nodded.

"Sometimes I write poems, lyrics for songs. I want to start up a group, you know what I mean?"

"You've certainly got something in you. That's clear."

"Listen," he said, moving so close to me that he was brushing against me, "Alberto's a good guy, but sometimes he loses the plot. Don't go getting into an argument with him, okay?"

"Run along, away with you," I said, pushing him away with my fingers, "and, when you get your group together, don't wear that cologne."

He took me by the arm, worried.

"Don't you get it into your head to talk to him like that. He doesn't understand these things. I like you, little girl."

Little girl? Where did this cretin crawl out from? He said little girl, has the handwriting of a nun, but what he's done to his head is really scary. I pushed him right away from me with my hand and went upstairs wondering what I could wear that wouldn't make the Eel lose the plot.

By the time I came down, Fred and Karin had been informed about my date. Martín had left. They looked at me all smiles. They relished anything to do with love. I'm sure they liked the idea of me getting together with someone from the Brotherhood. It would be the ideal way for them to get me under their control, or not to have to do anything to keep me under control. In such circumstances they could certainly name me heiress to all their worldly goods.

I'd put on my other pair of jeans, the boots and a white blouse with embroidery at the neck and cuffs that Karin had given me. It was something I wasn't going to be wearing on any other occasion and I was planning to throw it away as soon as all this was over, but now it would serve my purposes of getting a bit of an idea of how things looked from the Brotherhood's perspective. I picked up the anorak and draped it over my arm.

"They're very good boys," they said, taking the words from each other's mouths.

"Do you want some perfume?" Karin asked.

Fortunately the Eel tooted the horn from the other side of the gate just then and I could dash out. I was grateful he hadn't come to get me at the door.

"Hello," he said when I got in the car and he headed off towards the main road.

I didn't say anything, didn't know what to say until I heard a mixture of whimpering and yapping from the back seat. I couldn't believe it. It was Bolita in the gift basket. I leant back towards him.

"You little wretch," I exclaimed. "You've got so fat!"

"Because I look after him well," the Eel said.

"I would never have imagined it. I thought that…"

"That I'd taken him to the dog pound and got him put down? That I'd killed him with my own bare hands? That I'd eaten him?"

"I don't know," I said, playing with the pup. "Having a puppy and looking after it doesn't suit you."

"Yeah, it suits me to have a great big ferocious dog to scare the shit out of people."

"Precisely," I said, disregarding Martín's advice.

Now I was getting a closer look at him. He hadn't taken any particular pains over getting dressed up to be with me, so it didn't seem very logical to think that he wanted to get off with me, or it might also be that he thought I didn't deserve anything better. He was wearing a long-sleeved shirt that looked as if he'd been wearing it for a while, grey trousers that didn't look recently ironed, and he'd thrown a dark-blue everyday jacket on the seat next to Bolita. He hadn't even tried to run his fingers through his hair, which was tousled by the wind. He certainly had no intention of trying to impress me. He had delicate features and light-brown to blondish hair, a receding hairline, wasn't ugly and was about thirty-five.

"Might I know where we're going?" I said.

"To the lighthouse. It's very nice there."

He looked at me sideways and I looked back at him.

"I'd prefer to go somewhere more lively, where we can see people. If it's all the same to you, I'd rather go into town," I told him.

Thank God he didn't insist on going to the lighthouse. Why did he say that about the lighthouse? Would that have been intentional?

We went to one of the pubs in the town and had to leave Bolita in the car.

"How do you manage things with the dog?"

"I try to make sure he doesn't die of hunger."

He ordered a beer and I asked for a fruit smoothie and a slice of cake. I was starting to go hungry living with the Norwegians. They didn't eat much, not enough, I'd say. The only decent meal of the day was breakfast. At their age, a feast probably meant certain death and sometimes they forgot that I was young. So, even though I was nervous about this encounter with the Eel, I guzzled the cake and the smoothie.

"What do you want with me?" I asked him straight out. I didn't want to beat around the bush, because he had more experience than I did of life in general, and situations like this in particular.

Instead of answering, he got up and went over to the display case, which had some delicious-looking goodies inside. I wanted to make the most of this pause to think, but with a full stomach it was a very uphill job.

He came back with a plateful of different sorts of little cakes and another smoothie. He ordered another beer. I was going to tell him that this was much better than the ice-cream parlour at the lighthouse. Luckily I stopped myself in time. The best thing would be to speak as little as possible.

"I don't want what you think I want. I just want to know you. You're something new in our lives."

"And what did you think I was thinking?"

"That I wanted to get into bed with you or something like that."

"Hold your horses!" I said with a start that pepped me up a bit. "If I thought that, I'd need to have reasons."

"And what reasons have I given you?"

"Your eyes, your way of looking. You're strange, and it's impossible to know what you're thinking."

"You see? You're just like the rest of them, getting carried away by appearances."

"Yes, I'm just like the rest of them, so why do you say you want to know me?"

"Okay," he said, "what I want to know is how you ended up living with the Christensens."

"It's very simple. I met them on the beach. I'm alone and they need me. I'm glad to have the money they pay me. That's all."

"That's all? There's no one else?"

I sipped the smoothie so I wouldn't have to answer.

"How come you gave that dog to Karin? Precisely that dog?"

"I've asked myself that over and over again since that day. I don't understand anything and that's the truth."

"Yes, you do understand. Don't try to fool me."

"And if I'm trying to fool you, what do you plan to do to me?"

"The worst thing you can imagine."

"I'm not scared of you or of Martín either."

"Well, you should be. Don't act too smart. I know what I'm talking about. Do you want something else, something savoury?"

"I'd like to go for a walk. I've eaten too much."

The Eel wasn't as terrible as I'd imagined, based on present appearances. Though he said these things, I didn't believe he was capable of killing me and I'd even say there were moments when he gave the impression of looking at me with concern. In any case, I couldn't let my guard down and had to be very mindful of Martín's words.

We wandered round the port. At one point we stopped and stayed there contemplating the sea. We looked at each other from the corners of our eyes, he at my profile and I at his. The sky was full of stars. It was a marvellous moment to be with someone I cared about.

"Why did Martín write the note and not you?" I asked, sitting on a stone bench.

"Because... Never mind."

"Is he a good friend of yours, Martín?"

"We're in the Brotherhood. We're more than friends. A friendship can be broken but not the bonds of the Brotherhood. You should know, for your own good, that Martín isn't as patient as I am. I don't know if you get what I'm saying."

"Well, it's difficult to understand everything. I only just arrived."

"I know. What I don't know is whether you know what that means. Why do you think we're together? Have the Christensens explained that to you?"

"No, I don't think so. I thought you got on well, that you helped each other and that people try not to be alone. Don't tell me it's a cult."

128

"Something like that. Oh God!" he burst out. "Why didn't you just stay home with your husband, your partner, or whatever he is?"

"I'm going to be a single mother," I said.

And then the Eel stroked my hair, moved swiftly over to me and, without giving me time to think, kissed me.

I didn't react. It all happened so quickly and unpredictably. I was embracing him for at least a minute. I noticed his lips, his tongue, his saliva, his hands on my head, his smell. When he moved away from me, his hair lightly caressed me and mine lightly caressed him. He moved away slowly. I still had the impression of his kiss, a long, warm impression. My mouth wasn't the same any more, the Eel wasn't the same and the world had suddenly changed. I didn't speak, stayed quiet because I couldn't be angry, because the kiss was the kiss I needed, the kiss I needed exactly as he'd given it to me and never, not in my wildest dreams, even if I lived a thousand years, would I have imagined that the person responsible for giving me that kiss would be the Eel.

I didn't look up. Also looking down, he said, "I'm sorry, I couldn't help it. You're gorgeous."

I still didn't make a sound, waiting for a cataclysm to shake me out of my stupor. Or a second kiss.

"Would you kill me now?"

"No, and not before either, but you mustn't tell anybody I said that. And when I say not anybody, I mean not a single solitary soul. Understood?"

I nodded. I looked at him. He wasn't the Eel any more and this change flustered me. Before he was a terrible being, an enemy, and now he wasn't. I felt attracted to him, to his jacket of a blue as dark as the night which had just fallen on us, to his creased shirt. I would have walked back to the car through the port clinging to him. I would have liked him to put his arm round my shoulders and press me against him. It was madness. What had happened was madness. It might have been the magic of the night, the stars above us, the lights of the port, the sound of the sea, the breeze, being alone together...

"This is madness," he said, this time daring to look me in the eye, unflinchingly.

Now I liked his eyes. I liked his almond-shaped eyes and that slippery look. I had nobody near me who could make me feel something like this. I hadn't even felt this with Santi, which should have been so easy. The Eel hadn't needed to do anything, except for not resisting, so I didn't understand why it had to be him and not the father of my baby that had lifted my feet off the ground. It wasn't Santi's fault. It was mine, because then I wasn't what I was now.

In the car we were on the point of kissing again, but we didn't. We were letting a good moment escape, and who knows if it would be repeated.

"Do you think I should give in, that I should join the Brotherhood?"

He took a minute to respond, pretended to be concentrating on his driving and then said somewhat curtly, "What matters is what you think. No one called you. You got into this all by yourself."

I got slowly out of the car. This might never happen again. And I wasn't the same person who'd left Villa Sol a few hours earlier. I was returning from a long journey and what I'd left behind here seemed less important now.

Fred and Karin were waiting for me in the living room. They were curious to know how it had gone.

"Goodnight. I've had a big dinner," was my only answer.

When I got to my room I lay on the bed. I could see stars through the window and, beneath the stars, the palm leaves were swaying. I was slightly giddy. It was something like floating.


## Julián

Sandra probably wouldn't turn up for our appointment after what had happened the other day. If I was her I wouldn't come. Why would I want to see somebody who'd deceived me and put me in danger? Yet it was my obligation to be here in case she did decide to come. The only thing I could do was to show her the deep contempt I had for myself.

I didn't get out of the car, didn't want to see the face of the waitress in the ice-cream parlour before I had to. I didn't want to take her into account but couldn't avoid it. You can't avoid seeing, hearing or feeling liking or antipathy for people you come across, five-minute people. You can't be dead before you die, however much you might wish it. So when I heard the wheels of Sandra's motorbike on the pebbly ground, I beeped my horn lightly, to get her attention. My heart gave a dangerous leap of joy.

Sandra appeared and came over to me. I opened the door so she could get in.

"Is it full inside?" she asked.

"I can't stand that waitress. I'm offended by her way of looking at me as if I'm a pervert."

Sandra laughed half-heartedly. Her face was gaunt. She'd lost at least three kilos and I couldn't think of anywhere else to take her so she could eat something. I only trusted the bar with the set menu and this place, because we ran the risk of being seen together in any other establishment in town.

"But, on second thoughts, I'm hungry," I said. "I could do with a toasted sandwich and a bit of chocolate cake. They don't make them anywhere else like they do here."

"Whatever you want. I'm not hungry."

It soothed me to be sitting at our table by the window. It gave our meeting a feel of normality.

"It looks like the Norwegians don't keep a very full fridge."

"Why do you say that?" she asked as she unenthusiastically picked up the plastic-coated menu. We knew by heart what they served in the ice-cream parlour, but we always spent quite some time perusing the menu as we spoke.

"Pregnant women put on weight. They don't lose it."

"I'm fine."

The waitress interrupted us, glaring at me with her customary hostility.

"Espresso coffee for me and, for the young lady, a toasted ham sandwich with wholemeal bread, a slice of chocolate cake and a smoothie."

Sandra didn't want the chocolate cake and the waitress crossed it out, aiming a compassionate look at her.

"They're sucking your blood. If you stay in that house, you're going to fall ill," I told her.

"No, it's not that. I'm nervous. Well, nervous isn't the word. I'm on edge, in suspense."

"In suspense about what?"

Sandra went quiet. The waitress brought paper napkins and cutlery.

"In suspense. I've got the impression that my life, my real life, is going to begin any time now. This journey has been very important for me. Imagine, I believed I was going to spend the whole time lying in a hammock, and now look…"

I listened vaguely. Deep down, I was thinking about Sebastian, about how I could locate his house without having to use Sandra.

"The puppy's fine," she burst out.

It vexed me that I took a minute to twig which puppy she was talking about. She looked at me with her greenish-brown eyes wide open. They'd got bigger and had lost some of their joy, but had gained in intensity. The puppy reminded us of the bad thing I'd done. I was so engrossed in the turn things had taken that I suddenly noticed the things we'd ordered on the table. They'd apparently appeared by magic.

"And how do you know?"

She kept looking at me, giving me time to remember and pick up the thread. According to what Sandra had told me, the Eel had taken the puppy the night of the party and, besides, he'd wanted to go out with her one day.

"Don't tell me you've been seeing that fellow, the Eel."

She nodded, her expression transformed.

"He's called Alberto," she said, nibbling apathetically at her sandwich.

"So, it's Alberto then."

"He came to pick me up at the Norwegians' house and brought the dog so I could see him. He's got really tubby. He's very well looked after."

"So you think he's a good guy because of that?"

Guy? I'd been picking up Sandra's vocabulary. I felt odd saying the word "guy", as if I was turning into someone else.

"I haven't seen him since. He hasn't been there or left me a note. Nothing," she said, looking gloomy.

This time I didn't even need a minute to understand. Her eyes were shining dangerously.

"You're not scared any more."

She shrugged. She'd finished the smoothie and had only nibbled at the sandwich.

"Things have changed. Those people can't hurt us any more. At best, the least old of that lot will last five years more."

I had to raise my voice a little to get a reaction out of her. The waitress, who was keeping an eye on me from the bar, would think we were a couple having a tiff.

"Things go on being exactly the same, or worse, and precisely because both they and I have one foot in the grave, old scores need to be settled."

She looked at her watch. She was wearing a large watch with a wide blue leather band and she had lovely hands. There was usually nothing languid about Sandra, yet now she was one step away from being so.

"You don't understand... Alberto would never let them harm me."

"Why, if I may ask?"

"He kissed me in the port."

That was the end of the thread. She needed to tell someone that she'd fallen in love. She preferred forgiving me to not being able to say it.

"And did you kiss him back?"

"Yes."

"And what did you feel?"

"That everything that's happening to me is the best thing in the world."

"Everything? Now we've really got a problem," I said, but she didn't seem to hear me.

"But I haven't seen him since and I don't know where to find him. Why is he doing that to me?"

Until that point, I'd been concerned about Sandra. But now she had me really alarmed, especially because I found her a little distant. She was moving away from me and our objectives. I told her that by the time she saw him again she would probably have come to her senses and realized it had all been a mirage. I told her that soon she'd find a man who really loved her. And I told her that, maybe, after all her recent experiences, she'd be able to see her baby's father with new eyes. I told her that the Eel was no good for her, even if his name was Alberto and they'd kissed. I told her that he'd taken advantage of her because she was alone and needed to be loved. But Sandra didn't hear me.

What could Alberto's real feelings towards Sandra be? However cold the blood he had running in his veins, he might have fallen in love with her. Only a fool wouldn't fall in love with this big warm soul, her clear gaze, her sincerity and her strength. She was infinitely better than all of us put together, and the fact that the Eel could have got so far inside her heart was worrying, because it's very difficult to defend oneself against love. He'd managed to get Sandra still more entangled in the spider's web. If Sandra stayed in the group because she'd fallen in love with one of them, it would be very hard to get her out again.

I left this encounter more upset than ever, and with more feelings of guilt than ever, because, if I hadn't behaved like such a moron, Sandra wouldn't have felt so helpless and wouldn't have thrown herself into the arms of anybody.

## Sandra

I think that – just as I was becoming one of them – Fred and Karin were gradually becoming wary of me, prey to doubts if not paranoid. I played at acting in the most ingenuous way I could. I played at being the way I was before I met them, before knowing who they were. I tried to bamboozle them. What did I have to do with their nightmare world? They'd found me on a beach, I was pregnant (and what mother would put her own child in danger?) and I'd gone to live with them because I urgently needed money and I was alone. These were sufficient reasons for them not seeing clearly that I'd found them out. At the end of the day, our relationship had begun purely by chance, with a fluky meeting on the beach. That's why I didn't realize that the venom of suspicion had really got into their heads until I came back from my last meeting with Julián.

When I arrived, announced by the noise of my motorbike, Fred was there on the ground floor, watching television as usual, while Karin was reading one of her romantic novels. When she raised her eyes from the pages, I found her expression strange but, since I still didn't know anything, I stayed there for a while talking about how good it had been walking around on this marvellously cloudy afternoon and how I'd felt the air on my face while I was riding the motorbike. To tell the truth, since my encounter with Alberto I'd been producing lots of happiness hormones, so I wasn't able to interpret Fred's semi-smile and Karin's penetrating stare. They were looking at me from a different angle of their brains. But there came a point when my bladder was about to burst and, instead of using the downstairs bathroom, I preferred to go up to mine and, while there, have a shower. Then the world changed.

I went up to my room humming some song or other, softly because I can't keep a tune, and took off my boots and pants. I mechanically opened up the wardrobe to get out a clean T-shirt. Something in the mirror on the wardrobe door caught my attention or, rather, stopped me dead in my tracks. I was paralysed because I had to concentrate to the maximum in order to take in the situation. I felt a fiery heat shooting up from my neck to my face in something like shame or fear, and I decided to stop looking in the mirror and to check the bed where what was reflected in the mirror was located.

I couldn't believe it. Now I was well and truly done for. Right before my eyes, placed like a pillow, was the newspaper clipping with the photo of the Norwegians that Julián had given me. The Norwegians had surely put it there or Frida had surely found it in my bag. I didn't as much as dare to touch it, as if it was going to set off all the alarms in the house. I stood there staring at it without knowing what to think and feeling quite dizzy. The cutting could only have got here if somebody had pulled it out from underneath my clothes and, in order to do that, they had to poke around in the depths of my bag.

And what if it had been me? Maybe when I was rooting around getting out clothes the page had slipped out and somehow dropped on the floor and Frida found it and left it on the bed.

It was hard for me to respond to this, so I remained in my room as long as I could without having the nerve to go downstairs and face them, or to escape through the window. It occurred to me that there was no need for me to put up with such a tense situation, so I'd just wait in here, putting my clothes in my bag and backpack until they were asleep and then head for my little house, as Julián called it, and stay there till the new tenant arrived, or I'd ask Julián to give me shelter in his hotel. My mind was blank and I was confused. I've never been good at confrontations and I had no idea of how to lie to these two. After all, I'd come here to escape having to deal with the father of my baby, my family, my lack of a job, a future and reality in general, and now I was faced with this, as if it was impossible to escape from problems. However, now I'd met Alberto, who'd become another type of worry, the only kind of worry I liked. Why was he showing no signs of life?

I sat on the bed for a while, totally flummoxed. Then I took three deep breaths and decided to have a shower as planned. When I was wrapped up in a dressing gown with fresh skin and wet hair dripping, things started to look less tragic, and the solution to this uncomfortable affair came heaven-sent, as if in some part of the world an emergency cabinet had met to think fast about this mess and had telepathically sent me the result because I was in no condition to be making such an effort. So I got dressed, left the page on top of the chest of drawers and went down those increasingly infernal stairs (made, according to what Karin told me, of pink marble brought from the Macael quarries).

They were still on the sofa doing what they'd been doing before, he watching television and she reading her eternal romances. They shot the same look at me. I understood its meaning now and it intimidated me. But I might as well be hung for a sheep as a lamb. Gathering all my strength, I told them that I was very tired, that I was going to have some yogurt and go straight to bed. Then I got the velvet bag, took out the pullover and showed it to Karin. I asked her if it would be very difficult to work in some design on the front to brighten it up. She'd kept staring at me, trying to suss out my intentions, and all I could think of was to shove my work in her tortured hands and say something.

I could see from the look in her eyes that they'd gone in to search my room when I went shopping, or just to get out for a while, or to see Julián. They searched even before suspecting me of anything, as if it was a kind of duty for them to mistrust everyone. Worst of all, they didn't care if I knew that they were monitoring me, that they didn't trust me and that they didn't entirely see me as their friend, maybe because, with this find, the cards were well and truly face up on the table. It was all so open now that Karin averted her gaze. Suddenly her eyes and her age-twisted face were those of Nurse Karin sixty years on. Youth and beauty were no longer there to hide her true soul.

"If you want a design on it, you'll have to start again. You'll have to undo what you've done. It would be better if you tried with another one. Finish this one first."

Her words rang with some kind of occult meaning: you'll have to undo what you've done, she'd said. I sat on the sofa to have my yogurt and when I took my leave and wished them goodnight, they didn't insist I should stay, which would be the usual thing.

I hadn't undone what I'd done but felt relieved at not having to face them. I took my trousers off, left my T-shirt on, removed the satin negligee from under the pillow, flung it on the chair and got into bed. I did what people advised and opened the window slightly so I could breathe better and to improve the flow of oxygen to my brain. Then I began to read for a while. Tomorrow would be another day.

## Julián

I still didn't know where Sebastian Bernhardt, the Black Angel, lived. I hadn't seen him around the Nordic Club and neither had he turned up when I was following Fredrik or Otto. Evidently he led another life unless he was practically obliged to meet up with them. He was another cut of person, more intelligent and less fanatical. Everything people said about him suggested that he might seriously have believed that what he was doing was for the good of humanity. He was an active man, a man of vision, with a plan in his head that required suffering, because every change entails pain, and changing the world wasn't going to be easy or comfortable for anybody. He was all the more frightening precisely because of this. He wasn't a sadist, but he'd done the groundwork for sadists like Heim to give free rein to their instincts and run amok.

At this time of my life, I had a pretty good idea of what they were like. Their mindset was rigid and self-centred, with a totally instrumental idea of life, devoid of all understanding. They were sociopaths and the ones that weren't infected had ended up getting infected. I had no interest in speaking with them, but Sebastian was another, more complicated story and, at bottom, more dangerous. He wouldn't enjoy doing evil, or grinding his boot in the necks of his fellow humans, but he'd think of it as a necessary evil, coming from the same packet as good, and the greater the good one wished to attain, the greater the evil had to be.

I went to keep an eye on the floating home of Butcher Heim with a sense of foreboding. It was a sort of presentiment or sixth sense I developed in the camp. Maybe I developed it at an age when such talents tend to emerge but it came upon me in that death-serving place. The fact is that I learnt to notice in my soul or spirit when something worse than usual was going to happen, and also when something good was coming. One never felt good there, but when they were going to gas a friend or suddenly called us to the infirmary to check whether we were still fit for work, which is to say, fit to stay alive, the previous day I felt unbearably bad for no particular reason. All of a sudden, in the quarry, in the hut, or naked in the courtyard among the human livestock, the shadow of evil got inside me and the world went dark, like dusk falling. At first I didn't relate one thing with another but then I started to realize it was like my grandmother's arm, which started hurting whenever it was about to rain. The day I tried to kill myself was the day my soul or spirit had collapsed and I couldn't take any more, the shadow was too big and inside my head there was nothing to be seen. Salva caught me just in time and the following day was horrible. The chimneys smoked so much that it was impossible to breathe with the smell of burning flesh. A grey pall hung over the camp and then I thought that this cloud would watch over those of us who were left and I asked the molecules comprising the cloud to protect us from all evil, and to see to it that Salva, who weighed thirty-eight kilos, wouldn't be judged unproductive or useless. And they heeded me. Somehow, Salva turned invisible until we left the camp.

Until then, I'd had to invent all kinds of strategies to protect him. I managed to stand in front of him, keep him concealed from the quarry overseers and had studied where he had to go so as not to be seen. I got desperately exhausted when we climbed the one hundred and eighty-nine steps leading to the camp, trying to carry his load when they weren't looking, and I attempted to pass myself off as him whenever possible. It was hell, Salva was at the limit, I couldn't keep going like that and the time was coming when I'd have to abandon him to his fate and then, then, that ashen sky understood me, heard my pleas and, from then on, nobody noticed Salva, to such an extent that I stopped fearing for him. I got used to the fact that the guards didn't realize that he wasn't carrying the stone up the steps. He only went down and up once a day, at the beginning and end, and, meanwhile, pretended to be busy. Sometimes he even sat down for a while.

Exhausted as he was, he didn't realize what was happening, but I couldn't believe my eyes: looks went right through him as if he was a ghost. They probably saw him but he never interested them because there was always someone or something that was more eye-catching. The baptism of fire came on the day (and I'm not sure whether it was morning or afternoon) when a guard was staring at him. I saw that skeleton through the eyes of the guard who, when he impulsively went straight towards Salva, looked as if he was going to push him, shove him over the edge of the quarry. I was so terrified that I wasn't even thinking about what I was seeing, because the end was happening, we'd come to the finale, the moment in which you realize that, whatever you do, you're a puppet. And right then, the guard walked straight past Salva, who was comfortably leaning against a rock waiting for them to come and kill him, towards a poor fellow whom he finished off with a bullet, on the spot. That was my moment of greatest amazement about Salva's new nature, and after that I stopped worrying. Whatever was going on, neither Kapos nor dogs got a whiff of Salva. He was going to be saved, and I, who was inside his magic sphere, was going to be saved as well. And, in particular, I liked being in his magic sphere, which required no walls or doors. It was others who'd lost the power to see him. And I'm the one who's saying this, I who do not believe in such things.

Neither did I believe in the shadow of evil, yet I could feel it more than my own arms and legs. There was no shadow when something good or, at least, nothing especially bad was about to happen and, right then, I felt the warmth of summer inside me, bringing me to life again, giving me strength. Salva looked at me ironically and told me to grab hold of anything I could, that this idea of heat to combat cold was a good one. Naturally, I didn't tell him what his situation really was, didn't tell him that he was living in a magic circle, because I feared it might break. Nonetheless, that day of total absence of shadow, the day in which I confessed to him that I felt so good I thought I was going mad, something happened that made me think that strange things do happen sometimes.

I don't know whether I went so far as to hum under my breath. It was the day Raquel arrived in the camp. As soon as I laid eyes on her, I knew she was the reason. She came in a consignment of Jews and marched past among them, in a brown coat and with her black curly hair rather tangled. She looked around astonished and horrified. We, Salva and I, our skeletons draped in striped rags, were part

139

of the horror. She couldn't know that she'd bewitched us and filled us with sun. Neither could she know that, in no time at all, she was going to be like us.

Please don't have any gold in your mouth, please be healthy so you can work, but please don't let them notice you, please let them see you as a useful number and not assign you to prostitution. Please survive long enough to enter Salva's magic circle.

That day, Salva, seeing her coming in, looking around her with her huge black eyes, said, that girl's beautiful. And I said, didn't I tell you that something good was going to happen today?

Good for us and terrible for Raquel. We knew that because of what was going to happen. We thought that if she got through the first few days alive we'd take her under our protection. Salva fell in love. He said that never, but never, in all his life had he felt anything like this. He said it might be a means to feel he was human but, whatever it was, it was an emotion he'd never experienced before. I asked him why he was so sure he'd fallen in love.

"Because she makes me fly, because she lifts my feet off the ground, because she makes me so nervous when she's nearby that my hands shake, and because I'm desperate to kiss her," he said shamefaced.

Lamentably, Raquel fell in love with me, and I with her, though I've always doubted whether my love was as great as Salva's. I don't know if I've flown high enough, and now we shall never know.

Later on, after we were liberated, I didn't know much about Salva's private life. He threw himself into taking revenge for all of us. He hunted down all the Nazis that he got in his sights. Me too, but I was also as happy as I knew how to be. Would Salva have been happy with Raquel? Would he have carried out his mission with the same single-minded tenacity if he'd been happy? Life has no answer to that. And now neither Raquel nor Salva were here any more, but out of that came a daughter whom I love, and loving someone frees you from a great deal of despair. Out of that, I'd met Sandra, whom Salva had probably enclosed in a magic circle while I was pushing her towards the brink of disaster.

Although I could park in a place where I could stay in the car and comfortably observe the *Estrella* with my binoculars, I wanted to have a breath of fresh air, so I strolled down to where she was moored. The sun was shining most agreeably. I sat down on a stone bench three moorings before Heim's, as I thought it was a good idea to stay as close as possible to the car in case I had to make a quick getaway. Heim was sunbathing or just finishing his tanning session in the hammock, because he suddenly got up, went down the cabin steps, stooping half a metre to do so, and came back with a notebook that looked ridiculously small in his huge fist. I was irked that I'd left the binoculars in the car. What would he be writing down? Probably what he'd eaten. He liked to leave an account of what he was doing, of how he'd influenced the world. Thanks to his meticulousness, we knew, in his very own handwriting, the bestial things he'd done in the surgery, and that catalogue of his was proof that he was a war criminal. He wrote slowly and at one point he looked up at the sky, either to help him think better, or to describe the clouds perchance.

A minute later the writer Aribert Heim dropped into the background when I saw a familiar-looking four-by-four pulling up between me and the *Estrella*. A few years ago I hadn't needed to memorize things, hadn't needed to dredge my mind to come up with a damn four-by-four. It would have identified itself, would have shot out like a ray of lightning from among all the four-by-fours I'd ever seen in my life. Now, by contrast, I had to wait a few minutes for light to be shed, and in extreme situations a few minutes can be too long.

A four-by-four and a German shepherd with its head stuck out the window. Elfe's car and dog. A woman with a blonde plait got out. She was certainly one of them. Seeing her, Heim got out of the hammock. In fact he'd had her in his sights long enough to have reacted earlier, but what was happening to me was also happening to him.

With a jump she was on the deck. They didn't greet one another or exchange any kind of friendly gesture. They talked but I couldn't keep watching, because the dog picked up my scent, recognized me and went crazy. It was barking in my direction and looked as if it was about to shoot out through the half-open window. It was the dog that had saved Elfe's life; it wanted to greet me, it already had half its body out and the blonde woman turned round to look at it, so I decided to retreat. She and Heim were talking about something more momentous than the dog's excitement and would be thinking that anything could have set it off.

The dog kept barking in my direction until I got into my car. I could still hear it in the distance as I drove off. This didn't look good. I already knew, had already noticed that something bad was happening. The shadow of evil disappeared from my life many years ago but its memory had remained. I checked the fuel gauge and headed for Elfe's house. It was total rashness, because the tracks around there were very narrow. It would be a real rat trap if they discovered me, but I needed to confirm my suspicions.

The problem with this zone was that it was very easy to take the wrong track. The same vegetation was everywhere and getting to the faux-rural houses would involve some desperately tricky manoeuvres. I got lost twice and, with my third try, recognized Elfe's house, where the carport was now empty. The silence was absolute and I didn't dare to hang around for long, but then again I was there and I knew there was a trapdoor through which I could get into the cellar. I scratched the back of my neck almost to the point of abrasion. Obviously I couldn't leave the car where it was and suicidally call attention to myself, so I took the plunge and drove into a nearby vegetable garden, squashing lettuces and tomatoes as I went. I walked back to the house, removed the weighty flowerpot and opened the trapdoor, closing it behind me as I went down the steps. The most important thing was not to get agitated. I didn't want to die in that cheerless house with its stench of alcohol and stale vomit. I turned on the cellar light and something on the floor caught my eye. On the clay tiles they'd painted a black sun, which meant that they'd performed ceremonies in this cellar. I went up to the house fearing that the door that separated it from the cellar might be locked, but it opened, so they weren't expecting any intruder to get in.

The kitchen and living room were in a terrible mess, much worse than last time. They'd opened drawers and cupboard doors without taking the trouble to close them. God knows what they'd been looking for. The album I took? Probably more things. I ventured upstairs not wanting to think that if they caught me they'd kill me. I stepped carefully, though I was certain there was no one there. They'd eliminated Elfe. She was living a life she didn't deserve to live, in the view of her friends. I looked into her bedroom, which had been ransacked. I didn't bother to do a search, because I wouldn't have known where to begin. Whatever they were looking for, they would have found it and, if not, I wouldn't be capable of spotting it. I had a quick glance in the wardrobe. Some coat hangers were bare and the drawers half empty. I opened the doors of the other rooms, but didn't detect anything special except marks on the walls where paintings had hung. They could have been Rembrandts or Picassos.

It was time I was on the road. I made the return trip more quickly. I hurried down the main stairway and opened the door, fearing I'd run headlong into someone coming in. I replaced the big flowerpot over the trapdoor, and went into the vegetable plot where I'd left the car. Luckily it was still there. Before going back into town, I went by the house that was supposedly Frida's (perhaps the blonde who was with Heim right now), and saw Elfe's other car parked there.

They'd got rid of Elfe and they could get rid of anybody else. They were still active and I hadn't found a safe place to keep the album or my notebooks. They could ransack the car any moment and keeping them in my room was unthinkable.


## Sandra

Sometimes solutions appeared in my dreams, because now I knew what I had to do and I wanted to do it. I downed a milk coffee as fast as I could. I had no desire to drag things out for ever with slow sips of tea. I told them I wanted to check out some prenatal classes, that I'd been awake all night thinking about it and I was leaving now. They didn't raise any objections or even remind me that Karin had to go to the gym that afternoon. They were still mulling over the situation. Fine. I had the newspaper page in my anorak pocket. I could have sought Julián's advice, but thought it was childish to consult him about every step I took, and anyway it would only prolong things.

Two hours later I was back. Fred was making more tea, which was as good as a meal for them, and, despite the coolness of the day, Karin was sitting outside. For a Norwegian the concept of coolness is not what it is for us. Neither Fred nor Karin were in long sleeves yet, or closed shoes, and they didn't need any kind of heating.

I waited until we were sitting at the table, and then I got up and took a gift-wrapped object from my backpack. I held it out to Karin, saying that I'd never given them a gift and I hoped they'd like it. Karin unwrapped it and was rendered speechless when she saw before her the newspaper piece with their photo, now behind glass and in a lovely gilt frame that would go very well in their bedroom.

"Ever since I came across this photo I've been keeping it so I could get it framed. I wanted it to be a surprise, but I suppose you've already seen it. You're famous! It's incredible. You're famous."

They didn't know what to say or what to think. I looked at them, beaming my best smile.

"Thank you," Fred said. "It's a very nice thought, but you shouldn't have taken the trouble."

Karin was very tough. She didn't blush or apologize for poking around in my things.

"We'll put it here," she said, placing the photo on the mantelpiece. "It's quite an old newspaper," she added.

"I saw it by chance in the gym while I was waiting for you and took it. Someone must have left it there."

Finally I was lying to them. In all likelihood they'd find me out. They were experts at interrogation and, when they were speaking with desperate people capable of anything in order to save themselves, you'd expect that they wouldn't believe such lies, but neither could they be completely sure that I wasn't telling the truth.

"It was a fluke," I concluded, raising a bread roll to my mouth. "I couldn't have imagined that they'd be publishing newspapers in Norwegian here. By the way, what does it say?"

"I was thinking about the design that could go on the baby's pullover," Karin said with an expression that put an end to the matter. She'd decided to believe me.

## Julián

I didn't know whether or not to tell Sandra what I'd found out about the Eel (that's if I'd got the right man).

I'd discovered that he was avoiding her. On Thursday afternoon, when I was going to have a quick look at Otto's and Alice's house to see if Sebastian Bernhardt was there or if they were going out so I could follow them, two young men in a car I'd seen before pulled up in the small square of El Tosalet. When I turned into the first street on the right and was parking by a pinkish-coloured stone wall, I realized that it was one of Elfe's cars, the newer one. I could watch what was happening in my rear-view mirror. I saw Martín getting out of the car with a small package in his hand. The other one, who must have been the Eel, stayed in the car. Judging by the route taken by Martín, he would have been going to the Norwegians' house, and yet the Eel preferred staying in the car to going to see Sandra. In all likelihood Sandra would be there now, in this strange prison that she had imposed on herself with my help. She'd be waiting for the Eel to give some signs of life. When she heard the doorbell and footsteps that weren't Fredrik's or Otto's coming inside, her heart would be filling with hope. The Eel must be thinking along these lines too, yet he stayed here, far enough away for her not to see him. It hurt me to think that Sandra was suffering because of this moron.

Ten minutes or so later, the moron got out to smoke a cigarette leaning against the car. He was nothing to write home about, very ordinary, if it wasn't for something in his movements and features that made him sinuous and frightening. He had a long pale face with a receding hairline that would soon be leaving him without his fine light-brown locks. I thought him more than capable of leading on a girl like Sandra. He wasn't the first I'd known who could turn from a toad into a prince, and still more so if he was kissing Sandra's marvellous mouth.

If I was Sandra's father and if I was young, I'd take him by the ear and make him go and see her, although in fact it's impossible to disabuse anybody of self-deception. If you shed one illusion, another follows, as if there was a quota reserved for every human being. If the Eel didn't betray Sandra, somebody else would, just as she had betrayed Santi and, if she hadn't, another woman would have. It was better that such a contemptible creature wasn't just a little contemptible, or only half contemptible, but that he should be totally contemptible, like the Eel.

When he'd finished his cigarette, he crushed the butt with his foot and ran his hands over his head, pushing the hair off his face. He breathed in deeply and gazed into the distance for a few minutes. This wasn't the way of looking of someone who wasn't thinking about anything. He was thinking with great concentration about something, barely moving a muscle. Then he got back into the car and spent a quarter of an hour writing in a notebook that he rested against the steering wheel.

I was patient enough to wait there almost an hour, until Martín returned. But before he entered my field of vision, the Eel put the notebook in his pocket, wrapped his arms around the steering wheel and put his head down as if he were sleeping.

I took a chance on following them. It was almost suicidal because they were young and agile. If they spotted me I was lost. They'd realize that I was tailing them. I'd only be safe if I caught them with their guard down, when they weren't interested in being alert to anything. I followed at a good distance but having the same car constantly behind you can look fishy, so when I saw that they took the turn-off leading to Elfe's and Frida's houses, I stopped at the corner, parking between some other cars among the weeds of a vacant lot. It was too hazardous to enter such a narrow track. It would be a trap. If the car didn't appear again within half an hour I'd leave. In the opposite case I'd follow them again.

The car was back within ten minutes, driven by the Eel, now alone. I'd surmised that at this hour of the afternoon they weren't going to stay indoors until the next day and I was right. There was still plenty of daytime ahead for everyone. The Eel was driving like a madman. I only hoped that my contact lenses wouldn't start giving me trouble in this sprint.

He parked next to the Bellamar restaurant, which was under lock and key until next summer, and went to sit on the sand quite close to the water's edge, but not close enough to get wet. Then he lay back with his arms outstretched in an expression of freedom. I watched him from the car. After a few minutes a girl approached him, he got up and they hugged. They sat together contemplating the sea, her head on his shoulder. They had their backs to me and I couldn't see if they were talking. I imagined they were.

They spent half an hour like that, after which they strolled along the water's edge. I felt enormously sad for Sandra and wondered if she should know this. Maybe it would help her get him out of her head. Maybe she should know that she was just another girl for him, that she'd been the port girl and this one was the beach girl, and there were probably more. The Eel took off his shoes and socks and rolled up his trousers. A couple of times he put his hands on her shoulders and she put hers on his waist. Shortly afterwards they said their goodbyes. The Eel walked back along the water's edge until he was level with the car and then turned towards it. I pretended I was asleep, with my head on the wheel so he wouldn't see me. When I raised my head again, he was sitting in his car with the door open and his feet dangling outside as he brushed the sand off them and put on his shoes and socks again. He then adjusted the rear-view mirror and I had the impression that he glanced towards me, but it was probably just my own apprehensive imagination.

Would that girl on the beach be one of them too? I wasn't sure that I'd recognize her again if I ran into her. I stopped tailing him. Dusk was falling and night would soon hurtle down on us and I didn't want to be driving in the dark around places I didn't know. I'd have to call it a day and return to the solitude of my room, though I still needed to find a discreet place to park where my car wouldn't be noticed, and that took time. All my valuables were in the car and I didn't have the money to pay for a car park. Then again, my enemies would find me more easily there. As I parked, images of the lovebirds on the beach came into my head. There was something that didn't make sense, something disconcerting in that farewell. Why didn't they go off together? Who was preventing that?

## Sandra

Julián signalled to me from his car when I was bringing Karin down to the gym in the four-by-four. He was saying that when I dropped her off he'd be waiting for me double-parked and that I should follow him because he knew where I could leave the car. Now he knew the town like the palm of his hand, including the most tucked-away streets. Thanks to the fact that there was never a free parking space near the gym, I was free for an hour and a half, more or less. Sometimes when I came back, Karin was already waiting for me at the entrance with her sports bag in her hand and hair still damp from the shower. On those occasions I explained that I couldn't risk coming too early because then I'd have to drive round and round.

As soon as Karin disappeared through the gym door, I rushed off to follow Julián. I left the four-by-four in a small vacant lot and got into Julián's car, which he parked somewhere else. He offered me water from the arsenal of bottles he had in the car. Besides water, he had notebooks, binoculars, a blanket, his hat, a cushion plus a beach towel and another towel from the hotel. He also had apples and the car smelt slightly sweet. I put the cushion behind me at kidney level and asked what he wanted. I was hoping he wouldn't ask me about Alberto, hoping he wasn't going to get up my nose about that matter, which was exclusively my own business. But no, he said nothing about him. What he said was that they'd killed Elfe. He didn't want to scare me, but he didn't have the right to hide something like that from me either. Julián had met her by chance. She was the wife of Anton Wolf, who'd died of a heart attack while playing golf, a woman who was given to boozing big time and who talked a blue streak about things she should have kept quiet about, so they did away with her. She was a hopeless case, a nuisance, a danger. If they'd killed so many people who bothered them, why not Elfe too? Did I understand what he meant? Yes, I understood, although I thought they respected their own people.

"Elfe wasn't like them any more. She was human dregs. They couldn't stand her."

Now Elfe's lovely house was vacant and the cars and the dog had been taken to Frida's house, although it seemed that at Frida's everything was for everyone, because Martín and the Eel were using Elfe's cars as well. I felt something bittersweet in my stomach. If Alberto wanted, I could be happy, but since he didn't want it I was feeling a bit sorry for myself.

"Have you seen Alberto?" I asked.

"In passing. He was heading for the beach in one of Elfe's cars."

"To the beach?" Elfe didn't matter any more. Their killing each other had stopped mattering, and even if they killed other people it stopped mattering. I was only wondering why Alberto hadn't come to see me, or left me any sign, or sent me any note with Martín. Why?

I could see that Julián knew more than he was letting on, that he wanted to tell me but knew he shouldn't tell me.

"I followed him to the beach."

"Ah, did you?" I asked nervously, knowing that what was coming wasn't good.

"As far as that locked-up restaurant, the Bellamar."

"So he didn't go inside the restaurant."

"No, he stayed on the sand. He lay down fully dressed, without taking off his jacket, and opened out his arms, as if he wanted to purify himself."

How I wished I'd been there and that he was embracing me with his body, purified or not. I knew it was an illusion and that I couldn't really be in love with someone I'd seen so little of, without even knowing what he was like, or if he was a killer, or some poor sod. He'd only kissed me with a kiss I was afraid to forget. This story couldn't end well. I couldn't keep going with only the memory of a mouth. Everyone has lips and a tongue, and that was the terrible thing, because there was no other tongue like his and I'd probably never find another one the same. And, especially when I was lying on my bed or watching television with Fred and Karin, images kept coming to me of scenes that had never existed in which Alberto was naked and me too, and he took my head in my hands, gazed at me and then closed his eyes, because it was time to make real, deep love. Sometimes I imagined it in so much detail I couldn't bear it and I had to get up and go out into the garden. And it was even worse in the garden, because at least when I was sitting with Fred and Karin I had to swallow my disappointment and struggle against it.

"And what happened on the sand?" I asked, not trusting Julián a hundred per cent for the simple reason that he had a different way of seeing things and clearer objectives than mine. My objective now was Alberto.

"When he was on the sand, a girl came along and they went for a walk."

My heart flip-flopped.

"Just a walk?"

"I don't know how to put it. You young people are different nowadays. Friends kiss like sweethearts. I wouldn't know how to tell you what kind of relationship they have. They were together less than an hour."

How ridiculous I was. A thousand times ridiculous. I meant nothing to him and that's why he hadn't appeared again; he didn't want any commitment with me, and he might even be regretting what happened.

I couldn't help feeling sad, and sadness put things in their place. The world suddenly stopped having this layer of meringue that had covered it since the port and the kiss. It was real and serious again. And in the real world terrible things happen, like them killing Elfe. You could almost say that Elfe's death came to my aid, was balm for my spirit.

I got out of Julián's car and into the four-by-four. All these precautions for what? I was fed up. I didn't check the time. When I got to the gym, Karin was waiting for me looking really pissed off, but the one who was more pissed off was me. I didn't open the door for her or help her to get in, but let her sort it out herself as I watched the birds flying by and the people walking past and my life escaping from me. My son kicked. At least I had him and all the compassion in the world for myself. I felt Karin's twisted, difficult gaze on my profile. She couldn't harm me now. Any harm she was capable of inflicting was nothing compared with what Alberto had done.

# 6
## Eternal Youth

### Sandra

Karin took some alarming turns for the worse. She'd have four good days then five bad ones, until Martín turned up with a packet about the size of his hand, which she bore off to her room. At first I didn't make the connection between the packet and Karin's health, but one thing gradually led to another. My eyes saw that the packet arrived and that Karin improved, and then my mind got to work and I couldn't help but suspect something fishy. What was in that damn packet? They never left it within my reach. If Karin was in bed when Martín arrived, he himself or Fred took it up to her, or she came down. If they were out, he opened the library-den with a key that he took from his pocket, left the packet inside, locked up and tucked the key away again. What at first had looked like simple habits started to turn into real mysteries: the uniform, the packet, the Gold Cross, the locked door. Maybe I'd been so busy looking for the Gold Cross that I hadn't twigged to something so straightforward. This is what Julián must have meant when he told me over and over again to keep my eyes open, saying that you believe you're not seeing anything when, actually, you're seeing lots of things. No doubt there were a lot more interesting signs like the packets, which is why they were always on guard because of what I might have discovered. When they took me into their house, into the lion's den, it wouldn't have as much as entered their heads that someone as young as I was, so removed from their world, someone so lost she didn't know what to do with her life, who vomited on the beach, all alone in the world when they found her, someone who hadn't even gone to university – no, they couldn't possibly have imagined that this somebody was going to bump into somebody else like Julián, that this Julián was going to pull back the veil, and that behind the veil lay the truth.

At the beginning of November, Karin had spent several rock-bottom days, extremely fatigued and with her arthritis giving her hell. She couldn't even get up the stairs. Fred said they'd have to think about installing a chairlift, something that Karin had always refused to do because those chairs gave out a message of decrepitude. She spent the day in bed. I didn't feel well either. I was coughing and sneezing and sometimes I thought I had a touch of fever.

Fred was very worried about his wife. His face, serious enough in itself, was now even more serious, as if every feature, every wrinkle and every small muscle weighed like tons of cement. He spent the whole day observing Karin's decline and going up and down the stairs, twitchy all the time. Every ten minutes he asked if someone had brought a packet and sometimes he thought he heard the doorbell. I assumed that Martín hadn't come with the packet as arranged and it was vital for Karin's recovery. The cat was being let out of the bag and, depending on the changes of atmosphere from one moment to the next, I'd find out everything. On the one hand, I really wanted to know, to satisfy my curiosity, while on the other hand I was afraid they'd find out that I knew. I put on my anorak and told Fred I was going out.

"You can't go out now," he said, sounding annoyed.

"I've got a few things to do. I need to go to the chemist's to get something for my cold."

"Forget about your cold. It's not important."

I didn't like Fred's tone or his contained rage, which might explode any moment.

"I really need to. I'm sorry," I said. "I'll be back as soon as I can."

"No!" Fred exclaimed. Then he added something in Norwegian or German, which gave me the creeps.

I thought that if it came to a struggle I'd be more agile, but he was bigger and, despite being so old, was strong. He could open jars that I couldn't, and if he'd been a top-ranking SS officer he'd know plenty of ways to immobilize me. I could give him a kick in the balls with my mountain boots, but wasn't sure I'd hit the target and, once I'd tried that, the situation would turn terrible. I stayed where I was, with my anorak on, looking at him and coughing. It was more a nervous cough than one related to my cold.

"I need you today. Until today you've needed us."

"What?" I said, intuiting that he meant something more than the fact they'd given me a job.

"Yes, little one, you would be at the bottom of the sea now if Karin and I hadn't protected you."

I dropped onto the couch trying to think fast. How could I get out of this? They already knew what I knew. Did they think it was more or less than what I knew? Was it worth continuing to play the idiot?

"I don't get it," I said, testing the waters.

"I've got no time for fooling around. The time for fooling around and happy ingenuous girls with body piercings and tattoos has come to an end. We're all in the same boat now."

"I want to know why I'm in danger and who wants to kill me."

"There's no time for that, but you can be sure that if I abandon you to your fate you'll be getting on your motorbike just a couple more times at most. I'm not messing around and you shouldn't either, take it from me. You're going to do what I tell you," he said, without my having pronounced a single word because I couldn't think of anything to say. "Karin and I don't want anything bad to happen to you and that won't happen if you heed my words."

While Fred was talking, I was wondering if they'd discovered Julián. I'd come to Dianium out of fear of losing my freedom, only to feel I was someone's prisoner, and now not only my freedom but my life was in the hands of a whole bunch of people I didn't really know.

I felt cornered by Fred. He'd never spoken to me like that. I had no alternative but to do what he asked. I had to go to Alice's house and find a way to steal one of those boxes containing the ampoules that had revived Karin.

The motorbike was a better idea than the four-by-four, which was too associated with Fred and Karin, so I took it out to go to Alice's house. I was tempted to go and tell Julián everything, or to run away and forget the whole story, but now I was in the thick of it and it wouldn't be too easy to walk out of it. They'd be after me. And anyway, I then immediately thought that if life had presented me with this challenge there must be some reason for it. I parked and rang the bell at the gate of number 50, crossing myself as one does in life's tragic moments. I did it with my back to the surveillance cameras

153

and breathing in deeply. It wasn't good for me to be putting my son in danger, but I'd also be doing the right thing if I could get rid of scum in the world where he was going to live. Nobody answered on the video entry system, which was almost a relief. I rang again and was just on the point of leaving when the gate opened. It was cold but I started to sweat, at which point I recognized I was a coward. I would never have recognized I was a coward. That's why I was doing this, so I could pretend I wasn't. Only cowards are capable of doing such things.

It was Frida who appeared between the garden and the street.

She gave me the coarse stare of someone who does what she's ordered to do. I stared back and informed her I'd come to see Alice.

"She's at yoga," Frida said, "but you can wait for her."

"Does Alice know I'm here?" I asked, imagining they would have phoned her.

"Yes. She'll be here in twenty minutes. I can make you a cup of tea."

"That's fine," I said as we walked towards the columns. "And Otto?"

"He's in his office. He's not to be disturbed."

"No need," I said.

No sooner was the front door open than Alice's rowdy little dogs dashed out to greet us. Since she wasn't there, I didn't mind petting them. They were cute but I didn't feel anything for them. I sat down in the living room while they nipped at my boots. Despite the heat, I didn't take off my anorak. When Frida was serving the tea, I passed my hand over my belly and asked if I could use the bathroom. She pointed at the guests' bathroom next to the stairs. I went into this loo, which was small with a very pretty handbasin made in the local rustic porcelain. I didn't know what to do or where to start looking and, anyway, they'd catch me red-handed. It was too risky with Frida and Otto in the house.

Fred had told me, or ordered me more like it, to look for boxes containing injections, a colourless liquid with no name appearing either on the ampoules or the box. I might find them in the bedroom, which was on the first floor. As soon as I entered the bedroom, I'd see a chest of drawers on my right. It was possible that some boxes were kept there because Alice was constantly injecting herself. They could also be in one of the cupboards of the main bathroom and certainly in the safe, but there was no way I'd be able to open that. I was at a loss to find any excuse that would get me up to the first floor.

I looked at myself in the mirror. You're not cut out for this. Let Fred do it if that's what he wants. I left the bathroom and walked towards the front door. I had everything with me and didn't need to go back to the living room, but, when I had my hand on the doorknob, Frida stopped me, blonde Frida, who I could easily imagine gassing people without batting an eyelid.

"I can't wait. I don't feel well," I said.

Then Otto emerged, taking off his reading glasses and replacing them with distance glasses. He held out a small packet, half the size of the ones that Martín tended to bring, but a packet after all.

"Here, take this to Karin. She needs it. I'll call in ten minutes to be sure you've arrived."

"Okay," I said. "My regards to Alice."

I got on the motorbike thoroughly disconcerted. I hadn't needed to go snooping or to steal anything in Alice's house. They'd given me the packet voluntarily. They considered me one of them and I'd been about to put my foot in it because of Fred. He'd told me that the friendship with Otto and Alice was strained and it was my fault. The Brotherhood didn't approve of them having me living in their house. I didn't ask anything, didn't ask what I already knew and I'd been about to beg him not to tell me any more.

Though Otto had said he'd call in ten minutes, I was tempted to stop for a moment and open the box. After all, I'd had a bad time trying to be a thief. I thought I deserved to see the famous ampoules, that I should get a good look at them.

I knew there was no way the packet would be exactly the same as before and they'd notice it had been opened, but curiosity got the better of me, so I detoured down a side street. I stopped the motorbike, got off, put the packet on the seat and then began the operation of untying the string, unwrapping the paper and opening the box, praying all the while that it wouldn't fall and smash the ampoules to smithereens. I also prayed that none of the cars cruising slowly by were those of the Brotherhood. It was hard to untie the knot in the fine string that tied up the box. I had to sharpen my nails, so to speak, and, having dealt with that, I still had to open the wrapping paper, very carefully peel away the sticky tape that sealed the edges, and then I'd have to try to wrap it up again, making sure that the creases in the paper were in the right place and the sticky tape was back exactly where it had been.

There were only four ampoules inside, quite large ones. The fluid was colourless and there was no name, as Fred had said. What if I took one and kept it to give to Julián so it could be analysed in a laboratory? The idea almost drove me crazy. What was I doing? Should I take a slightly bigger risk? But the dose might be all four ampoules and then Fred would immediately see I'd taken one. What was certain was that he'd tell Alice and Otto and then they'd know at once that I'd swiped it. But if I didn't keep this sample, what was the point of everything I was doing? What was the point of putting my neck on the line? But what if this was a test? It was very strange that they should have trusted me with the box. Otto could have brought it, or Frida herself. Something didn't make sense, so I wrapped it up again as best I could. If you looked hard you'd see that the string had been untied and tied twice, but at least the four ampoules were there.

When I arrived, Fred came half-running to open the gate himself. Then he ran back again behind the motorbike. I gave him the packet in the garage.

"Otto called ten minutes ago. He told me you should have been here by then."

"I had to stop to pee. I couldn't hang on."

My explanation satisfied Fred. We went into the house. Karin was lying on the sofa in the horrible baggy jeans she wore when she wanted to be comfortable. She'd probably got herself ready in case she had to go to the hospital. Fred opened the box in my presence, took out a syringe from one of those bags people use for keeping cosmetics in, broke an ampoule, sucked the liquid into the syringe and stuck the needle into her now bared thigh. Karin then lay back and closed her eyes with a sigh. Fred threw the syringe and the broken ampoule into the rubbish bin and then looked enquiringly into the box.

"That's all he gave you?"

I shrugged.

"She wants it all for herself," he said, and as soon as the words were out he regretted them. If he wanted to let off steam he could have said it in Norwegian, but he needed to share his displeasure with someone.

"Forget everything I said to you about this affair," Fred said. "I went too far. This medicine is still being tested. It's not patented here, we get it through a friend of Otto's and I was suddenly afraid that they weren't going to supply it any more. I got too worked up. I'm sorry."

"That's okay. It's all right," I said, making light of it. "The main thing is that Karin gets better."

"I don't think I need to tell you that this is something you mustn't talk about."

I made a gesture saying he didn't have to worry about that.

"You're very strange. I'm really surprised that you agreed to go to Alice's house under instructions to steal."

"Yes, I don't know why I did it either. Maybe it was because I didn't want to see Karin suffering."

Fred observed me with his eagle eyes. It was possible that he didn't know exactly what he saw in me either. And I was wondering where these injections came from and what they consisted of.

At last I managed to get the couple off my back and go to meet Julián at the lighthouse, among the wild palms. I said I had to go to the chemist to get something for my cold, because, even though they hadn't asked what I was doing, it was better to be one step ahead of them and not give rise to suspicions. It was getting dark earlier and earlier every day, and it was cold. Soon we'd have to meet somewhere with a roof over our heads. I went as fast as I could through the bends, hoping with all my strength that Julián had waited for me, if not sitting on the bench or inside the ice-cream parlour, then sheltering in his car. If only he had the patience to wait the forty-five minutes, more or less, of my delay. I had so much to tell him. My information was so juicy that it was boiling inside my head. Deep in my heart I thanked God for my being caught up in this adventure. I knew things that none of the inhabitants of this town could imagine, yet did I really know or did I just imagine I knew, with Julián's help?

As always and out of precaution, I rode past the lighthouse then parked next to the ice-cream parlour, which at this time of year was serving everything except ice cream, and walked towards the stony area. I couldn't see the sea but only hear it and smell it. It was like being blind. I'd barely begun my walk when a horn tooted. I went in that direction and found Julián's car. What a relief! What an incredible relief! I'd become the plaything of high-speed emotions.

"I was worried," he said when I opened the door, and I believed him, because for both him and me these appointments were sacred. This was the time in which the most absurd details and the behaviour

of Karin, Fred, Otto, Alice and Martín (but not Alberto) finally got
to make sense.

"I can't stay very long. Before I go back I have to drop by the chemist's to pick up something for my cold."

"I've been thinking," Julián said, "and I believe I'm a fool. I've got
you mixed up in a right old mess and I'm putting you in danger. In
short, what's the point? However much we get to know, it won't be of
any use to us. We're alone and there's a lot more of them and they're
organized. Nothing we find out will send them to prison. They're very
old, leftovers of something that happened in a nightmare."

"And what about the young ones? Martín, the Eel" (when I said Eel,
part of my tongue held back) "and the rest of them?"

"There are a lot of people belonging to some or other secret organization but, as long as they don't do away with people… like…
well… Elfe… Listen, I'm serious, I don't want you to go back there.
We don't know what they're capable of doing."

"The time hasn't come yet. I can feel it. My life's always been chaos,
I've done things without rhyme or reason, without thinking, and now,
all of a sudden, things are falling into place and any move I make
helps to create another link in the chain. Today, for example – and I've
been dying to tell you about this – something happened and it seems
important, but I'm not sure how important."

And yes, it was important, because, as I was telling him about the
injections, the astonishing improvement shown by Karin, the vitality
of all of them in general and, in particular, of Alice, Julián was moving
his head, not much but enough, an unconscious sign that what he was
hearing fitted with something he had on his mind. He stopped moving and remained stock-still when I commented that this liquid most
probably had something to do with Alice's spectacular youthfulness.
And now, right now, it was dawning on me that, in all probability,
Otto and Alice were taking their time in dispensing the medication,
not because of any fault of mine, not because the Christensens had
taken me into their home, but because the product was in scarce supply and they didn't want to share it.

When I told Julián what I suspected, saying that Fred was a manipulator, that he'd tried to get me to steal something, which would
be much worse than stealing cocaine or heroin, he only said maybe
yes or maybe no.

"What do you mean, maybe no?"

"Until we know what it's made of, we can't be sure that they're fighting over this liquid. It might have a placebo effect. People will take any concoction doing the rounds outside the normal channels."

"But if they believe it works for them, it's the same thing. They might be fighting over something worthless thinking that it's really effective, especially if it gives results. And I can assure you it works with Karin. She can have a massive attack of arthritis and when they inject this liquid all her problems melt away."

"If it was really such an incredible formula, it would cure her for ever."

That said, he went quiet. I went quiet too. We left the matter there. It was clear that the next step would be to get hold of one of those ampoules. Julián wasn't going to ask me after having pleaded with me to leave that house, and I wasn't going to offer to do it voluntarily. I didn't even tell him I'd been on the point of nicking one of the injections from the packet.

"Have you phoned your family?" he asked, still mulling over the new information I'd given him.

I shook my head. What was I going to tell my family? And anyway, with each week that went by I had less to tell them. They were there and I was here, in two completely different worlds.

"You should speak with them and hear their voices so you can remember the person you were."

And I was left still wanting to talk to Julián about what mattered most of all: Alberto and flying.


## Julián

After our meeting at the lighthouse, we went back into town, me first in the car and Sandra following on her motorbike. Sometimes she disappeared in the rear-view mirror and then reappeared. She had to go back to Villa Sol with something from the chemist's in her hand to justify this afternoon's outing. Unfortunately for Sandra, the door of pretence, of deceit, of attention to some details so as to cover up others, had been opened. The chemist's bag would hide our meeting in the same way that Fred's and Karin's age hid their evil.

I suggested that I should ride the motorbike down, but Sandra flatly refused, saying that she was more used to that heap of scrap metal, that I might get a speck of something in my eye and she didn't want anything to happen to me. Nonetheless, I wasn't worried about her and took it for granted that if she'd survived thus far, she'd keep surviving. Basically, I didn't want to be worried unnecessarily and lose sight of the objective that had brought me here, especially now that I'd discovered something essential or, truth to tell, Sandra had discovered it. I'd just understood that the line in the letter my friend Salva sent to me in Buenos Aires, in which he told me I might find eternal youth here, wasn't empty words. It was a clue that would have remained a dead end if I hadn't run into Sandra. It was possible that Salva himself only had a hint of this compound they were bringing from some part of the world, and he didn't want me to get obsessive about it. He could very easily have told me in his letter everything he knew to spare me from starting from scratch.

I stopped when Sandra parked her motorbike opposite the green cross of the chemist's. I was a few metres in front of her, watching through the rear-view mirror as she entered and left the shop, after which she got on the motorbike, glanced in my direction and rode off. She was returning to Villa Sol and would have to keep seeing the faces of those two doddering monsters who knew a thousand ways of getting rid of people and for whom a life wasn't sacred but something to be used as a weapon.

Salva and I saw a lot of things in Mauthausen. We saw walking skeletons and masses of naked bodies walking on the snow in the courtyard, a strange, ashen, pinkish-toned kind of livestock. Our bodies became our shame. Pains in the stomach because of hunger, illnesses, lack of intimacy. It was all about the body. It wasn't easy to rise above one's own mortal frame, so one thought of suicide every other day. It was a form of liberation for me to think that all this could have an end and that, if I wanted, it could be all over for me. Death was my salvation. Hitler was sick and had destroyed all of us in his terrible mind. We lived in the vile brain of this man, where the most monstrous atrocities occurred, and there was only one way to get out of his head. Either he died or I died. I couldn't bear to see this marvellous life, with its sun, its trees and its songs, being turned into something so dreadful. But I didn't want his dementedness to kill me. I had wanted to do it of my own free will, looking at the sky if I could. I had sat down next to the hut, taken from my pocket a bit of the stone that we'd broken off in the quarry and cut my veins. Someone who saw me told Salva and Salva saved me. I don't know how he managed it but he saved me, he healed my wounds and said that, whatever happened, although we were up to our necks in shit, although we were humiliated, and although we were the lowest class of slaves, my life was mine. Of course it wasn't a good life, wasn't a decent life or a life worthy of living, but it was mine and no one else could live it for me. And okay, Salva, Hitler died before us, but he left so much evil behind him, so much evil in my heart. I often dream they won the War and wake up sweating.

Salva, you were referring to the ampoules of this stuff these decrepit old Nazis inject themselves with when you mentioned eternal youth, weren't you? Maybe they stumbled upon some anti-ageing formula with their numerous awful experiments, a formula they only apply among themselves. Where could they be making it?

My understanding of Salva's intentions was increasingly clear. He'd left a great project in my hands and I'd have to make it more and more mine with my enquiries and my own motivations. No doubt Salva knew a lot if he'd managed to light on the elixir of eternal youth, but he didn't want to set my course, didn't want to use me for his own revenge. I think he wanted to put this toy in my hands, to give me this gift. It was his wish to give me one last chance.

If there was any firm basis to all this surmising, I now knew how to hurt them. It was a question of cutting off their supplies of the elixir. Karin would contract until she ended up as a twisted heap in a wheelchair. Alice would shrivel like a raisin and the men would lose all their vitality. I wondered if their whippersnappers, if this Martín, for example, knew what he was carrying when he took the packets from one house to another.

The problem was Sandra. Sandra was a matter of conscience. Sandra, if I pressured her, would be capable of bringing me one of the ampoules, whose content we could get analysed. This might then lead us to the laboratories that produced it. But was I going to consent to a girl who had her whole life before her, who'd tried to protect me from having an accident on the motorbike, putting herself in such danger? However, I had to get to the end. I owed it to Salva,

who'd remembered me in his last moments and who'd given me the
opportunity of victory.

## Sandra

They'd stopped hiding the packet with the ampoules. They were
stashed in the chest of drawers with a couple of syringes for when
Karin needed them. If any one of them went missing, they'd know
I'd taken it and that would be no joke. I'd basically been shedding
lots of things, including a lot of fright, but good luck doesn't last
for ever.

When I arrived I put the plastic bag on the kitchen workbench, took
a spoon out of the drawer, opened the bottle of cough medicine and
took a dose in front of them.

"We were worried," Karin said. "You took such a long time."

"I didn't know," I said, slightly jumpy. "I didn't look at the time."

I coughed so they'd stop quizzing me. And one cough led to another,
a real one. I couldn't stop coughing.

"We don't want to meddle in your life, but the thing is, we're worried. At night, that road, all those bends and in your state. You've got
to look after yourself. We only want good things for you."

Karin had recovered. Her expression was alert and scary. She
watched me coughing without doing anything. I had to hang on to
the kitchen sink as I kept coughing. It was Fred who got up and handed
me a glass of water.

"You should get to bed. You're not well," Karin said.

She didn't tell me to sit down with them. But I wanted to spend the
least possible amount of time in their company. They didn't seem
so nice any more. Behind these faces were the ones of their youth,
insolent and unscrupulous. Perhaps age and what she'd learnt along
the way to this point had softened Karin somewhat, and her own
weakness would have made her more human too, or at least would
have obliged her to recognize that she needed the help of others. But
even if she lived a thousand years, I'd never have any idea of what
this woman was thinking and feeling, a woman who with a steady
hand had injected all kinds of shit into prisoners' bodies and helped
to carry out experiments on twins. If all that had seemed normal to

her, if between one atrocity and another she could enjoy reading her love stories, I would never be able to know what she was thinking and what plans she had in mind for me.

I said that if I didn't get better I'd have to go back to my family.

They looked at me, both of them very serious.

In order to escape their eyes, I went to the fridge and poured myself a glass of milk. I put it in the microwave while I was trying to think about what else I could say without blurting out anything that would give me away.

"You have a future here," said Fred. "Your son deserves to have a chance. You'll always have your family. You can't keep hiding under their skirts – is that the expression? – all your life."

"We don't have children or grandchildren," Karin added, "but somebody has to come after us and somebody will have to keep planting this garden and filling the pool with water in the summer. I don't know if you understand what I'm saying."

I took the glass from the microwave and started sipping the milk. They were acknowledging that they would be my longed-for grandparents, the ones that would sort out my life. The problem was that the idea of them being my longed-for grandparents no longer appealed.

"What you did today," Fred said, "was a very brave attempt. Before Otto handed over the packet, you went to the bathroom and checked it out. Frida told us. We'd like to believe that, if it had been possible, you would have stolen to help Karin."

I didn't say anything but just smiled a little as I drank. It wasn't true. I wouldn't have taken the risk for Karin and neither would I have gone so far as to steal. I did what I did because I wanted to know, because the idea of going back to my previous life, leaving things as they were, was unbearable. Not many people have something as important as this in their hands. I didn't know anything about Nazis before meeting Julián. Julián had come here looking for them and I'd found them without looking for them, or they'd found me, and here we were, the three of us, in the kitchen, playing the game of me being their favourite granddaughter.

"You can't go through life alone," Karin pronounced. "When you're alone, everything is much more difficult, you're restricted to what you can do by yourself, whereas if you have the support of others, of many others, what was once impossible can become possible. The group gives power. The hard part is finding a group willing to accept us and protect us."

I didn't say anything. I looked at them and kept sipping.

"You have a family that you love, and you should be much closer to it," Fred continued. Whenever Fred spoke, Karin observed him very intently, opening her eyes as wide as she could. Now I realized that she was jumpy because she was afraid he'd make some kind of blooper. "And apart from your family, you can have us and all our friends."

"Otto and Alice?" I asked.

Karin held out her arm and took hold of my hand. I shuddered feeling her skin, her fingers on my hand. I managed not to make any movement that might betray my revulsion until I could gently remove it and pick up the glass.

"Yes, you already know a few."

They looked at each other in apparent agreement over revealing something important. Karin took the floor.

"We've knocked at several doors and people have given us their opinions of you. It wouldn't be impossible for you to join our Brotherhood. It wouldn't be easy of course. We'd have to convince some very stubborn people. We're all very old, very conservative, and it's hard for us to get used to new faces and yet ... I don't know if I should be telling you this, but it's the young people who are most against your joining."

"I don't know what a brotherhood is. Is it like a cult?"

"Something like that." Fred nodded his head.

Karin rebuked him with a glance. There was no way she'd ever put him down in public. She'd never do that to her great work, her officer with a Gold Cross, but it didn't stop her wanting to.

"We're talking about helping each other, having dinners all together, parties and, when somebody has a problem, helping that person. I don't know what a cult is," Karin concluded.

"I'm quite tired," I said, letting out another cough. "You both know you can count on me for whatever you need, but this Brotherhood thing... I'm not sure if I'd know how to be part of a brotherhood, I don't know what I'd have to do..."

Karin got up, came over to me and stroked my hair. I didn't twitch a muscle. She really was acting like a grandmother.

"Get a good night's rest and think about it. Tomorrow you'll see things more clearly."

"Goodnight," I said getting up and going over to the stairs. On the first step I remembered the cough medicine and went back to get it. I thought it better to keep an eye on it.

"In case I get a coughing attack," I said.

Karin raised her voice so I'd hear her as I moved away.

"We're neglecting the baby clothes."

I dropped off to sleep thinking I'd have to tell Julián all this as well.

## Julián

When I got to the hotel after leaving Sandra at the chemist's, things turned ugly. Although, according to my reckoning, Roberto was supposed to be on duty, there was nobody in reception. It crossed my mind that he might have gone to the toilet or to smoke a cigarette, mechanical thoughts that pop up all by themselves without your having to make any effort. I'd been thinking about injections, about Sandra and how her hair had grown quite a lot, and how she was wearing it in a ponytail, which made her look younger. She'd lost her spontaneity and her gaze now lay somewhere between seriousness and incredulity. She'd discovered fear, not the fear of not knowing what to do with her life, but fear of other people. There was no going back now. Sandra was jumping over a precipice with no one holding her back, no one helping her, not even me.

The surprise came when I got to my room and saw Tony, the hotel detective, coming out. What would he have been looking for?

I asked if there was some problem. He moved aside so I could go in, but I didn't go in. I didn't want to be in there with him and nobody else.

Without batting an eyelid or looking in the least discomfited at having been caught in the act of illicitly entering my suite, he said he'd come to check that I was all right. It was pure routine, he claimed with every bit of his moon face. And he ended with a question to which there was no conceivable answer.

"Everything in order?"

The transparent scraps of paper were on the floor and nothing had apparently happened inside, except that I perceived Tony's hand on the knobs of the drawers and doors and his rotten-egg gaze on the papers (inconsequential jottings) on the table.

165

## Sandra

The next day I woke up wanting to phone my parents, my sister and even Santi. I was moving too far away from my normal life. It was as if I'd gone travelling to another planet and the homeward-bound spaceship had broken down, stranding me there. I was overwhelmed by impotence, especially since if anybody asked me if they'd harmed me, or ill-treated me or tried something against me, I'd have nothing objective or specific to say for myself. I'd have to talk of looks, words with double meanings, suspicions, and it would all add up to total vagueness, suppositions and apprehensions. If I took the step of joining the Brotherhood maybe I'd find out about everything but Heaven knows what I'd have to do. I didn't imagine they'd let me become one of them without my getting my hands dirty, and once I'd dirtied my hands I'd have to cope with having that on my conscience. It wouldn't be so easy to get out of the clan or sect or brotherhood. I wasn't finding it so easy to get out of my relationship with Santi, and leaving this weird group was going to be even less so.

Now that Karin was feeling better again, she'd probably want to go running around all over the place in the four-by-four, but I needed some time for my things. After I'd showered, made my bed and tidied up a bit, I went down for breakfast and, as I'd guessed, Karin had beaten me to it. And, more than I could hear her, I could smell Frida cleaning. As soon as she saw me, Karin told me she had a plan for today, while making me a milk coffee. The dreaded plan.

It was sunny and I drank my coffee looking out at the branches of the trees. There was a beautiful long window over the sink and the marble worktop, which made the kitchen very bright and cheerful. Karin set about making me some fruit juice – well not for me but for her, because she wanted to soften me up so I'd do everything she wanted. She squeezed the oranges herself with a vitality that made me suspect she'd had another shot from those ampoules. In that case, she'd only have two left so it would be far too risky for me to take one.

The plan was to go shopping in the department store. She loved checking out all the different sections, being amazed by how low the prices were and by all the beautiful things that people thought of designing. She loved the household-items section and I always had to drag her away from there. It killed me, it bored me, but she loved working off her energy like that. It was all about her feeling alive. Then we'd go to the gym, where I'd leave her, which would give me an hour to try and see Julián. I'd have to postpone calling my family until I had more time. At least the syrup was working and I was coughing less.

What I had on my mind now were the injections. As soon as I remembered them, they colonized my head. Fred had gone off to play golf with Otto and a few more "brothers", Frida was downstairs, making her usual noises of moving furniture in the library-den, and Karin had decided to wait for me on the porch. I told her I was going to get my bag, which was true, but, before going to my room, I slipped into Fred's and Karin's, leaving the door open in case Frida came up. Frida had a very highly developed sixth sense and intuited when somebody was about to break the rules, as I was doing now. I went straight into the bathroom and looked in the rubbish basket. I had to use my fingers to move aside tissues stained with snot and Heaven knows what else, and there was one of the syringes. I dug further down, and there was the other one. Karin had gone for two jabs to get a bit more pleasure out of life.

I was really nervous. If Frida caught me in there I was done for. I tore off a bit of toilet paper and wrapped up the syringes, then jumbled all the rubbish up in the basket and went into my room just as Frida started polishing the stair rail. I came out with my bag, the smallest one I have, hanging diagonally across my chest. In a little pocket inside it were the syringes wrapped up in toilet paper. I prayed that something more pressing would have attracted Frida's attention so she wouldn't have caught on. A couple of things occurred to me, like going back into Karin's bedroom, opening the flask of perfume on her dressing table and having a splash, just enough for the bloodhound Frida to detect it and to explain my presence in that rosy gilded sanctuary, but then that would be absolute and utter proof that I'd gone in there and had most probably nicked the syringes. It was better not to do anything and not to make any more blunders than necessary.

The banister was mahogany and very intricately carved with all sorts of ins and outs and cracks that gathered dust, so when Karin and I left, Frida was still polishing it. What was she thinking about when she threw herself into these jobs with so much zeal? I picked up the velvet bag with the little pullover I was making plus the knitting needles, giving Karin the message that at some point I was going to sit down and knit while I was waiting for her in the shopping centre.

Karin was enjoying the scenery. The sun wasn't very hot, but it warmed the glass of the windows and created a very pleasant feeling of cosiness inside the four-by-four. Karin sometimes closed her eyes, seemingly trying to soak up more life. Would she ever think, at times like this, of the people she'd killed or helped to kill, of the people she'd denied the warmth of the sun, of her own free will and not even in a fit of rage? I could see her out of the corner of my eye, almost smirking with the pure happiness of feeling well. It didn't look as if she was having any remorseful prickings of conscience. It looked as if, for her, she was the only one that mattered. It was this absence of guilt that made me wonder whether Julián had got the wrong people. It made me have my doubts as to whether everything he was telling me was totally true. Julián might have suffered so much that he couldn't tell the difference between good and bad people.

In the shopping centre, after half an hour in the gardening section, I told her my feet were swelling, that I needed to sit down and that I'd go and catch up on a bit of knitting in the car. She insisted on my staying, insisted that walking around all over the place was precisely the way to reduce the swelling of my feet, and she insisted, because she liked making comments about everything she saw. But I wasn't going to let her twist my arm and headed for the four-by-four. It was great not having to listen to Karin's voice. I took out my knitting, which I hadn't touched for days, and got into it. I almost forgot to think about Alberto. Absent Alberto. I opened the window to let some air in along with the clatter of shopping carts trundling out to the cars. Life could be so simple, a peaceful life of struggle-worn pensioners pushing their shopping carts and enjoying the small everyday things.

A couple of hours later I spotted Karin in the distance amid metallic gleams and got out to go and help her. She let me push the cart, didn't ask if I felt better, didn't speak to me. It made me suspect that this whole time, without having anyone to talk to, she'd started thinking about me and what she'd been thinking wasn't very good. I kept quiet. I opened up the boot, put her things in, then praised some terracotta flowerpots. She told me she'd hurt herself lifting them into her cart, but luckily some dark woman (did she mean black?) had finally come to help her. She said "dark woman" with contempt and she said "help" with the intention of making me feel that I'd abandoned her. I was about to tell her that there was no point in buying flowerpots if she couldn't manage them, but that would have made things worse, would have made me look worse in her eyes. So I opted to apologize.

"I'm sorry. There was a moment when my stomach was quite upset."

Did she relent with these words? I wouldn't call it relenting, because she wasn't thinking about me. She was thinking that I hadn't stopped liking her after all, thinking that I liked being with her, and that only feeling ill could drag me away from her side.

"When we get home, you'll be able to see everything I've bought."

I told her I was dying to see all her lovely things and we made our way to the gym. This time, she had a morning appointment and, luckily, at this hour too there was no parking spot nearby and she had to get out at the door while I went on to look for somewhere to leave the car. I'd been praying that this would happen so I could go to the hotel to see Julián or leave him a note. Otherwise, I'd have no choice but to go in with her and, if I left while she was doing her exercises, she'd know about it and then I'd have to come up with some explanation.

I went directly to the hotel. A minivan left a free space right at the door just as I arrived. I asked for Julián in reception and they called his room, but he wasn't there. He wasn't there, and I didn't want to go back with the syringes. I'd throw them away rather than go back with them on me, but, first of all, I had to try to get them to Julián.

Where would he be? What did he do when he wasn't with me at the lighthouse? I had to do everything all by myself. I was fed up. Fed up! I rushed out and went down to the seafront where there were some flower stalls. I went to the first one I found and bought the cheapest bunch they had. They were seasonal flowers, hothouse of course, and had no smell at all, or at most they smelt of wet cut stalks. The Chinese florist pulled them dripping out of a bucket and wrapped them in transparent paper. I asked her for an extra piece of paper, telling her to hurry, although now that I was buying the bunch of flowers I didn't want it to end up looking weird either. She also gave me a card and envelope so I could write something.

I sat down on a bench looking at the port and wrapped the two syringes, still wrapped in toilet paper, in the cellophane the Chinese woman had given me. I stuck this small package down among the stalks. You couldn't see anything at all. The bunch was also tied up with a great big ribbon that would cover up anything. I wrote on the card:

*Happy birthday! I hope you will always find unforgotten youth in the tender stems of these flowers.*

Instead of "unforgotten youth" I was going to put "your eternal youth", but that seemed too explicit if there was any possibility that the flowers were going to fall into the wrong hands. That was total paranoia, of course, but I wasn't going to take any chances for the sake of a few words. I hoped that, after the risk I'd run, the syringes would still contain a drop or two in good enough condition to be analysed. I went back to the hotel and left the bunch of flowers in reception for them to be given to Julián when he came back.

Next I went to a nearby bar and phoned my mother.

She almost squawked out loud when she heard my voice and said they were worried about me and wanted to know where had I gone after my sister had kicked me out of the "bungalow". When my mother was angry with my sister, she called the house a "bungalow", so I deduced that they must have had a fight over me. I told her not to worry, that I was sharing a flat with some girl friends and having a great time.

"Don't you have anything else to tell me?"

"No. That's all."

"Are you sure?" she asked in the inquisitorial tone she just loved putting on when she'd caught somebody out.

"What do you mean?" I said.

"I'm referring to… you know."

"No, no I don't know," I said to mortify her, or to mortify myself.

"For God's sake, Sandra! I'm your mother. You weren't found under a cabbage leaf, you know."

Cabbage leaf? When she lost it she used to say these stupid things, so I thought this was as good a time as any to come clean.

"Are you talking about babies, babies coming into the world?"

"Yes, that's what I'm referring to. Your sister told me. She couldn't have this secret on her conscience. What if something happened to you?"

She started to cry. It had taken quite a while to get to this, given what the subject matter was.

"I told your sister that she shouldn't have rented out the bungalow, that she should have let you have it till you came back."

"Mum, she needs the money. Leave it. I told you. I'm in great shape."

I told her that I'd had an ultrasound and that her grandchild was going to be a little boy. I told her that he was a very healthy, perfect little boy, and that my walks along the beach in the open air were fantastically good for me. She was now in floods of tears. Nothing I ever did fitted with her idea of the way things ought to be.

"Do you need money?" she asked in a choking voice.

"I've got a job. I'm living very well," I told her. "When my friends leave, you can come and see me."

Basically, I felt relieved. I'd only forgotten to tell her not to say a word to Santi, but time was running out and I had to go and pick up Karin. I didn't know whether going back to Karin was going back to reality or to the utmost unreality.

When I pulled up she was waiting at the door with her sports bag slung over her shoulder. As usual, her twisted face – all the more so since the sun had contracted it – expressed all by itself the question that I had no intention of answering. I didn't even resort to my well-worn excuse of having to leave the car miles away and then driving round and round till she came out. I limited myself to asking her how her session in the gym had gone.

"It was just great," she said.

Fred and Karin spoke Spanish very fluently, but with their accent it was quite funny to hear them using these colloquial expressions.

Karin was tired and we didn't talk much until we got home, when she said that the instructor had really worked them hard. All of a sudden, Karin stopped being a witch and turned into an old lady with problems. She couldn't carry as much as a single bag into the house. Her energy was running out faster and faster. I had to do it all. As soon as she got inside, she lay on the sofa. Frida had left some soup she'd made. It was incredible that she had time to do so much and, on top of that, to be on the lookout for the slightest sign that anything out of the ordinary was happening.

As I was taking things out of the bags, putting them away and telling Karin how beautiful they were, she asked me if I'd thought about the proposal of joining the Brotherhood. Right now precisely, Fred was trying to convince Otto and the rest of them to accept me.

"That's where golf and lunch and dinner with our friends are useful," she informed me.

I told her the truth. I told her that I'd forgotten about it, that I hadn't given it any thought, that I was really grateful for all their efforts but that they should understand that all of this was a complete surprise to me, something I'd never as much as imagined I might do. She started to nod off and I covered her with the tartan blanket she tended to use for her siestas. I went on putting things away, fearing that Fred would be turning up any moment, possibly with his friend Otto.

Now Fred wasn't like he was before. A great gulf had opened up between the man who helped me on the beach, who lifted me up with his big hands, who burned the soles of his feet bringing me water, and this one. This one was simple and obedient and I thought him capable of anything. If Karin told him to kill me, he'd kill me. If the Brotherhood ordered him to do it, he'd kill me then too. Ever since his and Karin's courting days, they'd lived in a group, and for him true law and true justice were what the group decreed. Anything outside the group had to be accepted grudgingly without any public protest.

## Julián

I spent the morning running around still trying to gather more information about Fredrik's and Karin's friends and what I was turning up looked like some sort of dream, of the nightmare variety. Salva had discovered a nest of Nazis, Nazis about to kick the bucket, but still Nazis. My question is why he hadn't left me the information he'd managed to put together in the old people's home. He must surely have left express instructions for them to hand over to me the box, the briefcase, the envelope or whatever in which he kept it. I'm certain that when he wrote to me he must have known how many of them there were, who they were, the kind of life they lived and what they were up to, apart from their shared bent for torture and murder. He would have told me about this business of eternal youth and would have known a lot more too, so as soon as I could I'd make a trip to the home. For the moment, I needed to rest for a while. Eat and rest.

I went to my usual bar and asked for the set menu. By this time the waiter knew me and had taken a shine to me. As soon as he saw me coming in, he came out from behind the bar with a fistful of cutlery in one hand and waving a paper tablecloth in the other. He was going to set, if it was free, a table at the back facing the door. This was something I couldn't avoid, one of the tics that had stayed with me after my work at the Centre. Never sit with my back to the door; turn round suddenly in the street if someone was hovering too close to me; cover up the number they'd tattooed on my arm, even in summer. Sometimes, when my daughter was small and we went to the beach, I put a bandage or sticking plaster over it so that the other children wouldn't ask me what it was. I didn't like people feeling sorry for me or seeing me as different. I had been different but, then again, I didn't want to make children feel threatened or to start deceiving them either.

Children immediately notice what really matters, however insignificant it may seem at first sight. There was a time when my daughter was crazy about the sand in her school playground and she used to put the most golden grains in a plastic bag and bring them home to me. I still have some of those little bags and I'd brought one with me on this trip, as a talisman. Fortunately, I always had it with me, in the pocket of my jacket, so when they went snooping in my room they couldn't take it from me.

My daughter told me that I could probably get the numbers on my arm removed by laser, but I told her it was one thing to cover them up and quite another thing to remove them. That number was part of me and my life could not be the same after they'd marked me with it. I'd be fooling myself if I had it taken away. And, anyway, why? My future was here, and what I was doing now would be what was left of my future.

I'd moved on from the French omelettes of the first days to having the set menu. What with one thing and another, the price was almost the same, I was well fed for the whole day, the waiter made sure they didn't put salt on my food and recommended what would be best for me. Some days I left him a decent tip. They knew in the bar that I was staying in the Costa Azul Hotel and told me I did well to eat with them. They didn't want to say any more, didn't want problems, but I did well not to eat in the hotel, and that was that.

I found the hotel slightly unappealing and didn't feel the same way there as I did in the bar. The last straw came when I came in after lunch to lie down for a while and tidy up the notes I'd been jotting down in the library, the town hall, the land and property registry and the deaths registry. One place led me to another and I was now seeing clearly that some Nazis had been living here since the Forties and Fifties, others had come here to join them after being called by those who were still here, and several had left or had pretended to leave. The fact is they'd led a gilded existence and had even set up some very prosperous businesses in real estate and the hotel trade. One of them had gone into private practice as a gynaecologist. I didn't know exactly what year Salva had come to live here, but he must have accumulated a vast amount of information. He must have had an infernal feeling of impotence when he realized that he was going to die before many of them. He didn't believe in God or the afterlife, and neither did I. We were republican atheists all our lives. After what we witnessed, we denied the existence of any being that might have been concerned about us. Nonetheless, I would have liked my friend to be buried somewhere, so I could take some flowers to him in the cemetery.

As I said, it was the last straw. To get to the lifts I had no alternative but to go through reception, and there was the hotel detective with a bunch of flowers in his hand. They more or less knew my habits and timetable. This is one of the things about old age, when it's impossible to survive unless it's on the basis of routine and ritual. When I was young, I'd never given it a thought, but anyway, there was Tony, handing me a bunch of flowers.

"What's this?" I asked.

"Happy birthday," said Tony.

I was admiring the flowers and kept doing so, making no movement that might betray me, but why would he say such a thing to me?

"Thank you," I replied with a festive gesture that would do the job both if it were true and if it were a joke. "You're really on the ball."

Tony smelt a rat and I did too, but he didn't say anything. He just looked at me. It was Roberto, the receptionist with the big freckle, who couldn't stand the tension.

"We're sorry, Don Julián, it's not us. A girl, a punk, brought them," he said, staring into my eyes so I'd understand whom he was referring to.

They were both still waiting for an explanation.

"Well, well, what a lovely thought. This is why I've been missing my country so much, because the people here are so extraordinarily nice," I offered, attempting to sidle off to the lifts with the bunch of flowers.

However, though I'd been taken by surprise and was rather full after the delicious meat and potato stew they'd served in the bar, I still conserved a modicum of lucidity, so I started looking inside the transparent paper for the card that they always include with a bunch of flowers, and by means of which nosy Tony must have learnt of my bogus birthday.

"Wasn't there a card with this?"

Roberto hastened to hand it to me. He didn't want problems. It wouldn't have bothered Tony in the least if he'd kept it. He'd been born and raised for this.

I took the card out of the envelope, had a quick glance at it, planning to read it at my leisure in my room.

"Don't tell me you read the card," I said to Tony, looking him in the eye. I've had enough experience with these animals to know that they have to be made to understand you're not afraid of them.

"The envelope was open," he answered, not taking his dead-fish eyes from mine. "We did it for reasons of security. We can't be in receipt of anything strange without guarantees."

Be in receipt, what crap!

"A bunch of flowers is strange?"

"If I were you," Tony said, "wouldn't it seem strange to me that a young girl, who doesn't exactly look like a nun, should bring me a bunch of flowers? We could be talking about some terrorist plot or some sort of threat. I'm responsible for everything that happens here."

"Try to understand," Roberto chimed in. "If we knew who this girl was, if we knew that you approved of her, then we wouldn't find it so strange if she turned up here with another bunch of flowers. After what happened in your room, we're concerned about you."

"She's not a terrorist and, as you've already seen from her card, she's not making any threats," I said, realizing that it was better to go along with them. "She's a normal girl. I helped her one day on the beach when she was having a dizzy attack. At some point I must have told her that my birthday was coming up... It's her way of saying thank you for what I did."

I was finally in the lift. In normal conditions, a person wouldn't have been subjected to such an interrogation and, in normal conditions, it wouldn't have entered their heads to go poking around in my affairs, but we all knew we were in the thick of a covert war. I wasn't at all happy – I was most decidedly unhappy – that they'd seen Sandra. This was the second time she'd come to the hotel, and I'd have to tell her to be more careful, because I didn't trust Tony. After all, we were in a small town, and in a small town everyone knows everyone else and spends the whole time making connections until, in the end, people put two and two together.

I dropped the flowers into a vase waiting on a small table as if it was taken for granted that sooner or later bunches of flowers would be coming into the suite. I looked at the bathroom and looked at the card. What should I do first, read the card or put some water in the vase? Still wondering about this, I took off my shoes but, since I took them off sitting on the edge of the bed, I then lay down and reached over to get the small envelope.

I read it carefully. I read Sandra's words several times. They sounded like poetry, but it was an specific message. She spoke of stems, of eternal youth among the stems. I jumped off the bed and took out the flowers. I broke the ribbon with the corkscrew that, in suites, seems to be forever waiting for a bottle of wine. It was difficult for me to break it and there was no sign that anyone had been tampering with it. Thus, fortunately and protected by a huge amount of luck, the good luck that Tony wasn't as smart as he thought he was, I would be the first person to see what was nestling among the stems.

Inside a cellophane wrapping there was another package, and its contents nearly pricked me. Good God! Inside were the disposable syringes Karin used to inject the mysterious liquid – white gold, because if it wasn't so mysterious you'd be able to buy it here in any chemist's shop.

In a laboratory they could extract a sample and analyse it. I'd go down to the hotel phone box and look in the yellow pages for clinical labs. I'd call a few to see if I could find any that were open.

This indeed is what I did, but first I closed my eyes for twenty minutes, trying to relax and rest, because it was stupid trying to force the body and end up being no use for anything. Nothing was going to change because of twenty minutes more or less. Next to the toilets in the hotel vestibule there was a telephone box encased in mahogany panels either side. I looked in the phone book and started to call the three labs I found listed. They were open to the public until lunchtime and only one answered with a human voice. I explained that this wasn't a blood or urine analysis, but another substance extraneous to my body. The voice informed me that they analysed all kinds of organic and non-organic fluids and gave me an appointment for nine in the morning.

Now I had some time to go over my notes before leaving to meet Sandra. After Raquel, she was the most marvellous, the bravest woman I'd ever known. My daughter was another story. I never compared my daughter with anyone. I would never have been objective.

## Sandra

When I finished putting away all the junk Karin had bought and while the soup Frida had left was warming, I went up to have a quick peek at Fred and Karin's bathroom. Going into that bedroom was always impressive, thanks to the headboard of the bed, the satin bedspread and curtains, their portraits on the wall and the framed newspaper photo I'd given them on the mantelpiece over the fireplace, which suggested that they must have preferred to have it in here so the others wouldn't see it. The wardrobe was spectacular inside with Karin's long, low-cut dresses over which the hand of the Führer himself might have passed, and Fred's massive trousers and jackets. There was a special atmosphere, full of the thoughts of these two monsters, full of their nightmares, although I'd never observed that they had any problems about sleeping. They only stayed awake to bonk or if they were doing something out of the ordinary the next day. I wouldn't say they were people who suffered from any kind of remorse.

Sometimes I was surprised to see them, surprised that they were real flesh-and-blood people I could actually look at, because the atrocities that Julián told me about couldn't have been committed by any human being. So, after that, when I heard someone saying that someone was very human, I didn't know whether that was good or bad.

The bathroom was impressive too. It was made of marble from the Macael quarries, like the stairs, which always made me think about

177

the quarry at Mauthausen, where Julián had been locked up like all those other poor people I'd sometimes seen in documentaries. This was very fine marble, cool and pink, and Karin's bottles of perfume were luxuriously conspicuous on top of it. Inside the cupboards were pots of cream with gold tops and indecipherable names. But now I wasn't concerned with any of that. I'd heard the street door opening with the typical noise of Fred's keys. He liked to rattle them for a while in his hand, and from the jingling they made you could tell whether he was in a good or bad mood.

I opened up the metal lid of the sanitary bin, or whatever you call it, and, to my surprise, saw that Frida hadn't emptied it. It looked as if all the crumpled paper, the cardboard cylinders from used toilet paper rolls, an empty shampoo bottle and several other things were more or less as I'd left them. It seemed that the way the contents looked now fitted with the way they'd looked the last time I'd seen them that morning, but I couldn't be sure that Frida wasn't playing with me, because this oversight didn't square with what I knew of her. Frida was the cleaning champion, she never skived, she never left anything undone, she was conscientious. She was a cleaning storm trooper. I felt a trembling inside me that quickly took away any desire I might have had for soup, because of the mere thought that Frida was on to me and that she was going to tell Fred and Karin the next day – that's if she hadn't already got hold of Fred and squealed. If so, what excuse could I come up with? It was her word against mine and they'd believe her.

But then something happened. It shook me out of my mental block and made me think that before taking any drastic decisions like confessing or throwing myself out of a window I should wait, should wait in silence for something else to happen, because something always happens. You just need to have patience.

What happened was that Fred was talking to Karin in Norwegian in a way that startled me. Fred never raised his voice at Karin. Fred was Karin's dog and that's why I was so shocked. I tiptoed out of the pink-and-golden room just in time to see the two of them making their way upstairs. Fred was practically pushing Karin and Karin was lurching from one hip to the other, grabbing hold of the banister as tightly as she could. At first I thought it was because of me. Karin must have been protecting me, and if they hadn't caught me spying on them until now it was because they hadn't wanted to, or because I had a special gift that made them blind, or because according to the laws of probability it was highly improbable that a girl they'd found throwing up on the beach should turn out to be a spy. Luckily, the fit of anger had nothing to do with me. Fred was so pissed off he hardly even saw me in the passage heading from his room to mine.

Karin came towards me half-crying, and clung to me when she got to me. Fred looked at us with a softer expression. I could see that Karin was pretending to be half-crying. I moved away from her a little and stroked her hair, looking at Fred, asking him with my eyes what was going on.

They told me. Karin with her half-crying act sobbed that Fred didn't understand what a woman's jewellery meant to her. Fred wanted to give hers to Alice.

I nodded, as Karin wished, despite the fact that we both knew I was a woman without jewels and that they were the last thing I'd be thinking about.

"For God's sake, Karin," Fred said. "Some things are more important than jewels."

Karin said nothing and Fred went on.

"Life's more important, isn't it? Life in exchange for jewels."

"That bitch..." Karin said. "She's taking everything I've got."

I understood that the injections Otto and Karin were giving them had a price in jewels.

"I want you to go to their house," Fred said, opening the built-in safe inside the wardrobe, "and tell them that you forgot to give them this little present and that you're sorry. I've never been so embarrassed in all my life as I was when Otto brought me to heel."

"Can't you go?" Karin asked.

"No," he said, opening the safe and taking out the jewel box, which I'd seen before. At that point I walked out. It didn't seem a good idea for me to hang around there looking at Karin's jewels, especially since I didn't want to see them.

"Let Sandra go with you. Then you can both have a walk."

The soup smelt as if it was burning. I ran downstairs and then started coughing as I'd been doing the past few days. A cold sweat ran down the nape of my neck. I took the soup off the fire and lay on the sofa, practically in the hollow that Karin had left a moment before.

They must have been choosing which jewels to take to Alice, which gave me time to pull myself together and serve out the soup in some wooden bowls that Karin had bought in the shopping centre.

We had the soup in the presence of the plastic bag I'd brought from the chemist's, into which Fred put the jewellery for Alice before dropping it with a clunky sound on the table. They talked for a while in Norwegian, telling each other off, maybe because Fred hadn't managed to get control of this product that was costing them so dearly. Then he announced that he was going to phone Otto to tell him that Karin was coming to see Alice because she really wanted to give her a gift.

He got up, made the call and said she was expecting us at five. Precisely the time I'd agreed to meet Julián at the lighthouse.

"Don't you think that you two should go? I don't feel very comfortable being involved in such a private matter."

"That's why I want you to go," said Fred, "because I want them to understand for once and for bloody all," and here he stunned me by thumping the table, "that you are family, that you deserve to join the Brotherhood, that you deserve it much more than many others who've earned their stripes as street louts."

Karin looked admiringly at her husband and then smiled at me.

"He's right," she said.

It scared me that they wanted to share so much stuff with me. It scared me that Fred could rebel against his tribe because of me. I hadn't counted on this. They'd probably been keeping their secrets and plotting things between themselves for so long that they desperately needed a third player to come in and save them from boredom. The Brotherhood gave them security but no fun. The little parties of the past were all very well but they fell short of the mark. More than anything else, the idea that I wouldn't be able to meet Julián was making me really nervous.

"I have an appointment at five to enrol for a course of childbirth classes. Could we go a little earlier to Alice's or, better still, tomorrow?"

Fred and Karin shook their heads.

"Earlier than that," Fred said, "Alice is resting. It's impossible to see her between two and five. I'm sure it won't hurt if you put your childbirth classes preparations back a day."

"The thing is they might be fully booked. That's the problem," I said.

"Don't worry," Karin said with her diabolical smile. "In my gym they do childbirth classes too. I only have to talk to the director. Then, when I'm doing my exercises, you can do yours. I'll speak with him tomorrow morning."

It was impossible. It was impossible for them not to do what they wanted to do, whenever they wanted to do it. It infuriated them to have to fit in with anyone else's needs.

At five on the dot, I parked the four-by-four at Alice's gate. We rang at the bell and they took five minutes to open it for us, which was humiliating for Karin. Without my wanting it (I didn't care about Karin any more than about Alice), this put me on her side. Living in Karin's house, I had closer contact with her. I knew her better. Even though the time had come when the two of them had started thinking about getting rid of me, it was impossible not to take sides.

I didn't say anything, as I wanted to avoid mortifying her any more. I didn't even look her in the face.

"This Alice is going to pay for this," she said as the gate slowly opened.

And while we were walking towards the Doric columns, I wondered which would be the worse of the two, which one would win. On the face of it, Alice was more youthful and stronger, and she was the one who controlled the liquid, so there wasn't much Karin could do except hang in and swallow her pride.

Frida, who apparently cleaned this mansion in the afternoons, came to greet us, and we had to wait a little longer in the living room. I was eager to see if I could read in Frida's face whether she'd discovered my theft of the used syringes, but she barely looked at me. Now I was paying more attention to her, I could see that she saw me as an intruder in the Brotherhood and that my presence in the Christensens' house would have been bugging her a lot.

"What bad taste!" Karin muttered, her eyes passing over bronze clocks, silver candelabras, gold-framed mirrors, extremely old tapestry and museum-piece paintings.

"Are they the real thing?" I asked.

"Even if they are, they might as well not be," said Karin, showing her contempt.

181

I asked her if she'd brought the bag of jewels and she touched her handbag to confirm that she had. It's not that Karin had exquisite taste herself, but at least it was more personal. She liked nice things even if they weren't expensive or luxurious. Alice's thing was pure luxury, a total glut of luxury, which meant that nothing special stood out from the rest. I felt as if I was in an antiques shop where you go around looking at the different things, picturing them in a different place. I'd never bought an antique, didn't have the money to buy one, or a house to put it in but, of all the things I could see here, I liked a Chinese urn that must have been two thousand years old.

Alice suddenly made her appearance at the top of the stairs. She started a leisurely descent, like an actress. She was wearing some exquisitely cut black velvet trousers that made her look really classy as she came down. Apparently she loved velvet, because the curtains were velvet too, turquoise in this case. She'd also put on a tight jacket of the same material as the trousers, and the only prop she needed to complete the transformation into the perfect old-fashioned vampiress was a long cigarette holder. Seeing me, she changed her pose. I didn't know whether that was good or bad. She fluffed out her hair with her hands, so I supposed it was good. She was happy to see me and they knew it. Fred and Karin knew that seeing me would soften her up and then everything would go better. I'd just realized that her gesture was better for them than it was for me. Maybe when they were massacring Jews and people like Julián these people thought they were doing them a favour.

Even so, I was on Karin's side, not Alice's. She offered us tea. They were always having tea. I passed. I said that tea gave me insomnia.

"You're so young," Alice commented, "I don't believe you. You don't even know what that is. I'll make you some camomile tea."

I regretted not having accepted her tea, because the camomile would mean further delay. It was five thirty already. To add insult to injury, she wouldn't let Frida make it, which probably poisoned Frida against me even more. I was lost. She went to the kitchen herself, put the water on to boil, dropped the sachet of camomile in the cup, and brought it back on a small tray which she set down in front of me with something like adoration. She scared me. Then she sat down, elegantly crossing her long legs, and sipped her tea from a very beautiful porcelain cup. Heaven knows who'd drunk from it before.

She stared at Karin over the top of her cup.

"Ah!" said Karin, pulling out the plastic bag bearing the green cross of the chemist's shop. "I hope you like them. This is the best I have and what would suit you most."

"Let's have a look." Alice tipped the contents onto the glass top of the coffee table amidst cups, sugar and teaspoons. Karin shot me a look as if to say: she's common and doesn't even deserve to look at these jewels.

"A ruby necklace," Alice pronounced, holding it up in her hand, "matching earrings, a pearl bracelet, a sapphire ring, if I'm not mistaken, and an amethyst ring. Is it white gold?"

She picked up the pearl bracelet. It had four strands.

"What a shame about this bracelet. It needs the necklace to go with it."

"The necklace?" said Karin. "Ah, yes. It must have dropped out into my handbag."

Before Alice's pitiless gaze Karin pretended to rummage in her bag and then fished out a two-strand pearl necklace that must have been worth a fortune.

"Thank you," said Alice as she took it. "I know you're not so keen on pearls, but I love them."

She got up and put it on, looking into a gold-framed mirror.

"It's a bit heavy," she remarked, "but very pretty."

Karin drained her cup, I made an effort to swallow the scalding camomile and we stood up. I glanced at my watch. It was five to six. Julián might still be waiting.

"None of that," Alice declared. "You're not leaving yet. You're going to have a slice of sponge cake that Frida made."

We said we weren't hungry, that we'd had a very late lunch and that both of us were still too full to fit in a slice of sponge cake.

"Just a little, only a taste. It's spectacular," she said, not getting up and still wearing the pearls. "Frida!" she screeched. "Bring some of that delicious sponge cake you made."

We had to sit down again. Alice too was used to getting her own way with every bloody thing that came into her head. She poured more tea for Karin and, to stop her from going to make more camomile, I said that now I'd have a sip of tea. Frida appeared with the same sponge cake she usually made in Karin's house and served everyone with a gigantic slice, a chunk so big that it almost over-lapped the plate.

"You surely can't be thinking we're going to eat all that." Karin flashed her diabolical smile.

Alice then said something in German, Karin answered her in German, and they were at it for about ten minutes in what looked like a slanging match until Karin got to her feet.

"Now we really are leaving," she decreed. "This girl has things to do and so do I. You make an excellent sponge cake, Frida."

I also mumbled that it was very good, even though I had it for breakfast quite regularly. From the expression on Alice's face it looked as if Karin had won the day with their chat in German. And, from the look on Frida's face, she seemed satisfied, as far as I could tell, being unable to get through the barriers of German and big secrets.

"Just a moment," Alice said as we were about to leave.

Karin huffed and puffed and looked at her watch as if she had something pressing to do. During our visit, she might have got the idea of going to the shopping centre, which wouldn't surprise me. Alice opened one of the doors on the ground floor and after five minutes emerged with one of the usual packages.

"This is a personal gift, something of mine."

Karin took it and clasped her in something like an embrace or more like a pressing of shoulders. They were reconciled. After all, as an endangered species, they were doomed to get on.

There was a moment, just an instant, as this scene was unfolding, when I instinctively looked to my right and caught Frida watching me. I looked away at once and couldn't draw any conclusion from it, but it was clear that Frida was studying me or keeping an eye on me, and it was also evident that she hadn't said anything to Alice about my taking the used syringes, so either she didn't know or she was keeping this trick up her sleeve. It was possible that all the time I'd been paying no attention to Frida, Frida was already observing me.

Saying goodbye, Alice squeezed me against her as she'd done the night of the party. I could feel her hip bones digging into me.

When we were at last sitting in the four-by-four, I didn't dare to look at my watch or alert Karin to the fact that I had a life of my own to lead.

"Looks like you put her in her place," I commented with some admiration, real admiration.

"I had to remind her of one or two things. People are very forgetful. And, now we're in the car," she said, "we could go for a drive, couldn't we?"

"Okay," I said, tired of the cat-and-mouse games.

"This woman drives me mad. She wants everything that anyone else has. If she found the biggest, most beautiful diamond in the world lying in the street, it wouldn't interest her. She'd only want it if someone else was wearing it. And you. If you weren't with us, she wouldn't have even noticed you."

The predator Alice. The whole lot of them were predators, each in his or her own way. Except Alberto. Alberto had given me more than he'd taken. Love is a double-edged sword that can make you happy or make you miserable. Then I remembered the Black Angel, who seemed to be the most intelligent of the bunch and who might be the leader of the Brotherhood. He'd only appeared in our house for Karin's party, giving the impression that he was fed up with all of them. It occurred to me to ask Karin about him.

"What about Sebastian? That really elegant man who was at your party."

"Sebastian... Yes, he's got class. He's got nothing in common with Alice. Alice is just another upstart, nouveau riche, as you say here, and you will have noted it in her manners, but Sebastian's in another league. I still watch what I say when he's around."

I drove towards the lighthouse. Karin kept looking out the window. It was getting dark.

"Where are we going?" she asked.

"I don't know. The town will be crammed full of people and at Alice's I started getting a headache."

"Yes, Alice was a real pain in the neck."

To get to the wild palm trees at the lighthouse I had to take a dirt road, make a detour. I tried to see if I could make out Julián's car from the road, and naturally he wouldn't be waiting for me at this hour, but we were already there and it was stupid not to go and look. Karin wouldn't be able to relate our visit to this place with anything else.

I parked next to the ice-cream parlour. Its lights cast phantom shapes on the trees around it. I liked this sensation of peace and solitude, but knew that it terrified Karin. She needed hustle and bustle.

"What are we doing here?" she wanted to know. She preferred to be in the shopping centre looking at people and pretty things.

"I need to pee. There's sure to be a toilet in here."

"You could have done it in the countryside. No one would have seen you." She burst out laughing.

"Yes, it's true. That tends to be the custom. If you don't want to get out, I'll be back in a moment."

"I'll wait for you. Don't be long," she ordered, getting cranky now because I wasn't doing everything she wanted.

It had been too much of a risk bringing her here and now I was regretting it. I was counting on her getting addled with her idea of going to the town.

I went inside, not expecting to see Julián and not knowing how to make the most of the situation. There were two or three couples sitting down and a couple of men trading jokes at the bar. When she saw me going to the toilets, the usual waitress looked at me and I looked back at her. I went over and asked if anyone had left a message for me.

"For you?" she asked, considering whether or not to give me the information.

My heart was thumping hard. If Karin got it into her head to come in, I was lost. The waitress looked under the bar. I heard a car door slamming and was about to run outside when Miss Nosy took out a bit of paper and stared hard into my face, wanting to bend my ear about her opinion of my relationship with the old Julián, which is what she did. I put the note in my pocket and was about to ask her to keep this to herself please, but then I didn't say anything, because it would be blowing the whole thing out of proportion and would end up making her remember the incident more clearly. I went out again without going to the loo and, once outside, saw another car parked next to ours. I checked to see whether Karin could have seen me through the window talking to the waitress and stuffing the note in my pocket. And it was possible.

"Done?" she asked.

I didn't reply, but simply sighed as if I was feeling pressure on my diaphragm and started the car.

"All those pieces of jewellery were beautiful, but the pearl neck-lace…" I said as I nosed the car down, heading for the town.

"Those pearls would have looked very good on you, but they don't on that old woman. I don't know who she thinks she is. Pearls are for young women. Do you plan to take that ring out of your nose some day?"

"Well, I got the hole made so I might as well use it."

She wriggled happily in her seat. She enjoyed being with me. I drove past to the El Tosalet turn-off and got us in amongst the tumult of the town. I could feel Karin's growing enthusiasm, but she said nothing, in case I hadn't realized and was taking the long way home. I stopped in the shopping-centre car park.

"Didn't you say you had a headache?" She was getting excited.

"Yes, but it's gone now, and we need to forget about the Alice thing, don't we?"

She was like a kid with new shoes, as they say. She didn't expect that the idea of going to the shopping centre would come from me, without her having to ask. I trusted that any doubt, any suspicion, any shadow that might have crossed her mind at the lighthouse would disappear now. When we were inside and we'd got a shopping trolley and her eyes were roving around all the pretty goods, I told her that I thought I might have left the car lights on. I'd be back in no time. I'd know where to find her.

As soon as she was out of sight, I took the note out of my pocket. He'd drawn some circles, three to be exact. Each one had a letter, A, B, C. Inside circle C was a cross. There was also a rectangle and some palm trees. I closed my eyes to calm down, and when I opened them again and looked at it carefully, the drawing started to look familiar. Stubby wild palms, bench, stones. It was the place at the lighthouse where Julián and I used to sit before it got too cool, which might mean that he'd left me some kind of message under stone C. It could be a way of telling me not to go to the hotel but to the lighthouse. But it would be complicated to go now. It would take too long and Karin would be surprised and get tetchy. But I could also invent something along the way. When Karin was happy, she was ready to believe anything. Karin knew the good life was run-ning out on her, that when the tap of the magic liquid was turned off she'd shrivel up and be prostrated in a wheelchair, unable to go

187

out any more. Her jewels would dry up one day too. She had to live for the moment.

I zoomed out of there, tooting at any car that crossed my path and held me up. On the motorbike I would have been there in a flash, but with this tank everything was complicated.

I finally got to the lighthouse. It was madness to have left Karin alone. It took me a quarter of an hour to get through the bloody bends on the road. I left the lights shining on the bench and the palm trees and, when I located stone C, I threw myself at it. It was quite heavy, but I finally managed to turn it over. I picked up the bit of paper he'd left wrapped in plastic and rushed off. It was like being in one of those obstacle races on telly where you've got to get through all the problems at top speed. Would all this rushing around be bad for me? In a couple of months, of course, I wouldn't be able to do it, but luckily I still could now. I got into the car and started it up. At the traffic lights I prayed they'd go green soon, begged for it with all my heart, and then I prayed for a space in the car park. At this hour the shopping centre was filling up and if I didn't find a spot to park in there'd be no human explanation for it. And my prayers were answered. I found a place one floor down. On this point, if Karin had any questions I might be able to make her doubt herself. I was sweating out of every pore in my body and my heart was racing. As soon as I set foot in the supermarket, I tried to get control of my breathing. I didn't want her to see me in a state. I wiped the sweat off my face. It had taken me almost three quarters of an hour. One more prayer. I swore that this would be the last one for the afternoon. I prayed I'd be able to spot her in the midst of the multitude.

I took up position near the centre, concentrated and swept the scene with my eyes, section by section. My prayer included her not being hidden behind one of the columns. I saw her. I saw her in the books section buying several gilt-lettered volumes.

I went to her side and took the bag with the books in it.

"Where did you get to? I was worried. You haven't been feeling sick again, have you?"

There was a trap in her comment, as I very well knew, so I told her that, no, it was a simple matter of not being able to find her. It was impossible with so many people and I'd been about to throw in the towel and get them to call her over the public-address system. And then I'd seen her at last.

"Are they good, these novels?"

"I'm keen to get started. I'm not going to watch television today."

That was good to know. Then I could go upstairs and run into my room too. I didn't want to be left alone with Fred. There were so many things I had to hide now that something might slip out.

In order to distract Karin's attention from the fact of having to take the lift down one floor and the short time that would figure on the car-park ticket, I told her I'd like to learn German. I thought that learning German would open up doors for me and that maybe she could teach me.

"For example," I asked, "how do you say, 'I live in Fred's and Karin's house. Fred and Karin are my friends'?"

Karin let fly a couple of sentences in German and then stopped for a moment to think. "I don't think I'd have the patience to teach you. You'd do better going to an academy. I know a very good one."

So simple, so simple. Karin had paid for the ticket and I'd taken it and thrown it into a waste-paper basket, we'd gone down one floor and were opening the boot and putting Karin's purchases inside. This time, besides her usual caprices, she'd bought practical items like fruit and milk. It was then that she looked around her and said that we hadn't parked there before. I said yes we had, but this time, instead of taking the escalator, we'd come down in the lift.

She looked around again and said nothing. I could have told her that when I'd gone back to check to see whether I'd left the lights on, I'd realized that I'd parked the car in an area reserved for the disabled and that I'd had to move it, but I took the shortest route. If she believed me, fine, and if not, she wouldn't have swallowed the other story either.

"Shall we go home now?" I asked, to shake her out of her thoughts.

"It'll be more for your sake than mine. I'm not tired."

I asked her, to shake her out of her thoughts again, if she'd mind calling by my sister's house to make sure everything was in order and to pick up a folder I'd left there, a folder that didn't exist of course.

# Julián

I was waiting at the lighthouse for an hour and Sandra didn't turn up. Any snag could so easily appear and prevent her from being able to meet me. When this happened, I didn't know whether to hang around or leave. It made me feel bad to think she'd find that I'd gone when she was inventing a thousand stories in order to come. What seemed really dangerous was her turning up at the hotel again. More than anything else, I wanted to warn her not to go there looking for me, and to tell her that when she needed to speak with me she should do it here, at the lighthouse. Our problem until now had been where to leave my messages for her and hers for me. Sometimes I'd been tempted to get hold of a mobile phone here and give her some money so she could call me, but phone calls end up betraying you, they're indiscreet and you never know the situation of the person you're calling. It was better like this. The fewer possibilities they had of tracking our ways of making contact the better. That's why the Norwegian couple didn't use mobiles and many of the invisible ones didn't have a home number either. They tended to use the phone of someone they knew or go to a nearby bar. It was then that I got the idea of what could be the simplest letterbox for us: the place we knew best, the stone bench where we'd sat so many times. That was the place where we could leave our messages and, while I was having a milk coffee and a bun loaded with butter and sugar in the ice-cream parlour, I drew a small map of the site. It was very rudimentary but, if you didn't know how to put two and two together, it wouldn't be so easy to decipher either.

I folded the piece of paper and wrote, "Please deliver to the girl with the ring in her nose."

## Sandra

I drove slowly to the little house so that Karin would be putting a good distance between the parking-lot episode and our arrival at Villa Sol. When we left the town behind us, the landscape was lovely, dark, with little lights here and there, shadows of trees and a sky that was swallowing us up. And there I was sharing that moment with a creature that had killed hundreds of people without batting an eyelid, without remorse, and sadistically. I could smell her perfume and I opened the window.

"You're very romantic, aren't you, Karin? You're really crazy about love stories."

"I couldn't live without them now that I'm old. But there are stories that remind me about things. I love them. It's the spice of life, love, conquest, seduction. You can't begin to imagine what Fred was like when I met him. He was a spectacular man. Tall, handsome, indomitable, he was the man I'd been dreaming of. He was an athlete, good at all kinds of sports, riding horses, skiing and mountaineering. He was a superior man… complete. I fell in love with him the moment I laid eyes on him. It was as good as being in a novel or a film. Now we're two old people. How old are your parents?"

"My mother's fifty and my father's fifty-five," I told her, thinking that the description Karin had given me of her Fred was like the one I'd had from Julián, though his was less idealized. In Julián's opinion, Fred was the raw material that Karin needed to move up the ladder and, I would add, to give shape to her sickly-sweet romantic dreams. From what I'd managed to deduce so far, Karin could be both terribly practical and also given to fantasy.

"What about your grandmothers?"

"They're not alive any more. I hardly knew my grandmothers. Sometimes I don't know if I remember them or imagine them."

"Now you have me," she said.

Without wanting to, I gave her a smug smile. Although I knew that this was a show put on by the two of us, I felt comforted. Even in her moments of greatest weakness or those in which she managed to feel more human, Karin would never give any more than she received. She wasn't used to generosity. It didn't enter into her scheme of things.

The lights were on in the little house, as Julián called it. I stopped the four-by-four and told Karin she could wait for me there if she liked, but, as I imagined, she didn't like that idea. When she was feeling well, she wasn't going to miss a single thing. She got out of the car, leaning on me, and waited with me for the gate to open. Basically, I'd brought her here to fill her head with so much stuff that she'd end up getting muddled. I thought that, in her head, this stop would assume greater importance than the fact that we'd stopped at the lighthouse or that she'd had her doubts about which floor we'd parked on at the supermarket. If she wanted to tell Fred anything, she'd have her conversation with Alice. She'd only turn Fred against me when she no longer needed me, or if I let her down and, meanwhile, I was willing to put on a show for her.

A man in shorts came out, his hair all over the place, the sort of man who carries on like a pig when he's at home. He listlessly opened up the wrought-iron gate. He was barefoot despite the cold, the sort of man for whom going into his house is the same as getting into bed. He was a secondary-school teacher. I knew from my sister that he was running away from a divorce and had asked for a transfer to somewhere by the sea. I informed him that I'd called in to see if he needed anything and to pick up a folder I'd left behind. He stood aside so we could take the few steps that would get us to the front door. I couldn't bear to think about the state the living room would be in.

"A folder, you say?" He laughed like a lunatic.

As I feared, the whole place was swamped with folders, papers, not to mention about an inch of dust.

"If you let me look for it, I'll recognize it."

"Let's do a deal. You let me look for it and come by here tomorrow." He cackled again. Either the divorce had unhinged him or his wife had divorced him because he was unhinged.

"Do you live alone?" I asked to cut the tension.

"Be very careful about what you ask." He moved over to me in an intimidating manner. "Then you won't be complaining about my answer."

Bloody hell! He was a complete mess.

"Very well," Karin intervened in her foreign accent. "Tomorrow at this time we'll send somebody to fetch the folder."

She then let fly with a few words in German, with a seriousness and cadence that not only threw the teacher but me too.

"I didn't get a word of that," the teacher said.

"I said," Karin told him, gazing at him very sternly with her difficult face, "that you should stick your tongue up your backside and go and have a shower. This place stinks of manure."

I was very embarrassed by Karin, by the crazy teacher and by humanity in general, but very relieved too, because a dodgy situation like this was exactly what I needed to make Karin stop thinking that I was acting strangely.

"If my sister could only see the state that this house is in," I said as we got into the four-by-four. "She hasn't got one good bit of furniture in her house, but she looks after it as if was Alice's."

"There are some things that can't be tolerated," Karin said angrily. "Does he think that his horrible folders are the only ones that matter? He was laughing at your folder. It had better turn up, for his own good."

I suddenly felt frightened by Karin's instant loathing of the poor crazy teacher.

"Karin, he wasn't laughing at my folder. No one can laugh at a folder. He's just gone bananas, that's all."

"He made sexual advances towards you, in very bad taste."

"He was only trying to frighten us. I'm sure he wouldn't harm a fly. Thanks for standing up for me, but really, he's inoffensive."

"Tomorrow someone will go to pick up the folder and ask him to behave himself. It's not just for you but for his students too. What sort of education can he be giving those young people?"

"Don't worry about it, Karin. People change a lot when they're at work. And who'll go to pick up the folder? Fred?"

"We'll send Martín. Martín knows how to deal with scum like that."

The night had taken a spectacular turn. Now I was worried about the life of this scruffy man we'd just approached in his house and who was in great danger, without his having done anything to deserve it. Who was to say that some of the unsolved murders happening in this zone weren't the work of the Brotherhood?

"We should be more charitable. My sister told me that his wife has left him. He was head over heels in love with her and he can't handle it. He's gone a bit mad."

"Madness is a terrrrible blot on society," she said evilly, dragging out her Rs.

It looked like Karin was dying to get stuck into someone, and that poor man was the one who was copping it.

I parked near a bar and, while Karin sat there having a decaf with milk and analysing all the people around her, I phoned my sister from a public phone box and told her what the tenant was like, adding that he might end up causing her problems. My sister listened to me as I spoke, less chatty than usual.

"You sound different," she said.

"I'm fine," I told her without knowing how to respond to this remark.

"It's your voice. You sound older. It must be the pressure on your diaphragm."

"Well, I haven't given it much thought. I think I'm pretty much the same as usual."

"You're not," she said, coming out with her authoritarian voice. "Your voice is kind of sadder too. You haven't got into some kind of mess, have you?"

"What sort of mess would I be getting into here? I've got my troubles."

"Well, let's see if you take the trouble to provide a father for your baby."

I was going to say what business was that of hers, that she should stick to her own affairs, and that I was doing her a favour by taking on the job of keeping an eye on the tenant and watching the house, but of course I didn't say it. I just wanted to listen to her voice, which is as old as I am. She's only two years older than me and to be honest I wouldn't know whether I like her or not. I'd simply grown up with her and was missing her, which was why I'd phoned. Now she'd started telling me that Mum and Dad had been fighting again I wanted to hang up. My body was telling me to get out of there fast.

"You're a stirrer. Mum's criticizing me now for not letting you stay in the house until you got it into your damn head to come back. You've managed to get her angry with me."

She made me remember the way I was before meeting Fred, Karin, Julián, Otto, Alice, Martín, the Eel. It reminded me that there's a life in which nothing out of the ordinary ever happens, tragic or otherwise. Karin was a few steps away, sitting on a stool with the cup in her hands, watching people who, luckily, she could no longer load onto a carriage of a train en route to a concentration camp.

I would have said more to my sister, would have sent her a sign that, yes, I was mixed up in a mess, in a mess and a problem of conscience, but then she would have started asking me for all sorts of details, and I didn't want her to know. I just wanted her to intuit, to guess. So I asked about my brother-in-law and my nephews with a huge sense of distance, as if I was eighty years old all of a sudden and was trying not to let the past escape me.

"Tell them not to worry about the motorbike. I always put the chain on."

194

When we got back, Fred ticked us off for being some four hours late. He said he was on the point of getting the forces out. Forces? Karin sent me a complicit smile and I sent one back. She wanted to play naughty little girls, with Fred as our protector. Deep down, he was happy to see his wife so exultant. She asked me to bring her handbag over and she opened it. She showed the little packet to Fred with a smile that really was diabolical this time. I was about to chip in, to tell Fred that Karin had put Alice in her place, but some sixth sense prevented me. There were things, some details that were for her and me alone. Karin opened the packet, fumbling because of the deformity of her fingers.

She said it in Norwegian but I got it. Three. Alice, in her infinite stinginess or generosity, I couldn't be sure, had given her three ampoules. Less is nothing. Three more shots of energy. She probably wouldn't wait till she started feeling off colour but would inject one tonight so it would take effect while she was sleeping and – hallelujah! – she'd throw the used syringe into the rubbish bin in the bathroom, and perhaps Frida would see it and get a bit confused. I should forget about Frida. I couldn't be on top of everything. I'd done what I had to do, in full knowledge of the risk involved.

# Julián

I got up very early to have some breakfast and take my pills so I could be at the laboratory first thing. I had the syringes, just as I'd taken them out from among the stems of the flowers, wrapped in toilet paper and then in a bit of cellophane. I didn't want to take them out of the packet and let the air get to them in case it affected whatever small traces of the product that might remain. I was hoping that they'd be highly skilled experts in the laboratory and able to do the tests with such a small sample, and I also hoped they'd want to do it.

I'd asked Sandra to meet me at half-past three at the usual place. Had she lifted up the stone and got my message? If only I could have the result of the tests by then.

I couldn't. I was first greeted by an assistant and then, when she saw what it was about, the boss of the laboratory came out to talk to me, a man nearly as old as I am. There were a couple of patients in the waiting room and I'd told the assistant that I would like to speak in private, so she ushered me into a mahogany office that looked as if it had been torn away from some lawyer's practice from the previous century. I took out the wrapped-up syringes.

"They've been used," I said as he unwrapped them, "and I'd like to know if there's anything left that might be tested."

"What kind of product are we talking about?"

"That's the bad bit. I don't know. I have no idea and I'm very worried. It's about a son of mine. I've caught him injecting himself several times. I don't want him to end up a drug addict."·

"What age are we talking about?"

"Thirty-eight. He's an adult now, but a son is a son. I can't pretend it's not happening."

"I understand," he said. "Do you live here?"

"No, we're staying here, having a holiday. I thought that the sea and the sun might help him to stop taking things, but it hasn't worked."

"Very well. I'll do what I can. I'll see if I can find a drop to use. Your address?"

"Right now we're in the middle of changing hotels. My son creates difficult situations for us. I'll come back whenever you say."

"It will be ready tomorrow afternoon or the day after, depending on the difficulty involved."

"Very well, I'll drop by tomorrow and see if we're in luck."

I was nervous. I knew this experienced man was going to find something truly surprising. Salva most probably hadn't had access to the product. He would have known of its existence but had never had a drop of it within his grasp, although he might have learnt where they produced it. It could be one of many Nazi experiments. They were very interested in immortality, and the Führer himself had ordered expeditions to discover the elixir of eternal life, just as he'd ordered searches for the Ark of the Covenant and the Holy Grail. It could be a full-blown genetic experiment.

For the time being I had nothing urgent to do before my appointment with Sandra, so I decided to sort out one thing that was still pending: a visit to the Tres Olivos old people's residence to make further enquiries about my friend's belongings. I spoke with the same lioness as on the previous occasion. She was even more feisty, if possible, than what I remembered. She was insultingly brunette.

"Back here again?"

It said a lot in her favour that she remembered me. It meant that she paid attention to details, and we old people are very dependent on the small needs and details that need attention.

"You have an enviable memory."

"I have no choice. Otherwise this place would be bedlam."

"Listen, I came a long way to see my friend and, when I arrived, it turned out he had died and only left me a note. Would you recall what happened to his belongings?"

"I think I told you. The clothes went to the parish church and we burned his papers."

"You burned them? All of them?"

She was getting prickly. She didn't like going round and round the same old track.

"Is there no box of his things still here?"

She didn't say a word, but just stared at me, saying it without speaking: I've already told you all I'm going to tell you.

"Salva deserves a bit more care from us, even though he's dead."

"I'm in no doubt about that," she said, "but just look at what's going on in that dining room. They also need me to take care of them."

Then a bizarre question occurred to me, or at least one that was right off the track of our conversation.

"Excuse me, but who finances the home? Is it state-funded?"

Then she began to look at me differently.

"It's private, with a small grant from the government, but it's subject to the same monitoring as any state-run home. Everything's in order. Nothing could be done for Salva and he knew it. He was very well aware of his situation till the end. He was an exceptional person. I felt his loss greatly."

She let me go into Salva's room, which was empty, with the blankets folded on the mattress. From his window I could see a vegetable garden and then the horizon with its mountains. Here Salva was thinking, here he wrote me the letter and here he spent the last days of his life. I opened up the wardrobe and cupboards without any luck. They were empty. I looked under the mattress with the same result. Yet Salva was far-sighted, very far-sighted and I had to assume that, if he wanted to leave me some kind of information, he would have found some place and it was up to me to discover where it was. Salva hadn't been paralysed by the knowledge that his death was nigh. He knew death, had looked it in the eye and had challenged it. The Salva I knew wouldn't have been daunted by death.

I was convinced that Salva had considered the possibility that they'd get rid of his things and that I wouldn't find anything on my arrival. Then again it was also possible that his legacy wasn't in his room but outside, in some part of the garden or some place where papers were usually kept. In the library perhaps. I closed the door with the sensation that I was seeing something without knowing what it was.

I didn't expect a library with so many books, some five thousand – a donation, the librarian told me, from a historian who'd spent his last years here in the home, abandoned by everyone. "There are a lot of people here," the librarian said, "who breathe their last without anyone remembering them, and the friendships they make here, and we ourselves, are their only consolation. Then the family protests because they've left us their library or they've made some financial donation."

I asked her what books Salva tended to read.

"Salvador... he was a highly intelligent man and his head was very clear. He was the only one who didn't bother you with his stories. Mostly he read history and some books on medicine. In general what most interests elderly people who lived through the civil war is history, and also the fascicles – and she showed me several shelves full of well-thumbed examples – on how to look after yourself and prolong your life. I think Salva read them all, because there came a time when this library didn't have what he wanted and he went off to the university. Until he got bad, really bad, he spent his days there, taxis here and taxis there. The man must have spent a fortune on taxis."

It seemed to me that the finances of the elderly people (as she called us) certainly mattered to her, but this wasn't the right time and she wasn't the right person to be asking about Salva's money. I went to the history section and picked out two volumes on the Second World War. If he'd jotted down anything, or left some special sign, he would have done it in the part that was most familiar to me, some section on Mauthausen.

Not much space was given to the camp, and neither did I find any-thing underlined. I checked the chapter titled "Spanish Republicans in the Death Camps" but found nothing significant there either. It would be a question of checking, going from book to book, but I was afraid that some problem on the road might prevent me from getting to the lighthouse on time, which would be inexcusable. Then again, it was also possible that Sandra and I had made more progress in our enquiries than Salva had been able to imagine. It was unlikely that he'd actually got hold of this liquid. That would have been his dream. Basically, the only things Salva had bequeathed to me were suspicions. Furthermore, if I was a believer, I'd think that Salva, in the afterlife, had sent me Sandra so I could finish the job he had started.

Then again, it was also possible that I was overrating Salva. When I thought of him, I always saw the forty-year-old man who'd turned into a Nazi-hunting machine. Like any other human being, his faculties were diminishing, and perhaps he knew less than I'd believed. Even so, he'd been able to discover all by himself that there was a brotherhood of Nazis in this area and that they were still testing on themselves an experiment of self-rejuvenation that dated back fifty years. Or maybe it wasn't so many years. We'd taken it for granted that the Nazis were content with not being discovered, growing old and dying in peace, but they still might have continued working on some inventions for their own use and for sale.

On my way back to the town, I wasn't sure whether or not to go to the bar. Today they had pasta with tomatoes and grilled salmon, all very heavy stuff, and besides, my visit to the home had killed off any hunger I might have had. If, as they said in the home, Salva had asked them to send me that envelope after his death, he should have told me everything in the most minute detail and sent me any information that could help me, and not left me with these half-truths, I thought yet again, but this time quite exasperated by his perplexing behaviour. I got a sandwich and a big bottle of water and went straight to the lighthouse. I ate half the sandwich and took my pills on the bench surrounded by wild palms, where Sandra and I used to sit when the weather was good. Then I started to feel cold so I got in the car. I'd use the time until she arrived to have a quick nap.

## Sandra

By two, according to a timetable that was half European and half Spanish, we'd already eaten the customary light lunch. We'd had time to go to the gym and have a drive along the beach. Karin told me she'd spoken with the manager at the gym and there was no problem about my enrolling for the childbirth classes. As she was saying this, I realized that I'd almost forgotten the baby inside me and wondered if I wasn't an unnatural mother, and whether I'd got into the fix I was in so I wouldn't have to be thinking constantly about what lay in store for me. It's not that I'd forgotten that I was pregnant, which was impossible, because that would be like forgetting how to walk, but I'd stopped giving it any importance. But, all things considered, in real and practical terms, whether I thought about it or not, the gestation was running its course and neither of us was standing still. Each of us, in our own worlds, was doing what we had to do. The future was an unknown, as people tend to say. When they told me I was pregnant, I imagined nine months in a world apart, the world of pregnant women, full of new and intimate things. And now look at the life I was leading. Of course I wasn't leading the life of the pregnant woman, and maybe no one leads that life. Maybe that life doesn't exist.

Karin also told me that if I decided to go to the gym it could go on her account. I didn't say yes and didn't say no, didn't make any commitment, but had decided that both this and anything else related with my son would be paid for by me, with what I earned working for them. For the moment, my own body separated him from them and they couldn't do anything about it, and when this was all over they'd never have any contact with him. Only the little pullovers I was working on, less and less frequently, would be some kind of memento. Of course I'd never put anything Karin made on him. In this, too, Karin had shown her true colours. Once she'd lured me to her with the bait of showing me how to knit, she'd hardly touched her knitting needles again. Her pullover still lacked sleeves and neck, and it didn't look as if she had any intention of finishing it, even though it was so tiny. Karin was no homemaker. When she was at home it was because she had no choice in the matter. Today she'd bounced back with a vengeance, because she'd got the idea into her head of having a little excursion to an antiques market in one of the inland towns of the region. I had to tell her that they packed up the stalls at midday, and in addition Fred might get angry again if we got back too late. Karin shrugged. She didn't take Fred seriously. Then I had to tell her something that in some sense was true: that Fred was with her through thick and thin, that Fred was there when she wasn't feeling well, and that Fred didn't care about getting rid of jewellery in exchange for a medicine that was very good for her. Fred lived for her, and she had to reward him by not making him worry.

"You can see for yourself, can't you?" she said. "I got the best. They all envied me. There were times that even Alice envied me. She would have liked to snatch him from me but she couldn't. She only managed to get hold of my jewels."

I wondered if she'd ever loved the real Fred, if she'd really loved him with all his defects, or whether the romance-novel Fred had elbowed out the real one. He really did seem to love her just as she was, with her arthritis, her witch face, her fantasies and her evil. Well, perhaps if it wasn't for her, the abyss would be waiting for him. The important thing was that after this little chat she agreed to go home and I could keep my appointment with Julián. The fact that, right now, someone from outside this house who bore no resemblance whatsoever to Fred and Karin was waiting for me gave me wings and the will to fight.

In order to keep talking about Fred, and so she wouldn't come up with another of her excuses to keep on having fun, I asked her how she'd realized she was in love with him. She had to think about it. Maybe she was trying to dredge up some words she'd read in one of her novels.

"I don't know," she said. "It's something you can't explain."

That's the kind of thing I'd say if someone asked me about Santi. But what I felt for Alberto was like doing a parachute jump. I just knew it, even though it was too long since I'd seen Alberto and I'd never done a parachute jump.


## Julián

In my dreams I heard someone knocking on the door. I opened my eyes and it was Sandra tapping on the window with her knuckles. I cursed myself for having gone to sleep. If she hadn't seen the car...

Then again, it was also true that I felt more alert after my little snooze. Sandra had got back a bit of colour in her cheeks, as if she was getting used to her unrequited love and, since she'd taken to wearing her mountain boots, she looked taller. We went into the ice-cream parlour and sat at our usual table. We already had our usual bench and our usual table. In the midst of so much uncertainty, so many doubts and suspicions, we'd been creating some small degree of order. I didn't know whether it was because of what was happening, but Sandra seemed much more mature than when I saw her on the beach for the first time and subsequently in her little house. It was as if five years had gone by for her, or maybe ten, flying by.

"They'll probably give us the results of the tests tomorrow. I bow down before you, Sandra. You're very brave, but I don't want you to go on being so brave. Has anyone noticed anything about those used syringes?"

She shook her head, but Sandra hadn't yet learnt to lie categorically. Those greenish eyes of hers – slightly downwards-sloping so some people mightn't find them beautiful, but I loved them – weren't so categorical. They had that sparkly flash that eyes sometimes have when someone is trying to deceive someone else.

"Has Frida noticed anything?" I didn't give her time to answer. "Frida's a lethal weapon. I've been checking her out. Her name is Frida... Well, it's better that you don't know what she's called as you might let it slip. She lives in a farm with several other young people who probably belong to the Brotherhood. Two of them, Martín and your beloved, are low-level members, at the orders of this gang of old crocks they're so devoted to. The old crocks reward them handsomely. Probably each and every one of them has to prove that he or she is worthy of a tidy sum in some tax haven somewhere and, meanwhile, they belong to a group with ideology, with weapons, with its own religion and a past, which is what makes them feel special. I've seen Frida, I've followed her, and have confirmed that she's cold and pitiless and would do anything they ordered her to do, because, for her, the only law that exists is the law of the group and anything outside that is unreal. I'm not sure if you understand what I'm saying."

In fact I hadn't seen Frida killing anyone, but it was very easy for me to imagine her killing Elfe or anyone else the bosses told her to kill. Who would be her immediate boss? Heim, Sebastian, Otto, Alice? It was unlikely that she'd have to defer to the authority of a foreigner like Fredrik Christensen.

Sandra nodded and said something. It took me a couple of minutes to get the whole picture. They wanted, at any price, to bring her into the Brotherhood, which meant that Fred and Karin understood that she was seeing too much and they needed to get her more embroiled. Otherwise, Alice and Otto could have given the order to liquidate her, which wouldn't bother Frida in the slightest, since Sandra hadn't been obliged to prove herself as she had, or to go through the same training, or to work as a cleaner, however much they trusted you, or to lead an almost monastic life in order to join the Brotherhood. She'd be very jealous of Sandra and would be dying to do her in or beat her up.

"The thing is," Sandra said, "I don't know whether or not she's noticed what happened with the used syringes. You can't tell what she's thinking."

"My advice is that you don't go back there today, and that you go to Madrid, to some friend's house where they can't track you down. Have you told them about Santi?"

She nodded.

"Go to some neighbourhood on the periphery where it will be impossible for them to find you."

"I don't want to run away," she answered. "I don't want to have the sensation that they're after me. I'm going to wait a little longer. If we have more proof, the police might act and do something about them. Why didn't you want me to go to the hotel?"

"Because you never know who's watching. It wouldn't be good if they connect me with you. They might discover who I am and then you're lost. Leave your messages for me under the stone and I'll leave mine for you there too."

"I have to tell you something," Sandra continued, looking really crushed. "Yesterday I brought Karin here. She didn't get out of the car. I told her I needed to stop to use the toilet. It was after the episode with her jewellery. We were on our way home, but then I thought that you might have left me some kind of message. And, lo and behold, you'd gone and left it under a stone. What an idea!"

"What's this about the jewellery?"

From what Sandra told me, she was in it up to her neck. She'd witnessed the wheelings and dealings of Karin and Alice, injections in exchange for jewels stolen from the Jews. Karin was still buying more life for herself with the lives of the people she'd helped to kill or that she'd killed herself. I made no comment. Sandra described the scene between Karin and Alice in the presence of Frida and herself. I told her that they most probably still saw Fredrik as a second-rate Nazi and that's why he didn't have direct access to purchasing the liquid. It might also be that Otto and Alice had cornered the market for themselves. It was said that Karin, in her splendid malevolent youth, had got into the Führer's good books and had wormed her way up to his inner circle. First, she managed to bring her husband to his attention as being worthy of the Gold Cross and then, as a result of that, it seemed to be substantiated that Karin had had some sort of relationship with Hitler, to whom she might have dropped a word in favour of Otto at some delicate point of their lives. Karin might have some moral advantage over Alice, but Alice had everything. She had the elixir of eternal youth.

But where did they get this liquid from? From some laboratory in the area or did they get it sent from outside? In my tailing of Otto I never saw anything strange, but that was probably because I hadn't realized he was after something.

# 7

# The Talisman

## Sandra

Julián told me that if I didn't get out of there, and fast, I'd have no alternative but to join the Brotherhood, and if I did, it would mark me for the rest of my days as a Nazi sympathizer, and he wasn't going to be around to tell the world that I was a mole, a heroine who'd worked to unmask a criminal gang. He could perhaps write to the organization for which he and his friend had worked so long pursuing Nazis, but they'd think it was some sort of lunacy, wouldn't even remember that he was still alive and wouldn't even be aware that Salva, his friend, had died after devoting his whole life to seeking justice. I said that they might listen to me and he obstinately shook his head.

"Then... it's just us two," I concluded. "You're old and I'm less and less agile. We can't handle this."

"There are three of us: you, me and Salva. He got me on the track and would have somehow found a way to help us a little more. The organization, with all the means it has at its disposal, hasn't been capable of discovering what you and I have found all by ourselves. Opportunity and courage together can do more than an organization. At this stage, anyone coming in from outside could make some error and destroy all our work. Either you go, or you stay, but we're alone."

"If anything happens to me, I'd like you to call my family and tell them what I've done." I took the turquoise napkin from under my cutlery and wrote down the address and phone number of my parents, and Santi's too. "If something bad happens to our son, I don't think Santi could ever forgive me, but I'd like him to understand that I didn't go looking for danger."

Over these past few weeks, I'd learnt that it's impossible to live without danger. Neither my son nor I, however much I tried, could be completely safe. Everything is danger, and you can't know which of the dangers will be the one that kills you. There are dangers that fly up in your face and others lurking in ambush behind the scenes. You can't know which kind is worse.

Julián listened to me with a great deal of attention, looking at me as if it was the first time he'd ever heard me speak. Then he put his hand in the pocket of his jacket, which was hanging over the back of his chair, and pulled out a little plastic bag with something inside it.

"This is for you. It's a talisman. It will do you more good now than it can do for me."

What the bag contained was simply sand, sun-toasted sand. Some of the grains were still shiny. I put it in my trouser pocket. It was some time now since I'd stopped thinking that Julián was crazy. He was a very wise man and very practical too. What was crazy was the world.

We agreed to meet the next day, here, at eight when the results of the tests would presumably be available and, if we had any message, we could leave it under stone C. I went back to the house feeling relatively happy, because the situation I'd got myself into was moving in the right direction, because I wasn't alone, because Julián was there and because, for once in my life, I wanted to finish something I'd started. What I wasn't counting on was a new scare.

I walked cheerfully into Villa Sol. It was half-past five and Fred and Karin looked as if they'd just got up from their siesta, stretching, yawning and trying to get their wits together. I offered to make them some tea and they thought that was a great idea. Fred turned the television on and tuned in to a game of tennis, probably the Davis Cup, while Karin went up to her room to change after having her usual siesta on the couch, filling the whole place with her snoring.

When I'd put the water on to boil, I needed to go to the loo, so I went to what the magazines call the guest bathroom. On the way, I had to go past the library-den, and I saw that the door was ajar, which meant there was some visitor, perhaps Martín working on the accounts. It wasn't good for me to be on bad terms with Martín, so I stuck my head around the door thinking I'd greet him, say hello Martín, how are things, do you want a cup of tea? But I saw that there was no one there. Fred was totally into the match, shouting away to himself, and Karin hadn't come down yet, maybe because she was curling her hair, imitating the ancient ringlets of her youth. I crept in, very stealthily, alert to the slightest sound but knowing that I had to overcome my fear and make the most of this chance. I was walking on the Persian rug, the one I'd seen Frida beating, so I wasn't making a sound and I didn't dare to open any drawers, though I did want to check out what had been left on top of things. I went to the writing desk, the writing desk that was taboo for my eyes, and my heart missed a beat.

Lying on it was a photo of Julián. I looked and looked again. There was nothing written on the back, just the photo. He was wearing his present clothes, the beige jacket we'd bought together, with its brown leather cuffs and collar, and his cravat. He looked like an old film actor. No one would ever guess he'd gone through so much suffering in his life. The photo had been taken in the street, in one of the streets in the town. I retreated from the forbidden territory with my heart thumping at a thousand beats an hour and left the door as I'd found it. Fred was still talking to himself and I couldn't hear Karin. I went into the toilet, peed, flushed and washed my hands. I almost screamed when I opened the door and found myself face to face with Karin.

"Are you all right?"

"Yes, I'm fine," I answered, surprised.

"I took the kettle off the fire," she said. "It was whistling non-stop."

"Time really flies, doesn't it," I commented by way of explanation.

The den door was still ajar, just as I'd left it. Karin apparently hadn't noticed and hadn't closed it.

Fred was still caught up in the match and Karin sat down at his side. As I prepared the tray with the gold-decorated cups, the sugar bowl, even though no one took sugar, and teaspoons, I was wondering whether they hadn't closed the den door because they already considered me a member of the Brotherhood, or because, and this had my hair standing on end, they wanted me to see that they'd discovered Julián. Of course it would have been worse if the two of us had been in the photo together. So, the way things stood, there was still a chance that they hadn't connected me with him. Would that really be possible? I caressed my pocket where I was carrying the little bag of sand so all its magical power would be transferred to me, and started to pour the tea. Then I sat down in what had come to be my armchair.

"I think I'll go to the hairdresser's," I said, running my hand through my hair. "It's months since I had a haircut."

It was true, my short hair had turned into long hair and the reddish streak had faded. Now I sometimes pulled it back in a ponytail. Julián was so right: if you have truths to hand there's no need to resort to lies. You forget the lies you tell and then they get you into trouble. Truths don't. What I hadn't counted on was that Karin loved the idea of going to the hairdresser's.

"Me too," she said. "I want to come too. I want them to give me a perm. I'm sick of using rollers."

Karin always had the words "I want" in her mouth, as if just by saying it she was going to attract everything she desired towards her.

Fred looked sideways at us without paying too much attention. In spite of everything, he was grateful to me for keeping his wife entertained.

The fact is I was trying, by whatever means I could, to go and see Julián. After our meeting he most probably would have gone back to the hotel to rest and, despite all his warnings about my not going there, this was more important. I needed to find a way to alert him, to tell him that he was now being monitored by the Brotherhood, and they knew what he looked like. Yet I couldn't go back on this business of Karin and the hairdresser. Karin had got herself excited. When the injections were still having their effect, it didn't take much to get her excited.

"Let's go then," I said. "If you don't have any particular preference, I think I've seen one that looks very good on the seafront."

"I'm fed up with my usual one. I want to try something new," she said, laughing and looking at Fred.

Fred joined in the joke.

"Good luck, darling," he said and laughed too.

Fred didn't seem to need the injections. He probably tried not to need them so Karin could have them all.

The fact that monsters can also feel love did my head in, because if they knew what love was they'd have to know what suffering was too.

The four-by-four yet again. I was tired of so much driving around and so much road. Why shouldn't I just forget about this Julián thing for a while and take it easy in the hairdresser's? I'd chosen a hypothetical hairdresser's on the waterfront, because it was near the hotel, but I didn't know if there really was one in that part of the world.

I was driving slowly, trying to summon up a memory I didn't have. Karin said that if we didn't find one, we could go to her usual place. Then I passed my hand over my pocket and the little bag of sand and a few minutes later the word *Coiffure* popped up. The place was nothing special, but it was more or less where I'd imagined it was and that was marvellous. I was very worried about Julián and preferred taking a little more risk to coping with this uncertainty.

Luckily I had to leave the car half up on a footpath, although I knew that two or three more streets towards the centre I'd most probably find a parking space. And luckily we had to wait our turn at the hairdresser's, so I said that, since a perm took longer, it would better if they started with Karin. Meanwhile, I'd go and park the car in a more secure spot.

I drove off towards the hotel. I parked easily and rushed inside, ignoring the concierge, and didn't turn my head, but I noticed that he was following me with his gaze. I decided to go straight up to Julián's suite and, when I was inside the lift, I saw an apparition. It was like being in a film. Martín was walking past with a brawny, thuggish-looking individual. I knocked at the door and, since nobody answered, wrote on a bit of paper, "It's me, Sandra," and then slipped it under the door. Julián opened it then and asked me to come in, after checking to make sure there was nobody in the passageway.

"You're mad coming here," he said angrily, really angrily. "Only this afternoon I told you never to do this."

"I know, but there's no time to argue about it. When I got back from the lighthouse, I saw your photo in Villa Sol. They're keeping an eye on you. Someone's following you. And, right here in the hotel, I just ran into Martín and some other hoodlum. Don't worry. I was in the lift and they walked past without seeing me."

Without especially wanting to, without paying attention, because I didn't have time for such things, I could see that the room looked pretty good. I'd never imagined it would be so big and so light.

"Was this bruiser wearing a suit and did he look like a cretin?"

"Yes."

"Were they walking towards the exit or the cafeteria?"

"To the cafeteria."

"In any case, you can't expose yourself any more. This is getting more and more complicated by the moment."

Then the phone rang and Julián hesitated a moment about whether to pick it up or not. In the end he took it and hung up again.

"No one there," he said. "That's a bad sign. Are you sure they didn't see you?"

"Fairly sure."

"Come on," Julián said. "You've got to get out of here, but not through the main door. Follow me."

Instead of going directly down we went up a flight of stairs, and then into a machine room which led to a staircase going down. We didn't talk. Julián had worked out an escape route. We finally got to the kitchen and went out through the back door.

Julián would have to cover the same route to go back and I was worried his heart wouldn't hold out when he had to go up so many stairs, although he could go up only as far as the first floor and take the lift there. He had no reason to hide.

Once out in the street, I ran to the car, pleading with my talisman to make sure it was still there, that no tow truck had whisked it off and that there'd be no parking fine. The talisman did its job. I started the car and parked behind the hairdresser's. I was sweating when I got inside. I took my anorak off and, after telling Karin that I'd at last found somewhere to park, went outside again. I was suffocating and the cough I'd had a few days before came back, as if it had just been keeping quiet without being cured. I was comforted by a blast of cold damp air.

The hairdressers were clustered around Karin with their dye at the ready, wondering what else they could do to make her hair look like it was in the photo. Karin had taken them a picture of herself when she was young, with another face and wavy blond hair. The hairdressers were telling Karin that they could see what beautiful hair she'd had and she was thrilled, as she always was when her own person was the centre of attention. I joined in the chorus of praise and she didn't seem to have anything else on her mind. I coughed and soon started to shiver, which obliged me to put my anorak back on, but after a while I was too hot again and had to take it off.

We were in the hairdresser's for about three hours. Karin had taken one of her novels, but was so well entertained hearing her praises being sung that she hardly opened it. She paid for my hairdo too, which consisted in removing the red streak, making the colour an all-over light brown and adding some honey-coloured streaks, which they said brought out the greenish colour of my eyes, and trimming the ends. It was a good idea not to draw too much attention to myself and to let them do it their way, let them take me to a more neutral terrain in terms of my appearance. In addition, Karin left a hefty tip when she paid. Everyone was happy for the time being.

On the way home she told me that she really liked the change and that from now on she'd always go there to have her hair done, because after this session our hair had turned into nice hairstyles. She couldn't stop looking at herself in the rear-view mirror the whole time. She liked what she saw. She must have seen herself as half what she was now and half what she was in that photo from her youth. I wondered if the injections they were using weren't making them all gaga, if they weren't creating in their sick minds some completely warped image of themselves. Except in Fred's case, of course, since he didn't seem to be injecting anything. Only one thing was bugging Karin, and that was that I was sneezing, and sneezing such a lot. She wasn't at all embarrassed about covering her mouth with her hand so none of my microbes could get her.

## Julián

After Sandra's alarm, nothing appeared to be happening in the hotel. I got to the first floor via the escape path, or the alternative route, and then took the lift downstairs, went to reception as if I was coming directly from the suite, and asked Roberto, who had called me because nobody answered when I picked up the phone. Roberto shrugged and said that no one had phoned me from reception. I only half-believed him. Roberto would more plausibly be on Tony's side than mine. Heading for the lifts and reaching a point at which Roberto could no longer see me, I went on to the cafeteria, and from outside spied Tony with Martín, who was strong but not as strong as Tony.

Close-shaven, tattooed head, very fine sideburns going down under his chin, a well-cut, dark-grey or black suit incongruously paired with trainers instead of formal shoes – the fashion maybe – and, instead of a shirt, a polo-neck jersey, also black. Tony was conservatively dressed and, next to the other brute, his suit looked like he'd picked it up in the sales. They were speaking with a certain hush-hush air and I couldn't work out what they were saying, but neither did I want them to catch me looking at them, so I sidled off to the lifts and that was that, for the time being.

After all the effort of rushing around passageways and stairs my body was feeling the strain. I had a French omelette for dinner in my usual bar and, when I got back, phoned my daughter from the public phone box at the hotel. It was so long since I'd spoken to her that I suddenly feared that something might have happened to her. I was too concerned with people I didn't know and was neglecting the really important people, the people for whom I meant something. It was always the same with me. This "always" came after the camp. I was always more involved with the people who'd harmed me than with the ones who loved me, and there was always something more urgent than lying on the beach and watching how my daughter was growing up, and how my wife applied the sunscreen cream so unhurriedly and meticulously.

She used to say, you'll be sorry when your life's gone by and you realize what was really important. The important things are the ones that inadvertently stay in your head – a sunny day, a pleasant meal, an evening stroll. Raquel was right. Until the time's gone you don't realize what's been important in your life. Engraved on my mind was my daughter as a little girl playing in the schoolyard as I watched from the other side of the fence, and Raquel too, getting dressed up on Fridays when we used to go out to see a film and have dinner afterwards.

My daughter was fine, but very worried about me. She begged me in the name of all the saints to get a mobile phone so we could be in contact. She asked if I was eating well, if I was taking my medication, if I'd had my blood pressure taken, if I was watching my sugar intake, all the typical things one asks dotty old people. I said I'd never felt better and that the plans for the summer house were well underway. I told her I'd made a few friends, and was about to tell her about Sandra and that she could be my granddaughter, but my daughter couldn't have children so it seemed cruel to say something like that. I told her I'd found a group of people who lived in an old people's home and that, in these parts, there were a lot of senior citizens still wanting to fire their last rounds.

My daughter only partly believed me but didn't say anything, because she wanted to believe me. She wanted with all her heart for me to be just a widowed pensioner hoping to have a bit of fun and to make the most of the time I had left. The problem was that she'd hang up and start thinking, because she knew me, knew that it wasn't like me to have fun just for the sake of it. Before the "always" I might have been able to do that, but after the "always" it was impossible. Anodyne, mediocre creatures like Hitler couldn't stand the idea of other human beings knowing how to get more out of life and how to enjoy it more than they did, so they not only wanted to terrify and exterminate people, but also to snatch away the will to live. Hitler wanted the world to be horrible. And it was for many people. For me too the world turned into a place that could be horrible when someone in power got it into his bloody head to make it so.

I opened my room. Nobody had been in. Tonight the world might be quite peaceful. Through the glass doors opening onto the terrace, the stars and a laser ray from some nightclub were visible as storm clouds melted away in deep blue darkness. I turned on the little lamp on the bedside table.

With the new day, however, with light, the action started. I didn't want to get too impatient about the results of the tests so waited till the afternoon, as I didn't want the people in the laboratory to get more suspicious than necessary.

To make good use of the morning I went to the Nordic Club, where Fred and Otto tended to play golf with other old foreign Nazis and their Spanish sympathizers. Martín was there and the Eel joined them later. The Eel was playing. He was very well equipped and was mild-mannered. Martín was only watching, but they were all talking, talking about Sandra maybe, because at one point Fred banged the ground with his golf club. They were enraging him. The rest went on without paying too much attention to him, and one of them hit the ball, a very long shot. I kept watching them until they moved off to some other holes and then I returned to the car. I couldn't let them see me now that I knew through Sandra that they had my photo. At least I could avoid unnecessarily goading these types into wanting to get me out of the way.

I was going to wait for them to leave, until it occurred to me that, now they were all here together, it would be a good time to go and see what cold-blooded Frida was up to. First I'd drive past the communal house she shared with Martín and others of his ilk, although this was the time she'd be cleaning Fredrik's and Karin's house. I'd have to move very carefully, because, from what Sandra had told me, they must have distributed the photo of me among the members of the Brotherhood. It would be one way of warning them about me or of asking for my head. I didn't know how much they knew about who I was, when not even my own people knew that, although they might easily have deduced it from that fact that someone of their own age was so interested in them, somebody they weren't going to be able to deceive.

Sandra had told me that Frida worked there three hours a day, from eight to eleven, and that sometimes she stayed longer if necessary. Hence I took up position next to the square looking towards Villa Sol. It was ten to eleven and I only had to wait till five past. Then I saw her closing the gate and getting on her bicycle. I let her get quite some distance ahead and then went after her. I immediately realized that she was on her way to Otto's and Alice's house. The big black gate of number 50 opened up; she went in. I waited for a while until I thought it would be stupid to stay there keeping watch when Frida was probably cleaning this house. But, no, I did well to wait. Sometimes intuition's more powerful than reason, and this was confirmed when I saw a solidly built gleaming Audi coming out. Frida was driving and Alice was sitting beside her.

Where could they be going? I was afraid that Frida would see me and recognize me, so I hung behind as far as I could, with my heart in a knot until we got to the main road. In one of the streets near the port they stopped in front of a small arts-and-crafts shop called Transylvania. The first to get out of the car, with astonishing agility, was Alice. Her straight hair, somewhere between brown and blonde, hung down to her shoulders, so perfect that it looked like a wig, and she was wearing jeans with a three-quarter leather jacket, which may have been excessive in this climate, but it was perfectly in tune with the Audi. From the way she walked, nobody would have said she was any more than fifty. Frida caught up with her at once, showing off sturdy legs in black tights under shorts. Unnerving attire. She looked back as if to check the street, but couldn't see me. Alice went in first, with Frida following. After a while they came out with a cardboard box carried by Frida. The box was closed. It wasn't the typical box that you only use to carry things out to the car, the kind I'd used a lot. For a while I hesitated between following them and going into the shop. On this occasion, I thought pretty quickly and concluded that the shop would still be there in the afternoon. I got the car out with an expertise that amazed me, without worrying about touching the one behind me, or anything for that matter. If I told Leónidas, my friend in Buenos Aires, about the adventures I was having while he was there playing cards, he wouldn't believe me. I didn't take the trouble to hide the fact I was following them. They were having such a heated discussion that they wouldn't be taking any notice of me.

It took us almost half an hour to reach the Bremer apartments. Pure luxury, a fortress with iron-clad security at the entrance. Even the smells and noises that escaped over the flower-covered walls had a more affluent style than the rest.

But how could I know if I was right, if what they'd picked up in the shop was the famous injections? This was all just suppositions. I was so wound up about the laboratory results I could barely keep still.

The guards at the Bremer complex raised the barrier to admit Alice's large shiny Audi. Somehow, it seemed that Salva was still guiding me from the past. I settled down to wait in the car with the bottle of water at my side. I didn't have anything better to do or any better place to be. Would my friend Salva have covered these same tracks? I don't know how he would have managed when he couldn't drive and had to depend on taxis. It must have been very difficult. I at least had a car and didn't depend on anyone. I believed that in my shoes Salva would have done what I was doing.

After an hour I was getting sleepy in the car, so I turned on the radio. From time to time they gave news of what was happening in the world, in contrast with this world where things were also happening but they weren't news. I was in no hurry. Alice couldn't stay in a place that wasn't her own home for ever and sooner or later she'd have to emerge. And indeed, at about half-past one she did emerge, now with an ageing playboy in a dark-grey suit with cuffed trousers, the lapels of his jacket turned up, a black scarf knotted the way they do it in magazines, and sunglasses.

There are times when you don't need to think, because the world falls into place all by itself and, without further ado, all the bits click together. There, before my eyes, I had Sebastian Bernhardt, the Black Angel as Sandra called him. I recognized him instantly, as if his presence had sparked something in me. Today was turning out to be quite a resounding success: the most invisible of the invisible, and probably the most important member of the Brotherhood, the one who had the last word, was practically under my nose, just a few metres away. He and Alice were chatting as they walked down the street. They looked young and attractive, obviously much more than they really were. I started my car and went down to the end of the street where they'd turned. I saw them sitting in the covered terrace of a restaurant looking out over the sea. He took her hand and kissed it and she was laughing. They could be lovers, hence Alice's control over the fabulous liquid and hence too the fact that right now Otto was caught up in his game of golf. Then it looked as if they were talking about something serious. They both had salad and coffee and, after an hour, walked back up the hill. I stopped halfway up the street, quite a way from the two of them. They were now standing at the entrance to the apartment complex, still talking non-stop, especially Bernhardt, who seemed to be giving her instructions. She was nodding. After five minutes, Frida came out and she and Alice left in the Audi.

This time I didn't trail them. They'd be going back to Alice's, straight into the garage, and I wouldn't be able to confirm whether or not they took out the box they'd carried out of Transylvania. In all likelihood they'd handed it over to Sebastian.

I didn't know what else to do. This was maddening, but then I thought of something. Watching Alice and the Black Angel eating had made me feel hungry, so I went off to my bar and asked for the set menu. I had lentils, grilled cuttlefish and some custard for dessert, with still mineral water to drink. I left feeling quite bloated and ready for a short nap, until it was time to go and get the results of the tests.

At half-past five I couldn't stand it any longer, so I went to the Transylvania gift shop. This would help to calm my nerves. I was really on tenterhooks over the lab results.

There was only one assistant, who was about thirty-five and with little to do. I told him I wanted to give someone a gift but didn't know what to buy.

"This is craftwork from Romania and the Balkans," he offered, without the slightest interest in selling me anything, or in the wares he had on display. He had a Romanian accent.

I looked at the prices of some of these items, some of which hadn't even been dusted, and chose quite a pretty lacquer box to give to Sandra. With the box in my hand I kept poking around in case anything interesting happened. The shop assistant took a call and in the unintelligible chatter I made out the names of Frida and Alice. It may also have been my imagination. In my desire to hear something familiar, I could have forced the names. It could also be the case that they were merely carrying objects from the shop in their cardboard box. Then again, it was curious that it hadn't been gift-wrapped.

The Romanian unenthusiastically took the lacquer box and clumsily wrapped it. To cap it all, when I only had fifteen euros in cash, he said it didn't matter, that he'd prefer to accept fifteen than to go through the rigmarole of a bank card. The place certainly reeked of a front for something. They could be the ones who brought the product from wherever it was and who kept it in the back room until Alice came to pick it up. It was highly likely that, owing to her special relationship with Sebastian, Alice had been given the job of safeguarding and distributing the treasure. And – another doubt – did Fredrik and Karin know where the collection point was? Even if they knew, they probably didn't dare to make the slightest move, because if Alice had been granted this power, it was because she had other powers that effectively covered her back.

The laboratory was on the outskirts of town, near the industrial estate, and although the director was almost my age, the installations were new and up-to-date. They asked me to come back in an hour, just before closing time, since the director wanted to see me personally and explain what he'd found with the tests. The patients sitting in the waiting room were also there to get their results and they looked at me pityingly but with a certain degree of relief. They thought I was in such a bad way that my tests called for comment by the director himself, and at the same time they were happy that I was one of the rare few to require this level of attention, rather than them.

I went for a walk around the estate, admiring the original design of the new factory premises, which bore no relation with those empty concrete hulks that used to be filled with greasy machinery. Nowadays, it was all glass, steel, plastic and luminosity. I was jumpy. Today was going to be a great day. I went into a DIY store and watched them cutting planks. It smelt very good, of sawn pinewood. Raquel would have loved this place. She liked anything that was half ready to take home, wooden things that had to be mounted and painted, ceramics that needed decoration, leather that required dyeing. She drove me crazy with these things. I walked around. It was a pity I was never going to be a client of this store and that I hadn't made the most of the years when these things made sense. Beautiful chests that only needed sandpapering, cupboards artificially aged to look a hundred years old. I sat in a chair with a bulrush seat while I was waiting. Couples got excited over unvarnished bookshelves while trying to restrain their children. Students were looking for a flawed, cheaper table for some provisional lodgings. There was no better place in the world to be waiting for the past, for the test results that would take me back to a time that no longer existed but that still struggled to keep existing at any price. Everything should smell like this store.

When there was only a quarter of an hour to go, I walked back to the laboratory, admiring the trees and the people who were working, who earned their living doing something for other people, making things they could see and touch.

Back once again in that oasis of peace, I was as jittery as I'd been when they were doing my heart tests. The doctor ushered me into his mahogany office and closed the door. He was very pleasant, asked me how I was and remarked on the good weather we were having. He apparently had all the time in the world. At last he opened up the folder and some typical-looking test results appeared. I'd had so many tests myself that I recognized them straight away. At least, I thought, they've been able to extract a bit of the liquid.

"Well," he said, "we'd need to repeat the tests. We've worked with a minimal sample which we assume has been contaminated, because we haven't found anything special."

"Nothing?"

He shrugged.

"And you say your son's been injecting this? There's nothing to worry about. It's a potent vitamin complex."

"Doctor, I'm not a doctor myself, though I spend my life surrounded by them, so let me ask you without beating around the bush. Is it possible that this compound might have effects of rejuvenation or of giving an old person like myself the energy of a young man?"

"The concentrations of vitamins and minerals such as phosphatidylserine, taurine, B-group vitamins and others are very high. Of course they can improve concentration and give a feeling of vitality, but they can't work miracles. It's certainly a compound that's much more effective than the stuff students tend to take."

"Sometimes," he went on, "people will pay a fortune for some vulgar formula, whether it's something to be taken orally or for local application, and here I'm referring to cosmetics. They let themselves be taken in by the illusion of becoming younger and more intelligent. I hope your son isn't one of them. What works best in many cases is the placebo effect."

The doctor settled more comfortably in his chair. Like all people of my age he was something of a windbag.

"We're appalled by death. We're panic-stricken," he said. "This is completely stupid and a waste of time, because death never misses an appointment. Death is punctual. We can't stop it or detain it. Delay it? Well, maybe, but I'm not so sure. And you know why? Because death is good. It's necessary for life. The death of a cell means its renewal. If some cells didn't die and others weren't born we wouldn't be able to stay alive. Tell your son to eat well, do some exercise, make love as much as possible, enjoy his life and that he shouldn't complicate things."

"And what about me, doctor? He's young, but I..."

"The same thing, but in small doses."

When it came to paying, I had to get out my gold card. It had turned out they'd had to do some very fine-tuned analysis and two assistants had worked until early morning. It cost me two thousand euros and he asked me if I needed the invoice. I told him that with something like this it wasn't necessary.

I walked out with my head spinning even more than when they told me they had to replace a valve in my heart. In the end, the sadistic experiments of Doctor Death and Himmler had been of no use in the quest for immortality or eternal youth, or even in prolonging life. Packing up the magic potion in those suspicious ampoules and distributing it from Transylvania was pure stagecraft, just a swindle.

I couldn't wait to tell Sandra. What with my conversation, it was now after a quarter-past eight and I didn't want her to think I hadn't been able to come. My pulse was racing. I had a good drink of water in the car and tried to calm down. If anything happened to me, they'd be able to go on sleeping like logs and believing they were the elect until the end of their days. Pull yourself together, I ordered myself and drove off to the lighthouse.

I was carrying the folder with the test results and was thinking that I'd tell Sandra we should go somewhere else in case they'd followed either her or me. I thought that we could go separately to a church near the entrance to the town. We'd have some peace and quiet there. But she wasn't there when I arrived. It was eight thirty and sometimes Sandra had no room for manoeuvre because of Karin's damn whims. I went to stone C. There was no one around. I lifted it and there was nothing there. No note. She hadn't come. If she had, she would have left some sign for me. I went inside to have a cup of herbal tea and to pass the time.

I sat down at out usual table and the waitress came over.

"She came and she's gone."

"Excuse me?" I said.

"The girl came and didn't even wait ten minutes. I know I'm getting involved in something I don't care about, but don't waste your time. That girl doesn't love you."

I was about to burst out laughing.

"And how do you know?" I enquired.

"It goes without saying. She could be your granddaughter. Look, if you were her, would you go for somebody like you?"

"Thank you for the advice. I'd like a camomile tea."

"She's out to get your money," continued this woman of some fifty badly weathered years, whom I didn't want to offend because of what might happen.

"Well, she should have chosen somebody else, because I don't have much. I live on camomile tea and set menus, and the days I have lunch I skip dinner."

"That's something, but that girl couldn't care less."

"You don't think it's possible that there might be just the remotest possibility that she could fall in love with me?"

"Hell no. You're crazy if you're under that illusion. It's pathetic the ideas that people get into their heads."

"A lot of things can go through a head. Don't tell me that you never dreamt about some famous actor that you were never going to meet."

"An actor? Like who?"

"An actor, well I don't know… like Tyrone Power, for example."

"Like who? Didn't he die ages ago? I wouldn't even know what he looked like."

"He was your classical ladies' man."

"That girl doesn't like ladies' men and she doesn't like you. Go back home. I wouldn't have had a clear conscience tonight if I hadn't given you a piece of my mind."

I was going to tell her that I'd always thought she was on Sandra's side and it had been a big surprise to find that she was worried about me.

I was grateful that the camomile tea was steaming hot, so I could hang around, because I knew that Sandra would be rushing here as soon as she could. Something major must have happened for her not to turn up for the most important appointment we'd ever had, and that we were probably ever going to have: the revelation about the Great Treasure. Without Sandra, without her pluck, it would never have happened. Some day her courage would have to be recognized. In comparison with what she'd done, everything I'd done didn't count, because I was full of hatred towards those people and any action of mine would only be personal revenge, yet she was doing it for everyone. The waitress didn't have the faintest idea of who she was talking about, or of who the person she'd judged so grossly really was. I looked at her with contempt when she came with my bill.

I wrote the word *success* on the serviette. "Waiting for news and hope you're well."

I put the serviette in my pocket, picked up the folder and went out. I sat for a few minutes on our bench and then put the serviette under stone C.

221

## Sandra

I had time to wander round the shops before going to meet Julián. I'd got to the point of finding some pleasure in the simple fact of being able to walk at my own pace and not having to adapt to Karin's tiny steps, or Julián's for that matter. We were always seated when we were talking, but he took for ever to put his cup down on the saucer, to pay and to get his jacket on. Feeling free, without Karin's weight hanging on my arm, was delicious. I walked towards the street full of artisans' and artists' shops where you can find all sorts of one-off items, handmade shoes, some really original dresses and objects in wood and leather.

I was window-shopping and diving in and out of the shops when I felt like it. This, which I used to do before meeting the Norwegians, before Villa Sol, before Julián, before the queasiness in my stomach that never left me now, without even thinking about it or giving it any importance, now gave me a feeling of independence, of being my own woman. One of the shops I liked most had handmade clothes for children and sold pullovers like the one I was trying to make in Villa Sol. And I was studying an armhole when, walking past the display window, which was decorated with baby baskets with delicate embroidered sheets, towels with lace edgings and a thousand other ways of making a child feel pampered, I saw Frida.

It wasn't surprising that I should come across her in any part of the town, yet seeing her outside of the realm of Villa Sol startled me, and the sick feeling in my stomach went berserk. Frida didn't fit into the normal world, although I was the only one in this street who knew it. My first impulse was to step to one side so she wouldn't see me, but then I realized she was obsessed with something else and wasn't looking anywhere. She probably thought that I didn't exist outside of Villa Sol or outside the grip of the old people, and now she could take a break from having to keep an eye on everything. I left the pullover on the counter and went outside. I was almost certain that Frida wouldn't look back. It was cold and she was wearing a padded navy-blue sleeveless jacket over a red pullover with a miniskirt and suede boots, and she'd done her hair in a plait.

She went into a small gift shop called Transylvania and came out with a big bag. For once she didn't have the face of a killer. She almost looked like a normal girl with something like excitement in her expression. She went on her way without taking any notice of what was happening around her, and I could quite comfortably follow the strong calf muscles that bulged out of the boots as she went up the street. I only hoped she wasn't going to get her bike, because I'd parked the motorbike quite a way lower down. She turned off towards the fishermen's quarter, walking increasingly faster. Either she was running late or she was keen to get to wherever she was going. Though it got difficult for me to breathe at some points, I didn't want to lose sight of her. Instinct had made me pursue her and instinct forced me to find out where she was going. I could have stayed where I was, looking at baby clothes and feeling free, but wanting to know what Frida was up to was stronger than my sense of freedom.

She stopped in front of a bar to look at herself in the glass of the door. She ran her hand over her plait and went inside. The glass had an octopus etched into it and it was hard to see inside, so I went round the corner and, as I'd anticipated, there was a large window, and through the window I could see Frida from behind and the Eel facing me. The Eel! I moved away a little so I could see them better without them seeing me. The Eel! She was speaking. He was looking at her. She produced what she was carrying in her bag. It was a very nice leather jacket. He took it and, after barely looking at it, handed it back to her. She took his hand and gently, without any brusque movement, he removed it. They talked, he leaning back in the chair, sometimes running his hand over his hair, and she with head and shoulders inclined forward, towards him. I was half concealed behind a car and didn't plan to move until this scene came to an end. How could I trust someone who had solitary trysts with Frida?

After half an hour Albert paid and they got up. Frida held out to him the bag with the jacket. He hadn't taken it at first but had put his hands in the pockets of his jacket so as not to take it, but she insisted, begged him with her whole body not to reject it, and he had no choice but to accept it. Even I had become so tense with the situation that I was glad when he took the bag and put an end to the scene. It didn't seem prudent to follow them. They'd most likely go their separate ways, so I went to get the motorbike.

I went up to the lighthouse as fast as I could and waited ten minutes for Julián. I thought he might have left, but since there was no note under the stone, he may not have been able to come. I was about to

ask the waitress and fortunately changed my mind immediately, because it would only have brought us even more to her attention, and
the only real information I was going to get out of her was whether
Julián had already been and left.

# 8
## Soap, Flower, Knife

### Julián

The day Sandra found the Gold Cross and confirmed that Fredrik was Fredrik, I was hugely relieved. I imagined how hard it would be for him not to be able to flaunt it on his chest, not to be able to show it off to anyone who wasn't one of his "brothers". His brothers would be sick and tired of the damn cross because Fred was an upstart. He was Aryan, well yes, but at bottom he was somebody who'd got to the very heart of the Reich to snatch the glory from others and to claim a place. They'd despised him a little and they'd feared Karin, because when she had embarked on this project she was very clear about her aims: get close to the Führer, seduce him, get herself infused, defiled with his power and rule over the world. The story went that she'd tried to oust Eva Braun herself from Hitler's heart. Would the Führer really have been capable of falling in love when even his slightest movement created waves of death? Would he have been sighing over Eva or Karin while, in Auschwitz or in Mauthausen, he was killing thousands of people just by wishing to? What did Karin see in his eyes? Would she have seen in them all the evil of the human world, and of the universe, of the stars, of heaven, of hell, of the future and of the origin of life?

Not even Satan, who was supposed to be evil incarnate, would have dared to be all evil at once.

But I didn't want such thoughts to distract me from the basics, and the basics consisted of knowing the movements of Aribert Heim or, rather, the Butcher of Mauthausen. He was part of the group, yet led a slightly separate life. He spent practically all his time on the *Estrella*, which was anchored in the port with its eye-catching, beautiful timbers gently creaking. He spent his free time polishing her, looking after her and, when not on the boat, he was at the fish market buying the best fish at the best price. When they were offering good lobster, red prawns and turbot, he scurried back to his boat more quickly in his haste to try them.

It was evident that he'd placed the boat and food at the centre of his life. Even in winter he wore shorts. His life, constantly out in the open air, had kept him strong, especially his knotty, muscular legs. Mine, by contrast, are skinny and white, almost bluish. He walked with a stoop, which made him look like an animal set on some fixed objective. He didn't look around, or if he did look at anything, it wasn't evident. His destinations were the boat, the fish market and the supermarket. That was all he needed. The boat frequently gave off an intense smell of grilled fish, and he tended to eat his extraordinary meals alone with a bottle of wine, probably quite a good one. After his feast he lingered there, lolling around, gazing at the firmament, before going down into the cabin to watch television, turned up full blast because he must have been somewhat deaf.

I was sure that Salva had pinpointed him here, had been observing him as I was observing him right now, and that he'd been thinking of me as he watched. And he would have been wondering how a psychopath like this would have behaved in his private life with his women – both the legitimate one and the lover – and his children. Did he forget his killer instincts at such moments?

He was the dullest of the Brotherhood gang, methodical enough to turn your stomach. I'd ascertained that it took him an hour to walk to both the supermarket and the fish market, although sometimes he tarried a little longer at the fish market, never less. And he took an hour to have dinner and enjoy his stargazing. He had a car parked in the garage of a house belonging to some people living in the port area, but I only saw him get it out once, perhaps to go and meet up with his friends. While I was watching him, everything he needed fitted into two bags that he carried one in each hand.

Two or three days ago, making the most of the fact that he'd headed off towards the fish market, I sneaked onto the boat. Somebody might have spotted me but I took the risk, did it fast and naturally. I'd more or less seen what he had on the deck, so I went down the steps, which were gleaming like everything else in sight. A safe haven for a pig. I could smell recently brewed coffee. The curtains were in red-and-white gingham. In the kitchen drawers, the cutlery was perfectly organized, as were the crockery and glassware in their little cupboards. I took out a knife in case he came back before time and I found myself face to face with him.

There were Tupperware containers in the fridge, with labels detailing what was in them, and he'd even installed a glass wine rack. There was nothing lacking in the bathroom and it smelt like flowers. In a silver soap dish he had a collection of those little bars of soap they give you in hotels. I took one and put it in my jacket pocket. I went into the bedroom-cum-living area. There were some small fresh flowers in a vase and I took one of them too, to keep the soap company. In a small wardrobe he'd organized his underpants and socks in pristine piles. Some reading glasses lay on a shelf and I thought about putting them somewhere else in order to flummox him, though I knew he'd notice the little flower and the soap. I was hoping he'd think he was getting senile.

Where would he keep the hundreds of notes he'd taken of his experiments? The handwritten notebooks must be somewhere, because he wrote down absolutely everything he did. Some of his notebooks had been used in the legal case against him, but there had to be more. He would definitely have fixed things so that he could take with him the material that reminded him of his days of glory, when he was God and human beings were his guinea pigs. Even now, he was still jotting down what he did, because not ceasing to be what he really was, even though he couldn't do everything he viscerally craved to do, would permit him to go on living better than other people who'd never killed. I too took notes of what I did, so we were alike in that, and I asked myself where I'd hide that information myself. Of course he was counting on nobody understanding the information, because it was written in German, and he'd assumed that nobody would go looking for it because nobody knew who he was. An old foreigner on a boat? What would he be calling himself now?

I wouldn't keep the notebooks in drawers, or on top of the little wardrobe, or in the folds of a blanket. If no one was going to be looking for them, why should I need to hide them? I'd put them among similar objects. I came out in goose bumps when I took one out. They were in the shelves, all in order, like books. He'd put adventure-novel covers over them.

I'd be back.

I left as I'd entered, cleaning the steps with my handkerchief and, when I was out on the wharf, I realized I hadn't put the knife back in its place. I'd put it in my jacket pocket and there it remained. I was the one who was getting senile. I was going to throw it in the sea, but then decided not to.

I went off to meet Sandra.

## Sandra

As I didn't find Julián at the lighthouse, I couldn't tell him that I'd discovered that Frida was in love with the Eel and that this could make her an even more dangerous foe. I got into bed thinking that I'd have to be increasingly tactful with the Norwegians and with Frida. Dealing with them was like walking on a wire. The best thing would be to let them think they were manipulating me more than they were. Julián neutralized the power with which Karin was constantly trying to dominate me, though it must be said she was very often successful. She was used to imposing her will and to treating other people like her playthings. The tension was affecting me physically. And, on top of that, after what I'd seen in the afternoon, I wasn't at all certain about what Alberto was playing at.

As soon as I turned out the light, I saw monsters hiding inside the normal human bodies of the "brothers", saw that I was just a toy for them and that, when they completely took over me, they'd also be taking over my son. But when daylight came again, everything changed as if by magic, as if a veil had been drawn back, and they stopped being so dangerous. I thought I'd got carried away by panic. I also blamed my tendency to exaggerate these situations on the fact that I didn't really know them and I'd never experienced such things before. Then again, the hormonal revolution that was going on inside me was making me all the more unstable. At least, everyone talked about this so-called hormonal revolution, and it might just be that this revolution had changed the whole world for me.

I got up late by Norwegian standards. Fred had gone off to do his Brotherhood things and Karin asked me if I'd go down to the town and fetch her some face and body creams and magazines. It was her way of giving me some freedom and I seized the opportunity. I was dying to know if we had the results of the tests yet. At bottom, I wanted the famous liquid to be worth all of that running around and all the spells of incredible nervousness and fear. I hoped I hadn't made a mountain out of a molehill.

Since it was an errand for Karin, I took the four-by-four, and within fifteen minutes I was reading a note that Julián had left me under the stone, saying that the test results had been a success. I left him another saying, very briefly, that I'd come by again at the usual hour in the afternoon to see if he was there.

I did the errands in a flash. I spent what remained of the morning walking in the garden, breathing in the fresh air and drinking lots of water trying to wash away the phlegm. Karin was inside writing letters and slathering cream on herself till Fred got back, and then we had some soup that Frida had made and left ready to serve. I set the table with the little embroidered serviettes and waited for them to try it first. This gave me a strange sensation. Did I suspect that they wanted to poison me? Was I going nuts? Was I a hundred per cent in my right mind? Was it reasonable to have listened so much to an old man like Julián? The continuous fighting of my parents had disturbed me a lot. Maybe such a long life had unbalanced Julián too. Crazy people don't know they're crazy. I watched them take a couple of spoonfuls to their mouths and then I tried the soup. It was good. It had bits of chicken in it, and vegetables. There I was, having this soup made by someone I didn't know with some old people I didn't know but who, whether I liked it or not, were now part of my world. And, while they were having a siesta (Fred dozing in the armchair with the television turned on and Karin snoring on the couch covered with a blanket), I went off to the lighthouse on the motorbike.

Julián was there. He'd come in case I'd left any message for him, thinking that he might even find me there. We'd both had the same idea. We were in luck.

He was dying to tell me that there was no mystery about the ampoules that had cost Fred and Karin a fortune and that were going to end up ruining them. The stuff was easy to make. Basically, time hadn't gone by for these old Nazis, they were dreaming that their scientists, who belonged to a race superior to that of other scientists, had managed with their experiments to discover the secret of eternal youth, among other things. They were still living out fantasies of grandeur that made them fall for their own self-deception. They'd tried to warp the world in order to make their far-fetched ideas come true. Probably only one of them knew that they weren't as powerful as they believed.

I didn't tell Julián that I'd stumbled upon Alberto and Frida together, because it was difficult to talk about that. If I told him that, I'd also have had to confess that I no longer knew where evil ended and where my imagination began.

Instead, I said that after he'd told me about Elfe, his suspicions that they'd killed her and the things he knew they were capable of doing, I'd started to worry about the well-being of the tenant in the little house. Karin had taken against him and had told me that she was thinking about sending Martín there to teach him a lesson.

## Julián

I had a demon in me and there was nothing I could do about it. Why was I doing these things? Why was I behaving like this with Sandra? The demon had been asleep for many years and had just woken up. I'd felt it when Salva fell in love with Raquel in that hell, and I was feeling it now, with the difference that now I couldn't handle it. It was acting alone, was faster than me, and smarter. The demon wanted Sandra to go on being as she was when I'd met her, a mixed-up girl who didn't know what she wanted. The demon didn't want her to be in love with the Eel, hated the idea that the Eel might take her away from old Julián. Until now, Sandra and I had been a team, had shared a secret. Suddenly all this could change, and my selfish demon didn't want me to be left alone. But despite the demon, I didn't want anything irrevocable to happen to Sandra, didn't want her to suffer a tremendous disappointment that would leave her marked for the rest of her life. I preferred to keep laying out the truth before her eyes in the hope that she'd decide to go back to her usual life.

I'd promised Sandra to call by the little house, even knowing it was foolishness. Sandra was afraid that the tenant, a teacher who couldn't possibly have the remotest idea of who had him in her sights, might meet the same fate as Elfe. Neither Karin nor any of the rest of them could permit themselves the luxury of eliminating

230

people they didn't like, especially when these people were no obstacle to their plans. However, I definitely didn't want to let Sandra down again, so I went to the "little house" to make sure that the tenant was still alive.

It was like going back into the past. I left the car on the patch by the roadside and walked along the path, letting myself be overcome with the fragrance of flowers and the chirping of birds, so loud it was deafening. The street sloped slightly downwards and the peaceful-ness was absolute. On this porch I'd spoken with Sandra for the first time. I stood there looking at it and it seemed as if the real Sandra of the piercings and tattoos was going to come out, the girl on the beach who'd drifted where life took her, because life was clear and fresh like the water in a river. But now we were in another life and on another river.

Behind me somebody asked if I wanted something. It had to be the tenant. His hair was all over the place and he had a briefcase in his hand. He must have come from the high school.

"Sandra sent me, the owner's sister. She wants to know if every-thing's all right and if you need anything."

"If I need anything? What a question. I need more tables and more shelves. This place is like a dolls' house."

I followed him in.

He opened the door without using the key, just by pushing it. He threw the folder on the couch and gestured at the piles of folders on the floor, the heaps of books and all the papers covering the dining-room table.

"Well, these are summer holiday houses."

"And what am I supposed to do?" he asked, cleaning his glasses with a shirt-tail. "Tell her I haven't been able to find her folder."

"Well, I don't know... Do you actually read all this?"

"Nobody reads everything, but you have to have it all in case you need it at some point."

"My name's Julián," I said, holding out my hand.

"Juan," he answered without holding out his.

"Forgive me for asking, but don't you lock the front door?"

He looked at me a little crestfallen, as if I'd caught him out and was going to punish him.

231

"I lost the key. You can tell her to throw me out of here, and I'll go looking for another house as absurd as this one, and then I'll have to move all my things."

"Don't worry. I'm not going to tell her anything. I don't think anyone's going to come in here to steal your books."

"In that case," he said, sitting down at the table before a million sheets of paper, "it's been a pleasure."

"How are the classes going?" I asked as I moved towards the door.

"A bore. They're dimwits."

"And you teach every day?"

I got out of him that his timetable was from three to seven in the afternoon, sometimes three to six, and occasionally three to eight.

I didn't have to think any more about what strategy to adopt, what steps to take. The plan had worked itself out. A world had slowly been building up around me, one that was invisible for other people, a world in which I had something to say and do. So having done the job for Sandra, I knew what I had to do when I got into the car.

I had to go to the Butcher's boat again. He'd be out shopping now or having a walk and this was the only home or dwelling of all the Brotherhood members that was accessible, probably because he'd spent so many years living like that without anything happening that he had no reason to be wary. Getting around unnoticed, camouflaged, being one of many, apparently not having anything to hide, this was more secure for him than being surrounded by high walls and guards. Yet all of a sudden one bar of soap had gone, one small flower was missing, one knife had disappeared. But who would have boarded his boat to take these things? He would only be able to explain it by his own absent-mindedness.

I took my shoes off and went down the steps in my socks. Everything was the same as last time. Being so intensely organized must give him a sense of stability and the feeling that nothing could change in his little world. I understood, because it was the same with me. If I put my glasses in another pocket, I got flustered. So I put the soap back where it belonged, the knife too, and didn't touch the flowers. Then I took from the shelves as many of the notebooks filled with Heim's handwriting as I could carry. I went out, put my shoes on again and sat on a bench facing the boat, waiting for him to come back.

He went on board with his strong knotty legs, his head looking down, and descended into the sacred precincts. I was cold, but I waited to see him come back onto the deck. He strode from one side to the other. There was nobody on board the catamarans either side, so he couldn't ask anybody if somebody had got into his boat. Why would somebody get in to do something so stupid? He'd try to be sensible. He'd assume that he hadn't seen things properly and had thought something was missing when it actually wasn't. So he decided to go down once more. When he came up again, he checked the boards of the deck in the same way as he must have checked inside the cabin and the steps. At one point he shook his head as if telling himself that this was stupid and not worth thinking about any more.

But the next day, before I went to meet Sandra, I saw that he didn't leave the boat at the time when he usually went to the fish market or to have a stroll on dry land. No doubt he wanted to see if anything was moving around, disappearing or appearing when he was there. The seed of mistrust in himself was sown, and now I only had to wait for it to grow. I was certain that he'd start doing to himself what I'd done to him. He himself would be responsible for watering the plant of suspicion. I'd go by every couple of days as I didn't want to lose sight of the Butcher. It hurt me to see him, and yet I couldn't give up watching him going about his daily tasks, like washing his beloved deck, as in former times he'd gone about his other daily tasks of killing human beings, with the same attention to detail and organization.

Sandra's going into the bunker of Villa Sol meant that we were out of touch, so I didn't know when I'd be able to set her mind at rest by telling her that the tenant was fine and, however demented they all were, they weren't going to take any chances with him because of some whim of Karin's.

I had to wait to meet her at the lighthouse at four o'clock every two days to exchange news, unless Sandra managed to work out a way to leave me some message at the hotel, in our lighthouse letterbox, or of getting to see me when she brought Karin to town and dropped her off at the gym. The good thing about being creatures of habit is that we end up having a more or less fixed timetable. Even I, despite not having to offer explanations to anyone and needing to make the most of every opportunity to continue with my enquiries into the

Brotherhood, had no choice but to take a rest break at lunchtime and to go to bed early at night.

I had to husband my energies and not skip my medication. And thanks to this trip I'd realized that I was able to look after myself. I watched over myself as if I was outside my own skin, obliging myself to drink a lot of water even when I wasn't thirsty, to eat even if I wasn't very hungry, and to do a few stretches when I got up, a few minutes of Swedish gymnastics, which Salva had taught me in the camp when we first arrived there. In the end, we hardly had enough strength to breathe, but until that point Salva said that the workout was very good for the head because it activated the blood circulation and the transfer of oxygen to the brain. And after I had tried to kill myself in such a pathetic, lamentable way, I didn't let a single day go by without doing the exercises.

I didn't know how I could penetrate this other world of Sandra's, but then I recalled Karin's enthusiasm for going to the shopping centre. It was half-past seven, so it was quite likely that Karin had asked Sandra if they could go and have a stroll around there. Although I'd been thinking about going to the Nordic Club to see if I'd be lucky enough to spot Sebastian Bernhardt, I drove towards the shopping centre.

It was crammed with people. There was one near our house in Buenos Aires and Raquel loved going there every second afternoon. At first I hated it, thought it a waste of time. I had better things to do, like following the trail of this or that Nazi, but with time I found that it relaxed me. Simply thinking about all the things I was seeing, I felt it was like strolling round inside the horn of plenty or Ali Baba's cave. Everything was there, all you could ever need, and all you would never need. So I didn't mind using the occasion to buy myself some socks and handkerchiefs. My daughter told me it's more hygienic to blow your nose on paper tissues, but I liked the touch of soft cotton on my nose and wasn't about to give that up. I don't know if it was a taste for luxury or my own fads, but I couldn't stand normal socks made of synthetic fibre. They had to be natural fibre and my underpants had to be a hundred per cent cotton, like my shirts. I needed my body's musculature to feel soft and comfortable and to be as minimally perceptible as possible. And when I saw the old men of the Brotherhood I thought that they must have their fads too, like Fredrik's abnormally wide shirts. We'd come to the same point, then, some along the path of the executioners and some along the path of the victims. We'd reached the edge of the precipice.

I didn't get to go into the shopping centre, strictly speaking. I'd only just parked between two columns when someone came up from behind and pushed me up against one of them. My head and back were bashed against the cement. Since I still had the car keys in my hand, I jabbed the madman in the stomach as hard as I could, but he was so close I didn't manage to do any damage. He moved away and twisted my wrist. It was the Eel.

I asked him to let me go.

"I'll let you go if you keep away from Sandra."

"Sandra?" I asked.

"Yes, Sandra," he answered, hurting my hand a little more.

"All right," I said, freeing myself as much as I could, because if he damaged me any more I certainly wouldn't be seeing Sandra again. "All right," I repeated. "What's all this about?"

There was no anger in the Eel's expression. It was full of tiredness, sadness even.

"Get away from here and don't go near Sandra again."

With one of his hands he pressed my neck and I begged him to let me go if he didn't want me to die on the spot. Once free, I cleared my throat and held my damaged hand in the other one. This was going to cost me dearly. My whole body would be aching for several days. I opened the car and sat down. He watched me.

"Who are you? Why have you come to this town?"

"A friend invited me to come, but when I arrived, he'd died. Either I made the long trip home again or I stayed for a while. I decided to stay as I hadn't had a holiday for a long time."

The Eel knew I wasn't telling him the whole truth. He sat on the seat beside me and lit a cigarette without asking permission. Evidently, someone who'd just beaten me up wasn't going to observe such niceties.

"How do you know Sandra?" he asked, looking around. He was thinking I had too many things in the car. He saw the hotel blanket, the water, the apples, the binoculars, the notebook and the newspapers. If it didn't occur to him to do a search now, it would eventually.

"I met her on the beach and we became friends. When we see each other, we say hello."

"It's much more than saying hello. You spend a lot of time together. You meet up frequently."

His tone was malicious. My hand and wrist were hurting quite a lot.

"Maybe Sandra's lonely and needs someone to talk to. I'm not the man of her dreams but she can count on me. At least I don't deceive her, I don't give her any false illusions, and I don't spend my time checking to see how hard she's taking it while I'm getting on with my Don Juan existence."

The Don Juan bit brought a derisive grimace to his mouth.

"You're causing Sandra problems by letting yourself be seen with her. I can imagine what you're after, can imagine that Sandra's crossed your path and now you've thought of a thousand things Sandra could do to help you, but I can also imagine that you wouldn't want to die precisely now that your dreams might come true, or at least now that you have dreams."

"For a while now, every day I've stayed alive has been a pure bonus."

"That was before. Now you don't want to lose her. And believe me, if we see you with her again, it's curtains for you. Do you get me?"

I nodded, and at last the Eel got out of my car.

I didn't feel like going into the shopping centre to buy socks any more.

The best thing would be to go back to the hotel before my body got cold, because then I wouldn't be able to move.

I drove with my good hand, the right one, gripping the steering wheel, and using the bad one to change gears. I found the strength, Heaven knows where, to leave the car as well-hidden as possible. Before going up to my room, I went to the hotel bar and asked for a glass of hot milk to take up with me. My hands were trembling, not from fear but from tiredness. It was still early, but I only wanted to take my medication, remove my contact lenses, put my pyjamas on and get into bed. I wouldn't fold back the padded bedspread, because I was going to need all the warmth possible. I wanted to forget about Sandra and about what might be going on with her so I'd be able to function the next day.

When I'd got my thick-lensed glasses on there was a knock at the door. This didn't seem to be the most appropriate moment for the end to come. If they'd really wanted to do away with me, they should have done it in the shopping-centre car park, when I was dressed in street clothes and next to my car, as if it was a robbery. It wouldn't even have merited as much as a note in the newspapers. In contrast, it would certainly get people's attention if they killed a totally defenceless old man in a hotel room. So I asked who was there.

Roberto came in, looking around the suite as if wanting to check that nothing was missing. To me, it no longer seemed as impressive as before. I'd got used to it and found that it was a just wannabe suite.

"Are you all right? The people in the bar told me with some alarm that you looked terrible and your hands were trembling a lot."

He saw the glass of milk on the bedside table and then noticed that I was holding one hand with the other one.

"I slipped over and hurt myself."

"Let's have a look," he said.

"It's only painful because of the bruising, but it's nothing to worry about."

He insisted that I should have it X-rayed, but I told him that now I was in my pyjamas I wasn't going to leave the hotel.

"I just want to rest."

I began to think that Roberto, with his big freckle, might be my friend and that I could tell him what I was doing here and deliver into his care Elfe's photograph album, Heim's incriminatory notebooks and my own. Too easy, too friendly and too much weakness on my part. I had already thrown out the idea when he came back again with some ointment and a bandage, which he strapped on very well, and I was most grateful to him for that.

I dreamt that the Eel was twisting Sandra's hand, that he was hurting her, that her joints were throbbing with pure pain and that I was bandaging it. But when I woke up I was the one with a sore hand and I couldn't do anything for Sandra if she didn't want to save herself. She could flee from Villa Sol, taking advantage of any of the moments when she went into town. She could go to the bus station and disappear. Even if I could get into the house, immobilize them all, and take her by the hand to get her out of there, she didn't want to go. She'd been poisoned by ideas of revenge, justice, or wanting to finish what she'd started, or falling in love. So I had to think about more practical matters.

Any time now they'd ransack the car. They knew I was keeping evidence and that I wasn't going to be hiding it in the hotel, so that car had to be the best option. I didn't need to think about it a lot. Since I'd been in the "little house" chatting with the tenant, the chaos of books and papers in which the teacher was submerged came into my mind again and again. The notebooks and the album wouldn't attract any attention. Or not his. He had so much to read that he wouldn't be looking for still more papers.

I took a Gelocatil with my breakfast. I wasn't hungry, but I couldn't afford to get weak and, since it was sunny and windless, I thought that it would be best to go to the beach and let the sun's rays fortify me. I'd sit down by the wall where the sun was strongest, come back to the hotel to rest for a while on the bed, and then go over to the little house shortly after three.

Everything went as planned. I waited for the tenant to walk out with his briefcase, get into a third-hand (at least) Renault, and I went in without any problems. If he surprised me, I'd tell him I was taking measurements for bookcases. However, there was no need for that. I opened the small gate, and in a few steps I was at the front door, which opened easily. Making my way through mountains of papers and folders, I managed to reach the stairs. Of the upstairs rooms I immediately deduced that his was the one with the tangled bedclothes and newspapers and magazines scattered round the floor. There were a couple of copies of *Playboy* and I didn't want to look more closely. It seemed that he didn't go into the other rooms very often. One of them, the larger one, had two beds (I vaguely remembered having seen it when Sandra showed me the house), two desks with drawers down the sides and, on one wall, a bookshelf with school books that must have belonged to Sandra's nephews. I didn't believe these things would attract the tenant's attention, and if he did have any interest in them he would have investigated them already, so I opened up one of the drawers. Inside were notebooks and some bound folios of drawings going back to primary-school efforts. Only parents could be interested in these, so I put Elfe's photo album underneath them and stashed Heim's notebooks and mine lying on their sides behind the textbooks. Nobody who wasn't expressly looking for them could possibly find them. And if they stumbled upon them they wouldn't be able to interpret Heim's notes or know what to do with the album.

I left feeling quite relieved, certain that neither the Eel nor anyone else connected me with the little house, or at least it wouldn't occur to them to suspect that it was my strongbox. What I wasn't so crazy about was that anyone could get in, so the next day, when Sandra and I had arranged to meet, I'd tell her that the tenant was perfectly fine but that it would be a good idea to give him a new key.

Then I went to the casualty department at the hospital to get my hand looked at.

## Sandra

I gave the new key of the house to Julián and he offered to take it to the tenant. I had no intention of telling my sister that, right now, anyone could get into her house and raid it, because I didn't want her to come and disturb my world any more than it was already disturbed. Julián was a wreck, because he'd slipped over in the shopping-centre car park and twisted his hand, though it wasn't serious. They'd put an elastic bandage on it in the casualty department.

I wanted to spend the minimum possible time with him at the lighthouse in case Alberto went to the Norwegians' house while I was out, which would have upset me a lot. Then again, spending so much time in the house, only to be left without his putting in an appearance, sometimes made me even more upset. Sometimes I even thought about sending him a message via Martín, when the latter came to bring Karin's injections or to speak with Fred in the library-den, but then I desisted, somehow sensing that Alberto himself was asking me not to say anything. All I had was that kiss in the port, Julián's confession that he'd seen him with another girl and no show of interest from him since that night, and there I was, worrying about what he might want me to do. Was I some kind of cretin?

What would he want me to do?

"Have you done many stupid things because of love?"

The question took Julián by surprise. And he couldn't have done many, because he had to think about it for too long. The night on the coast was black and clammy, with damp creeping into your bones.

The estates of summer holiday houses were barely lit, dotted with isolated lights, giving an even more intense sensation of darkness. It was all stars, the waning moon and the invisible sea roaring. Every minute, a flash lit up the lighthouse in the darkness. There, you were outside the known world, completely alone on the planet, with others, but they were also alone.

"Not many, actually," he said. "I didn't need to, because I only loved one woman and she loved me back straight away, so I was never in the predicament of having to do anything out of the ordinary."

"And what you're doing now, why are you doing it? Why did you come here?"

"Out of friendship and out of hatred," he said, raising his cup of coffee with the bandaged hand. "I came out of friendship for Salva and I stayed out of hatred for the monsters you know."

"And that's all?"

I don't know why I asked that question. It made Julián look away, towards the waitress.

"I'm living, I feel alive, I'm taking risks, I have something to do here, and I'm doing it without needing to lean on my daughter, although I suspect that Raquel, tucked away in some corner of my head, is helping me a lot."

"And that's all?" I repeated, without any particular intention.

"You're right. I'm not doing it alone. I'm doing it with you. I never imagined something like this was going to happen. When I got here, Salva had gone, but you were here, and I didn't mind the change." He looked up a bit as if to ask forgiveness from his friend Salva. "Situations are never repeated exactly the same, and, in this one, one of the two of us was superfluous, so one of us had leave a space for you."

"Do you believe everything's planned, rather than things happening just because? Do you believe it was part of this plan that you and I should be here having a fruit juice and a coffee?"

"No, no, I don't believe that. It's just a manner of speaking. We're the ones who are linking this up with that, trying to give things some lovely meaning, but, at bottom, it's all savage and brutal."

"Feelings can't be controlled. Either you have them or you don't," I said, thinking that I could never feel for Santi what I felt for Alberto, although Santi deserved it much more.

"Sandra, I've been very ham-fisted with you. I'm not good enough for you. I'm a selfish old man."

When I was going to ask him to stop mortifying himself and to point out that somebody had to teach me the things he'd taught me, the waitress banged the plate with the bill on the table. It was a little dark-brown plate, with a clip to hold the bill. In good weather, when the outside terrace was set up, it would stop the wind from blowing it away.

I took back to the house the image of that plate and the small tip Julián had left. When I got there, I tried to find out what visitors they'd had, and they tried to find out where I'd been, so we were even.


## Julián

Salva, if only you could have seen me going in and out of Heim's boat whenever the mood took me. Salva, if only you could have seen this, I was thinking as I was watching the spectacle of Heim, the *Butcher*, going mad. I knew how he was feeling, because losing my memory was what terrified me most about all the morass of old age in which you end up wallowing. And, however different Heim and I were, on that point we had something in common. First, it was the bar of soap, the little flower from the vase and the knife. They disappeared and then they reappeared, which for such a methodical and organized man, who ordered the world around him down to the last millimetre, must have been quite unnerving. And now the notebooks detailing his bestial acts in Mauthausen. Where had he put them, he'd be asking himself, and why would he have taken them down from the shelves where they were camouflaged in the covers of normal books? Had someone got onto the boat? No, no one had ever done that and, even if somebody had, that person would have to know very well what he or she was looking for. And even if Heim assumed that somebody had stolen the books, that would never explain the business of losing and finding the knife. Most probably he'd more than once weighed up the possibility of changing the place where he kept the notebooks. What if he'd actually done it and didn't remember?

It was one Tuesday morning, a nice day but a bit chilly to be wearing shorts as Heim was, and I was whiling away the time watching how

241

he took up on deck practically everything he'd kept stowed below. It was strewn with books, sheets, blankets, casseroles and more oilcloth-covered black notebooks that I hadn't found. He was going up and down. In the end, he sat down in the foldaway hammock in which he tended to have a nap after his meals in order to go through every item, one by one, writing it all down in yet another notebook with black covers. Sometimes he clasped his head in his enormous hands and then got on with the job. Everything he was noting down went back to its proper place, and he was at it for several days, morning and afternoon. I watched him at different times, for a while in the morning and then again in the afternoon, always savouring a good espresso in the bar over the way and thinking about Salva and what I'd give for him to be here with me. I'd been tempted to tell Sandra about it, but thought it was better for her not to know. Finally, on the last day, when he'd taken up all his things into broad daylight several times and noted them all down several times, he came to the terrible conclusion that his inventory wasn't panning out the way it should. Looking very purposeful, he left the boat and went off to the garage where he kept his stately black Mercedes.

I was waiting for him. He nosed slowly out of the garage, looking straight ahead without blinking, his face a stony mask under his cap. It was easy to follow him. He might have been driving an impressive tank, but his reflexes were worse than mine, and still worse now that he was feeling so insecure. Bastard, I thought, I hope you start feeling like a pile of shit, a useless crock. I hope you feel your life isn't worth living and that now you have to take some of your own medicine.

He drove out of town and for some twenty minutes after that towards the next town, but before reaching it he turned into a residential zone that I already knew, heading for the Bremer Apartments where Sebastian Bernhardt lived, surrounded by security guards. The Butcher was probably coming to consult him about his problem, which confirmed that, in the hierarchy, the Black Angel ranked above Otto, Alice and Christensen. I felt very agitated. I was starting to understand how this community of invisible people functioned. All this time it was Sebastian who'd prevented them from doing too many stupid things, from exposing themselves unduly, Sebastian who'd found a way of bestowing on them an excessively long life so he wouldn't be left alone in an alien world. He must have suffused them with confidence and kept them united by the bonds of the Brotherhood. He was the one who instructed the young people. He had to be the queen bee and, when the queen bee was dead, the others wouldn't know what to do. In order to give them confidence, he'd had to make them believe that he was invulnerable and that he could make the rest of them invulnerable with a product that was exclusively for them.

After three quarters of an hour Heim came back out from where he'd gone in. His black Mercedes glided through the streets of a planet to which they'd adapted like insects.

I remained there in case Sebastian came out.

## Sandra

I saw him unexpectedly on Thursday when I was leaving for my meeting with Julián. On this occasion I didn't have to give too many explanations when I was going out, because Martín had just turned up with something to tell Fred and Karin in the library-den – their business, Brotherhood things, the usual crap. It was half-past three and, for once, I was going to get to the lighthouse on time. I left with the sensation that this story couldn't last much longer. Julián's money was running out. He didn't want to complain, but sometimes he let it slip that he couldn't afford to keep paying at the hotel and that he practically had to put petrol in the car with an eye-dropper. A man of his age couldn't stand all this hassle for too long either, and I couldn't go on being entangled with these people and their alien world. The time would have to come when the whole thing exploded or we each went our separate ways. I didn't have to decide anything. It would be decided in due course.

I came out of Villa Sol and in the street I felt something whipping my eyes, lashing my brain.

That car!

Inside the car was Alberto doing a crossword puzzle, resting it on the wheel. I stopped, paralysed, sitting on my motorbike.

Alberto!

I called him without moving my lips and he heard me without hearing. He turned his head towards me.

It was still him. The same eyes, the same mouth. He got out of the car. He was wearing dark-blue jeans, a check shirt and a pullover thrown over his shoulders. I was pleased to see he hadn't put on the jacket Frida had given him. He stopped in front of me and I stayed there sitting on my motorbike.

Tousled light-brown hair, forehead and nose red from the wind and sun. He was no beauty. His wallet was sticking out from his back pocket and one of his moccasins was coming undone.

"Your shoelace is undone."

He looked at it without paying attention or bending down to tie it.

"Where are you going?" he asked, as if we'd seen each other only five minutes earlier.

"What's it to you?"

"I'm asking you because it means something to me."

He was only a few metres away from the house, yet hadn't been capable of coming in to see me. It hurt so much that I stopped loving him.

"I don't believe it," I said. "I'll pretend I haven't seen you."

My last shred of pride prevented me from calling him a pig.

"And I'll pretend that I never got out of the car, right?"

"Up to you. You seem to be so sure about what to do and what not to do."

"Yes, I am sure. And you should be too, but you prefer to act like a madwoman without thinking about the consequences."

"You're always threatening me."

"You're being threatened, but I'm not the one who's threatening you. I told you to go, to put this behind you."

I fancied him a lot, wanted him to be the father of my baby, and I also knew that the day I stopped fancying him I'd hate him.

"Everyone's saying the same thing, telling me to go, but where?"

"Everyone? Who else is telling you to go?"

"It's a manner of speaking. I can't go. I have more ties here than I have anywhere else."

"Come on, let's go for a ride on the motorbike," he said, getting on behind me.

"Where do you want to go?"

"To the lighthouse. There's a lovely view from up there."

It was then that I remembered Julián, who, precisely then, would be waiting for me at the lighthouse.

"The lighthouse? Are you sure? You wouldn't prefer to go to the beach or the port?"

"The lighthouse is a quieter place. Besides, there's an enormous cliff and I can throw you over it. Nobody would find you. It's not true, this story that the sea throws up everything it swallows."

I'd started the motorbike. It was windy and it got stronger with speed. I went in the direction of the lighthouse. I couldn't hide the fact that I knew the road very well, that I could almost do it with my eyes shut. Yet I went as slowly as I could. I loved feeling Alberto behind me. He took away the wind, he protected me. It was impossible that he could ever think of doing anything bad to me. It seemed that the whole time I hadn't been with him was lost time, a test.

When we got to the level ground by the lighthouse, the only place to park, I saw Julián's car and knew he'd be in the ice-cream parlour, and that maybe he'd seen me coming through the window. If I told Alberto I needed to go to the toilet and to wait for me a moment, I'd be able to send some sign to Julián, but I didn't want to waste as much as a minute of being with Alberto. I left Julián to get bored and then to leave and go and do whatever he wanted to do. What I certainly wasn't planning to do was to mess up this moment that had dropped on me out of the blue, when I least expected it.

We walked among the wild palms, stepping on pebbles and little rocks, until we were nearly at the edge of the cliff. Immense, mostly blue but green in some patches, the sea spread out from its base to meet up with the sky, far away in the background. Only the two of us were there.

"It seems unreal," he said, referring to the spectacle we had before us, or to us two, or to life in general.

"It seems unreal" were three marvellous words. He took me by the shoulders and then kissed me. It was the kiss I knew, the kiss I was waiting for. I knew it better than the first time because it wasn't a surprise, just the pleasure of its softness and warmth. I could feel his penis pressing against me. He pulled back.

"It can't be now," he said.

I took one of his hands in mine. It was squarish, with strong fingers, rather an insignificant thing in that glorious beauty of sea and sky, but it was the only really important thing, something capable of giving sense to life.

"What about your husband?"

"I'm not married."

"Okay, the father of your baby," he said, slipping his hand out from mine and putting it in his pocket to bring out his cigarettes. He lit one.

"We're not together. I wasn't sure whether I loved him."

"And did he love you?"

"I think so. I feel bad about that."

He suddenly turned his back to the sea.

"I have to go back. This will be our place."

I didn't want to ask him about the girl he'd been seen with on the beach. I didn't want to ask him about Frida either. The other one could be the girl on the beach and I'd be the girl at the lighthouse. I didn't want to spoil my moment, my little spell of happiness.

Julián's car was no longer next to the lighthouse. I wondered if he'd seen us. I would have liked him to have seen us, so I could talk with him about it later, to prolong these sensations somehow. He might have left me a message under stone C, but I couldn't check that now.

Alberto drove and I sat behind, hugging him.


## Julián

The waiting was worthwhile. In the end, when I was about to throw in the towel and go back to the hotel, I saw Sebastian come out accompanied by Martín and the Eel.

Sebastian was more or less the same height as me but not so skinny. He had an elegant style. He was wearing a knee-length black coat with the lapels turned up and an artistically knotted scarf. Adapting to Sebastian's pace, they walked slowly down the street to the cliff and entered the glassed-in restaurant overlooking the sea where I'd watched him and Alice. You could see them from outside, eating oysters and drinking champagne. They were talking and sometimes they laughed. I took up my position next to a car, got the mini-camera out of my pocket and took their photo. At one point I thought Alberto looked in my direction, but then he turned to face Sebastian again.

I went away happy. I was getting closer and closer to Sebastian and I wanted to celebrate it with Sandra somehow, so I went off to the lighthouse feeling more chipper than usual.

She was late and I waited sitting by the usual window. This time I asked for a Diet Coke, and the usual waitress banged it down on the table. I was used to her treating me badly. Despite what people believe, you can adapt to the tyranny and despotism of others. If you think otherwise, go and tell all those people who acclaim their dictators and torturers. The offensiveness of this harpy was becoming familiar.

I drank my Coca-Cola slowly, making it last, as I'd have to pay for Sandra's juice and slice of cake and my funds were at rock bottom. I didn't want to sink all my savings into the Costa Azul hotel and this place. I'd have to keep something in case of emergency and, most important, I had to think about my daughter's future. If only I could have paid for Sandra's snack. I wouldn't have felt as bad about that as I did when I saw her with the Eel, leaning against his shoulder and contemplating the terribly blue and romantic sea.

Through the window I saw them arriving on Sandra's motorbike, but they parked outside my field of vision. After a while, realizing that they weren't coming in, I paid, went out and walked to our bench, and there I saw them, among the palms, facing the sea. I saw them kissing and, right then, I was very happy for Sandra, because, whatever happened, she could take that with her. At the same time I felt a huge emptiness. As is understandable, I would never have dared to look at Sandra as anything but a granddaughter. I swear I've never looked at her in any other way. It was the fact of being left alone, seeing myself being totally and irrevocably excluded from a joyful, marvellous life that left me feeling empty inside, lifeless. I wondered whether I should leave her a note under stone C after they left, but in the end decided not to. I left as I'd come, or rather I left worse than I was when I'd come, and yet, deep down, I was glad, because something that Sandra really wanted had happened to her.


## Sandra

I had another relapse. When I was going back to Villa Sol on the motorbike with Alberto, I kept shivering, which I put down to the emotion of being close to him. When you've waited so long for something and it seems as if it's never going to come, it's too much when it does come. On the cliff near the lighthouse Alberto disarmed me, left me defenceless in every sense.

When we got to the car near the house we found Martín waiting, leaning against the bonnet of the car. It was clear that he wasn't exactly amused about being kept waiting, but it was also clear that Alberto was a little above him in rank, so he couldn't tell him off.

We didn't say goodbye. Alberto didn't give me a chance. As soon as he got off the motorbike, he went over to the car without looking at me. He started talking with Martín and I rode off to the house. We didn't have that moment, tiny as it is, that's always there at the end of everything, and that helps you to remember it all over and over again.

When I got to the gate of Villa Sol, I felt that, given the state of agitation I was in, I couldn't go inside, so I went off towards the beach. I needed to walk fast, to run and use up the energy that wouldn't let me forget about Alberto. I couldn't lock myself up inside four walls with this feeling, because I'd die if I did.

I walked fast along the shore for two hours and, when I couldn't go on, went back to the Norwegians. On the motorbike, my legs kept trembling. I could have tried to see Julián, at the hotel, or in the port where he said he spent quite a lot of time, but I didn't want to talk about anything that wasn't Alberto, or to be obliged to think about anything that wasn't Alberto.

I didn't take any notice of what Fred and Karin were doing when I came in. I couldn't get what they were saying to me either. I went upstairs and lay on my bed. I was sweating. I crossed my hands over my breasts and concentrated on the kiss at the lighthouse.

# 9
# Don't Be Afraid

## Sandra

All through my pregnancy I'd been developing something like a sixth sense. I noticed the changes in the weather and especially if something out of the ordinary was going to happen, something that was going to change me. The baby either seemed more active or went completely still, and this scared me. I had the impression of having been loaded up with sensors without my knowing it. It only took some setback or worry for all the sensors to light up and that was the only thing the child knew in his world. The sensors and the baby were on another plane, on another frequency that anticipated what was going to happen a few hours before it did. Very early in the morning I opened my eyes, totally awake and with a feeling of anguish. I didn't feel like getting up so early, because I didn't want to feel tired during the day, getting exhausted as I went along with all of Karin's whims until it was time to meet up with Julián. I started to read but couldn't concentrate. I had no objective reason for feeling so anxious, at least not beyond the people I already knew and with whom I'd learnt to wake up and go to bed, and yet this dawn was very disagreeable. It brought back the days when I was a little girl waking up to my parents' senseless fighting, after which life turned bitter, as if they had power over the sun, the sky and the plants.

It was also true that I'd been coughing in the night and that the cough itself had probably got me worked up. It could have got worse a few afternoons before, at the door of the hairdresser's when I'd gone outside without putting on my anorak. Maybe it was time to start thinking about a name for the baby. A name is basically useful for calling out to somebody in the street, in order to make the person turn his or her head. Names are nothing in themselves. It all depends on who's bearing them. Ernesto, Javier, Pedro, Jesús, Francisco and a thousand others. But I still didn't know what his face was going to be like, or his voice. Any name might do.

I woke up around ten. I'd gone out like a light as I was running through names. That was fine. The less time I had to see and hear Frida, the better. I got up slowly, put on some trousers to go downstairs and have some breakfast, and, when I opened the door, everything smelt of snow-capped pines. It was still an hour before the squeaky-clean forest sprite departed. Karin and Fred would have had their breakfast quite a while earlier and they weren't around. They must have gone out for a drive along the seafront, or shopping. I had the house all to myself, not counting Frida, who would be keeping an eye on me somehow, even if I couldn't see her. I got up to go and have my milk coffee out in the garden. The plants gave me very positive thoughts, but when I looked away from them something negative was lurking. With Karin and Fred absent, I could go and check out the house. I could go down into the cellar and have a look at the black sun now that I knew what it was. It symbolized, according to Julián, what's hidden behind the shining sun, what we don't see, and its rays were bent to form the swastika and runes. The Nazis believed in these things, in what they invented themselves and what they made use of for their fantasies. Basically it was all about having the upper hand and doing whatever they pleased, and all of the ones I was getting to know had this same trait.

I didn't want to be hanging around there with Frida, so I tidied myself up a bit and started up the motorbike. I might come across Julián in the town or I could go and have a walk along the beach. But just as I was about to head out, Frida appeared. She'd done two small plaits, one on either side of her head, and was wearing rubber gloves.

"You can't go out," she said.

I stayed there staring at her doughy face. I looked her in the eye.

"You have to stay here till they come back. They want to talk to you about something important."

I saw the malign spark flashing in her sky-blue eyes, which would be able to hold my gaze for three or four hours.

"Thank you," I said, going back inside.

I collapsed onto the sofa and picked up the velvet bag with the knitting and the little pullover, which seemed condemned never to have sleeves or a neck. I started to knit. I knitted and coughed, coughed and knitted. I took off my anorak. What did Karin and Fred want to say to me? Frida's face had been fiendishly impenetrable. With those rubber gloves on she was scarier than ever. She could chop me into pieces and then take them off and throw them in the rubbish together with my remains.

I drank some water because the cough was irritating my throat, and I put the anorak on again. I was hot and cold. I didn't want to knit, didn't want anything. There was nothing there that could make me feel at home enough to enjoy stretching out on the sofa and reading a magazine. But I wasn't there for that, and I wasn't going through all this apprehension to throw myself on a sofa and read a magazine. I had a mission, a job to do. Frida and I were struggling on the same ground but not with the same weapons. I had none.

I went up to my room to pass the time. The bed was still mussed up. When I was late getting up, Frida didn't clean my room any more. It was her way of punishing me for my laziness. She couldn't stand me. I'd caught her watching me out of the corner of her eye when she saw me lazing around in an easy chair, or on the sofa, or yawning my way round the house. She hated people like me, parasites probably in her understanding. Frida had such clear ideas about everything that she made you both envious and afraid.

Through the window I saw the Mercedes coming into the garage. That was strange. They hadn't taken the four-by-four but the car they used when they wanted to make an impression or look more formal. They almost always took the Mercedes when they visited Alice and Otto. They knew each other very well, knew what belonged to each person, but even then they didn't want to give any ground when it came to presence and power, so they might have gone to Alice's house or somewhere similar. Maybe they'd gone to sort out some paperwork or simply to the bank. Then I heard snatches of conversation, worked out they were speaking German, and finally I captured Frida's voice mingling with theirs. The situation was making me uneasy. I lay on the unmade bed to think.

I didn't understand what could have happened, but everything in-dicated it had something to do with me. Would it be because of the hotel? Would they have seen me going into Julián's hotel while Karin was at the hairdresser's? I could always say I'd gone nearby looking for somewhere to park and I needed to go to the toilet. They might have seen me with Julián at the lighthouse, or in the town. It could be so many things... But... oh my God!... Perhaps they'd also found out about the syringes. That's what it was. I'd defend myself, saying I didn't know what they were talking about. What was this about used syringes? Surely someone must have thrown them out with the rubbish and the rubbish into a container. I'd ask them how I could possibly join the Brotherhood if they were thinking such things about me. Why would they want to bring into the Brotherhood somebody they believed was capable of stealing used syringes from a rubbish bin? What would I want with used syringes? Did they think I was a drug addict and that I'd used them to shoot up heroin?

I heard light footsteps approaching my door. They weren't the enormous, heavy, slow, solid footsteps of Fred. They weren't Karin's dragging footsteps. These seemed hardly to touch the floor, like a low-blowing wind, like big autumn leaves falling, one after the other. They were like the footsteps of a fairy, or a witch.

She knocked, or rather brushed the door with her knuckles and opened it before I answered. Frida was making her declaration of war, which irritated me, scared me and was going to make my life a lot more difficult. She caught me lying on the bed with almost no time to react.

"Get downstairs," she said. "They want to see you!"

"Why didn't you knock at the door?" I asked as a way of getting my act together.

"I did knock, but you didn't hear me. You must have been asleep."

I could hear in her voice the contempt she had for me, and knew she'd harm me as much as she could. Maybe her feelings for Alberto had something to do with this. If that was the case, I was really glad.

"Why did you say I was sleeping? Were you spying on me through a hole somewhere?" I said, sitting up and speaking as loudly as I could. Something was telling me I had to rebel against Frida and make it clear to Fred and Karin that we didn't hit it off.

"Carrying on like that isn't going to help you," she said, without raising her voice so only I could hear her.

Then I had another coughing attack. Since the visit to the hairdresser's I'd been coughing almost non-stop and now my nerves were making my throat tickle, my chest hurt and my eyes weep, so I could barely get the words out.

"Ever since I came... to this house... you've had..."

I was going to say she'd had it in for me, but just then she went out, slamming the door. The coughing was choking me. I heard water running in the bathroom, which was on the other side of the passage, opposite my bedroom. Frida must have gone to get me a glass of water. I lay face down on the bed to cough better. More steps were coming up the stairs. I needed the glass of water, but I wasn't going to take it from her hands.

"Can we come in?" Karin asked.

"It's open," I said. This was absolutely true, because it was the only room in the house that didn't have a bolt on the inside.

Karin grabbed the glass of water from Frida and held it to my lips. I took a small sip and it relieved me. I mopped up my tears. I was tired and sweaty.

"Calm down now," Fred said. "I'm sure there's an explanation for all this."

"There has to be," Frida added.

"Please be quiet," Karin said, sitting on my bed.

I got up. I didn't want my bed to be full of monsters. I might sleep under the same roof but I needed to have a space as far away as possible from their bodies and their spirits.

"I'm better now," I said, going to the door.

They followed me. The heavy steps, the dragging steps and the rubber steps came down the stairs behind me. By comparison with theirs, my steps were the most normal. I listened to my steps, something I'd never done before, and they were more like those of normal people than theirs.

I went into the kitchen, to terrain that was a little more neutral than my bedroom, and got myself a big glass of cold water. They came behind me, not speaking. Only Frida said something in German, but nobody answered her. I could swear she was saying that I was putting it on so they'd feel sorry for me, that it was pure theatre. She'd be right to some extent, because I wanted to distract them from whatever it was that they'd caught me doing. I didn't want to feel like the condemned prisoner awaiting sentence.

I sat down to drink and they sat down too, except for Frida.

"I'm sure there's some explanation for this," Fred repeated.

Frida looked at the clock. Karin looked at Fred. I drank some more.

"There's an ampoule missing from the box you and Karin brought from Alice's," Fred said.

An ampoule missing from the box? That wasn't my work. I was so amazed I almost burst out laughing.

The three of them were looking at me with very serious faces. I took a while to respond, sitting there with the glass in my hand. Then I very slowly put it down on the table, and when I looked up I met the eyes of that bitch Frida. I didn't want to get my fingers burnt and tried to work out what I should say. Which would be nothing.

"What do you want from me? I don't understand anything."

"Maybe you took it without meaning to, or you took it and put it somewhere else."

"But why would I want to take one of Karin's ampoules? That doesn't make sense."

"We all have to try to find it," Fred said.

"And the other ampoules?" I asked. "Have you used them all up?"

"No, I've still got one left," Karin said. "I wasn't going to start the other box without finishing this one."

"I've never touched these things and I've never even been in your room."

"You do go in there," Frida said. "The other day you went in and dropped this."

She showed me one of the small coloured hair clips I was using to keep my fringe off my face before I got my hair cut.

"You come into my room and you could have taken it from there," I said.

"I found it," Karin said, her voice a little depressed, as if she was sorry to have caught me out.

I had to think fast because, to begin with, I was certain that no clip of mine had ever fallen in their bathroom. Frida must have put it there.

"The clip might have been dragged along by the broom. Frida sweeps my room too."

Karin looked thoughtful.

"Then again, Frida, you might have dropped the box on the floor while you were cleaning and an ampoule was broken, so you want to blame me."

254

I'd just guaranteed for myself the world's worst enemy.

Karin and Fred shook their heads.

"She would have had to take the box out of the chest of drawers for it to have fallen on the floor and, in that case, the box would have been wet with the contents of the ampoule," Fred said.

"I don't know what to say. I don't know anything about this. Maybe Karin used it and didn't remember."

Karin frowned. She didn't like me saying that. Probably Frida had noticed the absence of the two syringes in the rubbish bin and would have thought I had an alibi, so she'd preferred this dirty trick. I couldn't think of any other explanation. She wanted to incriminate me all the way. Then Fred spoke.

"What do you think is in these injections?"

"Vitamins. I suppose it must be a very strong, complete vitamin complex which I wouldn't dare to try because I'm pregnant."

"Maybe you wanted the ampoule for something else," said Frida.

Frida had made up her mind to put an end to all this and was trying to accuse me of being a spy who'd taken the ampoule away as proof. But Karin looked at Fred, and Fred said that was enough, they'd find a way of getting to the bottom of this situation and that Frida could go. Karin hadn't finished with me yet. She still wanted to suck a bit more of my blood and wasn't willing to let Frida spoil her fun before she was ready.

Frida said something in German. I didn't need them to translate it to know she was telling them that she was going to report this. The others nodded.

"If you did this, it'd be better if you told us," Karin said when Frida had closed the door behind her.

"I have not touched those ampoules. I swear it."

I was telling the truth, and I looked them in the face and held their gaze.

"I don't know what could have happened, but it had nothing to do with me."

"Maybe Alice," Karin said, "ordered Frida to take it, thinking that Sandra would immediately get the blame. So she gets one ampoule more and I'm left without Sandra. You know she always wants anything that isn't hers."

"I have to confess something," I said. "I want to be sincere. A few days ago I went into your bathroom. I wanted to put on a dab of

Karin's perfume. I love it, but I was there only as long as that took, and I didn't drop any hair clip. I swear it."

"That changes things," said Fred. "Before you swore that you'd never entered our bathroom and now you say you did. Now you're not to be trusted."

"I didn't swear. I only said I hadn't been in there and I said it to Frida, not to you. I didn't want her to use that information against me."

"You do well to tell us the truth," Karin said, looking reprovingly at her husband. "Since you live here, it wouldn't be surprising if you'd gone into our room and our bathroom sometimes, and it wouldn't be surprising, either, if you'd had a look at my dresses and tried them on."

"No, no, I haven't tried them on. I wouldn't dare do that. They're not mine."

"Do you like them?"

"They're really beautiful. I only saw them once."

"That's normal." Karin was addressing Fred.

"But what is it about this liquid that makes Alice risk putting your friendship in danger?"

"Our friendship is not in danger," said Fred. "We are not united by friendship but by the Brotherhood. There are members who can't stand each other and yet they can't stop being brothers. There is nothing that can separate us for ever."

"So what are we going to do now?" I asked ingenuously, knowing that someone was still testing me: them, Frida or Alice. It was like having to do an exam when you don't know a single answer, because you can't understand the questions either.

I told them I wasn't feeling well, I thought I had the flu and in this disagreeable situation it had got worse, so I was going back to Madrid. I couldn't take it any more, I felt lonely, I was going to have a baby and I was with a family that wasn't my own. And however much they said they were like my grandparents, they weren't, because my real grandparents would have believed me instead of a foreigner. Well, Frida wasn't a foreigner for them. I was the foreigner. They had more faith in their housekeeper than in me. I understood that. I was a new arrival, I wasn't their granddaughter, they'd found me alone and vomiting on the beach and they'd brought me to this house, which Frida had known long before me. As I was talking, my eyes had been filling with tears, and now I'd exploded. And I really wanted to explode. I wasn't their granddaughter. They weren't my grandparents. I was an employee, like Frida, whom they paid, and they paid me too, very well, it had to be said, and that's why I was with them, but not everything can be bought with money. They'd just accused me of stealing and I'd never stolen anything in my life. We'd come to that. I couldn't go on speaking, because I was crying and coughing all at once. Karin's crooked fingers pushed the glass over to me. I drank and I drank and calmed down a little.

"I'm going to play golf. I think better in the open air," Fred said.

I was still caught up in my coughing attack when he came back dressed in his checked trousers, black-and-white shoes and golfing cap. He took his golf bag out of the cupboard in the hallway and left. When I heard the Mercedes leaving, I said, "I'm going to get my things together. It's time to say goodbye."

I went upstairs with a great sense of freedom. They hadn't tried to detain me, I was leaving, and I was freeing myself from this nightmare. I'd eat somewhere, go and lie on the beach till it was time to meet Julián, and then say goodbye to him. Now we'd discovered that the famous liquid was a scam, I'd done my duty to humanity and I didn't have to engage in any more heroism for the rest of my life. I was going to a normal world where people take what a normal doctor prescribes.

I was surprised that Karin, who couldn't bear anybody acting under their own free will, had let me come upstairs. When I got to my room, the window was open, the birds were singing and everything seemed like it was before. I was exhausted by my physical discomfort and by having to get out of this predicament as sincerely as I could, but I had no choice but to pull myself together. The only friend I had here was a wreck and I couldn't trust the rest of them. So I got out my backpack, opened it up, and put my few things in it. I was thinking that Fred and Karin didn't seem anything like the old couple on the beach who helped girls like me and, in that case, how many times had I got it wrong and judged people too kindly or too harshly? But neither can you go through life suspecting everyone who crosses your path just so you can always be right. There are some people who see straight away what lies underneath a face, or a smile. I must admit that I was slow and that's why Fred and Karin had blown up in my face and, in some sense, Julián as well.

With what they'd paid me, I had enough to keep myself for a while. After all this, I was running my hand over the last shelf in the cupboard to be sure I hadn't left anything behind, when I heard Karin's knuckles rapping at the door. Come in, I said before she came in, which was exactly what she was going to do at any moment anyway.

"You mustn't go like this. You're not well, you've got a cold and you might have the flu. Stay a few days more, until you feel better, and when you've recovered we'll take you ourselves to get the bus or the plane or whatever you want. But meanwhile, rest."

I saw Karin's witch's face and it frightened me. I was younger and stronger than her and would win if it came to a tussle, but she frightened me. She knew about terrors I'd never seen and perversions that had never entered my head, and I intuited that, even if we were alone, it wouldn't be easy to win.

"No, I've decided to leave today," I said, putting on my boots and my rucksack on my back. "I want to go before Fred gets back."

"Not so fast," Karin said, grabbing my handbag.

It was a brown suede bag with fringes and a very long strap, so I could cross it over my chest. It was a soft, comfortable bag and very much my style. Santi had given it to me. Everything Santi gave me suited me very well. I was thinking about this stupid stuff as Karin was opening up my bag. It was as if I needed to escape from what was happening right then. I didn't understand why Karin was ferreting around in my bag. This act was too aggressive, even for Karin. And when I reacted, when I was about to tell her to get her dirty twisted hands off my things, she pulled out something wrapped in toilet paper. It was one of the ampoules that she injected.

"I didn't want to believe Frida. I refused to think you were betraying us, and now look... She was right."

"Frida put it there," I whispered. "She's crazy about Alberto and I'm in her way."

"Stop talking nonsense. Right now, Frida will be telling the Brotherhood about what has happened. And how am I going to defend you after what I've seen?..."

"I swear, Karin," I interrupted her, "that I did not take this ampoule or put it in my bag. I swear it by whatever you want."

I couldn't believe I was saying something like that.

"I can't be disloyal to them. You've put me on the spot. It's them or you."

"If I can't do anything to demonstrate that it hasn't been me, then I'm leaving."

"Wait," Karin said, blocking my way with the bag in her hand. "You're in such a bad way you won't even get as far as the corner."

Then she backed off, threw the bag on the bed, walked out and locked the door with the key.

I was dumbfounded.

"It's for your own good, dear," she said from behind the door.

I sat down on the bed and looked out the window. I couldn't see how I could get to the ground. I was on the second floor, quite high up, and there were no pipes nearby to cling to. I didn't want to take risks in my state. I could have tried to kick the door down, though I wasn't sure I had enough strength to break it. Karin had locked me in and was holding me hostage.

I lay on the bed. If only I had supernatural powers and could communicate with Julián. If only he would pick up that something was wrong and come to get me. But how would a man of eighty, who was so thin a child could break his bones, come and get me? If only Alberto would sense I was in a mess and come running to help me. If only he loved me. If only my parents would do what I'd never forgive them for doing in other circumstances and come here to get me, even going to the police if necessary. If only my sister would get pissed off with the tenant and come to speak to him, and he would tell her that I'd been there with an old woman he'd thought was my grandmother, and my sister would be curious enough to come looking for me. Please come and find me, I thought with all my strength. If only the spirit of Salva, this man that Julián talked about, was here in this room to send me signs about how to get out of here, because, being a spirit, he'd see everything and would see the weak point through which I could escape.

Salva, I said, you've been in a concentration camp, you, who were so many times on the brink of death before you really did die, send me the strength and wisdom to get out of this. I'm thinking of you, Salva, about how strong you were and how cunning you were when you had to overcome evil. Get inside my head, Salva, and tell me what I have to do. Let me think with your brain and let me not have to learn everything you learnt so I don't give in to fear.

I'm eighty-seven years old, I thought. I'm eighty-seven years old and I know you people. You've exploited me and tortured me and I know how to stand up to you. One, you are vampires from hell and you can't live unless you're sucking the blood of others. Two, because of that, I should never ever trust you under any circumstances, as you will deceive me and do everything you can to suck my blood. Three, I'll have to become like you so you'll leave me alone. Four, you're creatures of the night, and night cloaks real intentions, real desires...

I was still a daughter of the day and I saw things under the light of day, but let's imagine this light went out. What would these same things be like in the darkness? I closed my eyes. I took out the little bag of sand Julián had given me and squeezed it tight. No, no, it wasn't like closing your eyes, because with your eyes closed you don't see anything. In the darkness you keep seeing things but in another way. You don't see everything as you do during the day but you do see some things that have more luminosity or that stand out for some reason. I closed the shutters and pulled the curtains across, then lay on the bed to see what I'd see. A crack of light came in from under the door. And this line of light, these grains of light, concentrated in my belly. My belly.

The eyes of those who look in the darkness wouldn't see in me the shining of my eyes or the slope of my nose, but they'd see my future son in my belly. So it wasn't madness to think that Karin had exposed herself to my discovering her secrets so she could suck out my time and my energy, so I'd keep her company when she was living exactly as she pleased. Karin had not locked me in here because I had my suspicions about her and Fred and their famous transparent liquid. They could have got rid of me. They did it because they wanted my baby. I tried not to think about it, but the film *Rosemary's Baby* came into my head and I felt really bad. Five. Don't be influenced by evil. The great speciality of evil is making you believe it is more powerful than good.

My baby was protecting me. While he was inside me they wouldn't do anything. I should learn to move in the darkness of evil and see what they saw. I should be more cunning than I'd ever been before and not let myself be blinded by the light.

The only thing they needed was life.

They were looking for anything with life.

\* \* \*

An eternity went by until I heard the street door. Fred had just arrived. He and Karin were talking about me in low voices so I wouldn't hear them. I went over to the door and moved away again when I heard footsteps on the stairs, some heavy, some dragging, now coming along the passage to my room. The key turned and they came in. I was sitting on the bed. I lay down facing the window, turning my back to them.

"Karin has told me what happened and that you can't explain it. Or can you?"

I didn't answer. I was thinking about how I could jump up, run downstairs and get away.

"Let's be sensible. Karin locked you in because she didn't know how to react. She did it to protect you. If it was up to us, we'd let you go but it's not about us. It's about the Brotherhood. If the Brotherhood found out that you were thinking about taking the medicine outside our circle, the situation would get a lot worse for you. Do you understand? We have to think together about what to do."

"We're not even going to ask you about why you wanted the ampoule," Karin said. "To sell it on the black market? Or do you think it's a drug?"

I kept lying there with my back to them and not answering. I had to bite my tongue to stop myself telling them what I knew about the liquid, but when they came closer and I felt them nearer, their breath on the back of my neck, I turned round quickly and got up.

"You know very well that I didn't take the injection. I didn't take it. I didn't take it. This is a trap."

"It would be dangerous for people if this medicine was circulating without any control. It is made only for us," Karin added. "We run the risks of its possible contraindications. We don't mind. But it can't go outside our circle."

"The problem," Fred continued, "is that Frida would have told Alice and Alice would have told Sebastian and, when it gets to that level, everyone is going to be upset."

They couldn't deceive me any more. I saw into their darkness. I saw what they were seeing.

"We need to think what to do," Karin said, sitting on the bed.

"Yes, we have to come up with something," said Fred, scratching his chin.

261

"I've got it." Karin smiled at me. "We'll say it was an error of mine, that I put it in the box that only had one left in it, so there'd be two, and then I forgot."

I didn't say anything.

"But," Fred intervened, "they'll only half-believe that. You'll have to join the Brotherhood so we can keep this episode in the family. From the moment you join the Brotherhood you'll have to observe the hierarchy, the rules, and then we'll all feel more secure, you, us and them."

The darkness told me that if they were so keen for me to join the Brotherhood it was because they'd have me locked up in a prison without bars from then on. The locks would be in my mind.

"There's no other way out," one of them said.

They were in the darkness. In the light was Julián, who'd soon start worrying about me.

"And what do I have to do to join the Brotherhood?"

Both of them smiled. They drew closer to me and put their hands on my shoulders.

"You'll see how good it is," Karin said. "Your life's going to take a spectacular turn for the better. You won't have to worry about anything. You'll be our protégée, and all this," she told me, doing a half-turn around the room, "will be for you when we're no longer here."

"Tonight we're going to invite Alice and Otto to dinner so we can tell them the good news, and maybe we'll phone Sebastian as well. He might come too, since it's about you. We'll see."

At the dinner they talked about my joining the Brotherhood, although I didn't manage to take anything in because I was very tired and my vision was blurry. Halfway through, I said I didn't feel well and Sebastian stood up and pulled out my chair for me.

# 10

# No One Sees Us

## Julián

Martín was taking Sebastian to and from the Nordic Club, banks, a law firm and on longer trips. The Black Angel was spending a lot of time in the back seat of the car checking through papers. Martín also accompanied him to the cliff-top restaurant. Sometimes he ate with him and sometimes he waited outside. It was one of the times when he was alone that I took the opportunity to go over to his table. I told him my full name and asked if I could sit down for a moment.

Just as I imagined, Martín came rushing over, but Sebastian signalled with his hand that he was not to bother me. He reacted as I'd expected, like a gentleman. Martín whispered something in his ear as he kept looking at me. Sebastian grimaced in disgust, whether because of the close proximity of Martín's voice or because of me, I wouldn't know.

I formally introduced myself. I told him I was a Spanish republican who had been in Mauthausen the last year of the War and that I'd joined an organization that hunted down Nazis. He listened very attentively.

He took an oyster from the tray where they nestled in crushed ice and invited me with a gesture of his hand to do the same. I declined, also with my hand. He offered me champagne. I let him pour me a glass but I didn't drink it.

"It doesn't agree with me," I told him, and it was true.

"I am sorry you had to go through that," he said.

"Are you really sorry?" I enquired in the same tone, the tone of a conventional, even friendly conversation. To some, we might have looked like old acquaintances, which to some extent was true.

"Why would I not be sorry? It was never my aim that people should suffer. I was fighting for a better world. The world always improves

263

when some people take the reins and guide the rest. People in general don't know what they want."

"People didn't want what you wanted, so you lost."

"The world lost. The human species lost. We wanted to shun mediocrity, wanted to make a leap to excellence, which was achieved in many cases as many people have been favoured by our efforts. However, what you say is true. We lost the War."

"You're predators. You were robbers, taking for yourselves the efforts and talents of other people. You stole the lives of others, although, of course, you didn't call it life but human material."

"There was some immoderation. I never agreed with that."

"Was it immoderation to kill millions of people?"

He thought about it while he savoured the oyster flesh.

"Do you know who I am? You haven't made some mistake?"

"I doubt it. Fredrik and Karin Christensen, Otto Wagner, Alice, Anton Wolf, Elfe, Aribert Heim or the Butcher of Mauthausen, Gerhard Bremer and Sebastian Bernhardt and a few others. It's a good story. This town could become famous. Your guards, Martín, Alberto and the rest won't be able to gag the press."

"We have no fear of the press."

"And justice?"

"Who can bring us to justice at this stage of life?"

"I'm not referring to that justice, but to the justice that contrives to keep a balance in the universe, making sure there is the proper amount of helium so we can exist and the proper proportion of good and evil, of suffering and pleasure that makes life possible. You destroyed the balance."

"Nowadays," he said, inclining his body as far as he could towards me, "it is very easy for you to judge because we lost, it turned out badly, but imagine for a moment that we won. The balance you speak of would have been achieved because balance is order, beauty and purity."

"I've been looking for you for a long time now. I need to speak to you. I need you to understand me."

Sebastian assented and he didn't seem to think it appropriate to take another oyster. He crossed his hands on the linen tablecloth.

"There's no time to go backwards now. This is the moment of truth. I want to know whether you understand my suffering, my humiliation, my pain at being reduced to human material."

He looked me in the eye, taking me very seriously.

"It gives me no pleasure to think that you suffered, but in periods of thoroughgoing historical transformation of reality there is no time to sift the chaff from the grain."

"And your duty was to transform reality, to turn it into something else."

"Exactly. I always believed I came into the world to change it. My life had a goal, a mission. Otherwise, my birth would have been absurd. National Socialism gave me the chance to act."

"Did you have an ideal world in mind?"

"Yes, a beautiful planet."

"In the camp where I was there was no beauty. Do you think Heim's experiments on us were beautiful?"

"We didn't have time to see the results. The results are what count. Perhaps at some other point in history…"

"Neither one of us is going to see it."

"I visited your camp once," he said. "It was in the spring of the year you said you were there. It had snowed heavily."

It was terrible to share anything with that man, but I was one of the people who could barely lift a shovel that spring.

"I didn't think about your suffering. I didn't even think about you. I saw you all without thinking. That's how things were. I was wearing an SS uniform and you were in the striped prisoners' uniform. We were part of an established order that was impossible to break. There was nothing to think about. We had found a balance. Do you understand?"

"And what do you think now? The world has changed without you."

"It was a bitter blow, because I am absolutely convinced that society has erred. I am convinced that everything would have been more perfect now."

"And do you understand that I hate you and your people, and that, in these last days of your lives, I want to see you suffering more than I had to suffer?"

"Am I to suppose that I am being bitten by a rabid dog?"

"But I'm not a dog. I wouldn't bite you. I'd do something worse."

"What I did to you was not for personal reasons but for reasons of a higher order that are beyond good and evil. That is why you are behaving like a dog and I am not."

He was serious, convinced of what he was saying. All of them had clung to such ideas and programmes to exonerate themselves from guilt.

"Don't you accept any kind of responsibility for all those deaths, those millions of murders?"

"Guilt, remorse and repentance hold back human progress. Do you feel much remorse when they slit a cow open or shear a sheep to use its wool? If one sees the objective and the way there clearly, and the objective is good, globally, as they say nowadays, then one must not hesitate."

"And you think I'm supposed to understand you?"

"That would be all but impossible. You have been on the side of the victims."

"What I find impossible is that nobody, not a single one of you, has been tormented by having taken part in your atrocities."

He pondered that for a while. He'd finished his coffee and he sipped a little more champagne.

"Hardly anyone is tormented by what he has done, but rather by what he has not done, what will be left undone when he dies. Take the case of poor Elfe, who said she drank to forget, but that might not be true. One always looks for excuses to justify one's vices."

Poor Elfe. He said her name as if it was of no importance, because he couldn't imagine that I knew her. Sebastian, I thought, you don't know it all.

"She doesn't drink any more?"

"If she is still drinking, it will be somewhere else without obliging us to deal with her mental debility."

"I don't know if you're telling the truth, and if you don't tell me the truth now the mark you leave on the world will always be blurry. You won't have managed to be totally real."

He agreed with a slight inclination of his head. He was taking our conversation extremely seriously.

"You are not mistaken. Now, for better or worse, we are invisible. No one sees us, except you, of course."

"If you get your people to go after me now," I said, "your story of serving a higher cause will be a lie. If you kill me, it will be for purely personal reasons, because I've unearthed you and endangered your way of life."

He agreed again. I didn't know whether his affirmation meant that he was going to kill me or whether I was right. I waited for some sign.

"There is a girl who joined our group not long ago," and he gave me an inquisitive look that make my hair stand on end. "Her name is Sandra. She has little idea of what she has got into and she is not one of us. She is a fresh rose that will very soon be wilting in the mediocre world in which it is her lot to live. She will look for a job that does not fulfil her, a husband, she will have children – indeed, I believe she is pregnant – and she will grow old without enjoying her life. We may be able to save her from all that. One has to help. Not everybody knows how to find salvation. People do not know their destiny."

I didn't say anything, pretended not to be paying much attention, and that the name Sandra meant nothing to me. Would the Eel have told him that Sandra was secretly meeting me? If not, why would he have mentioned her?

I left him having another coffee. He had a cast-iron constitution. I was quite wound up. I'd had to restrain myself so much in order not to punch him or smash a glass over his head that my hands were shaking. Outside, in the car, Martín was waiting for him and, seeing me leaving, followed me with his eyes. I was almost certain that Sebastian wasn't going to tell him who I was, because, basically, I was from the world that he'd lost, and he'd be wanting to talk with me again. At some point in the conversation I wondered what Salva would be doing in my place and I think he would have partly approved.

Salva was much smarter than me and he would probably have had Sebastian on the ropes, would have seeded doubts and would have demolished him from within. In the same way as he'd known how to encourage me so often, just as he convinced me that life is always worth living that day I'd tried to commit suicide, he would have made Sebastian see that his plan was always, absolutely always, utter imbecility. I, in contrast, had offered him arms he could use to fortify himself.

I felt terrible. Another lost opportunity. I'd left him savouring his glass of champagne and thinking about how we, the winners, had actually lost, because we were fools. I got to my car then drove off past Sebastian's luxurious apartment complex, thinking that at least Operation Heim was bearing fruit. Talking had never been my forte. I liked talking trivia with Raquel, about what had happened when I went out to buy the newspaper, or discussing the television news, or exchanging views on a film, calling her darling and her calling me idiot in the same tone she used to call me love. Using words seriously had always intimidated me slightly, because Salva and his magnificent dialectics always came to mind. Salva should have been the one who spoke with Sebastian. Not me.

## Sandra

Karin rarely came to my room because she was scared of catching my flu. I coughed as loudly as I could so she'd keep that in mind, though the alternatives to Karin were the terrifying Frida or Fred, who tended to appear like a dear old grandfather bearing juice and chocolate. I only wanted to sleep and think about Alberto. My slight fever put me in contact with him, and I wanted to see him so badly I could hardly bear it. I felt in the grip of a passion I couldn't control, maybe because it was a way of fighting this over-the-top mess I was now in. So I got out of bed and got dressed. Was it morning or afternoon? Who cared? I went down the stairs, half in a trance. I wasn't asleep and I wasn't awake. When I got to the last step, a surprised Karin asked me where I thought I was going. I didn't answer. I asked her where I might find Alberto.

After thinking it over for at least five minutes, Karin asked me why I wanted to know.

"To talk with him," I said.

I could have answered her in another, more roundabout way, but I wasn't capable of such a feat, so I'd got to the point.

"About what?"

"I don't know. I'll think of something."

She smiled and got that crafty look in her eyes.

"You like that boy …"

And without giving me a chance to answer, she went on, "No, you don't like him. You're in love." She paused. "Well, I'm sorry, but you've fallen in love with the wrong person."

I listened to her with real anxiety. For once, what this bossy old windbag had to say interested me. It was a matter of life and death.

"He's got a girlfriend. He's been seen kissing a girl on the beach. I prefer to tell you before you get too carried away."

This information fitted with what Julián had told me. It seemed that everyone had seen Alberto kissing this girl, who, according to Julián's description, was nothing to take your breath away.

Karin was really into it. This was a new ingredient in her life. One of her romance novels was coming true.

"You're pregnant and it's not good for you to get upset. Aren't you aware of your state? How could you get it into your head that, out of the millions of girls your age running round here, he'd choose you precisely?"

Karin was going too far. She was a bitch, but she was dragging truths out of my head that I didn't want to face.

"I didn't say I wanted anything with him."

"Then why do you want to see him? You can't fool me."

I almost told her that he'd kept the dog I'd tried to give her, and wanted to know if it was okay. Luckily I didn't open my mouth but kept quiet and had enough time to pull myself together. I didn't let myself get trapped by the moment or by wanting to protect my self-esteem from any more battering. Before loosening my tongue, I preferred to get carried away by the fever and self-pity so I started to cry.

I sat down on the sofa and cried my eyes out. I was overcome with tiredness. She looked at me as if she was watching a film. She sat down next to me and caressed my hair. I could smell that very expensive perfume that impregnated any place she went and that I was hoping would go off to the next life with her.

"I want to see Alberto. I want to know if he feels anything for me," I said.

"If it was Martín, I could do something, but I can't in the case of Alberto. He's very much his own man, very serious, and I wouldn't dare to say anything to him. Although," she said with a nasty smile, "something does occur to me. If you joined the Brotherhood, he'd have to come, because he's the right-hand man of Sebastian, our leader."

I lay down full length on the sofa. I was dying to tell Karin that the injections that were costing her all her jewels could be bought in any chemist's shop. I was dying to tell her that they were pulling a fast one on her and if she didn't believe me she could get them analysed, and that maybe Alice was keeping the real ones for herself, but I didn't want to waste such juicy information. I wanted to keep it for some critical moment when I urgently needed to strike the killer blow. Then I think I went to sleep.


## Julián

Life is surprising. It was the only sure thing about life that I'd stowed away over the years. Life was cruel and surprising, monotonous and surprising, marvellous and surprising. Now it was time for it to be simply surprising.

It happened when I got back to my room after monitoring the *Estrella* and Heim's movements on deck. I came back happy, because I could see he was going downhill by the day. He kept moving up and down from cabin to deck in a state of confusion. He didn't take it easy after his feast like he used to and, whenever he set off to the market to buy the fish he was so fond of, he'd come back at least twice to make sure everything was well locked up. He looked around him to see if anyone was watching him – he wasn't far wrong about that – and the last time he took out his imposing Mercedes he scraped it along one side. He would have been going to see Sebastian, blubbering and begging for more injections. What he probably wouldn't tell him was that he suspected he'd been exposed, because if he was exposed, the rest of them would be too, and then he'd be a danger to the whole group.

What happened is that Roberto pretended not to notice when I greeted him as I walked past on my way to the lifts, and when I got to my door I surprised Tony, the hotel detective, slipping something underneath it.

He was startled to see me.

"I was asked to leave you a message. You'll find it when you open the door."

"That's very kind of you. The chambermaid could have brought it," I said, making it clear that I knew that, whatever it was, he was involved.

At least he hadn't gone in. The transparent bits of paper were in place. He must have been well aware that there was nothing of interest inside. When I went in, I picked up a folded piece of paper but didn't read it immediately. I drank some water first, then went to the toilet, took my shoes off and lay on the bed. At this stage of my life I knew that whatever might be waiting for you round the corner, it's better if it comes on you with some things shipshape.

And while I was doing all this, my head was trying to work out who the note could be from and, although I was almost certain it would be from Sandra and that it wasn't prudent to have let it fall into Tony's hands, to my surprise and relief I found it had been written by... Sebastian.

I gave a start on the bed. Sebastian wanted to see me. Would I like to meet him in the same restaurant as last time? Could I go there at one thirty tomorrow afternoon for lunch? He hoped I'd accept his invitation this time.

I folded the note over. I folded it twice and put in my trouser pocket.

A thousand stupid ideas ran through my head about how we should have arranged to meet in a place chosen by me, and maybe he'd repented after all...


## Sandra

I was so weak that they'd stopped locking me in. I got up and staggered to the bathroom. I had a stomach upset plus fever that I put down to the flu and was spending all day in bed. Frida was making me eat and drink and I started to fear that they wanted to poison me, although at bottom something told me that they wanted my son for the Brotherhood and they wouldn't hurt him. I threw up my breakfast and the lunchtime soup in the handbasin. It was very big, made of beautiful local ceramic ware with yellow sunflowers. The walls were covered with a nubbly silky material, also yellow, and there were some old-fashioned wall lamps either side of the mirror. I spattered the yellow fabric with bits of fish and tried to clean it up with toilet paper, but my head was woozy. I picked up as much as I could from the basin with a lot of toilet paper, cursing myself for not getting my head over the toilet bowl, and I couldn't stop thinking that Frida would have to clean it up. I was terrified she'd get even more pissed off with me.

I hardly saw Karin. Fred came up sometimes to make sure I was still alive. I only wanted to sleep and in my dreams I saw terrible things and had nasty sensations that made me open my eyes all of a sudden. I never dreamt about Alberto's kiss but, when I was awake, scenes of the lovemaking we should have been into right then kept sneaking into my head. I saw him naked above or underneath me, but I didn't have enough details to see him totally naked. Then I quickly imagined him dressed in the clothes I knew. I liked him a lot like that and his trousers, his slightly crumpled shirt and the memory of his smell got me very excited. In my normal life, before I went to bed with anyone, I wondered, without really thinking about it, what it would like with him inside me, what his penis would be like… Yet, with Alberto, no such questions occurred to me. With Alberto, what I liked was him and everything that made him the way he was. I imagined myself in perpetual embrace with him, glued to him, and ended up very frustrated because I had nothing, and then I went back to sleep.

Except now, right now as I was closing my eyes, I heard his voice scraping at the closed door, and I opened them again.

"Sandra, are you all right?"

I opened my eyes wider, not daring to breathe. It was very strange that Alberto should have come up to this room and that he should know I was in such a pitiful state. Who would have told him that this room was like a prison for me? I couldn't believe what I thought I was hearing.

"Sandra."

My name passed through the wood and came to me.

I sat up in bed. My head was going round and round, like when I drank more than two gin-and-tonics.

"Yes," I said.

"I want to see you. I think I love you," he said.

I love you? Had he said it or did I want to hear it?

"Me too," I said.

Then I heard a voice that was different to Alberto's. It sounded like Martín's. The two voices mingled as if in an argument and they moved away. I let my head drop onto the pillow and tried to remember Alberto's I-love-you as I'd heard it, spoken softly from the other side of the door. I love you. I love you. I love you. And what was I doing?

## Julián

Before going to see Sebastian, I drove past Villa Sol in my car. It seemed strange that so many days had gone by with no news of Sandra. I was seriously worried. I was apprehensive. She hadn't come to our appointments and hadn't left any message in our lighthouse letterbox and neither had I received any message from her at the hotel. She knew how to get in and go up to my room without being seen to slip a piece of paper under my door. Nothing. None of that had happened.

The windows of the second floor and the loft of Villa Sol were closed. I had no way of finding out whether Sandra had left unexpectedly. She could have found a way of leaving me some explanation. Then again, if she'd had to flee, that wouldn't have been so easy. If it wasn't for the fact that I might be putting her in danger, I was tempted to try to find the Eel to ask him about her. The truth is I didn't know what to do. They had my photo, they knew me and I couldn't turn up at their house just like that. I therefore went on to Bremer Apartments, which, as I'd suspected, belonged to Gerhard Bremer, another Nazi who played golf with them, a rich builder who'd got away without as much as a hair on his head getting ruffled. Sebastian would certainly have felt safe living there, yet it still seemed stupid for somebody of his intelligence, unless he believed that nobody would get the idea of looking for him there. It hadn't occurred to me of course.

I parked nearby. With the sun striking the glass, the restaurant looked as if it was about to take off and fly over the cliff. At the door, Martín informed me that he was sitting at a table at the back. It was very comfortable not even having to ask for him.

At the back table, in a nimbus of diabolical luminosity, Sebastian had a cigarette in his hand. I believe he was sporting it more to complete his image than to smoke it, and indeed, at no point did I see him take it to his lips. Seeing me, he gestured to me to sit down.

"I have ordered black rice with lobster," he said. "Naturally, if you prefer something else, I shall ask them to bring the menu."

I told him that his choice was fine by me, but didn't tell him that I had no intention of tasting it, not a single grain of rice, nothing paid for with his money.

"I didn't expect that you'd want to see me," I said. "Well, actually I did expect it deep down but I'm not sure why."

"We will never understand one another. Reconciliation is impossible. You do not forgive and I do not repent. I think there was a moment when we failed to keep reality in sight. That is all."

"And that's why you've got me to come here?"

The waiter started to fill the table with food. The only thing he didn't do was fall on his knees before Sebastian. He didn't look at me.

"I have got you to come here because I want to ask you to do something for Sandra, the girl who lives with the Norwegians." He too called them that, just like Sandra and me. "She is ill and I would not like anything bad to happen to her. That is all in the past now. We lost. Useless damage is not good for anyone. We know she is your mole, your contact inside the group. Take her away. We shall not live for ever. Take her away and get her to a doctor."

"I met Sandra on the beach when she was already living with the Norwegians. I was investigating you people and I came across her. We became friends but she doesn't know what I'm doing. She thinks I'm just some old man who reminds her of her grandparents."

He looked pensive. He passed me the trays but I took nothing, so he put them back where they were while he was pondering whether I'd told him the truth.

"She suspects nothing?"

I wasn't going to give him any ammunition against Sandra. I had no intention of admitting the truth. In cases like this you have to deny, deny and deny until you die.

"Nothing at all. She likes you a lot. She calls you the Black Angel. She hasn't got a clue about the SS."

"Then why has she never invited you to the Norwegians' house?"

"She has invited me. I was the one who made up excuses about not going there. You people will have to convince her to leave. I don't have any compelling arguments, and anyway, it's quite a while since I saw her."

"This girl is marvellous," Sebastian said. "Why does she call me Black Angel?"

I shook my head.

"Maybe because she saw you at night, in the moonlight, and she thought you seemed better than the rest of them."

"Better?" he asked with a sceptical, sardonic, disagreeable smile. "I am like them, and they are no worse than a lot of people walking round the street."

"Well, I've lived for a long time and I've never known anybody worse."

They filled our plates with an aromatic serving of black rice, which I didn't try. He took a couple of mouthfuls and left it. This time they'd served red wine and water. He wet his lips with the wine and drank water. I was thirsty but didn't drink any.

"Let me tell you something," he said, wiping his mouth with a linen serviette. It seemed a pity to crumple it. "We have a traitor in the group and I am glad it is not Sandra. I am glad that she will be spared some kind of accident. I am glad that she is pure and happy."


## Sandra

They took me downstairs with two of them holding me up. I was dizzy with fever and weakness. At the foot of the stairs some faces I recognized were waiting for me, and there were others I'd never seen in my life, but they must have been members of the Brotherhood. There were a few guys like Martín, and Martín himself, a man with white hair with two or three others who looked Spanish, a couple of other foreigners, and the rest looked familiar. I closed my eyes so the faces wouldn't melt together.

"Do you feel all right?" Karin's voice asked as sweetly as possible.

I shook my head. How could I feel all right? It was a ridiculous question. She knew perfectly well how ill I was, but she wanted to throw a party and any pretext was good enough for her.

I'd managed to get dressed, making a huge effort. Actually Frida dressed me. She put on one of the two dresses I had hanging in the wardrobe because all the rest was jeans, T-shirts and pullovers. On this occasion she, who normally didn't speak, made all sorts of comments about my clothes, my mountain boots, my hairdo, my piercings and my tattoos. Since it was difficult for me to raise my arms to get the dress on, she roughly shoved me around me until I got pissed off and told her to get her hands off me, and I wasn't in the mood for ceremonies. Fuck off, I told her. Fuck off the lot of you and leave me alone, I said, half-lying sideways on the bed, with the dress only half on.

"I'm going to give you an aspirin," she said.

"Forget about giving me an aspirin. I can't take anything."

Her eyes were bright. They were so blue and so shiny that they looked a lot like the little globes that my mother hung around the terrace at Christmas time. She wanted to kill me but she couldn't. There were a lot of people downstairs waiting to see me.

"Okay, let's have this party in peace. I'll treat you well and you do what I tell you. Let's see, one arm here… The princess is ready," she said, making me sit on the edge of the bed. Frida was very strong. The muscles in her arms were like balls.

Since, in her opinion, the mountain boots didn't go with the floral dress I'd worn for Karin's birthday, we settled for the platform-sole sandals, though this was no weather to be wearing them. But I already had the flu, so what the hell? Then she went to the bathroom and came back with some blusher and a brush, cussing me all the while.

"Now you look halfway normal."

She called Fred and the two of them got me downstairs. I looked for Alberto but couldn't see him. It was then that Karin cynically enquired whether I was all right. I was shivering and she put her shawl that reeked of perfume around me.

"It's always colder in the cellar," she said.

I didn't like hearing about the cellar. I wasn't mad about cellars. In films the cellar's where the worst things happen. It's where somebody is locked up or where they kill somebody or where they hide the murder weapon. In all the time I'd been living in that house, I'd only been in the cellar once, and I never went back.

The only good thing was that they were all being nice to me. They asked how I was feeling and the Black Angel came over and kissed my hand, after which he held it for a moment in his.

"She has a temperature," he said to someone. "I believe she is not well enough to go through with this ceremony. She will not understand anything."

"The time is ripe, believe me," Fred said.

Between the two of them, Frida and Martín got me down to the cellar.

It was certainly colder there than upstairs. It was a dank cold.

They all took up position around the sun engraved in the floor and stuck me in the middle. I saw Alberto, who was staring at me and very serious. Alberto had come. He was here. I ran my hands through my hair in a reflex gesture of trying to look as good as I could. I couldn't explain to myself how it was that I hadn't seen him before when I was seeing him now. Then the Black Angel (and now I understand why I got the idea of calling him that) pronounced something that sounded like a prayer. It went more or less like this: "Sun of wisdom that illuminates the true world, the world of spirits, through you Sandra consecrates her soul. You are concealed behind the golden sun that lights the material world. We wish to ascend to your light, to the light of wisdom, so we may reach illumination and true life. Beyond the heavens and in the depths of the heart, in a small cavity, the universe reposes, a fire burning within and radiating out in all directions. Darkness disappears and night and day no longer exist. Beyond the rampart that sustains the world there is no night, no day, no old age, no death or pain, no good deeds or bad deeds. Beyond the rampart the blind man sees, wounds are healed, illnesses are cured and night becomes day."

I started to tremble and thought I was going to faint, which obliged them to cut short the ceremony. It seemed that the most important part had been completed.

The Black Angel laid his hands on my shoulders.

"You belong to us and we belong to you. You will know our secrets and we shall know yours."

"All right, thank you," I answered, not having a clue what to say. They all looked at me as if expecting something more. Maybe I should have prepared something, but nobody had said anything about that or, if they had, it hadn't sunk in.

"I'm sorry," I added. "I am very happy but I'm cold."

Alberto took me by the arm and helped me to go upstairs to the entrance hall. Everything was set out for them to have a few drinks. Alberto didn't stop but kept pushing me upstairs.

"Now, get into bed and don't talk to anyone," he said. "Rest as much as you can."

"I love you," I said, answering the ghostly I-love-you of some days back. Days? How much time had gone by?

When we got to the door of my room, Frida was there watching us.

277

"I'll take care of that," she stated, pulling me out of Alberto's hands. "You get downstairs with the others."

Alberto didn't let me go. I felt how his hands stayed on my arms till the last moment. Then I felt how they'd gone and I felt utterly alone.

Frida dragged me over to the bed and I half lay on my side without even taking my sandals off.

"I need to see a doctor," I told her.

"Don't worry. One will be coming up later."

She was good enough to cover me with a blanket and then she went out. This time I didn't hear her turning the key in the lock. Not that there was any need to. Where would I go in the state I was in? How was I going to escape when I was in the midst of such a concentration of enemies? I curled up and tried to forget the whole thing, although something was bugging me and it was this story about a doctor coming up to see me.

I must have been fast asleep, because it was very difficult for me to move and open my eyes. I was dreaming about people talking. And, when I finally managed to get away from those voices and wake up, I thought I was going into another nightmare when I saw looming over me the faces of Fred, Karin and the Butcher, who was preparing an injection. This couldn't be real. This couldn't be happening to me. I laughed and, in a matter of seconds, switched to crying. I was burning.

"I don't want it," I said.

"My dear," Karin said, "this will make you better. He knows what he's doing."

No! No! No! I screamed with an anguish that, before this, I'd only ever known in nightmares. No! I screamed at the top of my voice and woke up. This time I really was awake. I pinched myself to make sure. Sometimes I'd pinched myself in dreams when I wasn't sure if I was asleep or awake, but never consciously like now, except that now I felt so bad that I had my doubts as to what my real state was.

Needless to say, Fred, Karin and the Butcher were standing there looking at me:

"Dear girl," Karin said. "You've got a high fever."

The Butcher stretched out his hand towards me. It was enormous and full of tendons, like tree roots. I wanted to hide under the blanket, I wanted to turn invisible and I wanted to go missing. He pulled the blanket slightly aside, looking for my arm, but my arms were glued to my body, like two bars of iron. Fortunately he didn't try to separate them. He took my wrist with finger and thumb. I closed my eyes and started thinking about possible names for the baby.

"She's got a high temperature. Thirty-nine point five degrees. You'll have to put her in a bath."

"Very well. I'll tell Frida to get it ready," Karin said.

I didn't open my eyes till they all went out.

Then I got changed as best I could. I put on my trousers, mountain boots and a pullover. I put my documents in the backpack. Then I threw up in the bathroom, on the floor I think, and washed my face with cold water.

I opened the window and threw my backpack into the garden. Now what? My head was whirling. I put my hand in my trouser pocket and tightly squeezed the little bag of sand Julián had given me. I could try to get hold of one of the branches near the window and swing down on it. How easy everything seems in your imagination, and how hard to do. The branch wasn't that close and the jump didn't seem a sure thing either, but I wasn't going to let them give me a bath. What kind of bath? A bath of water? Coming out of the Butcher's mouth, the word "bath" sounded terrifying. I went back inside, wet a towel and put it round my head. Fever, go away, I said. I sat on the window sill. From up there I could see a shadow with a red point, like a burning cigarette, moving around below. I waited for it to go and then started trying to reach the branch. Until some arms surrounded me from behind. I tried to get them off me. Then they felt familiar.

"Take it easy. Don't even think about jumping. You could hurt yourself."

It was Alberto, and if I couldn't trust Alberto, life wasn't worth living. I went back into the room. The wet towel had helped and I was thinking more clearly.

"I want to get away. They're going to give me a bath."

"It's to get your fever down."

"I've got it down. Help me. I've got to get out of here. I need to see a proper doctor."

He looked at me, very serious and sad.

I took off the towel and ran my hand through my wet hair.

"Okay. I'm going to help you get down. First I'll jump. Then I'll bring the branch closer to you. After that I'll get you from underneath by the legs. Let's go."

Alberto jumped for the branch and then dropped to the ground. I was scared the branch would break, but it didn't. Frida must be coming now, although she might have been waiting for all the guests to leave before giving me the bath. So when I found the branch with my fingers, I grabbed hold of it as tight as I could. With my last bit of strength I hung there swinging. In those few seconds, my body, my joints, my vertebrae were all stretching and it was a very nice feeling, but when I dropped, Alberto couldn't get hold of me in time so I fell and hurt my side. Then I panicked.

Alberto acted fast. He slung my left arm round his neck and put his arm round my waist. He was taking my weight. We left quickly. He'd parked the car some distance from the house and all the way there I was painfully repenting everything I'd done. It wouldn't have mattered if I'd only put myself in danger, but I'd involved an innocent creature whom I was supposed to be protecting.

We went into the hospital and, after Alberto explained to a nurse behind a counter that I had fever, possibly flu, that I was pregnant and that I'd fallen, she sent us to a waiting room. Five minutes later Alberto said he had to go. He told me not to worry about anything because they'd look after me here and he'd come back as soon as he could. Then I closed my eyes and everything started to spin.

## Julián

Even after everything that was happening to me, the last thing I would have expected was to see the Eel coming into my room. I nearly died on the spot. All of a sudden I heard someone fiddling with the lock on the door and, before I could even get out of bed, I saw him coming towards me. I saw death coming for me. I was leaning back on two big pillows, in my pyjamas and thick-lensed glasses, reading a newspaper. I'd had a light dinner and had taken my seven mandatory pills. I was so relaxed it was difficult for me to make any movement.

"Take it easy. I just want to talk to you."

The Eel watched how it took me an eternity to pull the blankets off, stick my spindly shanks out of the bed and get my feet into the slippers that were so precisely positioned I didn't have to look when I put them on. I didn't want my feet to be cold when I got up to go to the toilet.

"You've got to hurry," he said. "You must go to the hospital. Sandra's there. She's in a bad way."

He spoke like a telegram so I wouldn't get confused by any superfluous words, so I'd understand him as clearly as possible.

"What happened?" I asked, trying to grasp the situation.

"I took her there. She had to escape from Villa Sol, through the window."

"Through the window?"

At last I was waking up. I could picture the windows on the second floor where Sandra's room would have been.

"Through the window," I repeated. "And you, how did you get in here?"

"Very easily. There's no security in these places. Come on, get dressed and go to the hospital. I have to get back to the Christensens' house. Will you do that?"

I was getting the shirt I'd worn that day from the coat hanger. I had to take off my pyjama top in front of him and of course he stared at my scrawny arms. I thought I saw a flash of compassion and admiration on his face. When he got to my age he'd realize that you simply do what you can at each moment of your life, and there's nothing heroic about that.

To speed things up, he helped me to put my shirt on.

"Where are your shoes?" he asked, looking around as I took my pyjama pants off.

"In the bathroom."

I always left them there with the socks inside.

"She hurt herself when she jumped. She hit the ground in a bad position," he informed me as he brought my shoes to me. Then he hurried out of the room, giving me no time to ask anything.

I only had to put my lenses in. I ran the shaver quickly over my face and took two doses of my medication with me.

It was a damp night. When I got to the hospital, they told me Sandra was being examined. They asked if I was a relative of hers and I said I was. I told them I'd be looking after her.

I knew what an examination in the casualty department consisted of. They put you in a compartment boxed off by curtains. They take blood and urine samples for testing and put you on a drip. I asked if I could go in to keep her company, but they wouldn't let me. Suddenly I was afraid that she was unconscious and they hadn't realized she was pregnant. They might take an X-ray. They might be that stupid. I couldn't let that happen. Then again, the Eel hadn't told me she was unconscious. In any case, I went over to the counter.

"Please tell the doctors that this girl's pregnant."

"They know their job," the nurse answered. "Don't worry."

Don't worry, don't worry. The worst things in life happen because you don't worry. I sat in the waiting room. Why had she escaped through the window? She should have left through the door ages ago. Not through a window.

I was so anxious to know how she was, so wanted some doctor to come out and speak to me, that I didn't dare to go and get myself a coffee from the machine in the corridor. When I finally decided to go, I told the staff at the counter what I was doing, but there was no guarantee that they'd actually listen to me. So when I came back, at the risk of being considered a pain in the neck, I asked if they'd called me while I was at the coffee machine.

"I'll check," the nurse said, picking up the phone. "Yes, you can go in."

I downed the coffee in one gulp, burning my tongue, and went into the place I'd seen from a stretcher some weeks earlier.

Sandra was surprised to see me.

"Have you been conscious all the time?"

"Yes, I think so," she said.

"They haven't taken any X-rays, have they?"

She shook her head and lay there looking at me with immense tiredness.

"I'm OK and the baby is too. They've got my fever down and now I only need to rest. It's because of all the stress. And you, why are you here? How did you know?"

"The Eel told me. He's very worried about you."

"Where is he?" she asked with her typical apprehension.

I shrugged. In fact, I didn't know.

Before we left the hospital, they did an ultrasound scan, just to be sure. We left at six in the morning after she checked herself out. They'd got her fever down and started her treatment, which mainly consisted of resting a lot.

In the car she told me she had absolutely nothing with her. The backpack into which she'd put the money Fredrik had been paying her and a few other items had been left lying in the garden. I told her not to worry and asked her what we should do. She said we should go to my room via the alternative route in the hotel, but first we needed to stop at an all-night pharmacy to get her the syrup they'd prescribed and a toothbrush.

I did everything she asked, wondering how we were going to deal with the double bed in my room. If I'd been younger, I would have been fine with a bed made up on the floor with a folded bedspread and a couple of blankets, but I wasn't up to such things any more. If I tried that now, I'd be getting up with devastated bones and then it'd be Sandra who'd have to look after me. I could also push the two armchairs of the small living area together, but even more than that, I was worried about her seeing the real me, the one with the thick-lensed spectacles, the old pisser who had to get up five or six times in the night. I didn't want her to see me in my singlet. Perhaps this was the last lesson that Sandra would have to learn in our short friendship, and the lesson I'd have to learn too.

We walked through the passages and stairways we already knew, sometimes in darkness. We opened doors trying not to make a sound, although Sandra was limping because of the damage she'd done when she fell and I was afraid of tripping and falling too. We heaved a sigh of relief when we got to the door of my room. I got out my card, put it in the slot, the green light came on and we went in. Sandra fell onto the bed and started to cry, but not loudly. Tears were falling and she was biting her lip but that was all.

Within the hour they'd be opening up the breakfast buffet and then I'd be able to bring Sandra some good things to eat. I told her to get into the bed on the unused side, not to worry about anything, to rest, and that everything would look different tomorrow. It was just words, reasonable words, and they convinced her. She was fast asleep in five minutes.

I picked up the newspaper from the floor and settled down on the side where I always lay, next to the phone and near the bathroom. It was yesterday's newspaper. Other disasters were happening today. I didn't even take my shoes off. I didn't want to go to sleep before breakfast. After that I too would certainly be resting.

I didn't go down to the dining room too early. I wanted it to be fuller, so that after having my own breakfast I could make her a small ham-and-tomato sandwich and then put that, some fruit and two croissants into the bag I was carrying. I'd also take one of those instant decaf coffee sachets they leave on the table, put some hot milk in a glass and carry that in my hand next to my leg so the glass wouldn't attract attention. If they did ask me about it, I'd pretend I hadn't realized, which wouldn't be so surprising in a man of my age.

When I got into the lift, I reckoned I'd done a good job.

Although I nearly spilt the milk when I opened the door, I felt very pleased with myself when I could set out, on some paper napkins placed on the table-cum-writing desk, the croissants, the sandwich, the fruit and the glass of milk with the coffee and sugar bags. When Sandra woke up, she'd find it, with the milk gone cold, of course, but she might be able to warm it a little if she filled a wider glass from the minibar with hot water from the tap and put this tall narrow glass inside.

I hung the "Do Not Disturb" sign from the door handle and lay on my side of the bed on top of the bedspread. I took out my contact lenses, removed my shoes, covered myself with a blanket and slept like a baby. When I woke up it must have been about eleven in the morning. Sandra was still asleep. I changed my shirt and washed, making as little noise as possible. I didn't want to have a shower in case I woke her. I left her a note next to the breakfast.

The cleaning cart was still in the passage and I asked the chambermaid not to do the room because I was tired and would be coming back upstairs straight away.

I tried to locate the Eel. I drove past Frida's house at the time when she was supposed to be cleaning in Villa Sol. Elfe's old car, which the Eel had been driving recently, wasn't there. In any case, I waited for an hour at the corner with the main road, which anyone who lived

284

around here had to use to get anywhere. I now understood that the Eel hadn't wanted to hurt me in the supermarket car park that day. He'd wanted to warn me that it would be dangerous for Sandra if they saw us together, and was trying to convey the seriousness of the danger. He didn't know that he could have got me out of the picture with one single slap. I wanted to know if he'd helped Sandra only out of love or if there was more to it than that. But what could be more than love?

Then again, I was uneasy. If they were going to look for Sandra, they'd end up linking my hotel room with her, so the sooner she left the better. I had to act fast and not ask her what she planned to do, but just get her a bus ticket for early in the morning when not so many people are travelling.

## Sandra

I woke up with a start, as if someone had slapped me. It wasn't Frida who'd put the ampoule in my bag. It was Fred and Karin, and they'd done it to get me even more caught in the trap they'd set for me, and they'd set it so I'd have no choice but to join the Brotherhood. They wanted me there because I was going to contribute a new being that they'd educate in their own image. My side hurt but I didn't have a temperature any more. Now I only felt disoriented. Suddenly I didn't know where I was. It was a hotel room. I closed my eyes again. It was Julián's room and he wasn't there. It was one thirty in the afternoon. I remembered hitting the ground when I fell, and the hospital. I was free now. I got up to go to the toilet and saw some breakfast on the table and a note from Julián telling me not to leave the room. I pulled the curtains back. What a beautiful terrace. You could see the rooftops and the line of the sea in the background. I opened the glass door and breathed deeply. I was wrapped in a very agreeable coolness, which quickly turned to cold. I drank a glass of water from a bottle I found and lay down again. Maybe I should stop worrying about life making no sense. There are some people who realize very early on that it makes no sense and only plan things in the short term. Others take longer and live in fantasy land for a while, as I'd done.

I'd been clinging to illusion right up to this very moment, but from now on I knew that reality depended on me. I couldn't and didn't want to go back to Villa Sol, yet I didn't feel able to leave Dianium without seeing Alberto again, without asking him to leave this shitty Brotherhood to start a new life with me. And it pissed me off that my things, however few they were, should still be in the hands of the Norwegians. I would have preferred to throw them in a rubbish bin.

When I woke up again it was three o'clock. I was hungry. I ate the breakfast, showered and got dressed. I went out to get a breath of fresh air on the terrace. The adventure had really ended for me now. I had a terrible sensation that I wouldn't be seeing Alberto again. It felt like one of those summer loves of adolescence that are locked into a month of holidays, unable to move, like the butterfly I'd had tattooed on my ankle.

## Julián

Sandra was much better and even in good spirits. She'd had the breakfast I left for her in the room and was reclining on the bed calmly reading the newspaper. She said she'd heard steps by the door and feared that the chambermaid would come in.

"The longer you stay, the more insecure this place will be for you," I told her. "I've got you a bus ticket for six tomorrow morning. Until then, you have to rest and get your strength back. Does it hurt where you hit yourself?"

"I feel a bit mangled, but that's all," she said pensively.

"There's no going back now, Sandra. There's nothing more for you to do here."

"I'm not leaving without my things. At least I want my backpack. We left it in the garden with my money and documents in it, and I've got to return the motorbike. It's not mine."

"All that can be sorted out. You can get another identity card and the motorbike's very old. It's not worth the risk."

"I'm not going to leave without anything," she said, angry and determined. "I'm not going to let those two keep my things. They've lived off all the things they've stolen and they're not going to steal from me."

"It wouldn't be because you want to see the Eel again?"

"If I could, I'd take Alberto too, but he has to decide that. He knows where to find me…"

Her tone suddenly became more melancholic, dreamier, as if the very name of the Eel bore her off to another world.

"I'll go. I want to have a chat with Fredrik Christensen and this might be just the right time. If I don't give any signs of life before tonight, put the alarm clock on when you go to bed and leave the hotel via the alternative route with enough time to walk to the bus station in case you don't find a taxi. If that happens, forget about backpacks and anything else. Here's twenty euros to cover your costs."

"It's very selfish of me. I'd never forgive myself if anything bad happened to you," she said.

"Nothing's going to happen, but you've always got to think the worst so you can have a Plan B."

Sandra smiled at me, halfway between being in love with the Eel and being fearful for my physical well-being, apart from her worries about what was going to happen between now and tomorrow, and what would come next when she got back to her normal life.

I asked her if she was hungry and if she wanted me to bring her something to eat. She said she still had an apple and commented that she always seemed to be locked up somewhere lately.

The hours flew by until I decided the time was ripe for me to go to Villa Sol.

I parked right next to the gate of Villa Sol. Not a single soul could be heard behind the walls. A light shower of leaves sometimes fell down over them, sprinkling the street. It was getting dark and I rang the bell.

They asked who I was and I told the truth, that I was a friend of Sandra's.

Fredrik came in person to open the gate. He didn't open it wide, but just enough for us to see one another.

"I've come to collect Sandra's things. She says she left a backpack in the garden, some things in her room and the motorbike in the garden."

"Sandra," he repeated, stalling for time so he could think. "Where is she? We are worried about her."

"She's fine. She's left town."

He peered at me. Now he recognized me.

I looked at him, unblinking.

"Yes, I'm the one in the photo, the one who's been following you and the rest of you lot."

He opened the gate to let me in and it automatically closed behind us. The garden was very pleasant. Swimming pool, reclining chairs around it, an arbour, a barbecue. Trees towering up to the sky, semi-wild plants, the smell of damp earth. We sat in some cast-iron chairs around a very pretty table and I knotted my cravat a bit tighter round my neck. He was more used to the cold and was in shirtsleeves.

"I know who you are," I said, "and it's better to leave Sandra out of it. She didn't know anything about you till I told her."

"She's one of us now."

"You know she's not. Sandra will never be one of yours, or one of mine. She's in the hands of the wind. It was pure chance that she came to this house."

"Nothing happens because of chance. She is with us. She is part of our life, and nothing and nobody is going to change that."

Fredrik Christensen was a tough bastard, obstinate and with a disgusting air of superiority. He spoke holding his chin high, looking at me as if I were a cockroach.

"If you give me Sandra's things and leave her alone, I won't unmask you."

"How can I be sure?"

I shuddered. Someone was watching us through the living-room windows. Karin, for sure.

"At our age, we're never going to bring any of you to trial. At first, I was only thinking about revenge, but now I'm thinking of the future of people like Sandra."

"You can't fool me," Fredrik said. "If anyone had done to me what we did to you, there's no way I'd spare him."

"Don't forget that we're very different. Besides you're all going to die soon."

He smirked to himself.

"I know something, a secret that you certainly don't know," I said.

Evidently, it took a lot for Christensen to feel the cold. He lounged in the chair, stretching his arms full length and letting the air caress him.

"You're really that interested in the girl's bits and pieces?"

"Bits and pieces or otherwise, they're hers."

"Well, if the secret's worth it, I'll give them to you."

"It's about the injections you people use."

He was utterly disconcerted.

"I had their content analysed."

"That's impossible," he asserted.

"In the laboratory they managed to extract a sample from some used syringes. I found them in a rubbish container."

He didn't in the least like what he was hearing.

"I can show you the results. You'll be completely flabbergasted."

"You're in my hands now. If I want, you won't get out of here alive."

"Then you'll never know the truth."

"Tell me more."

"It's a very highly concentrated multivitamin compound, but at bottom it's like plenty of others sold all over the place."

"That is absolutely impossible," he said, incredulous. "Karin improves when she has the injection."

"You're talking about the placebo effect. First she improves and then she gets worse. Don't tell her the truth if it helps her. But it won't prolong your lives. One of these days you'll come down with pneumonia and you'll never leave hospital, and Karin's one step away from never getting out of a wheelchair."

"You're a bastard!"

"That's neither here nor there. The main thing is that what I'm telling you is the pure truth. Take an ampoule and get it analysed if you don't believe me. You might save yourself a fortune in jewels and works of art."

He laboriously heaved his huge bony frame out of the chair and went inside. Karin remained spying on me through the windows until he came out. My backside was freezing on the cast-iron chair, but I didn't move, didn't think. I didn't want to get distracted by thinking. I put up with the cold and stayed alert for half an hour. Great was my relief when I saw him coming out with the backpack in one hand and a travel bag of clothes in the other.

"Here you are," he said. "I've taken the motorbike out of the garage and put it next to your car."

I opened the backpack to make sure it contained the money Sandra had earned in this house. There were about three thousand euros, a magazine, her identity card and driving licence. I didn't look in the other bag. What I'd seen was enough.

I had to stand up to get my hand into the back pocket of my trousers and pull out the folded sheet of paper with the results of the lab tests.

"Look at that. I'm not deceiving you. In any case you can confirm it for yourself."

"You're asking me to believe that these tests have been done on our ampoules. They could have been done on anything."

"Think whatever you like but that's the truth."

I didn't sit down again. While he was perusing the bit of paper, I took the backpack and the bag and headed off. It was difficult for me to open the gate from inside, but it gave in in the end and, once outside those walls, I felt so free I wanted to sing.

I had to go to the little house and convince the tenant to let me drive him up to El Tosalet so that he could bring the motorbike down. I had my work cut out trying to make him see that this was not some subtle plot of his ex-wife to get him killed on the road. I relaxed when at last I saw it chained up to the bougainvillea.

Before going back to the hotel, I went to buy a roast chicken and some chips. By the time I got to my floor, the lift stank of chicken.

I nervously put the card in the door. I didn't know what might have happened during my absence. Maybe they'd come for her. Sandra! I called her name as soon as I closed the door. I clenched my teeth when there was no response. Not a peep.

Totally forlorn, in pain and crushed by the enemy, I put the backpack and bag of clothes on the bed. I was just going to check the bathroom before starting to search for her when she came in from the terrace.

"How did it go?"

Sandra will never know the happiness I felt. She came in from that terrace like the night that was closing in, like the dark-blue clouds that were streaming across the sky.

"Better than I imagined. Here are your things."

"I've had a terrible time thinking about what might be happening to you in Villa Sol, and all because of some whim of mine."

"I left the motorbike at the little house," I said in response to her marvellous words.

## Sandra

Julián lay on the bed fully dressed. He said he preferred to be ready in case we had to get out of there in a hurry, although I guessed it wasn't only that.

"Get some rest. Don't worry. I'll wake you at five. I don't sleep much."

Julián gave me peace, so much peace that I slept like a log. When I felt him touching my arm, it seemed that I'd only gone to bed five minutes before.

"It's time to go," he said.

We sneaked out of the hotel, taking the alternative route at the bleakest hour of the day, when people are still sleeping and it's neither night nor day.

There was time for him to have an espresso and me a milk coffee before I got on the bus. I asked him to give my address to Alberto. And then I waved goodbye from the window. He was wearing the jacket he'd bought in the town, with the cravat at his neck, and was as perfectly shaved as always. I didn't stop looking at him until he disappeared from sight.

## Julián

Stories don't end until you're done with them, until you finish them off in your head or with your heart. For Sandra, the end of the story came as soon as she got on the bus to go back home, although she was going to keep dreaming about the Eel. However, if that relationship was going to go anywhere, it would have to be in another world. Not yesterday's world. That, for the time being, was still mine. If all these shocks hadn't killed me off yet, it must be because I still had something to do. I had to keep going, had to keep in step, like a soldier. Would Fredrik Christensen have sounded the alarm after our conversation in the garden? If it came to taking measures, Sebastian would already have taken them after our first meeting. Basically, I was thinking about all this so as not to think about Sandra moving away in a bus towards a future that was totally unknown to me.

I let my legs take me wherever they were going, wanting to walk because I'd been spending too much time in the car lately. I did up the collar of my jacket, stuck my hands in the pockets and let myself be drawn by the sea breeze, by its dampness, its blessed dampness that opened up my lungs and made me breathe as if I hadn't smoked three packets a day for so many years of my life. And by the time I was ready to take stock of where I was I'd reached the port. The morning had now opened up completely and a few chilly sun rays were endowing everything with an air of normality. Guided by the memory of my own steps, I headed automatically for the *Estrella* and Heim, or rather to the place where the *Estrella* used to be moored.

I looked around, disconcerted. Perhaps my sense of direction was feeling the strain. It wouldn't be the first time that, one day, an old man like me suddenly didn't know where he was, or wasn't where he thought he was. Nonetheless, the only thing missing was the *Estrella*. The bar opposite was still in place, as were the two catamarans either side, the boundary stone with its two red stripes and a vacant lot I'd used for parking a couple of hundred metres away. The *Estrella* wasn't there and neither was Heim. This did put me on edge, especially because they'd whisked Heim out of my clutches. Realizing he wasn't in his right mind, they would get him out of the way, as they'd done with Elfe. The ones that were still able to fend for themselves didn't want any unnecessary encumbrance. They didn't have the strength to take care of the rest. However much Heim was Heim, he was now reduced to bothersome material.

I had another coffee, this time decaf, calculating how many kilometres Sandra would have covered by now. I would have liked to have gone to Madrid with her. I could still afford a bus trip, a few days in a hostel and a few more set menus. But if it was just for my sake, the journey wasn't worth it. It wouldn't have given me time to see a thousandth of the things I hadn't seen, so it was better to leave things as they were, not to move them either forward or backward. I'd stay here, in the place that Salva had chosen to end his days. Salva was more like me than anyone else in the world, and he'd prepared the ground for me, so why reject it? The moment I got on the plane in Buenos Aires, I knew I was setting out on an elephant's journey and wouldn't be coming back. Go back for what? My memories weren't separate from me. Tres Olivos was a good option. I could pay for it with my pension and nobody would go looking for me there. When life presents you something gift-wrapped on a tray, you have to accept it, because if you don't you pay a high price. Life always knows more than we do.

Once again my weary spindleshanks, whose memory was better than mine, left me next to the car, which I'd parked near the bus station. I went to the hotel without thinking about dangers of any kind. I took my lenses out, put my pyjamas on and got into bed, something I'd never done in daytime except when I was ill. But now my body was pleading for rest, needing to recover from all the tension, to go to sleep without thinking about anything as I tried to make sure that the images of Sandra looking at me through the bus window would upset me as little as possible.

## Sandra

It wasn't until we left Dianium and got onto the motorway that I noticed the passenger sitting next to me. I'd been absorbed in my thoughts while the lights of dawn, these lights scattered among the clouds, were fading. I was looking at Julián until I couldn't see him any more. It made me sad to lose sight of him for ever and, I don't know why, but I couldn't stop staring at the cravat at his neck. I had to breathe deeply. I couldn't avoid knowing how skinny his arms were. He was very careful not to take his shirt off in front of me in his room, but I could feel them when I accidentally touched him, and I saw the arsenal of medicines he had to take in the bathroom. He was on his last legs yet he wasn't afraid, and I don't think that fear respects age. For me, coming to the end of the journey was scarier than the danger I'd faced when I was in the hands of the Brotherhood. I was much more afraid of normality, of everyday life, in which I had no means of earning a living. However, I wasn't the same idiot who'd arrived in Dianium last September when I thought the world owed me something. Now I felt something different, something more bitter and yet more comforting. I wouldn't know how to explain it. When we said goodbye, I was about to hug Julián, to press him against me, but then I thought it wouldn't be good for either of us. What's good about saying goodbye? The man at my side must have been about twenty-five and had gone to sleep as soon as he sat down. Now his head was resting on my shoulder and his legs were so sprawled out that there was hardly any space for mine. I tipped his head to the other side and he came back to me for support, but I wasn't going to put up with that so I woke him up. He looked at me in surprise, as if I'd suddenly turned up in his bed, until he got his bearings.

"Sorry, I was out clubbing last night."

I gave him the slightest smile, to forgive him but not encourage him. I didn't feel like talking to him. I wanted to think about the Norwegians, about what they'd be doing today, about how they'd be taking my escape. It would be impossible for them to find me since they had no idea where I lived and they'd have too much work trying to find out. If they felt threatened, it would be easier for them to stampede off. If I told this boy at my side what had happened to me, he'd be gobsmacked. What would he know about Nazis?

I checked him out from the corner of my eye. He wouldn't be anything like Alberto, not in a thousand years.

We stopped in Montilla to use the loo and have a bite to eat in the roadside café, which was crammed with travellers. My fellow passenger did his best to invite me for a Coca-Cola and said, yawning, that he thought I looked sad.

"You're very observant," I said putting paid, to Coca-Cola and conversation. "What I like most in the world right now is being sad."

## Julián

I was paying the hotel by the week and, with the last payment, I told Roberto I was leaving the room. He was surprised that I should be leaving a suite for which I was paying a price so low that it was bordering on the ridiculous, and tried to explain to me that if I did a comparison with other hotels I'd see what a privileged client I was, and the disagreeable incident that had been the cause of my leaving a normal room could have happened anywhere, but he, personally, had undertaken to make sure that it wouldn't happen again and, as I could see, it hadn't happened again. I understood that this was low season and it was his job to keep clients, come what may. It was better to have a suite occupied at the price of a double interior room than letting it gather dust.

I had to interrupt his description of the marvels I was unwittingly enjoying in the hotel to tell him that it wasn't a matter of money. I was leaving town. Of course if I was going to stay longer I wouldn't have dreamt of leaving the hotel. My holidays were coming to an end and I was returning to my country. Roberto was baffled. We old people had all the holidays in the world, but he didn't say anything. He knew very well that he had to keep his curiosity to himself. I told him I was leaving the hire car too and that I had returned to the room a blanket I'd borrowed in case of emergency, and a towel. I'd be taking a taxi to the airport.

Roberto got them to bring down my luggage and insisted on calling a taxi for me, but I refused very firmly. I told him I preferred to stop one in the street because I had to kill time before the plane left. There was no way I wanted them to locate the taxi driver later and ask where he'd taken me.

"I'm sorry," I said jokingly, "but this is my last wish."

Thus it was that I walked out of the Costa Azul at eleven in the morning with my bag hanging from my shoulder and dragging a suitcase on wheels.

Once I was far enough away from the hotel to be sure that no one was following me, I stopped a taxi and asked the driver to take me to the Tres Olivos old people's home. On the way, I looked back several times but saw nothing. My decision had taken them by surprise, when Tony wasn't in the hotel, so they had no time to get their act together and find some way of keeping tabs on me.

This time when I arrived at Tres Olivos I sent the taxi away.

I liked the look of the garden. There were several people like me, all very rugged-up, playing pétanque, deliberating about whether one of them was clumsier than another and chatting about football. I went to the office and once again found the buxom lass I'd seen the previous time.

She pretended she didn't remember me, but she did remember. I didn't understand why she was denying it, unless she'd got into the habit of saying no to everything from the outset.

I was clear. I told her I didn't want to be a burden for my daughter and if they could give me a good price from now until I died, and if they gave me the room that my friend Salva had occupied, I'd stay there with them. She opened her mouth and then closed it again.

"You're very attractive and very intelligent and I'd like to spend the rest of my days in a place where I could see you. That would bring a lot of joy to my life."

"Good grief, you've got the gift of the gab too, just like Salva."

"Did Salva also stay here so he could see you?"

"That's why they're all here," she said and burst out laughing.

"That room's been occupied for a week," she added, a little more seriously now. "But I'll see what I can do to change things and get you in there. My name's Pilar."

I'd just entered into real senility. I was in Pilar's hands. Pilar had started to use the familiar *tu* form with me as soon as she knew I was hers. One more point notched up to Pilar. My pleasure. This was just what I needed, a Pilar, the pétanque and people who'd lived their lives and were still living out the bonus they had left.

I sat down on a bench and waited for Pilar to sort out the matter of my room. Then she walked past, right in front of me, like a vision, as if I were asleep and dreaming about the events and characters of those days and meaninglessly mixing them up. I saw, I repeat, I saw her walking right in front of me, going towards the grove of trees: Elfe.

Once I'd reacted, I went out after her but Pilar stopped me.

"Where are we off to in such a hurry?"

"I thought I recognized someone."

"Well, you'll have time for that. Nobody ever leaves here." She didn't laugh, as one might expect. "Now we're going to move you into Salva's room. You're in luck. And I'll show you round a little."

A chambermaid was just finishing tidying up the room. I left my suitcase in a corner and the bag on top of a small writing desk. The window was open. The air coming in was wafting away the humours of the last occupant and Salva's unseen presence was filtering in.

The installations weren't fantastic. There weren't many young oldies, so the tennis court and paddle tennis court were superfluous. The kitchen was clean and the best thing was an indoor swimming pool, a bit on the small side, which was the pride and joy of the home. Pilar assured me that once I tried it I wouldn't want to get out, but Swedish gymnastics suited me quite well and I wasn't sure whether I'd dare to change.

"Did Salva swim here?"

"No. He said he had more faith in the gym exercises he did. Swedish gymnastics, I think it was."

I was talking to Pilar, looking at her and paying attention to her words, but I was still thinking about Elfe.

I was about to ask Pilar whether there was a German woman in the home, my age more or less, a former alcoholic or ongoing alcoholic called Elfe and, if so, who'd brought her here. But I didn't ask because I didn't want to let the cat out of the bag as soon as I arrived.

She was right, this comely lady. I'd have time. Lunchtime was upon us. I certainly hadn't expected this. They hadn't killed her but had locked her away. Basically, killing was more awkward than locking her up in this reservation where anything she said could be taken as a flight of imagination.

I didn't have time to open my suitcase as the smells of soup and fish and the clatter of dishes were coming from the dining room. When I went in, I was a little hesitant because they all knew where to sit and I didn't want to take somebody's place and then have to stand up again. I waited, trying to spot a free place and hoping to see Elfe at one of the tables.

A thickset man signalled to me to come and sit next to him. He prattled on and on while we were eating. It all went in one ear and out the other, as I was so intent on watching for Elfe's arrival. How far away Sandra and her future son seemed now. She'd been a gift from the gods, like all the other gifts life had given me. Not everyone had been as favoured as I had been. I'd told my daughter that I'd discovered a sort of hotel for people of my age and that I was staying on another month. Unfortunately the owners of the little house I liked so much had let it out to someone else and I didn't feel like looking any more. She'd have to agree to stay in a hotel when she came to visit. I also told her that I missed her, but it was good to be giving each other a bit of space.

When dessert came, I told the stocky man that a friend of mine had asked me to give a message to a woman called Elfe, a German woman with certain problems.

"Sometimes she comes to eat and sometimes she doesn't. You know what I mean." He made an elbow-bending gesture.

## Sandra

I was sad for a while. It was the only way I had to retain everything
that had happened in Dianium and of not forgetting Alberto or Julián,
or even the Norwegians, or the terrible time I'd had in that upstairs
room at Villa Sol. It was on the right as you went up the stairs, ten
metres down the passageway, ten metres sounding with different
kinds of footsteps, which drilled into my brain. More or less opposite
was the bathroom, and I remember throwing up in that handbasin
decorated with beautiful yellow sunflowers and how I was terrified
at having soiled it, and because I didn't have the strength to escape.
Now I knew how important it was not to let yourself get weak, not to
let yourself be intimidated or manipulated. It wasn't easy to avoid it
but I knew the consequences of innocence. Now I knew that anyone
can be an enemy.

When I got to Madrid, I went straight to my parents' house. At
any other time I couldn't have borne the idea of what was in store for
me there, but that seemed stupid now. My mother crying, my father
giving advice, both of them yelling that the other one was wrong, a
hot dinner, a few reproaches and a nice bed. I went into my room and
left the backpack on the white cotton summer bedspread (my mother
still hadn't got out the eiderdown, as if, in their heart of hearts, they
doubted that I'd be back). I took off the boots I'd bought in Dianium
and looked around. My high-school books were still on the shelves.
The posters, the adjustable table lamp, the work table, all of it had
an adolescent air. My head started to get things clear. Obviously I'd
come back in order to leave again.

It wasn't hard. My sister managed to rent for a very good price a
small space in a shopping centre and we set up a costume jewellery
shop. It went so well we were even able to employ an assistant and
I started paying off a flat. Santi came back into my life in a more
prominent way than in the past. I appreciated qualities in him that
I'd never even noticed before and I thought he could be a good father. You can wait for the perfect love all your life. Perfect love isn't
real, and nothing perfect is real, so our relationship didn't have to be
perfect either, and we limited it to seeing one another from time to
time and taking Janín to the park together. I told him about half of
what I'd gone through in those days that were so spooky and so cut

off from everything, and I occasionally blurted out the name of the Eel, which I preferred to call him when I was talking to Santi so as to block out the emotion, to tone down what I felt for him because, moreover, Alberto was probably the illusion I'd needed to be able to stand the tension I'd had to deal with in Villa Sol. Yet his name wasn't just a name. It was his dark-blue jacket, his creased shirt, the cigarette ash dropping on his moccasins, the long hair, the forehead reddened by the sea wind, his smell, his worried looks, and the voice squeezing itself under the door when he said I love you. Then nothing. He didn't come back to the hospital or to Julián's hotel room. I fled and he stayed. Santi was happy that I'd settled down and said that the past was the past. But he was wrong.

For a while I was tempted to go back to Dianium, to find him and get him out of my head one way or another, but then the baby and my work kept me busy all the time. The present was devouring me and sometimes it seemed that I'd turned the page... until I fell into bed completely done in at night and went to sleep. Then those days kept coming back, as fresh as today.

## Julián

On my first day at the home, Elfe didn't put in an appearance until night-time. I went to have some dinner, not because I wanted to but only so my pills wouldn't play havoc with me and make me ill as soon as I arrived, and also in case I saw her.

Looking at the olive trees through the window, I thought about the bar with the set menus and the shabby suite at the Costa Azul. I thought about Sandra and the Eel. It all happened so recently and yet such a long time ago. When I decided to come here, I knew that this was a place where I could prowl around the past, because, when the body packs it in, we still have the power of the mind and imagination to recreate the best moments of our lives.

I was thinking about all this until I saw Elfe coming into the dining room, with a mad look on her face although she was certainly better groomed than she'd been the time I saw her in her own house, covered in vomit. Whatever she cared to say, nobody was going to take her seriously.

I signalled to her to come and sit with the thickset man and myself. We were starting to form a group.

She sat down and didn't recognize me. How could she possibly recognize me? This woman had managed to live like a ghost.

"Elfe's got some paintings in her room and they're worth millions of euros. Isn't that right, Elfe?" the man said, giving me a wink.

"A Picasso," Elfe said, "a Degas and a Matisse, I think."

Elfe sat there staring at the ceiling, trying to remember, and the man shook his head sorrowfully.

"It seems that all of us have come from a better life," he commented, without the remotest suspicion that, in all probability, Elfe's paintings were originals. Then Elfe asked with pitifully childish helplessness, "Do you know where my dog is?"

The man shot me a look saying she's as mad as a hatter, not imagining that I knew where the dog was. It was in Frida's house.

When we finished, I offered to see her to her room. When she opened the door, I saw the paintings hanging on the wall. They were so authentic they looked fake.

"Do you want to have a drink?" she asked, putting her hand inside the wardrobe as if into a viper's nest.

I left, shutting the door behind me. You should see what's happening, Salva. You wouldn't believe it.

It beggared belief too, a few days later, when a tall, stooped, ungainly man got out of a taxi pulling two suitcases on wheels behind him. I had some difficulty slotting Heim into the small garden of the home. And I had to struggle to make real the sight of Heim talking to Pilar.

So he'd had to abandon his beloved boat, the *Estrella*. That must certainly have been painful for him, but they would have convinced him that, given his alarming loss of faculties, he'd have to go into reclusion if he wanted to survive. And, evidently, more than anything else, he wanted to survive. Basically, he'd be thinking that, as a member of a superior race, he still had many years ahead of him, and he'd find some way to check his dementia. Would he know that Elfe was here too? How would Elfe react when she saw him?

There seemed to be no end to this. When I wasn't going after them, they were coming to me; coming alive again for me. There was some reason for this. I felt that they were in my hands and that Salva's spirit was guiding me.

When Pilar finally completed the formalities before leading Heim to his room, showing him the facilities, telling him the timetable, enquiring whether he was diabetic because of his meals, and asking all the other questions that had addled me at the start, I went to talk with her.

"A new resident."

"Yes," she said as she typed Heim's file into the computer, under another name of course, and I had no wish to memorize it. "Let's see if he's a proper German and, unlike Elfe, comes to meals on time. What a nightmare of a woman!"

"The punctual ones are the English, not the Germans."

"But the Germans are supposed to be better organized. You should see the suitcases this man's brought. They're so well organized."

I agreed with her. The Germans I'd known were very well organized.

"Listen, Pilar," I said, looking her straight in the eye, "I don't know how you can stand being around all these old crocks. A woman as attractive as you should be showing off her charms elsewhere."

She laughed, not very happily.

"Elsewhere, all that glistens isn't gold," she replied.

"That's true too," I said, "so how would it seem to you if an old man like myself suggested going to see a film or sallying out to see what's in the world?"

I did pretty well holding out as she took her time in answering.

"It wouldn't seem too bad. I'm sure you've got a lot of stories to tell."

"You don't know the half of it."

# 11
# Under the Ground, Under the Sky

## Sandra

I convinced my sister that we should all go and spend a few days in the little house. I told her that the sea air, having other kids around and the warm presence of the family, including grandparents, would be fantastic for the baby. He was six months old now and was very alert, or rather very observant. If it's true that the foetus receives sensations from the outside world, he must have taken in a lot of suspicion, fear, watchfulness and the clear message that nobody is what he or she appears to be. When he was staring at us, it was as if he was seeking the truth inside us, or as if he knew that behind whatever he saw there was always something else.

After lots of thinking about hundreds of names, I'd settled for Julián and we called him Janín. I wanted the old Julián to know this and I sent him a letter to the Costa Azul Hotel but it was returned. He wasn't staying there any more, so I imagined he might have gone back to Argentina.

I think that, if I decided to go back to Dianium now, it was in the hope of bumping into Alberto on some street corner. At first I dreamt about him. I dreamt that we were on the motorbike, going down together, away from Villa Sol, or that we were walking along the beach. I dreamt that this world was flooded in very bright light that blinded me and stopped me from seeing what was around me. I dreamt of the girl on the beach as if she wasn't me. And now I wasn't totally her. I remembered her as a little sister full of doubts. It's not that I was sure of everything now, but I'd entered the house of evil, I'd had a taste of evil as one has a taste of illness or wretchedness, of everything that sets you in a world apart, and you don't forget this.

I was quite affected when I went inside the little house. It smelt of flowers. A thousand years ago I'd come here with my backpack and a head that was all over the place. Now we shot out of the cars, filling the garden with shouts. No sooner had they arrived than my parents started fighting. Janín observed them with eyes like saucers. Traces of books and papers of the tenant still remained. My brother-in-law immediately started to come up with his excuses to do a runner to the town, without the troops, as he called us. What had happened to me could never have happened in these circumstances. Fred, Karin, Villa Sol and Julián couldn't have existed. Now Alberto couldn't exist.

I settled into the smallest room. My father installed my nephews' old cot, which he got out of the garage, and I opened the window wide. The birds were boisterous in the green branches.

# Julián

Once you got used to it and stopped being interested in what was happening in the outside world, the days slipped by peacefully in Tres Olivos. Sometimes they took us on excursions to Benidorm or Valencia, and that was pleasant if you didn't have ideas about doing things on your own. Sometimes somebody died and that was discussed in the dining room as if it was never going to happen to any of the rest of us. Heim was as out of place as an octopus in a garage and Elfe fluttered around here and there, half drunk, completely out of it. Elfe occasionally exchanged a few words in German with Heim, but I'm sure she never managed to work out exactly who he was.

Thursday was Pilar's day off and we went out. She drove her BMW and I talked about the concentration camp and my time as a Nazi hunter. I tried not to talk too much about Raquel.

It turned out that she found me an interesting old chap. When I realized that she was falling in love with me, I told her about my heart disease and that I was taking ten pills a day. I told her I was in no state to be satisfying her needs and that I could snuff it any moment. I told her I didn't even have enough money to pay for my burial and barely enough for Los Olivos. But Pilar was very stubborn. She was trying to make us into one of those couples where the woman's like the nurse or carer. That was fine by me. The last woman for whom I might have been able to do something was Sandra. Now I was looking for ways to mortify Heim. He'd always managed to escape from his pursuers but the one he couldn't escape from was himself.

One afternoon I asked Pilar to come with me to the little house at the time when the tenant was teaching at the high school. She stayed in the car while I sneaked in, made my way through piles of papers and went up to the room where, months earlier, I'd hidden the photo album and Heim's and my notebooks. They were there, where I'd left them. As if no time, no wind, no gaze had entered among those four walls. I picked them up and returned to Pilar.

"What's that?" she asked.

"This? Nothing. It's an errand. We have to go to the post office."

Pilar looked at me admiringly. She took it for granted that anything I did would be interesting. What a shame my life was beginning just when it was ending, or perhaps it was better like that. Right, Raquel?

I sent my old organization Elfe's photo album, Heim's notebooks and my own notes, amongst which were jotted down the addresses of Villa Sol, of Sebastian, Otto and Alice and Frida. As for Heim, I preferred to keep quiet. Heim was mine.

Pilar settled for not much, for my telling her that she was very beautiful, which was absolutely true, and that she was the nicest, happiest woman I'd known in all my life, which was also true. I ended up giving in when she set about passionate kissing and a couple of times I let her drag me off to her bed. She tried to pretend that she liked my body, which made no sense. Then I told her that this was over, that I'd got out of the habit of sex and didn't want to get back into it and thus acquire another need.

In the end, Pilar and I were a fine team. We had a good time without having to rip our clothes off in a hurry and flurry. It was better that she should undress with others and leave me in my pigeonhole of "very interesting". However, at bottom I think that any psychologist would tell me that I was trying to repeat my marvellous relationship with Sandra. What would her life be like now? I didn't want to know. I belonged to her past.

## Sandra

The motorbike was still there, chained to the bougainvillea. Even though I now had a car and didn't need it, I got on it. I happily started it, savouring the moment, and headed for El Tosalet. I felt free – now yes – completely free, knowing that my son had come into the world and that if anything bad happened to me it wouldn't happen to him too. Mission accomplished.

When I got to Villa Sol, some children with towels over their shoulders were hurling themselves at the gate, followed by their father. He ticked them off, telling them not to carry on like animals.

I went over to him and asked if he lived in the house. He was suspicious and asked why I wanted to know. I told him that it was for sentimental reasons, that I'd also lived there for a time. He stared at me incredulously.

"What are the upstairs rooms like?" he asked while he warned the kids to watch out for cars.

I described them.

"Come in, if you like," he said. "Come and wallow in nostalgia."

The hammocks were the same, but now they were full of towels and in the wrong place. The pool was the same but there was something different. It was the difference of now, when doors were wide open and Karin's face wasn't appearing in the kitchen window.

"I've rented it for the whole month. Come whenever you like. We'll invite you to dinner."

His eyes had got brighter. He was probably divorced and it was his turn to have the kids. I thanked him and went back to the motorbike. He didn't have the faintest idea of who the owners were, for sure.

I went past Otto's and Alice's house. It was silent and emanated a feeling of heaviness, suggesting that any moment it was going to sink and drag all the surrounding villas, the region and the whole world with it. I climbed up on the seat as I'd done that rainy night of the party and saw that the garden was a complete mess, with weeds springing up everywhere. I can't explain why, but the Doric columns gave off a tremendous air of neglect, like those temples that time chips away at, trapping them in the past.

On my way back, I went past the Costa Azul Hotel. I went in and walked around the vestibule. The receptionist with the big freckle was there. He looked at me, trying to place me. I'd taken out the piercings and my hair was longer and chestnut brown all over, the way I'd had it done the last time it was dyed, when I was with Karin. I'd opted for comfort. Since I'd got myself a job, I paid more attention to my clothes and to making a good impression on the clients. The only thing that mattered was that my son wouldn't go short of anything. I didn't care what people thought of me. I only cared about what I thought about life. I no longer had any sense of danger in this place. I went out again followed by the receptionist's eyes.

Was that all? No. There was still the lighthouse. I left that till last. The worst thing was that nobody could share this with me. I felt as if my head and my heart were going to explode. Now instead of the ice-cream parlour there was a small restaurant with a big terrace shaded by a vine-covered lattice, which took up part of the esplanade. I was afraid that they'd taken away the bench among the palms, but no, it was still there. A couple was sitting on it. It didn't matter. Right under their noses, I lifted up stone C.

They were staring at me, not knowing what to think. The corner of a plastic bag was sticking out. I removed the compressed earth and pulled it out. It was a plastic bag that said "Transylvania Souvenirs", and inside was a lacquer box, the size of about half a hand. There was nothing in it, and there was a lot in it. I never thought that my life could be so full of emotions. I sat on the bench next to the couple. They were invisible to me. I made them feel uncomfortable and had barged in on their magic moment, so they left.

Thanks, I said mentally to the couple and the whole universe. I touched my pocket and the little bag of sand that Julián had given me one day. I always carried it with me. I took it out and put it under the stone. I wanted him to have it, wanted it to bring him luck again. I'd had plenty.

On the way back, I filled up the petrol tank, surrounded by nonchalant people aimlessly wandering around wherever the mood took them, and then went back to the little house. I went up to my room. Janín was asleep, sprawled in his cot. The breeze was coming in through the half-open blind. I put the box on the chest of drawers.

## Julián

The truth is that most of the time the bits fit together too late, when you can no longer do anything. Then why should we know certain things? Sandra had gone back to her normal life and the rest of us had rushed off to our respective destinies. Mine, for the moment, was Tres Olivos and Pilar. Last Thursday, like every other Thursday, Pilar picked me up early. We had a nice drive in the car, listening to rancheras, stopped to eat in a very nice-looking restaurant where she paid as usual, and then went back into town to do some shopping. Our first stop was at her favourite boutique. It was incomprehensible to me that she should waste her time and money with someone like me, but there we were, Pilar trying on dresses for New Year's Eve and me looking for somewhere to sit down.

And it was between a black velvet dress and another in red silk, I think it was, that I heard a woman's voice at my side.

"Excuse me, could I speak with you?"

I turned around to face her. The dog she held in her arms barked at me.

She was young, between thirty and forty, with blonde hair pulled back in a ponytail. She was slim and strong, and you could see from a mile away that she did a lot of sport. She was wearing jeans and a yellow cagoule lined in navy blue, like the ones worn by sailors you see in films. I took a few paces backwards, to see her better. She looked very familiar. I'd seen her before.

"I'm a friend of Alberto's, Sandra's friend. You are… Julián. I've been trying to track you down for weeks and had given up hope. Then – it's amazing – I saw you coming into the shop."

"You're the one who was with the Eel on the beach."

"With the Eel? Who is the Eel?"

"I saw you with Alberto on the beach some months ago, carrying on like a couple of sweethearts. Would that be right?"

She nodded. Pilar came out of the fitting room and whirled around. The skirt must have been sequinned because it glittered when she moved.

"That's lovely," I said. "I'll wait for you outside."

We went out and instinctively crossed over to some benches opposite the shop. The damp cold seeped into my bones.

"My name's Elisabeth."

The tip of Elisabeth's nose was going red. She had a lot of presence, though you couldn't say she was pretty. She stroked the dog and put it on the ground, tying the lead to a bench. She stretched out her arms as if they'd gone numb.

"Alberto told me that if anything happened to him I should look for you and speak with you. I saw you too, that day on the beach. You were watching us."

We sat on the bench, both of us with our hands in our pockets. I sensed she was going to tell me something disagreeable, one of those things that casts a pall over life.

"Alberto is dead. Or rather, they killed him."

So that was it, the thing that turns life disgusting.

"He'd infiltrated the Brotherhood and I was his contact."

"Police?"

"Something like that. Detectives. They found him out and killed him. A traffic accident, you understand? But I know it wasn't an accident."

The news left me paralysed. It was hard to know how to react. The past was still getting fat on disasters. The Eel was left definitively in the past, while Sandra would navigate through the future. Only Heim, Elfe and I were locked in the circle of the present, until Heim went completely mad, until Elfe failed to emerge from her last attack of the DTs, and until I had the last heart attack.

"I'm sorry," I said. "He helped Sandra and, in spite of everything, I think he tried to help me."

"Now we're looking for the Christensens, Alice and Otto. They're scared and not only because of us. It seems that there are other people on their trail. We know they've gone into hiding. They might have remade their lives in any housing estate near any beach. The coast is very long. We believe Heim's fled to Egypt. There's no sign of Elfe."

I looked into her eyes without saying a word. They were blue, but they couldn't compare with Sandra's greenish-brown eyes that made you laugh inside. The Eel and Elisabeth didn't make a good couple. It was obvious that there couldn't have been anything between them. That long ago day on the beach they'd been acting at embracing and kissing. How I would have loved to say to Sandra, guess what: the Eel and that girl were only colleagues in a job that was too dangerous; I want to ask your forgiveness for letting my head go sometimes, for my thoughts about you that weren't as honest as you deserved, because there were some moments when I wished I was young too; and as we know, I abused your trust in the matter of the puppy. Sandra, I'm disgusting.

"Alberto liked this girl Sandra. He said that when he was with her he wanted to laugh and conquer the world, and that this had happened very few times in his life, but unfortunately he'd met her in the worst possible circumstances."

"It doesn't matter any more," I said impotently.

"Yes," Elisabeth said, staring at the ground. "It's very strange the way things happen."

When I saw Pilar leaving the shop and coming over to us, I got up from the bench. Elisabeth got up too and untied the dog.

"He's called Bolita," she said.

"I know," I answered. "And you don't know what to do with him. You've got fond of him but he's a burden too. Isn't that right?"

She nodded and, surprisingly, she blushed slightly.

I picked Bolita up. He weighed a lot. Dogs grow fast. He licked my neck and I put him down again.

"I'll have him. I have a lot of free time and a house with a garden, but you can't visit him. Agreed? He can only have one master."

Elisabeth stroked his head and flank for the last time and didn't look at him again. She knew how to leave behind the people and things she loved.

"It would be good if you could tell me anything I might not know." She went quiet for a moment, using the tactic of staring at me unblinking. "I don't want it all to end here."

"Coming," I called as I turned my back on her to go over to Pilar, tugging at the dog's leash.

"I know you're not living in the Costa Azul any more. Where can I find you?"

I limited myself to waving goodbye. I took one of the bags Pilar was carrying.

"Who was that?" Pilar asked, full of curiosity.

"An admirer. I don't think I ever told you I used to be a film star."

Pilar took my arm, looking at me out of the corner of her eye, wondering if it was true that I'd been a silent-movie star.

"And this dog?"

"A gift from my admirer. We could do with a dog."

The three of us started to walk. Elisabeth would be watching us and, if she didn't throw in the towel right away and forget the whole affair, she'd end up finding Tres Olivos and thus Heim and Elfe.

As for me, I spent quite a few nights with my thick-lensed glasses and the adjustable table lamp writing a long letter to Sandra, reminding her of all the events we'd gone through together. I gave it to Pilar to send it to her after my death, as Salva had done with me. I wasn't sure whether to tell her or not that the Eel had died in a suspicious car accident (in which I couldn't help seeing the hand of Martín), and that I'd never seriously thought he was having an amorous affair with the girl on the beach, but had suspected it was another kind of contact. In the end I didn't say anything because I was hoping that another love would appear in her life, a love as powerful as the one she might have had in her dreams of the Eel, without my having to drag her out of it. Neither did I tell her that I'd managed to find Bolita, that he'd been in Tres Olivos ever since, and that Pilar and I took him to the beach so he could have a good run.

Meanwhile, while the day in which the letter would be posted was still coming, I devoted myself to driving Heim mad. I knew how to do that. They had taught me.

# Endnote

Most of the old Nazis that appear in this novel are based on real people who, after the Second World War, found refuge under the warm, serene sky of our coasts, where they managed to live to a ripe old age without anyone bothering them. Only the fictional character of Aribert Heim, also known as Doctor Death or the Butcher of Mauthausen, keeps his real name.